ALSO BY
WENDY LAW-YONE

The Coffin Tree

IRRAWADDY
TANGO

IRRAWADDY TANGO

a novel by

Wendy Law-Yone

Alfred A. Knopf New York

19 🐕 93

THIS IS A BORZOI BOOK

PUBLISHED BY ALFRED A. KNOPF, INC.

Grateful acknowledgment is made to the following for permission to reprint previously
published material:

PeerMusic: Excerpt from "The Great Pretender" by Buck Ram, copyright © 1955 by Panther
Music Corp., copyright renewed. International copyright secured. All rights reserved. Used by
permission.

Random House, Inc.: Excerpt from "Autumn Day" from *The Selected Poetry of Ranier Maria
Rilke*, edited and translated by Stephen Mitchell, copyright © 1980, 1981, 1982 by Stephen
Mitchell. Reprinted by permission.

Library of Congress Cataloging-in-Publication Data

Law-Yone, Wendy.
    Irrawaddy tango : a novel / by Wendy Law-Yone. — 1st ed.
        p.   cm.
    ISBN 0-679-42192-0
    I. Title.
PS3562.A862177   1993
813'.54—dc20   92-45863
                                                                  CIP

Manufactured in the United States of America

First Edition

———————

This is a work of fiction. Characters, places, and events are the
product of the author's imagination or are used fictitiously and
do not represent actual people, places, or events.

For Chuck

Like to the lark

. . . either I'm nobody, or I'm a nation.

DEREK WALCOTT,
"The Schooner Flight"

My thanks to the National Endowment for the Arts. The progress of this book owes much to the encouragement of its generous award to me.

IRRAWADDY
TANGO

I have done as you have done; that's what I can.

Now that I'm near the end, it's time to return to the night of my homecoming, the night they poisoned the lion.

It was the breakfast boy who told me the next morning. A dazed little corporal with pus in his eyes and crud on his lips. A most obtrusively filthy little fellow, I was forced to notice. He planted his face up close, too close, to mine. He had a message, a secret too dangerous to whisper. I took it that I was to lip-read.

The secret he disclosed: the lion was dead.

But how, I asked—too afraid, I suppose, to ask why. Here my informer clutched his throat and stuck out his tongue—a long, thin tongue and none too clean. *Poisoned!* he mimed.

"But I beg you," he whispered, a shaky finger to his lips. "Never, never say I told."

It was the first clue to my whereabouts. If that was the lion I'd heard, the ruckus that had kept me awake, the lion house had to be close by. And the lion house, everyone knew, was a fixture of Government House. They must have brought me, then, straight from the airport to my destination—directly, so to speak, to the den.

But I couldn't count on it. Not when they'd removed the blindfold only after leading me to my room, bowing politely before locking me in.

The best thing about the room was that it was a room—not a cell, not a cage. A bed; a table; a deck chair; a spittoon in one corner; over it a stool; on that stool a tin tray holding an earthenware jug of water. And a window! Just a small one, well secured with bars, a screen, and an outer grille. Granted the view was hardly uplifting. Three sides of brick wall covered with moss and mildew—a deep window well, apparently—was all I could see. And all it let in was a whiff of sour monsoon air, a dim figment of light. But a window was a window.

That was my homecoming, then. The return of a stranger to a strange land. I kept telling myself it wasn't so strange to be a stranger anymore. Everyone, after all, was from someplace else these days, from across some border or sea. Or so I'd begun to believe, after all those years in America. What was home anyway but the horizon seen from abroad? A place, that's all, where life began. A ground fenced in by the barbed wire you spend the best part of your life plotting to break through, waiting to vault over, vowing all the while never to look back. Although . . . how you do look back.

Nevertheless, I was home. Just trodding the ground after all that time abroad felt familiar and true, as if the earth knew my footfall, recognized it from times past. I crossed the tarmac from plane to airport terminal under a gray-brown sky, gritty and curdled like rancid coconut milk. But the curds separated suddenly and let the sun through, shining a spotlight on me. A breeze whipped by and threw a bouquet: the scent of an almost-forgotten flower, a yellow-and-white blossom I could no longer name. From the open spaces around the airport came a steady background noise, part music, part static. That old frog-and-cricket serenade, the hum of the tropics. Just as I reached shelter, down gushed the rain.

Inside the terminal, what do I find but the same frantic mural from two and a half decades ago, featuring every major mythic figure in the land: birds, beasts, spirits, soldiers, kings, and queens. All painted in cartoon colors, and all grinning. Laughing their heads off, in fact, as if their separate tragedies, full of cruelty, sorrow, bloodshed, and sacrifice, all added up to one killingly funny joke on us mortals.

There's the *naga*, grinning away: the fire-breathing *naga* who turns into a prince each night in order to bed the queen. In the end the dragon deity is found out by his rival, a mortal. And how the mortal lets him have it here: gleefully hacking the *naga* to pieces with his sword, fairly cavorting in the fountains of blood. Meanwhile, off to one side, the twin sons born to the *naga* and the queen—blind boys whose names I once knew but can no longer recall—are merrily riding the raft on which they've been set adrift by their jealous stepfather.

The tiger is there too, smirking from ear to ear, gripping its victim by the throat in its bloody jaws. The victim is that famous paragon of virtue: a faithful wife. The beast, sent by her jilted suitor, has practically broken her neck; she's dripping a trail of blood, but she's smiling sweetly, even a little seductively.

And there's old Snooze Head—*his* name I remember—the imperial messenger. Now here's a character who smiles in his sleep, one plump cheek resting on a plump palm, while his white horse simpers at a round green moon. Snooze Head is the dolt who fumbles a crucial mission. On his way to the prince's camp with military intelligence of dire importance, he decides to break journey to nap. This catnap will cost him his head, but up on the mural he sleeps the dimpled sleep of the just.

Also present is Golden Face—rushing headlong into a flaming pyre. In the center, blindfolded and tied to a tree, is her beloved brother, sentenced to death by burning. But one of the executioners—a half-naked, heavily tattooed ruffian—has had the mercy to grab her by the hair and sever her head just in time to save her lovely face from burning. A jollier trio would be hard to imagine: the brother and sister as they're eaten up in flames, the executioner as he plucks off the loyal sister's head. All three are chuckling.

And there's Little Miss Lonely, the eternal child and patron spirit of orphans, to whom a hard-boiled egg must be offered when a child is born. Miss Lonely, in this rendering, has a trick up her sleeve. One hand hides behind her back while the other holds out the egg. And this egg, to judge from the mischief in her slit-eyed, fat-lipped laughter, might just be raw—the better to crack open on the skull of a newborn babe.

What a tableau! The screaming colors have held, and, good Lord, the cracks have held. The same zigzag cracks, the cartoon thunderbolts, were there from the start, at the mural's official unveiling, some twenty-five years ago, when they'd painted the plaster too soon, before curing. I know because I did the unveiling.

The thunderbolts point down at exactly the same angle now as then, I'm willing to bet—toward the head of King Maha Bala. King Blah-Blah-Blah, as we called him in school, was the First Great Unifier of the land. When not conquering new lands, he was known for stuffing himself. One hundred and twenty-five different dishes a day was the standard menu, while royal physicians stood by with emetics. (The Great Unifier met a fitting end. He expired on his chamber pot, although it wasn't gluttony but an assassin that did him in.)

The mural still shows the great gourmand in his apogee, all bounce and glitter, leaping over treetops in full battle regalia with spiked helmet and tasseled sword, the imperial embroidery on his jacket intact down to the last sequin.

. . .

There was plenty of time to reacquaint myself with the grisly fresco of burnings, beheadings, infant blindings, et cetera, all carried out to utmost hilarity. The airline officials had left me there, in a room with a glass wall, across the hall.

Had nothing changed since I left, not the mural on the wall, not the uniformed men in the halls below? There were more of them now, of course. And—wait the guns were new. They used to be great clunky affairs that gave the soldiers a toy-soldier aspect, some posing at attention, some at ease, toting their too-heavy weapons. The guns seemed smaller and lighter, much fancier now. But how the men enjoyed swaggering through the same old pointless theater of airport security.

At Customs, they were giving a Brazilian butterfly collector a hard time. The sweat stains around the Brazilian's armpits were darkening as he opened out each envelope for inspection, waited for the officials to peer at the butterfly, then carefully folded it up again. They meant business, meant to scrutinize every single one of his specimens, however long it took.

Farther down the table, another officer had dismantled the old portable Smith-Corona belonging to the turbaned Sikh in the shiny three-piece suit. The officer had removed the type-writer ribbon. He had a spool in each hand and was holding the black strip up to the fluorescent light in the ceiling, winding it slowly as he mouthed the words. Now and then he dictated to his assistant, a sergeant with acne and rickety legs. The assistant wrote with a pencil stub, painstakingly, on the back of a shoe box.

The Sikh had brought trouble on himself by carrying on his person a pen that doubled as a flashlight.

"What!" demanded the officer, thrusting the gadget at him. "Pen flashlight."

"Pen flashlight?" the officer barked. "Pen? Or flashlight? Which? For writing or for seeing?"

The Sikh inclined his turban meekly. "For writing *and* seeing."

"Writing *and* seeing? Hah!"

Without warning, the door across the hall flew open (the door marked VIP LOUNGE and crisscrossed with masking tape) and out swarmed a platoon of officials toward me, accompanied by a photographer trotting alongside and popping his flash. They were staring at me through the glass; I could see the ones in the back nudge each other. *There she is! Look at her! Will you look at that? That's her? That's all she is?*

An old feeling came over me: a surge of disgust and fear. It affects the vision, this feeling, and in the resulting blur those khaki-clad men receded into the wall and seemed to be mingling with the loonies on the life-size mural.

I looked from face to face, half expecting to see *him*. Ridiculous. Of course he wouldn't be there. When was the last time he had appeared in public? But my heart was still jumping when they came through the glass door. I stood near a wall, for support in case my knees gave out.

Yogis, I said to myself. *Remember the yogis who can slow their hearts down till they're practically dead. Slow down, heart!*

"Mrs. Tango?" asked the first officer, a colonel, extending his hand. A challenge, not a greeting. He cocked his head to regard me, squinting, looking askance just to see straight.

"I hope," he said, since I hadn't said a word, "you still speak our poor language?"

"I do." Good. My voice was intact; my knees weren't shaking after all.

"But you've been gone a long time," said the colonel. "A long time."

"Not that long," I replied, sensing accusation. "Just twenty-five years."

"Twenty-five yahs!" said someone in English, the only civilian in that uniformed crowd. His hair was greasy, his fingernails were dirty, and down the front of his faded black jacket was a sprinkling of either dandruff or crumbs. "Twenty-five yahs is quarter century!" he protested. "Long time. Long time no see."

"Kick, kick, kick!" he added, which turned out to be his way of laughing.

The colonel ignored the joke. He wanted to see my passport. I handed it to him. I might as well have produced a document of historic value. Heads crowded together, nodding, shaking.

"American passport!" said another voice, the voice of a child sneering at a toy he wants but can't have. The child in this case was a major.

"All right, enough," snapped the colonel. "We'll hold this. For safekeeping."

Then they ushered me out toward the main terminal. I followed through the exit marked by peeling arrows taped onto the linoleum floors, past the busy mural, past Customs, past the hand-lettered sign: WELCOME TO THE REPUBLIC OF DAYA.

The Land of Compassion, I added automatically, unable to let go of that silly guidebook phrase. In recent guidebooks, I mean. In the old days it was the Jewel of Southeast Asia. But what's not in the guidebooks, old or new, is that *daya*, the word for "compassion," is also the word for "wound." And that's how my countrymen, the odd stragglers in the airport, struck me now. The walking wounded.

Wait! Where was I? In an airport or a hospital? The operating room lights, the refrigerated air, the groups of moon-eyed starers and whisperers acting like relatives of terminal patients, the secrecy and gloom! *Let me out of this dreary waiting room! Who wants to linger with these hangdog families keeping vigil over their doomed?*

I floated somewhere between dread and disbelief, like waking with a pounding heart to the same bad dream—same in effect, same in every implausible but tangible detail.

Outside, the scene shifted but the dream continued. Behind the curious crowds straining against the barricades, a convoy was waiting: motorcycles, jeeps, and a single black Mercedes with the doors already open. More discussion and delay as they posed me for pictures *(Pictures! Like some state guest! A good sign, maybe!)* and argued about who should sit where.

Once I was wedged into the backseat of the limousine, they tied the blindfold over my eyes. With apologies, naturally. As I said, not much had changed. Not even our famed politeness.

The blindfold was a strip of crimson velvet. An elegant touch, but troubling, if you happen to recall that a sack of crimson velvet was what they'd used in the old days to swaddle the relative of a deposed king before clubbing the victim to death. Velvet for royalty, red to mask the blood. Of course the men responsible for my blindfold didn't seem quite the types to uphold the refined ways of the old monarchies. Still, it wasn't a soothing touch, that velvet.

The drive seemed long, but what drive isn't long when there's nothing to see? And I saw nothing. Nothing of the streets, nothing of what might have changed in my long absence and what might be the same. Hardly the welcome I'd expected, although it shouldn't have surprised me—if only because of the number of times I'd told myself not to be surprised by anything, anything at all, that happened.

So I was blind. What was a little blindness if I could still breathe? Better a blindfold than a bayonet. I concentrated on the air-conditioned chill and the hot garlicky breath of the official to my left (the man in civilian clothes who had engaged in a brief power struggle at the airport to sit next to me).

At last: a slowing down, a stop; a starting up again; the

sound of gates creaking open; dogs barking, then silenced by a harsh command; a sort of siren like the warning beep of a garbage truck backing out into traffic; the crunch of tires treading gravel. Somewhere at the back of my mind was the nagging of a duty neglected. I should have been counting the minutes, measuring distances, observing all available cues. I should have been making mental notes for future reference. Intelligent captives are supposed to do things like that.

I should be counting my steps, I thought as they led me down the twists and turns of echoing halls. But to what end?

Finally the blindfold was off and I could see again. . . .

And there I was in the dim room with the one fortified window.

I sat at the foot of the bed, exhausted, and counted my blessings. Home at last—so far unharmed. I also counted my money: the thin sheaf of traveler's checks they could have lifted from me but didn't. Not a good sign, that scrupulosity. The honest ones were the worst. They were the ones without a shred of humanity. The petty thieves had hearts at least. My bags weren't there yet, but I didn't doubt they'd be delivered later, as promised, "after clearance."

I stretched out on the narrow bed—that old smell of sheets in need of proper drying!—and listened to the rain. A roaring, angry rain. I'd forgotten the fury, the vehemence, of a monsoon. The eternity of rain that doesn't end with the downpour but goes on and on for hours, dripping.

This particular dripping sounded like a board game: the *shake-shake-shake* and roll of the dice; the wait for the player's move; the *shake-shake-shake* and roll of the next player's turn, and so on.

I must have dozed off to the steady clatter of the dice. The next thing I knew, the game had stopped and all I could hear was a shallow whimpering. My first thought was of a dog with a thorn in its foot. But a very large dog—the size of one of those mutant hounds that leap out of nowhere to chase you through the streets of ghost towns in your sleep. And the thorn in its flesh had to be a massive thorn—more like a sharpened bamboo—stuck not in the foot but in the ribs.

Then came the roar—a deep, sepulchral roar, as from the inside of a drum—that told me this was no dog but a much bigger beast.

It's the lion, I thought. *Something's happening to the lion.*

Lord, the torment. The bellows, the groans. Creepiest of all, the mutters. They sounded like human complaints, like *words* uttered in animal voice. Once I dropped off but woke with a jolt to the feeling that it was right on top of me, that suffering beast, crushing me under its dead weight. What a relief finally to hear the great mammoth snore. The death rattle—it had to be.

At last, the next morning, I discovered the cause.

But why the long agony, the cruelty of poison? Something to do with the prophecy, I imagined—the same prophecy that brought me back. I have the Board of Astrology to thank. It was the board that set the wheels turning, when it cast the prediction that the reign of the Lion was ending.

Of course any village idiot knows which lion's fate the astrologers had in mind. They meant the Lion of Daya, the leader of the nation himself. The same idiot knows what one does with a bleak forecast. One tries to forestall it, naturally. "Cancelling destiny," we call such measures.

Maybe that's all the poisoning is about. To head off the unhappy prediction, the Lion of Daya takes the first step advised by the chief astrologer: he eats crow and asks me home. But then he goes an extra step, for good measure, to try to thwart fate.

He kills the lion.

But why I should be informed of this unpleasant fact was

beyond me. To frighten me, maybe—to make it clear who was still in charge, holy prophecies or no.

So much for guessing. In fact all I had to go on was what I had been told: that they'd poisoned the lion on the night before.

How could I help but suspect it was somehow related to me?

Because we were related once, the lion and I. I remember the year, the event. It was the year I turned twenty, the year of the Revolution, the occasion of the first official visit by a foreign potentate, the emperor Haile Selassie. His Highness had come to congratulate Supremo.

In those days, Supremo was merely my husband the general's nickname, not his assumed title; not yet. Supremo was what we in the inner circle called him because of his passion for ice-cream sundaes. The delicacy was available at one place only. The new American ice-cream parlor was the first of its kind in the country. SUPREMO ICECREAM.

But at the time of Haile Selassie's visit, Supremo was still the general. He was also the new head of state.

The emperor came bearing the gift—a most felicitous gift—of a pair of lion cubs. The lion was Supremo's lucky symbol, an augury determined by his horoscope at birth. (True to forecast, he was operating under the code name Lion when he made his mark during the war by leading the troops that duped the occupying Japanese.)

The emperor reached into a slatted box that stank like a public latrine. He lifted out the first cub and handed it to Supremo. The tawny-haired cub opened its mouth and yawned.

"MGM," said Supremo, laughing and pointing at the yawn. "MGM, MGM!"

A flicker of puzzlement in the emperor's sooty-looking eyes. *Maybe,* I thought, *they don't have cinema halls in Ethiopia;*

or if they do, maybe the bioscopes don't begin with the roar of the MGM lion.

How to explain the MGM joke to His Most Gracious Highness? I felt an obligation to ease his discomfort, having danced with him at the gala banquet just the night before, when he steered me through a stiff-legged fox-trot. His beard had brushed against my cheek, and I smelled a most exotic ancient scent. I thought of myrrh. Perhaps it was his resemblance to one of the three wise men pictured in the Bible storybooks.

> *Myrrh is mine; its bitter perfume*
> *Breathes a life of gathering gloom;*
> *Sorrowing, sighing, bleeding, dying,*
> *Sealed in the stone-cold tomb.*

There was something sad about this musty monarch. Sad but forbidding. An emperor was an emperor, after all. (And here was one said to toss tender chunks of veal to his lions and leopards, while a full-time cushion bearer followed with a pillow at the ready. Another rumor had it that His Majesty's teeny feet needed propping; else they dangled from the throne.)

Then there was Supremo's mood to consider.

"Old blackie," he had said under his breath, after the ruler of the Abyssinian Empire returned me to my seat with a stiff bow, "feeling up my wife." My husband had a toothache that night, and when in discomfort of any sort, he began to suspect treachery.

After Haile Selassie left, I began wheedling to keep the lions at home.

"Not the zoo!" I said, thinking of our fun-loving crowds who pelted monkeys with stones and bottle caps, dropped inedible objects into the bear pits in hopes of seeing a bear gag, teased the wolves by poking bamboo sticks through the bars of the cages, and such.

What was the difference, anyway, I argued, between a gift to the state and a gift to the leader of that state?

Supremo gave in. While his men were still running around with their midnight knocks on the door, dragging out suspects and herding them into trucks bound for the interrogation centers and the lockups, I, the coddled bride, was rolling around with a pair of wildcats from Ethiopia.

And they were getting wilder by the day.

One day Emperor, the male, gave me a nip that drew blood. "Enough," said Supremo; "they're going to the zoo."

I thought at first he was afraid of rabies and reminded him that the cubs had come with health papers. "Rabies!" he snapped. "Never mind rabies. Think of the bad omen!"

Supremo was right, I see that now. What a bad end we've come to—all of us bound by the lion connection.

It was during Haile Selassie's trip to Daya that his Imperial Guard staged its ill-fated coup. By the time the emperor returned, the loyalists were busy snuffing out all traces of the uprising. While heads were still rolling and bodies hanging from trees, the emperor decided to count among the traitors his own pet lions. They had failed to protect the palace against the rebels; they had fallen down on the job. He had them shot.

We named our lions Emperor and Empress. Empress was the first to go, from a worm-infested heart. She was two years old. Some twelve years later—long after I'd left—the tanks rumbled up to the palace of Emperor Haile Selassie, the Lion of Judah, to put an end to his reign.

About the same time, *my* Emperor—by then a mangy old cat—was moved from the zoo to a specially built gilded cage annexed to Government House. There he survived all those years I was gone.

Now *I* was back and *he* was gone. To be poisoned by a piece of meat after an overlong life in a cramped cage—what a way for the last of the lions to go.

Next to the last, anyway. There was still Supremo, my former husband, the Lion of Daya.

Someone called Lazarus has made this possible. Yes, they granted me my request, had the pen and paper delivered by a boy named Lazarus. I'm not supposed to know the names of the many that come and go, but *his* I found out by accident. He'd just left the supplies and was on his way out when the telltale echoes leaked from one of the halls beyond. "Lazarus! Hey, Lazarus! You still there?"

Lazarus froze. I know that's his name by the way it stopped him in his tracks. I saw him hesitate with the door half-open. Should he hurry up and lock it behind him, or quickly lock himself in again with me, at least until the fool down the hall had shut up? He stepped out, and the door clicked behind him, the solid click of a heavy fireproof, soundproof door with a combination lock on the outside, like the kind found on bank vaults.

He was scared of me, so scared that he'd come and gone— even arranged the stack of paper neatly after tapping its edges against the table—without once looking at me. They're all scared of me, though not of course in the same way as I am of them—each and every one of them, from the big shots with their attendant bootlickers who click their heels and snap to attention while their bosses throw their weight around, down to the latrine cleaners who creep in and out to empty my daily wastes.

Yes: Bosses. Bootlickers. I can name what I see now, say what I mean; be as disrespectful as I feel, as brazen as I dare. That's the beauty of this place, the place enclosed by these four windowless walls. It isn't wisdom I mean; I never thought confinement brought wisdom, despite what the hermits of antiquity have said: "Go and sit in your cell; your cell will teach you everything." No, I don't expect wisdom; only the liberty that comes when there is nothing to lose. So little to lose, such freedom of thought. And now, thanks to Lazarus, I'm at liberty to think on paper as well. Liberty. What peculiar forms it can take.

And what peculiar types stop in, each intent on performing his little duty. Picture the pair who came for the body receipt. The lieutenant fidgeted, while the captain reached into his breast pocket and pulled out a piece of pink paper that he handed to me, with a ballpoint pen, to sign. At the top left-hand corner of the page was the familiar lion's head seal. Underneath: "Ministry of Internal Affairs." The same letterhead was on the receipt they had given me for my Timex. But beneath *this* letterhead was the phrase "Body Receipt." At the bottom of the page, a dotted line for a signature and the date.

"What's this?" I asked the captain, careful to strike the politest of inflections.

The captain tapped his finger on the piece of paper, almost knocking it out of my hand. "As you see. Body receipt." He had a big ring on his middle finger, a jade in a crude hexagonal setting with the look of a jagged weapon.

"Oh, *body* receipt. For whose body?"

The lieutenant shuffling his feet in the background blurted out suddenly, "Your honorable body." (Maybe the man secretly adored me; men have nursed weirder fantasies.) He coughed with embarrassment and took several steps backward, one arm hanging by his side, the other hand gripping the hanging arm by the elbow—the old posture of servility.

"Okay, okay, please sign," said the captain, impatient.

"But what does it mean, 'Body Receipt'?" I persisted, trying not to sound persistent.

"It means," said the captain, speaking slowly as to a child or a half-wit, "we need a receipt for your person. LOB, section five."

"LOB?"

"Law and Order Board."

"Ah." Just as I was signing, before I could continue to worry whether I might be initialing my own death warrant, a single bang shook the door. The lieutenant leapt to open it. In slithered one of the latrine cleaners, an old skeleton in a loincloth. This one swung his aluminum bucket and moved in a kind of battle crouch toward the spittoon that served as my chamber pot. He lifted it with an unsteady hand and slowly, noisily, emptied its contents into his bucket while I wondered if he'd been trained to prolong the humiliation. Then out he hustled with the slop, followed by the two men who turned to pay their respects to me, bowing and double bowing, Japanese style, before backing out the door.

The complaint collectors come in pairs, too. They come for the one complaint I'm entitled to each week. Those are the rules here. One grievance a week—no more, no less. But the right *must* be exercised: an enforced freedom, so to speak.

Last week I said I'd pass, said I had no complaints. Why go through the useless formality? But no, that wouldn't do. The man with the clipboard shook his head, refusing my refusal to complain. He had come with his assistant for the usual inventory. A weekly visit to take stock of things: the furnishings and fixtures in the room, my behavior and state of health, food consumed and waste generated, the daily routines, the weekly complaint. Number One put on a look of sinister distaste, pen poised over the clipboard to record the required complaint. *Don't!* the look said, when I declined to find fault. *Don't make us hold you to your rights. Just make your complaint and spare us the nuisance of enforcement.*

He had a point. Why invite a wrangle at this stage? So I mentioned the weevils in the rice. Bugs in the gruel were the least of my concerns, but it was exactly the sort of harmless gripe that met their needs. While Number Two nodded his

eager approval, Number One completed the form on his clipboard with a flourish. How little it takes to please little men.
But they'll be back, these little men, to make their other,
perhaps not quite so little demands.

By then they'd moved me to another room, a room without
a window. There was a clock in that room I could have
complained about. In fact it preoccupied me more than the bugs
in the rice. It was one of those battery-powered models found
on the back shelves of Chinatown supermarkets, above the
ceramic pandas, silk pajamas, and salted plums. A Chinese
clock, without question. The big gilt Roman numerals suggested ideographs. The power was on—the face was lit and
buzzed faintly—but it was a clock that ran without telling time.
The hands had been removed.

Of course I understood the purpose of the handless clock.
In addition to not knowing the time, how much worse to be
reminded that time still stares you in the face, that the clock
keeps on ticking while your world is stalled, in darkness. Still,
I felt grateful for the useless thing. It would give me something
to complain about.

With pen in hand, I made my first entry, a shorthand
account of the previous day:

*Transfer to new room. Blindfold again, then short
journey by car. Armored car to judge from the slamming
doors. On arrival, much more complicated procedure and
security measures, from the sound of things. Inside a
building. Damp air. Echoes. Wait for elevator—a
dinosaur. Problems with expanded metal door.*

*Which building? Maybe one of the old colonial
departments? War Office? Memory of Supremo calling it*
war 'piss; *calling "fatigue"* batik. *Climb up several
flights of deep stairs; opposite of descending into dungeon.
Ascent to hell?*

Now the arrival—hallelujah!—of paper, requested more than a week ago. A request I never dreamed they'd allow; but what harm in asking, I figured.

The delivery came with a form I had to sign, to confirm receipt of the paper and pen. With the form: an official note stating, of all things, the reason for the clemency.

"We are a civilized society, a country with one of the highest literacy rates in the world. We promote the written expression of ideas—a tradition since the Crystal Court Chronicles, *authored by the poet-concubine Kindra."*

No mention—no need for it—that Kindra penned those immortal lines some three hundred years ago, in prison, while awaiting her execution after charges of conspiring against her former lover, the king.

At the bottom of the receipt: "Received: Writing materials (including exercise books and ballpoint pen) for confession."

Confession: They can call it what they please, so long as I can say what I want.

All I want to say is what I have done and why.

1

Tango wasn't my given name—wasn't given to me anyway till I was eleven, maybe twelve. Until then I was called Mew. I wondered what sweet kittenish traits had earned me the nickname. I remember asking, and my father laughing. "*Look* like a cat? No, it wasn't how you looked. You *acted* like a cat. No love for anyone but yourself."

What did he mean, I wondered. I loved my mother; I loved my father. I loved small babies, their toe stubs the size of corn kernels, their ribbons of clear drool streaming out of mouths open wide with enthusiasm, their delicious, clean-baby smell.

But this was also true: from time to time I felt a hardening inside, around the very spot warmed supposedly by love and goodwill—a thickening, a cooling, a crust. As for example when Jewel annoyed me.

Jewel was a neighbor, a girl with a soft skull. Her parents were away in the U.K., studying to be doctors, and had left her in the care of her mother's family. Jewel appeared docile and eager to please, but she was a tyrant in disguise. *My head!* was all she had to say to win an argument, call a halt to any game, demand attention or sympathy. *My head!* and the world would come to a standstill.

The plea lost its urgency for me. What was so special about a soft skull anyway? I'd managed to touch it once—a thing that was strictly forbidden, but Jewel had let me, as a bribe. It wasn't anything like I'd imagined. It wasn't soft at all. But at the top, right on the crown, I made a discovery. The skull was thumping with a beat as insistent and alive as a heart.

She's stronger than the rest of us, I thought. When the adults were present I still had to humor her. But in their absence I stood my ground. It took Jewel's tears—more and more tears, an increasing deluge of misery—to win a favor or concession from me. I gave in out of admiration more than pity. It was skill, sheer skill, that induced her sobbing fits.

We used to play in a deserted godown on the riverfront. One day I was jumping off the gunnysacks of rice. Jewel, for whom rough play was forbidden, watched from ground level as I climbed and leapt and slid from stack to stack.

She called to me suddenly—from above, not below. I looked up; and there she teetered on one of the highest stacks, legs akimbo, arms outstretched, insisting, "Get me down."

I started to clamber up, scared she might hurt herself, for which I'd be blamed. I'd almost reached her when something stopped me: the sight of her holding out her arms, imperiously helpless, demanding to be saved. She wasn't frightened at all. I caught her sly smile, the pouty little thumb-sucker's smile. That curling upper lip with its mole above it (which she called her beauty mark); the big self-pitying eyes; the stringy hair fastened with her special rubber-tipped hair clips—all of it disgusted me, and I stopped where I was and sat.

"Get down yourself," I said.

The supplicating arms fell; the eyes, not soulful anymore, narrowed. "Get me down. Now!" She had a new, forceful voice. "Now. Or I'll hurt my head."

"Why didn't you think of that before?" I swung my legs along the side of the rice bags I was sitting on, to show I was staying put. Jewel began to whimper. I'd had my back to her, but it was too much to pass up the performance I was now familiar with. Sure enough, she stared into the distance without blinking, until her eyes began to water. Squeezing out the tears, heaving her chest and shoulders, entranced by the memory of some great sorrow, she let loose the wail, the thin plaintive wail.

Tears flowing, she belted out her song. I could make out a rhythm, and a tune of sorts. I was taken by the hint of clowning, the long lament broken up by elaborate sobs. It echoed through the godown, hollow and deliberate.

"My God, you're a witch!" said a voice from below, breaking the spell. There was Cloddy. (His name in fact was Claudie—French blood on his mother's side—but I didn't know that at the time.)

"What's wrong with you? Why don't you help her down? Can't you see she's begging you?" Cloddy was demanding.

"What's wrong with *you?*" I said. "Can't you see I won't help her *because* she's begging?"

I jumped down off the rice stacks, leaving Cloddy to attend to Jewel, whose wail had thinned to a whimper.

"Let her go," I heard Cloddy say about me. "She'll burn in hell."

The Clod reported me, of course. My father, resigned, looked up at the ceiling to pass the sad judgment on me. "Dogs will be dogs; cats will be cats. No love for anyone."

"Yes, cat," muttered Cloddy, sticking his tongue out at me speedily, before my father could see. "Grinning Cheshire Cat."

It was thanks to Carlos that they stopped calling me Mew. It was Carlos who taught me the tango. Carlos wasn't really Carlos, either. He was Gabriel de Brito, an Anglo. His family came from the Portuguese settlement across the river. Once upon a time they had come from Goa. "Goa constrictors," his mother called the clan—she being a local, not an Anglo.

"She's a fake!" said my mother about Mrs. de Brito. "Telling everyone she's a local. Just a local Dayan woman who happened to take up with an Anglo! Oh, the cunning of that woman!" My mother was swatting flies. I noticed that with the flyswatter in hand she became belligerent.

"But she *is* Dayan. I've seen pictures of her parents!" I said.

"Exactly!" My mother smashed a bluebottle. "So why say she's Dayan when she's in fact Dayan?"

I shrugged, unable to follow.

"She's only saying it to fool everyone, so people will think she's really an Anglo trying to be Dayan. Think about it. Why else would she be wearing dresses and speaking English like an Anglo? So people will say, 'Oh, that Anglo woman, posing as a Dayan!' That's what she's really after. She wants everyone to think of her as an Anglo."

"Then why wouldn't she just say she's Anglo?"

"Sometimes," said my mother, "you can be quite stupid. Wait, don't move!" And she whacked my forehead. "Because, then people would take her for a Dayan."

Whatever the truth, Mrs. de Brito did have Anglo airs. She wore frocks, kept her hair short and called herself Mamie, which wasn't her given name. When her son was a baby, he had called her Mamie, not Mama. Later, learning that Mamie was a proper name, she took it on as her own.

Mamie de Brito's only child was Gabriel, a k a Carlos. Carlos had credentials. He was a B.S. (agriculture) from the University of Buenos Aires—a B.A./B.S., he liked to say, giving people the wrong impression without actually lying. He'd gone to Argentina on a state scholarship. There, at the Instituto de Agronomia, instead of keeping his mind on his studies, he became a worshiper of Carlos Gardel, the Argentine tango king.

After graduation he turned professional. He took his idol

Carlos Gardel's name as his nom de plume. The mother of a friend, a seamstress specializing in wedding gowns, made him a Dacron tuxedo. He bought a pair of pointed shoes, which he paid to have shined once a week. With a lavender silk rose in his lapel, 4711 Eau de Cologne in his armpits, and Brylcreem in his hair, Gabriel/Carlos went out and danced for a living.

It wasn't much of a living, but he was happy to be able to stay on in B.A. after his B.S., happy to keep on dancing. He wasn't ready to return home and face the life expected of him there. But Mrs. de Brito—her husband by then was deceased— was worried about the stiff government bond that parents of students who went abroad on scholarships and didn't come home were forced to pay. She ordered Carlos home.

Carlos came home. And sulked. "Lying in bed all day," his mother complained to friends. "Lizning to the rayjo," she said, bunching her fingers and smiting her ear, "qua-qua-quack. Lying on the *flat* of his back. Sheikh of Araby. Just staring at his *records,* if you please. Life! You send your only begotten son to Southern Hemisphere. Result? He wants to go on shaking backside for a living."

Carlos decided it was time to leave his bed when he tried on his tux one day and found that after inhaling in order to button up the pants, he couldn't exhale. "No hard feelings," he said about the government rule forcing his return. A country needed such rules. "Otherwise," Carlos explained, lowering his eyes modestly, "brain drain."

For a time I thought that a brain drain was punitive surgery done on students who refused to come home from England or America or wherever they'd gone overseas. The idea must have come from Jewel, who once told me that the purpose of rubber tips on her hair clips was to prevent an accidental puncture of her tender skull.

"But what if her skull *were* punctured?" I asked Cloddy. He rolled his eyes, wearied by my ignorance. "Obviously!" he said. "Obviously, the brain will burst, and the stuff will all spill out."

"What kind of stuff?"

"Brain stuff, dopey. You seen porridge, right?"

Carlos happened to teach me the tango because of my second cousin Thurani. He adored her. Thurani was enjoying the adoration in her own way. "You know how Carlos walks?" she'd say behind his back. Then she'd do a funny knock-kneed walk that called attention to her backside. "Not everyone can walk like that. First, you must become a tango champ. Second, you need two turtledoves rubbing heads in a dark cave." Piles was what my cousin meant. She had a way with words.

And a way with men, too. In their company she was so correct that even her sneezes came in threes, like little stammers of apologies. *Its-its-its.* But when no one was around to impress, she sneezed her head off with deafening abandon. *Acheeee-hah!* The whoops were like buffalo calls. She played odd games with men. She'd egg them on with sidelong looks. But if they came on, she'd biff them. It was clear from the clench of her teeth as she punched and slapped them on the arm that she liked hitting them.

She herself couldn't bear to be touched. "I have extremely sensitive skin," she said in front of the mirror, slapping her cheeks quite savagely while rubbing in the Ponds cold cream. Sensitive skin, but she plucked her eyebrows and underarm hair without batting an eye. She was also famous for being ticklish—too ticklish to be touched at the waist. Since it was unthinkable for Carlos to teach her the tango, he instead taught me.

Carlos brought music. Not the kind of music I'd been aware of till then. We owned an old radio, an RCA, but it was meant for the news. It sat on the meat safe, behind the door to the veranda. In the afternoons I'd come home from school to find that door always open (except during heavy rain), and from the street I could hear my mother's favorite lady announcer delivering the three o'clock news in her velvety voice.

The only other program we tuned in to regularly was the English-language request hour. "Our next request is for 'You Are My Sunshine,' and it's to Juliet, with everlasting love from your Romeo. . . . For our dearest mama, wishing her a happy birthday from Mumu, Tutu, Lulu, Juju, Pupu, Susu, and Ba. . . ."

It was the messages my mother listened for; the music was incidental. She liked songs all right, but not enough to be bothered with the words. She hummed a lot—mostly English nursery rhymes. I could tell her moods from the tunes she hummed. Annoyed with my father, she would take up the flyswatter, humming "Baa, Baa Black Sheep." (Her handling of the flyswatter was another giveaway: she used it to keep time, not to swat.) But when she was pleased with one of her soups, she leaned into the thick, salty vapor, one hand on her hip, the other wielding a ladle to stir and taste and tap against the pot, humming "Goosey, Goosey Gander" after scalding her lips. It was "Yankee Doodle," though, that always alarmed me. I knew I'd be a target in some way then.

Jewel's family had an old horn gramophone. Her people were better off than most in our compound, with things like tablecloths and a sideboard to their name. The Victrola was put away in this sideboard, along with a set of seventy-eights, warped and badly scratched, on which I first heard "The Blue Danube," "Indian Love Call," and "Come Back to Sorrento."

Carlos was not my cousin's only suitor, but as the least likely one he was my parents' favorite. He was an Anglo, for one thing, and Thurani had made clear her distaste for mixed marriages. She knew *what* she was going to marry; she just didn't know *whom*. She was going to marry a diplomat. The other thing about Carlos was: How could you take seriously a man who wanted to dance for a living? And the third thing: the man didn't have two bad coins to rub together.

No, Thurani had other, bigger plans. She was living with our family now, but not by choice. Her father, my father's first cousin, was a former schoolteacher. After the war and independence, he'd landed a job with the foreign office. The next thing we knew he was something called an educational attaché, living it up in places like Belgrade, Karachi, Paris, and London.

Uncle liked to make it clear that these tours had left him uncorrupted. A man of simple tastes was how he presented himself. My father, whose own career had not gone as well, accused him of putting on "foreign airs" (he used the English phrase).

"Foreign airs?!" Uncle would protest. "*For-rain ayars!* Just give me rice, salt fish, sour bamboo, and I'll be happy in a hut here in my own birthplace, where my navel crumbled."

Thurani made no such claims. She liked the West. She had unfinished business there. Having attended international schools, she hoped to become a United Nations tour guide. What worried her father and led him to send her to us for a year was this very worldliness. Uncle wrinkled his forehead and massaged it as he confided to my parents that his daughter was calling herself Rani (as her friends abroad had done) instead of Thurani; she was lax with her mother tongue and her manners. The worst of it was the length of her sarongs. If she wore them any shorter, she might as well be wearing skirts.

Thurani pouted. "My God!" she complained to me in English. "There is nothing to do in this small-town dump!"

I began to see our situation in a different light. Before Thurani's arrival I'd always found a lot to do. We lived in an enclave of zinc-roofed bungalows housing the families of RTA employees. The River Transit Authority was headquartered there, in Irrawaddy Township. Our compound sat on a rise above the Yama River, and from the verandas of the bungalows we could see the endless activity of boats below: boats being built; boats being loaded with paddy, livestock, and sometimes elephants; steamboats; fishing boats; sailboats; rowboats; poling boats; and long narrow boats that could be sailed, rowed, or poled, depending on wind and current.

Twice a month, we heard the shrill whistle of the Delta Region bazaar steamer threshing upriver, towing its double-deck barge. Then the rush began—the dash to the riverbank, to wait impatiently for the ferry to berth and the gangways to come down. At last: the stampede on board to the little stalls jammed back-to-back along the narrow walkways, for the rummage and haggle over hand mirrors, plastic combs, piece goods, taffeta ribbons, marbles, spinning tops, celluloid dolls; for delicacies like toffee, biscuits, jaggery; for the latest junk from the city.

Most afternoons, I'd walk the few blocks to the center of town. In front of the dry-goods store owned by the Gopal brothers was a bamboo fence to which their beloved pet gibbon was tied. The ape was a joy to tease, plainly asking for it. It knew exactly what it was doing, unlike dogs or cats who, even though they were supposed to be intelligent, clearly had no idea how stupid they looked when they ran around in circles chasing their own tails or sniffing and licking their genitals. This gibbon was not only vain but calculating. It posed and preened and performed. Of course it had incentive. The silliest prank would get rewarded with handfuls of peanuts or brown-sugar jaggery from customers and passersby. The creature was shameless, fawning one moment and vicious the next. Having begged for a reward and gotten it, it would think nothing of biting the hand that fed.

It attacked me once when I went too close. It grabbed hold of my arm, looking up for a moment in a reflective way, as though thinking how best to do it, and bit. I hit it as hard as

I could until it bounded off, screeching. It had the nerve to turn and bare its teeth at me.

After that, I took great pleasure in eating things in front of it without giving it a morsel. It paid me back by feigning utter indifference. Or turning around to point its backside at me—a fleshy, hairless protuberance that resembled another insolent face I longed to slap.

The Gopal brothers, one fat and bald, the other womanish and excessively tall, were a stingy pair. They never gave anything away free—not even a paper cone's worth of the powdered crumbs from the birdshit bin. This was an old aluminum milk canister filled with tiny noodle and lentil chips that had been fried to a crisp and tossed in salt and spice.

Once they had caught me pocketing a handful of gobstopper sweets.

"You are a ge-*rowing* girl," the tall prissy Gopal said, his hand chopping the air.

"Growing"—the fat one leered—"like a cokkernut tree."

"Have you," the thin one inquired, "no *morality?*"

Not satisfied with prying my fingers apart to retrieve the sweets, they wanted me to apologize. Quaking, I refused—telling myself that anyone capable of kissing a gibbon on the lips had no right to lecture me.

When I'd tired of the ape, I'd make my way back to the compound for a game of hopscotch, jump rope, kick-the-can, rounders, or, my favorite, a "cockfight" contest. This last involved shuffling on your haunches and trying to push your opponents off balance before your legs cramped and locked. Years later, when I had moved to the city, I saw a performance by a dance troupe on tour from the Soviet Union. Their cossack dance almost brought the house down—mainly, I think, because it was just a fancy version of our cockfight games.

There was, as I've said, always a lot to do—until Thurani came along and made it all seem drab.

"Small-town mentality!" was one of her favorite English phrases, muttered about any person, idea, or thing she disapproved of. She thought us all backward—me, my parents, the neighbors in the compound, their babies. "Shouldn't baby be talking by now?" she'd ask the mother. "In Europe, you know, babies learn to talk much earlier. They even know how to feed themselves."

Another thing Thurani tried to spoil for me was teasing the gibbon. "Yes, go on. Keep tormenting little animals," she said. "And see how you like hell. See how you like being reincarnated as a pinmouth."

This always gave me pause. A pinmouth was the most miserable of all living organisms, a misshapen blob with a huge body and a minuscule mouth capable of taking in only one grain of rice at a time, so that its particular agony was to be eternally famished.

"That poor creature," Thurani said about the gibbon, "belongs in the jungle, swinging through the trees with its own kind."

I couldn't easily imagine this particular gibbon preferring the wilds. Whichever jungle it might once have come from— maybe it came from our own teak forests right outside town, maybe from somewhere in Bengal, the birthplace of its owners (the Bengali Babu brothers, as we called them)—wherever it came from, it was now thoroughly in its element. Captive, yes; but making the most out of captivity. Thriving, even. If someone had cut the string, far from swinging off into the bush it would have stayed, I suspected. Preening. Posing. Performing. Begging. Showing off. And no doubt aiming its buttocks at me.

"The gibbon isn't a *little* animal," I tried to argue.

"Of course it's a little animal!" Thurani said. "You as a

human being have the power to be its oppressor. Have you no pity?"

No pity. No charity. No morality.

And no hope for straight legs, it seemed.

"You've got to stop playing games that are making your legs crooked," she said. "Just look."

I looked at my reflection in the river. I'd heard the English expression "knock-kneed" and remembered a joke Thurani's father had told about an upstart claiming to speak English, then saying "k-nock k-need." But it hadn't occurred to me until now, seeing the silhouette of my legs, and finding it impossible to have them touch at the knees and the feet at the same time, that knock-kneed was what I was.

Thurani's sarong was wet from a swim and clung to her like a second skin. She peeled it upward to bare her legs for me. "You could have had legs like mine," she said. I didn't want to have legs like hers, straight as they were. The thighs were a little too plump and pale, with large goose bumps.

Seeing I was unimpressed, she asked me to turn around and look the other way. I heard her giggle and rearrange her wet sarong. Then I heard a soft whistle. "You can look now," she said. I saw nothing different. "You heard the whistle?" I had. And did I know where it came from? I didn't. "Turn around again," she said. I did. Another whistle—not shrill, not loud, but distinctly a whistle.

"Look at me," she said. Still nothing different. "Where do you think it came from?

"I'll give you a clue," she offered. "I'm not carrying a whistle, and I didn't do it with my mouth."

"Give up?" she said, seeing I was losing interest. "Here, I'll show you how I whistled." She did a funny little hop, then a quick crisscrossing of her thighs, and out came a noise, an exhalation.

"How do you do that?" I said, envious of my cousin's many hidden talents.

"Practice," said Thurani airily. "And a wet sarong."

She shook her head at my slowness. "If you can make a sound with your lips up here," she reasoned, tapping her finger to her mouth, "why can't you do it with your lips down here?" With the same finger she tapped her crotch.

Then she noticed my feet. "Your toes!" she laughed, and spread out her fingers to show how splayed they were. She dipped her own foot in the water and held it up for me to see what a real foot should look like. Except it didn't look real. It looked like carved wood, a very hard wood with a hard varnish. The foot itself was arched and narrow, the toes aristocratic. I noticed, though, that the one next to the big toe was excessively long.

"Hah!" I said, delighted to find a flaw. "You're going to boss your husband!"

"So?" said Thurani, smirking as if I'd paid her a familiar compliment. "Listen, I'm telling you," she warned, "don't go around with bare feet so much. Hang around with fishermen and you'll get webbed feet, just like them."

I'd made friends with some of the fishermen's children. They were looked down upon because they had worms, lice, and snot. Also because their fathers were routine takers of life—even though it was the fish they caught that we then bought and fried and ate. The children spoke a funny dialect I loved to make fun of—and they knew all kinds of interesting things about mud. From them I learned to roll mud pellets, which we shot from catapults made from tree twigs. I learned to shape mud into little fruits and vegetables and pots and pans. We made mud masks, mud poultices, and played hopscotch and hoopla in the mud. We laid mud traps for minnows and worms and scavenged for bottle caps and other shiny bits of garbage from the docks.

"How can we better ourselves," Thurani was saying, "unless we seek out our betters?" She was always prodding me to improve myself while hinting that it wasn't going to be easy or even possible to do so, given my fate. And that fate, like the fate of our small town on the Yama River, was to be backward.

Once, she caught me trying on something I'd fished out of her steamer trunk. A black shawl with an embroidered peacock flashing a tail of multicolored sequins and beads. Oh, the treasures in that trunk! The brocade jacket of shimmering gold bamboo leaves! The delicate blouses of nylon, georgette, lawn, eyelet, and crepe de chine! And lacy, fitted bodices to wear underneath! I would have stolen, had I known a way. But Thurani made regular inspections. She had a stack of fashion magazines saved from her trips abroad. *Vogue. Elle. Annabella.* These she studied like textbooks. Then, studious, she would spend hours sorting through, inspecting, trying on different outfits in varying combinations.

The day she caught me posing in front of the mirror with her shawl, she surprised me by being amused instead of angry. "Style, my dear," she advised in English, like a schoolteacher, as she took the shawl off me, carefully folded it, and put it away, "is not so easy as it looks. You must have *potential.*"

I didn't have to understand the word to sense that whatever potential was, it was beyond my means. It was potential, I supposed, that got you things like brocades and portable record players.

I especially coveted the record player. Thurani's father, back for a visit on home leave, had brought it for her, a bribe to sweeten her small-town stint. It was a portable the size of a small suitcase, covered in a fancy fabric like oilcloth with a moiré print. A small crowd had gathered for the demonstration that Carlos, as the compound's technical expert, had been charged with. I saw him quiver as he looked the machine over, stroking the cover longingly. At last he sighed. Taking this for disappointment, my father said, "This record player is not good?"

Carlos hesitated. "Well . . . good . . . ," he allowed, implying it was good enough, but he'd seen better.

"What luck to have this machine," my mother said with a loud clap of her hands. "Now, when it's broken, our expert B.A./B.S. can fix it." She poked Carlos in the ribs and hummed "Put another nickel in, in the nickelodeon."

Carlos gave a dutiful little jump. "Oh, Auntie, Auntie," he giggled, causing Thurani to snicker at him. It wasn't manly, in her opinion, to giggle the way he did. I thought this unfair. True, he clutched his waist and took shallow breaths as he laughed. But only because his pants were too tight. "What are you saying, Auntie?" Carlos went on gasping. "I don't know that much about machines. I'm just an unemployed leaf-eater." Leaf-eaters were itinerant theater folk who were reduced to eating their meals off banana leaves rather than plates.

The self-ridicule endeared him to my mother. But if he'd really been inept, he wouldn't have been allowed to hang around the house. He was tolerated because he made himself useful. He fixed broken things, carried my mother's heavy shopping basket as he followed her through the muddy bazaar, and gave my father hefty massages that produced groans of agonized pleasure. "Such a good boy," my mother would say approvingly, "so polite, so nice to order around."

Carlos had brought a record of his own for the demonstration. "Stand back!" he ordered, as if expecting an explosion. With the touch of a lever, the circular floor of the record player turned; the record shivered and dropped; the needle arm rose regally, taking its own sweet time, and alighted at last precisely at the edge of the spinning disk.

What a letdown! A male voice, scratchy and nasal and slightly off-key, sang solo—sang and sang in words we couldn't understand. "Spanish," Carlos explained, seeing our slack jaws. I picked up the record cover and studied the man on it—a man in a hat, with fat leering lips. The kind of man who might offer me sweets I probably shouldn't take. Across the top, in splashy purple letters, was emblazoned: CARLOS GARDEL—TANGO.

What a swindle, after "The Blue Danube," "Indian Love Call," and "Come Back to Sorrento."

But Carlos was leaning back on the veranda railing, listening with his eyes closed like a swami in bliss. One by one the audience left, but I stayed and watched him in his rapture, lost to the immediate world.

After that, it was hard to tell whether he was more in love with Thurani or her record player. He brought over his own LPs and played them as often as decorum allowed. A certain look would come over him whenever he was about to be left alone in our house. He'd grow fidgety, and I knew he could hardly wait for everyone to clear out so he could put on a record and listen to his heart's content.

I'd never seen records handled so reverently. He slipped them in and out of their jackets almost without touching them, his long dark fingers merely skimming the rims. Then he gently blew the dust off them and held them up to eye level to check for warps.

He was like a merchant, a man who knew his trade—like the piece-goods man who folded as he measured his fabric; like the jeweler who picked up his gems with tweezers and set them on their bed of cotton ever so delicately, as though handling live insects; like the Indian cooks in the night market who swirled parasols of dough over their heads; like the Chinese cooks who could turn out perfect oyster omelets almost without looking.

These merchants did only one thing well, but Carlos had so many talents. Not only could he speak Spanish, dance the tango, play the bandonion, sing "Donkey Serenade," and fix broken lamps, he could make his body do tricks. He worked his jaws, and his scalp moved back and forth. He wiggled each eyebrow and ear one by one. With his tongue and lower lip he made Negro lips. Like a Hindu dancer, he had a rubber neck that let his head sail the breadth of his shoulders, then turn almost back to front. He threw peanuts and plums six feet up into the air and caught them in his open mouth. He made his arms undulate like snakes, his buttock muscles twitch cheek by cheek. He could vibrate each leg so powerfully that once, when he tied a string of Indian brass bells onto his ankle, they trilled like temple bells in a storm.

When Thurani wasn't home, he'd try to teach me these tricks out on the veranda. We'd spend the afternoons there, Carlos perched on the railing where he could keep an eye out for my cousin, I on the palm-leaf mat on the floor.

Through the veranda rails I could see my friends at play in the afternoon heat haze, but I much preferred being with Carlos, listening to his stories of dancing the tango in Argentina, or trying to ape his tricks. Carlos was merely filling time between Thurani's appearances, which I prayed to forestall. Once she showed up, he'd become distracted, and I'd have to take myself off and settle for the games in the dirt yard below.

It was on this veranda that Carlos first taught me the tango—on one of those afternoons when Thurani was home and I was playing downstairs for a change. The boys had started a game of rounders, excluding me because Cloddy was on one of the teams and he wanted to keep me out. We'd had a falling out after the battery incident.

Cloddy had wanted to make the swap: I had something for which he was prepared to give me his transistor. This transistor was a small cardboard box about two inches square, fitted with a little jumble of wires and a light bulb the size of a berry. By touching together the tips of two of these wires—with a frown of concentration and expertise—Cloddy was able to make the bulb light up.

"Blooming genius, man," said another boy in admiration. I agreed to the exchange.

What I gave up in return, the thing that Cloddy seemed to value even more than his baffling little box, was a headpiece—a hood I'd made out of a plain gray fabric, one of my mother's old sarongs. It was inspired by *The Man in the Iron Mask*, the movie of the year (meaning it was the only movie to come to town that year). I'd cut the thing out myself, stitched the seams for double strength, and finished the eyeholes with black thread. The whole painstaking business had taken days.

And I'd as good as thrown it away. That's how I felt when we'd made the exchange and I found I couldn't get the light to go on in Cloddy's transistor.

"Battery's probably dead," Cloddy said, dismissing my complaint.

Battery? He hadn't said anything about a battery before. How could I have known that two wires, touched together, won't spark a light without a battery?

"Where am I going to get a battery, Cloddy?"

Cloddy looked at his friend, the one who'd called him a blooming genius. They both laughed.

"You need more than one battery," Cloddy said, tapping his head, "to turn the lights on there."

"Give me back my hood," I demanded.

"Fair exchange," said Cloddy.

"Is no robbery," his friend amended.

An idea came to me. "Keep the hood," I said, imitating my mother's tone whenever she informed me that she was letting me have my way, with every expectation that I'd come to regret it. "Keep the hood. And may you wear it the rest of your life. It's made from a woman's sarong."

I may as well have told him that something he'd been eating with great relish had been contaminated with shit. No male was supposed to risk the ignominy of walking under a clothesline on which an article of female clothing was hanging—much less wear one on his head.

That's how the feud began. We stopped speaking to each other—or rather we spoke in tongues. Some days I managed to stick mine out at him, then run or look away before he could stick his out at me, and on those days I slept better. But when he bested me, I couldn't rest until I had my revenge.

This was one of those days. I stood on the sidelines while the game of rounders went on, staring at Cloddy with all the patience of spite. After a while I realized it might be a long wait. He knew what I was up to. To pass the time I picked up a cane hoop someone had left on the ground near me. The Hula Hoop rage was yet to come, but I'd learned how to work the hoop and spin it around my waist and hips, up and down my arms and legs, and even around my neck.

Practicing every hoop trick I knew, I stuck my tongue out at intervals in Cloddy's direction, just in case he happened to break down and glance at me. I must have been there a long time, spinning the hoop and imitating a flycatcher with my darting tongue, unaware that Thurani had left the veranda and Carlos was leaning out over the railing, watching me, laughing. When I finally noticed him and dropped the hoop hastily, Carlos applauded.

"Girl," he called down to me, "you are born performer, you know that? Come here and I'll teach you tango."

Up on the veranda, when Carlos drew me to him, I began to giggle.

"No giggling, please," Carlos said. "Nothing to giggle about. First thing you must keep in your head about tango: two sad faces, four happy legs."

2

"You are *talented*, girl! *Talented.*" Carlos pronounced the word to rhyme with "relented."

His approval made me reel. I was already giddy from our spins and dips across the veranda floor, from the whiffs—part 4711 Eau de Cologne, part cumin—that came from his armpits, under which the top of my head fitted neatly. The swoon was unlike anything I'd known since diving off the rocks into the river. But even that wasn't as fancy as the way he'd flip me backward into a dip that flicked my ponytail across the floor. When he pulled me up to lean into his chest, my ear to his heart, there was that beat to steady and guide me. I could have sworn it kept time to the music we were dancing to.

At night, in my sleep, I let in the mosquitoes by kicking my foot against the mosquito net in time to the tango's rhythm.

"My God, Tango, you are certainly quick on the uptake, my girl," Carlos said. People came to watch us dance now. Our reputation was spreading.

"Oh, yes, why bother with school?" said my teacher at school, an Armenian Baptist named Mrs. Baba Sheen. She carried a special ruler whose flex she often tested on my open palm. "Why waste time on studies when you are Carmen Miranda? After all, tango is more important than school."

I couldn't have agreed more. I wanted only to dance. On days when Carlos didn't come, I felt weak and listless; I felt the emptiness of not dancing. All the old entertainments of compound life, all the games I'd played, had lost their appeal— hopscotch and hoopla, rounders and kick-the-can, the antics of the Gopal gibbon. Nothing else mattered now but the tango.

"You'll grow up to be a leaf-eater, like Carlos," my mother warned.

It didn't seem like the worst fate to become a leaf-eater in Buenos Aires. That, I took it, was where ultimately Carlos would go. "Biding my time," he'd say. "I'm just biding my time, Tango, till I can vamoose out of this dump. Back to my lovely B.A., the city of lights."

In my mind's eye Buenos Aires was a Xanadu of nightlife. Everything I already knew about life after dark was worth waiting for. Nights in Irrawaddy had a bloom, a hum, a pulse so tantalizing it seemed a shame to go to sleep. It wasn't just the flowers that released their perfumes only after dark, or the orange flames that blossomed in the kerosene lamps lit throughout the huts along the river, or the budding of the stars all across the black soil of the sky. It wasn't just the chorus of cicadas and bullfrogs and night birds, the rollicking breezes that fanned down the heat of the day. At the right season, on the right days, whole lives, whole dramas, unfolded at night—on the stages of our open-air theaters for all to see. The performers—clowns, comedians, actors, musicians, magicians—carried on in this season all night long, laughing and singing and dancing and wisecracking, crashing their cymbals, beating their drums, sawing on their fiddles, and shrilling on their flutes well into the first light of dawn.

In the Buenos Aires Carlos described to me, the intoxication of nightlife was routine, not seasonal. He told me the

difference between restaurants and cafés, nightclubs and caba-
rets, dance halls and concert halls, movie theaters and opera
houses. All came to life in Buenos Aires night after night after
night. And in my mind this bewitching city took shape in a
fairyland of wide, important avenues so extravagantly lit up
that it put our own light festival to shame, of street mazes
converging on jasmine-scented courtyards where lanterns hung
and nightingales crooned and someone played the bandonion
while a pair of star-crossed lovers danced the tango well into
the first light of dawn. . . .

Carlos's bandonion, that long-awaited, much-touted instrument, arrived at last by sea mail. I watched him attack the crate
with a crowbar, then lift out the precious cargo: a rectangular
box with shoulder straps and leathery folds that yawned and
collapsed with whispers and sighs. It had buttons on one side,
a keyboard on the other, and gleamed with polished wood and
inlaid mother-of-pearl.

Standing, one leg hitched up on a shaky stool, Carlos rested
the instrument on his knee. He began to play, swinging it this
way and that, squeezing out of its bellows a wheezy sort of
wail—foreign sounding, gloomy, but ecstatic. As he played, he
sang. He had a high voice with a catch in it. I couldn't make
out the words, but there was a story there, a heartbreaker to
judge from Carlos's watery eyes and quavery voice, which
hovered between a sob and a song.

"My God, Tango, you are certainly quick on the uptake,"
Carlos said when I could play my first tune on the bandonion.

But while I fell under the spell of the tango and its music,
my mother was falling under a spell of her own, the spell of
religious devotion.

"So your ma's off to the convent again, lah?" said Mrs. de
Brito during one of my mother's extended stays.

"Not a convent, Auntie Mamie," I explained. "A Buddhist—"

"Nunnery, right? Same thing. Off with the hair in both places."

"Yes, but no, not the same, really. Buddhist nuns can come and go; they don't have to give up their husbands and children," I said, eager to emphasize this point. Thank God my mother wasn't faced with the choice; I dreaded to think how she might choose otherwise.

"Fate, fate!" said Mrs. de Brito, yawning. I thought she was commenting on destiny, but what she meant was "faith." "Just be like me, Tango," she said, kicking up her leg gaily. "Free tinker."

"What's a free tinker, Auntie Mamie?"

"Well, use your logic, my girl. Free tinker is someone who is free to tink what he wants, do what he wants. Of course, you must have basic . . . basic character, like. You want to be a flart? Go ahead, be a flart. Flart with ten buggers. But only marry one. Diworce, annulment, not worte it."

I had been wondering about Mrs. de Brito's husband, her chosen bugger. I was curious about how he had died.

"Very sudden. Just like that," she said, snapping her fingers. "Cause of death was infart." She meant "infarct," but "infart" was the way she said it, loud and clear.

In fart. I had thought there was only one kind—the kind that went out, not in. Maybe, in Mr. de Brito's case, he had let it all build up inside, causing the implosion.

"A lovely, lovely man, my Gabby," she said wistfully.

Gabby was Gabriel de Brito, Senior, Carlos's father.

"Was Uncle Gabby free tinker, too?"

"No fear! Catlick as they come. Holy communion, holy this, holy that. His sister is worst of the lot. That Mercedes woman! Mass every morning, singing in the choir, playing the organ, but in her heart is no true charity. Blaming me, *me*, if you please, for being bad influence on her bro. In her eyes, he's angel Gabriel and I'm Lucifer. Some people, I tell you!"

"Ma been poisoning your mind?" said Carlos. "Doan listen to her. Ma's jealous of Auntie Mercy."

"What she jealous of?" I said.

"She jealous of Auntie Mercy's breeding."

"Auntie Mercy's breathing?"

"Not breeding, I didn't say 'breeding.' I said *breeding.*' Anyway, you better get along with Auntie Mercy, hear? She's going to teach you piano. You have ta*lent.* And wasting ta*lent* is sin."

"Piano! Why piano, Carlos? Just keep teaching me bandonion."

"Ah, bandonion!" His face softened; he sighed. "Bandonion is different kettle of fish. If you really want to play tango music, I mean. Of course you can learn bandonion like you can learn concertina; learn to sight-read, learn rhythm, learn technique. You can make noise like German polka musicians. But there is something else no one can teach you about tango music, and until you know that something else, you can't really play it. Trouble is, you get to know that something else only by playing, really playing, for tango orchestra. Follow?

"Anyway, my girl," he said. "Bandonion is no instrument for girls. Where's the future in it? Matter of fact, not much future for tango, period." He sounded pessimistic; it troubled me. There was a time when he seemed paralyzed by a longing for Argentina, by the dream to take up where he had left off—roaming the world of tea dances, ballrooms, and cafés. I learned the Spanish word for "earthquake" only because Terremoto was one of his favorite dance clubs, where he heard the great bandonionist Julio De Caro play.

"Let's be practical, Tango," said Carlos. "Piano is the instrument for you."

. . .

"So!" Mercedes greeted me. "This is the famous Tango." She looked me up and down and sniffed. Her smile was prim and off to one side of her face. She was tall and dark-skinned and elegant, with the bearing of a maharani. She wore extremely high heels, a chiffon scarf draped about her shoulders and fastened with a brooch, a pearl necklace, and a cloisonné comb to hold the French knot in her crinkly black hair.

Her house, unlike ours, was crammed. We had nothing on the walls except huge stains from leaks and mold, and our furniture amounted to one of every item: one chair, one table, one stool, one meat safe, and one standing lamp—a necessity, not a luxury, because the overhead bulbs in the bare sockets kept shorting out even before a person could step off the stool after changing them.

Mercy's walls were hung with framed pictures, her rooms crowded with chairs, stools, footrests, and tables displaying collections of boxes, figurines, dolls, and photographs in frames. The music books were everywhere: stacked and strewn all around the base of the walls, covered with dust balls and dead bugs.

This was no small-town dump. This was luxury; this was excess. If only Thurani could see!

The piano was in the living room. I'd seen pianos before, but in pictures. This one was an upright of reddish wood, with a lace runner over the top. "Come on, Tango," Carlos coaxed. "Give us a tune, what say?"

I found middle C and managed "Bill Groggin's Goat." When I looked up, Mercedes was wincing.

"What you think, Auntie? She got potential, or what?" said Carlos.

Mercedes stood up. "Budding Moseart," she said, winking at me. "By the way, you can call me Teacher Mercy."

That night I woke to a smell. My mother found it increasingly necessary now to cook late at night. She had taken to offering alms twice a week to the monks who came begging at dawn. The odors of her cooking were often strong enough to wake me: the smell of onions, ginger, and garlic sizzling in oil or of fat frying or of pickled greens steaming in a soup. Sometimes, when fish paste was involved, the fumes were enough to make me sneeze.

But it wasn't food I was smelling this time. It was some newly discovered substance I couldn't place. I tossed and turned, trying to identify the sweet, hovering fragrance. At last it came to me. It was the scent of Mercedes de Brito's piano keys.

I came to love that smell—a blend of varnish and L'Air du Temps, Mercedes' perfume, which arose from the felt and ivory. The first thing I did, sitting down to each lesson, was to bend and sniff the keyboard—a ritual Mercedes accepted without understanding. *Her* ritual was to begin the lesson with a complicated prayer to the Virgin Mary.

Remember, O most gracious Virgin Mary, that never was it known, that anyone who fled to thy protection . . .

Then she wheezed beside me, humming along huskily as I played, slapping her thigh to keep time.

"Not half-bad," she'd say with her dislocated little smile, "could be worse." She tapped me on the knuckles with a bamboo back scratcher—but playfully, in time to the rhythm I was keeping—a different sort of rap entirely from Mrs. Baba Sheen's.

"The time has come," she announced one day, "to concentrate on the three Bs."

"The three Bs," she repeated, widening her eyes. She seized the back scratcher. I flinched, thinking she was going to hit me with it, but instead she stuck the stick end of it into her French knot and scratched. "Bark," she explained. "Bark, B. Thoven, Brahms."

From once a week, after school, I was lured into going twice, then three times a week, then every weekday from after school to after dark, when she herself walked me home.

In time I wished my two separate lives—the life of piano practice and the life at home—could be brought together. If only we could afford a piano! If only it were the way it had been in my tango-dancing days. My family used to sit and watch then—my mother clapping in time; my father clucking and jerking his head to say, "Not that again!" but watching despite himself; Momo, a neighbor's child, off in a corner trying to imitate me by spinning round and round until she collapsed from dizziness; Thurani leaning against the wall, a hand over her mouth to stifle her amusement.

If only Teacher Mercy could just sit down and eat with us for once! But the most she'd been offered at our house was a glass of Vimto or a cup of tea. My mother couldn't bring herself to invite Mercy for a meal. "She won't like my cooking," she'd say. I wondered why, if her cooking was good enough for the monks, it wouldn't be good enough for Mercy. "Her kind doesn't know how to eat our kind of food," my mother reasoned. "We would have to put out spoon and fork just for her. Then *she'd* feel embarrassed about being the only one, then *we'd* have to eat with spoon and fork as well. You know how your father hates eating with gear. Food doesn't taste like food to him unless he's eating with his fingers."

My parents were wary of Mercy. Why that interest of hers in me? they wondered. She had managed to placate them somewhat by paying me what she called scholarship money. It was nothing—enough to buy two new comic books each week from the stand at the Gopal brothers' store, no more—but it helped justify my time spent with her. I was supposed to be assisting her with her other students. But in fact it was her way of keeping me practicing longer and longer hours, between (and sometimes even during) her other classes.

All those hours were producing obscure gains in my parents' eyes. And in Mrs. Baba Sheen's. "You are arriving at conclusions," she roared at me one day, flinging my test paper at me, "by guesswork. You are cooking without benefit of salt. Why is it you can remember wisecracks and rubbishy jingles like 'rasp-, cran-, blue-, black-, dingle-, goose-, and straw-,' but you can't remember *facts?*" (She was referring to something I'd learned from Carlos: the jingle berries.)

Behind me, the fat Chinese girl in glasses who never let anyone forget she got "hundred upon hundred" for every exam—was waving her hand and bouncing with impatience. "T'cher, T'cher, T'cher!" she insisted. Her father was a dentist called Doctor Dingling, a quack with a loud, unstable laugh. A quack and a cook. After attending to a patient, he offered a meal (for an extra fee), which he whipped up on the spot, turning to a wok that sat on a gas burner next to his sink. The patient remained in the dental chair to eat. It was nothing fancy: a plate of slippery rice noodles or bean curd or an omelet as a rule—but tasty enough. The practice had its dangers, though. Between the drilling and the stir-frying, wrong teeth had been pulled, and, as in my own case, the drill had been known to slip and injure the tongue, moving Doctor Dingling to shout with laughter.

I turned around now and said to his daughter, in a voice I thought Mrs. Baba Sheen wouldn't hear: "Fatty, fatty, boomalatty!"

She heard.

"Smart aleck, eh? Smart aleck with *superiority* complex!"

I didn't know why everyone was so eager to remind me

that I wasn't smart. I never said I was. My father put it another way.

"Look, you're not stupid," he said. "Why don't you just put your mind to it and study? Thurani used to study."

(I happened to know that wasn't true, but Thurani's name came up often in connection with success. Not only was she now working as a guide at the United Nations headquarters in Geneva, she was engaged to a Dayan diplomat, himself a graduate of the University of London. Thurani had sent photographs of him. In some of them a scar across the upper lip was visible. I showed them to Auntie Mamie, who held the pictures up to her nose, studying them intently. "Harelip!" she said, triumphant. She hadn't cared for Thurani, I could tell.)

"No," said my father, in a private aside, as if a chorus of voices had just contradicted his assessment of me. "No, she is not stupid." Then, turning to me, "You're just lazy. I'm telling you this out of love for you."

"What is all this for?" he asked one day when I came home from piano lessons too exhausted to eat.

When I relayed the question to Mercy, she said, "Tell your father a man's reach must exceed his grasp, else what's a heaven for?"

We burst out laughing at the same time, struck by how funny that would sound, translated literally into Dayan. My father didn't like me speaking English to him. Unlike Thurani's father, who had been educated, in English, at a Christian Brothers school, my father as a young boy had gone to a Buddhist monastery school where only Dayan was taught. Later on, of course, in high school, he *had* learned English, matriculating with sufficient marks to secure a clerical job with the River Transit Authority.

His accent was strong. He knew it and flaunted it—like many men of his generation, who compensated for their inferior grasp of English by deliberately mispronouncing words.

It was a mark of national pride among the insecure. It was proper to speak English like a true Dayan—not like an Anglo putting on "ayars." When he was in the right mood, I could persuade my father to say, "There is a bear under the stair," which he rendered as, "There-yar is a bear-yar under the stair-yar." He said "op*por*tunity" for "opportunity," "bokka-see" for "box," "bomping" for "bombing," and "wahtah" for "water."

But he could, and did, read English books—always a little furtively. He covered each book with newspaper before reading it. I never knew whether it was to protect the book or to conceal it. Sometimes a book would slip out of its cover, and I would catch a title: *Memoirs of a Midget* by Walter de la Mare; *The Circus of Dr. Lao* by Charles G. Finney. But let me address him in English, and he'd respond in Dayan. He looked at me a certain way—resentful but also envious—if I said something complicated in English or sang an English song. When Thurani's father complimented me, my father said, "Of course she's fluent. She eats and sleeps with those Anglos. She might as well be an Anglo."

I wished that I *could* go up to my father and say something like "A man's reach must exceed his grasp." But even if he did understand, he would have pretended not to; he'd have given me that blank look and said, "What, forgotten all your Dayan, your mother tongue?"

Come exam time, Mercy went to make her case with my parents. In those days, the national music exams for admission to the Music Academy were held only in Anika, the capital, and administered by an examiner sent out by the Trinity College of Music in Dublin. This year the exams coincided with another special event: the concert tour of the renowned pianist Niki-foros Focas. In addition to his performance at Municipal Hall, the maestro was to hold a master class, which Mercy had already arranged for me to attend.

Mercy successfully talked my parents out of their two chief concerns: the expense, and the hazards, of a journey by train. To my surprise they let me go. She assured them that once in Anika, we would be staying with her relatives, and as for the risk of a rail attack by insurgents, it was unlikely in this season when most rebel attempts to subvert transportation routes occurred along the riverbanks and were aimed at the ferry launches.

We left on a brilliant morning, the shower trees in full bright-yellow blossom, the sun fast climbing and spreading its dazzle across acres of green-gold rice fields. It was my first big journey: I'd never been as far north as the oil fields, or as far south to the mouth of the delta.

I pointed at a tiny pagoda on the west bank of the river. We had white pagodas and gold pagodas in quantity, and white ones capped with gold, but I'd never seen one like this, built out of silver, before.

Mercy was busy looking through her bags, making sure our lunch wasn't leaking. She had brought hard-boiled eggs, bundled with rice in banana leaves. At village stations, vendors rushed up to the windows of the train, balancing big bamboo trays of food on their heads at just the right height for passengers to reach down and help themselves: fried noodles, banana fritters, crispy sparrows, sticky rice; mangoes and custard apples and pomelos and guavas—always of course with hot tea.

At one big junction we were in our seats, having a snack, when we heard a commotion on the platform. One of the food vendors, a girl about my age, was standing with a tray on her head, crying her eyes out. The tray was empty, but the girl— by force of habit, apparently—kept it balanced on her head. The effort required an erect posture comically at odds with her misery.

The face under the tray was puffy and wet. Through her

sobs she was trying to tell some sort of story to the people who'd gathered around.

"How is happening?" Mercy asked, in her quaint Dayan, of someone below.

"She has been robbed," said the person on the platform, in precise English. He had a plump mole in the middle of his chin out of which grew three luxuriant hairs. "They have taken everything. They have taken the food, they have taken all her money. Now she fears going home because there she will be thrashed."

The distraught girl, the tray still on her head, was walking purposelessly along. People were pressing advice and admonition of every sort on her, but she was beyond reach. Right below our window she stopped to bawl out something in answer to a question from the crowd. I looked straight down at the empty tray. On the seat at my knee was my cloth bag and, in that bag, a clear plastic wallet Thurani had given me. I had money in that wallet—pocket money for the trip. I was planning to spend it on something available only in Anika: a Hong Kong clutch bag—the kind woven out of multicolored plastic string.

I looked at Mercy. She was still talking to the commentator below, who was now opining, in English, on the state of lawlessness in the country.

The train gave a lurch preparatory to moving on. There was just enough time for me to reach into my bag for the money and drop it onto the tray beneath the window. Such an act of charity would have been applauded by my mother. It would have bought me some merit, maybe spared me rebirth into one of the loutish existences—of a rat, say. Or a worm. Or a pinmouth.

I thought again of that Hong Kong–style bag I'd been wanting for so long. That bag was a desire of this life alone. What use for such a yearning in a later life as a rat or worm or louse? And with no such use, in those incarnations, for a woven plastic bag, where was the loss? Life as a louse would bring the consciousness of a louse.

In any case, there'd be just enough time to drop the money and maybe call the girl's attention to my gift before the train pulled away. It would all happen too quickly for anyone to get a good look at me—let alone for the girl to thank me. It would happen so fast that I wouldn't be recognized or acknowledged or thanked. I wouldn't like that at all.

By the next morning, on the last leg of our journey, the train had filled to overflowing. Bodies and bedrolls had lain in wait at every stop, all along the station platforms. Through every opening in the train came a crush of bedding and luggage and pots and pans and people. Our second-class compartment, only half-occupied until now, was filled with new passengers and their packages.

The occupants had settled themselves and the panic was abating when a last arrival came crashing into our midst as the train took off.

"*Japan*," said someone.

"*Japan*," someone else confirmed.

"*Japan*, it's a *Japan*."

The man who tottered in, almost falling on his face, was a Japanese gentleman with a very large suitcase of a delicate baby blue. A space opened up for him as people shrank back. One or two voices rose in complaint. But as the intruder appeared not to be able to speak either Dayan or English, these voices soon fell to mutterings, then silence.

The Japanese passenger, who had steadied himself after an apologetic bow, brought out from his breast pocket a crisp white handkerchief. With it he mopped his face, then cleaned his glasses. That done, he perched on his upright suitcase and affected an air of abstraction by gazing at the ceiling, where a warning was posted about the fine for improper use of the emergency bell. But every now and then he clasped his hands as if in prayer, cracking his knuckles in one rippling motion.

"Ma!" tattled a small voice from behind some bundles. "Ma, he's quacking his nackles! Ow, stop pinching me, Ma!"

Mercy and I turned our faces to the window, to keep from laughing. After I'd recovered I turned back to stare. I'd never seen a Japanese person before, but this one hardly matched my impression of what such a person should be. I was too young to remember the Japanese occupation, but stories I'd been told about the brutality of the conquering army came back to me now. Whenever my mother recounted the exchanges she'd had with one or another bullying Japanese officer, she mimicked their hoarse voices, demanding, threatening, barking out orders in broken English. More than once she'd reenacted for me the terror and humiliation of the moment when one particularly hateful sergeant had slapped my father—for no apparent reason—in front of a gathering of people. This was not a story she told in front of my father, and by this fact alone some of the shame of the incident was brought home to me.

Studying this fastidious-looking Japanese before me now, I recalled—or thought I recalled—the scene I'd always believed I was too young to remember: a group of people in an open field somewhere, my father being called out of the group, the Japanese officer barking out questions and accusations, my father's passive denials. Then the vicious slap across the face as the onlookers winced and averted their eyes.

I could go up to this distant cousin of that officer. Perched on his suitcase, he would be just about eye level with me. I could pay him back with a slap on the face. Or spit on him. Others, I noticed, were looking him over, too—maybe recalling other slaps, other wounds. If the Japanese struck back at me, would they come to my aid?

I lost my nerve for the revenge, but not the itch. As we approached Anika I got up, and, pretending to bend over and busy myself with something on the floor, I dropped a long dribble of spit down the back of his immaculate suitcase. He was first off the train; I felt I hadn't taken full advantage of the situation, but it gave me a little satisfaction to see him so innocently shepherding his blue suitcase through the crowds.

Down on the platform, someone was calling to me.

An eager-faced young man was grinning and waving in my direction. Thinking he was signaling to someone else, I looked around. But no, he was fixated on me, waving excitedly, jumping up and down so I wouldn't lose him in the throng and, yes, rushing to me.

In front of me he held out his arms in greeting and welcome. And broke into song. "A-beckon-silly-ahhhhh . . . ," he crooned, with such clarity and feeling that I couldn't believe those mysterious lyrics weren't meant specifically for me. But they weren't. The next minute he was bouncing off to serenade someone else. "A-beckon-silly-ahhhh . . ." I heard again and again as he disappeared into the crowd.

"Village idiot!" Mercy said, half in annoyance, half in explanation.

But what a village we were in now!

How lucky, I thought as we rode our trishaw through the city streets, that we'd arrived on a festival day: everybody in riotous cottons and silks; women with jewels in their ears, jewels in their combs, jewels on their jacket buttons, and jewels at their throats and wrists; children all dolled up and men in silks, too—silk sarongs and silk jackets.

Music in the air! Cymbals clashing, kettledrums rattling from some concert in the distance! All the while, a jamboree of car horns blaring, bicycle, trishaw, and gharry bells trilling!

The whole city was in rehearsal. Boys on bicycles did stunts. The trishaw peddlers rode in threes or fours, now in tandem, now abreast. Decked out like floozies with flowers behind their ears, garlands around their necks, ribbons in their manes, and bells on their bridles, the gharry horses were prancing. Even the beggars, cripples, and crazies along the pavements had talents to show off and tricks to perform: a ragged boy, his bare bottom covered with sores, somersaulted like the Gopal gibbon; a blind musician fiddled away, picking up the coins at his feet with his toes; a wild-eyed sadhu danced in a trance; a legless boy on a board with wheels whizzed up and down a sidewalk.

It was a dream. The streets beneath our trishaw wheels, so wide and regimented, took on the distorted dimensions of the streets in dreams. The storefronts and sidewalk stalls held a dreamlike profusion of food and merchandise: pyramids of saffron spices, red chillies, purple brinjals, green limes, pink melons; and, hanging from the awnings above, silk umbrellas, plastic boxes and buckets, nylon raincoats, and bolts of electrifying cloth. Even the office buildings we passed had fantastic façades suggesting dark interiors where in dreams a person's fate is decided.

And when at last our trishaw turned a corner and there, at the end of the street, was the Great Universal, this dazzling colossus seemed like the first and last pagoda of all time—studded, of course, with precious gems and, as in dreams, ablaze with gold.

"What's the festival, Teacher Mercy?" I asked.

Mercy laughed. "It's the festival of city life, my dear."

The maestro kept us waiting all morning for the master class, but we didn't dare complain. We had heard that Monsieur Nikiforos Focas, born in Greece and educated in France, was a direct descendant of a Byzantine prince.

"What's a Byzantine prince, Teacher Mercy?" I asked. Anxiety seized me. I wasn't sure how to greet a concert pianist. Especially a concert pianist with such a pedigree. Should I bow? Did he have a ring that required kissing, the way Mercy had once startled me by so fervently kissing the smoky topaz on her archbishop's crooked, arthritic finger?

"Not Byzan*teen*, dear. Byzan*tyne*."

"Byzantyne, then."

"Don't you know about the Byzantyne Empire? No? Don't they teach you anything in that Baptist school? The Byzantynes were, well, sort of Russians who made icons. You don't know what icons are? They're these holy pictures made of gold. Anyway, the Byzantyne Empire was a very great empire. And just imagine! You'll be meeting a direct descendant of a Byzantyne prince."

"A Byzantine prince!" I said.

"Byzan*tyne*, Byzan*tyne*! Remember it rhymes with 'Clemen*tyne*.'"

"O my darling, O my darling," I sang, "O my darling Byzantyne . . ."

"Mmm," said Mercy, trying not to laugh.

The maestro arrived at last, around noon, quick-marching down the hall. I could hardly believe my eyes. This Byzantine prince was handsome enough—with thick black hair and powerful shoulders and arms—but his legs were so short that I couldn't wait for him to come close enough to verify my suspicion that I was taller than he.

He was holding out his arms impatiently: it appeared we had something he wanted.

What he wanted was Teacher Mercy's hand, for a quick sniff.

"Madame!" he exclaimed. "Forgive me! I was laid on the way! But please! Before we start: let me offer you some lunch. The ministry have poot something for us to eat. That way."

"And you are?" he said to me, referring to a piece of paper he'd pulled out of his breast pocket. "Tango?"

"Tango!" he repeated, having made a highly amusing discovery. "Come, then, Tango and . . . and *madame*, is it? Or *Mademoiselle* de Brito?"

"Please call me Mercedes," Mercy said. On her cheek appeared a little spot I'd never noticed before: a dimple, of all things.

"And please call me Nikki!" said the Byzantine dwarf.

How they laughed and laughed over lunch, sitting at first at either end of a sofa, then drawing nearer and nearer. Finally Mercy got up and reached across the table to pour another cup of tea.

"Mercedes bends!" muttered Monsieur Focas, leering at her backside. "Mmmm. My favorite car." He caught my eye and winked.

"I have a proposal," he said. "Perhaps Tango would like to practice in the auditorium while we finish our lunch?" I looked at Mercy, who signaled me to comply, so off I slouched, dispirited, down the hall to where a monumental concert grand stood on the empty stage. After warming up, I had barely begun to play when Monsieur Focas startled me by slamming the door noisily behind him as he came into the auditorium. His mood had changed altogether.

"So!" he said. "Here we are. Shall we begin?"

I settled myself on the stool and got ready to play the Haydn sonata I'd prepared. And on the brink of playing, I foresaw disaster.

Unhinged by the premonition, I decided on a change. I plunged into the Rachmaninoff instead: the G-Minor Prelude. Racing headlong, I stumbled; but instead of pushing on, I backed up to correct the blunder. And blundered again. And backed up again.

"Stop!" he shouted at last. "Stop. Just stop, please!" He was holding on to his head as if it might fall off. "Thank God!

"Now what was that?" he said, baring his teeth at me unpleasantly. "Music? Maybe a little Irrawaddy music, eh?

Ting-tong, ting-tong?" I noticed he said "Irrahvahddy" for "Irrawaddy."

"Tchahhh!" he said, flinging his book onto a chair. "Why do they waste my time? Master class, ha-ha! One student shows up! One student out of the whole country! And he cannot play." For a moment I thought Monsieur Focas was referring to another, male student, but realized that he'd just got his genders mixed up. It was me he meant.

From out of the darkness of the auditorium a voice said, "That's it. That's enough."

Teacher Mercy stepped out into the light of an aisle. She clip-clopped her way toward the stage on her clownishly high heels, panting and limping by the time she reached us.

"That's quite enough," she said, pulling me up from the piano seat. "Thank you very very much, *Mister* Focas!

"You have no right," she said, her lower lip fluttering, "to take out your wounded manhood, your petty . . . pettiness on an innocent child. A talented child. No right at all. Come on, Tango. We've wasted our time."

"Talented?" shouted the maestro after us. "Talented, my foute! He's meediyok! Just like you, madame. Meediyok. You don't know, you can't know, what is talent. It's my time you have wasted. *My* time!"

"It was a successful trip," Mercy announced on the train back home. "Yes, successful," she insisted, folding her arms. "Don't look at me like that, Tango. You passed the exam, didn't you? That's the important thing."

"But I had a bit of difficulty," I said. That set us both laughing as we hadn't laughed in days. (The exam was on the day after the "master class." The examiner, a portly, good-natured Humpty-Dumpty in a black suit, had waltzed around the room making patient, soothing noises whenever I faltered.

At the end he had written on the exam card, under the passing grade, "Seemed to be having a bit of difficulty.")

We were on the last stretch of our journey home, where the train ran parallel to the river. Things looked so different now. The silver pagoda I'd seen on the ride down turned out to be a construction of corrugated tin. The familiar silhouettes of men poling boats went by in flashes. In that speeded-up tableau—the relay of each man briskly following the other up and down the length of the narrow boat for his turn at the pole— you could see the whole disheartening sequence: the men moving so fast, the boat moving so slowly. Even the sight of fishermen casting their nets was pathetic. In the setting sun, the river now was flowing gold in the distance—pure gold—and in their tiny boats they seemed set adrift on some fool's errand, flinging their stick-figure bodies forward, casting their gossamer nets again and again and again. I felt sorry for them; they seemed to be angling for gold, not fish.

3

"So you're back," said Mrs. de Brito when I'd got up the nerve to visit her again, after the fiasco in Anika. "Tail between your legs, eh?"

What I had between my legs wasn't nearly as amusing as a tail. It was a sort of loincloth my mother had handed me when I went to her with blood on my hands, so to speak. She made a sound with her tongue and teeth and turned away to set about fashioning the loincloth affair.

She was very preoccupied as she folded and wrapped, giving me no hint of what was on her mind. Then she handed me the thing, saying, "Well, Daughter, you're a young lady now."

Was that all? Why then was she swallowing hard, as if I'd just stuffed a big rice ball down her throat? Why end up looking so stricken and resigned? Had I come down with some unspeakable disease?

I'd waited as long as I could before telling her, because I couldn't decide what position to take. To pretend innocence would have required an act that might not come off. But if I did let on that I was already in the know, she was bound to ask me where I'd got my information. And I couldn't very well reveal that it wasn't Mrs. de Brito, or even Mercy, but Cloddy who'd explained the facts of life to me.

Cloddy had become something of a scientist, dissecting frogs, measuring rainfall, and writing down his findings in a notebook with graph paper.

"Blooming genius, man," said his friend whose job these days was to empty the rain buckets and soak the frogs in formaldehyde.

"Just you wait," Cloddy warned me. "One of these days you'll be pissing red. Bleeding. It happens to all women. Only women." He shuddered, to convey disgust.

I didn't know if I should believe him, since he'd said it in a huff, after I'd refused to touch his precious pet, as he referred to his penis.

"What's that?" I said, the first time he proffered it to me. Of course I knew what it was, but the blooming genius took me seriously.

"It's my little pet," he said.

"No! You keep a worm for a pet?"

"Touch it," he said, as if what he had in hand was an exotic creature he was eager for me to experience while fearing I might mishandle it. He was behaving just like the tout with the two-headed snake I'd seen once at the bazaar.

I touched it—the worm, not the snake—and it moved a little.

Cloddy seemed satisfied as he tucked it into his pants, jumping a little to get it back into place. But then he kept wanting me to touch it. Again. And again. Finally I refused— mainly because of the way he *ordered* me to touch it, implying that only a fool would resist. I didn't like being ordered to do things on grounds that they were irresistible. That's when he told me about the blood.

For this, too, I went to Mrs. de Brito, whose reaction was as I'd anticipated: different.

"Is it true, Auntie Mamie? You're not supposed to eat sour preserves when you're, uh, bleeding?" was the way I introduced the subject.

She was playing solitaire. "Ah!" she said, looking up at the ceiling and waving a card at it in friendly acknowledgment. "The curse.

"So you've come of age, lah?" was her bored remark as she went back to her cards.

It was in the same offhand manner that she enlightened me about Mr. Sanders's peculiar smell. Mr. Sanders was an American missionary I'd once had the privilege of sitting next to during a bioscope at the church hall. In the dark, he placed a hand on my thigh—while I placed a finger horizontally (but discreetly) under my nose, to block his strong wet-dog smell.

I told Mrs. de Brito about the smell—leaving out the part about being stroked, of course. I thought the fault might have been partly mine because when Sanders had said, "Will you sit next to me?" I had replied, "*Avec brassiere,*" which Cloddy had told me meant "with pleasure."

"Oh, *that* smell," she said, as if I'd just described one of the oldest smells on earth. "Smell of white man in heat."

Did she mean the smell of a white man afflicted by hot weather, or by the same urges that overtook our compound dogs when they went around humping the nearest thing in sight? I wasn't sure.

"You becoming a flart?" She studied me with a squint. "Making eyes at men already, hnn? Just be careful, girl. Playing with fire is dangerous pastime, if you want my honest opinion."

But there was approval in her warning. And approval was hard to come by these days. Approval from women, anyway.

Ever since the day of the loincloth, my mother was nursing

a grudge I couldn't fathom. One afternoon while the radio was on, I sat on the floor leaning over the low, round table, reading a poem I was supposed to memorize:

Bright Flower!
whose home is everywhere
Bold in maternal Nature's care
And all the long year through the heir
Of joy and sorrow;
Methinks that there abides in thee
Some concord with humanity
Given to no other flower I see
The forest thorough!

How full of surprises was the English language! All this time I thought "thorough" was pronounced "thurra"—and here it rhymed with "sorrow." And yet: "The forest thorrow"? It didn't sound quite right.

Then I realized my distraction was coming from another source: from my mother's clapping. She was keeping time to the radio, which was tuned in to the "Strictly Classical Hour." She was clapping to Bach's "Badinerie." Maybe it was the flute that got her going: flute music recalled the festivity of our outdoor theaters. Certainly it was a piece to which a person might whistle along, or even tap his foot. But clapping! You clapped along to carnival music, not to Bach!

Deaf! She was deaf to these distinctions.

But she wasn't blind. Just observing my posture roused her suspicions.

"What's the matter?" she asked, still clapping. "Anything wrong?"

I shook my head without looking up. *Bright Flower! whose home is everywhere, Bold in maternal Nature's care . . . Of joy and sorrow . . . The forest thorrow . . .*

"Look at me when I talk to you!"

I looked, trying to remain expressionless. I hated the way she clapped and hummed to put on an insouciance I knew she didn't feel. Her nursery rhymes sounded far from lighthearted of late. She made them sound like veiled threats.

"You disapprove of something?" She kept up the clapping—a bad sign. I knew the difference between rhythm and threat. But we were at the edge of some sheer drop-off, and it was either push or be pushed.

"This is," I said, using the full English phrase, "Western classical music." As soon as I'd said it, I felt puffed up. "Please don't clap along"—and then it came out—"like a yokel."

Bold in maternal Nature's care was the last thing I remember before the shocking slap across my cheek.

"Who do you think you are?" she demanded. Whoever I thought I was, I was clearly mistaken. We glared at each other, breasts heaving as if we'd just run a race. Even her sarong had come loose around her waist, as if she *had* been running.

"Nobody," I said at last, "just your daughter."

"What do you mean by that?" she said. Frankly, I didn't know what I meant.

"Peacock!" She sneered. "So you think you're a peacock. Big *Western* peacock! Big performer. Big tango dancer. Big piano player. Big fancy music. *Ting-tong, ting-tong.*"

But those were the very words of the Byzantine pianist! Had he conveyed them to my mother? Or did everything I play come out *ting-tong, ting-tong?* The humiliation of that encounter returned in a tingling heat that spread through my arms and face.

"Sparrow!" my mother said. "The truth is you're not a peacock, you're just a sparrow trying to be a peacock."

"Why do you hate me?" I asked suddenly.

"Hate you?" my mother squealed, the sarcasm overtaken by fury. "Hate you! You don't know the difference between love and hate, you don't know anything."

"Yes I do, yes I do! You keep on saying I don't know how to love, I don't know what love is. You've said it enough so that I believe you now. Fine. I don't know what love is. But I know what love *isn't*. It isn't what you feel for me. You never loved me!"

"Oh? Poor mistreated child!" she said, but I think I had startled her.

"I never said you mistreated me. I said you never loved me."

"Love! Love! Love!" she wailed, gripping her temples. "It never comes out right, no matter how much you love, no matter what you do!"

She turned her back on me and began pounding the wall, crying, "What do you know about a mother's love? What does anyone know what I've suffered for love?" She was upset in a way I hadn't ever seen, and my first thought was to touch her. But before I could reach her she turned around and, with her back against the wall, slowly, rhythmically, began banging her head against it. She looked past me, over my head, while I watched her crumpled teary face.

"I . . . did . . . what . . . I . . . could!" she repeated, between sobs.

Her sorrow captivated me. It was so large, so misplaced. I couldn't help but stay where I was and watch, while the familiar crust began forming on the inside somewhere in the vicinity of my heart. It made me think of Jewel and her tyranny, the tyranny of the weak. My mother turned her bitter, bloated eyes toward me then and stopped her crying long enough to say, "All you can think of is yourself. Your vanity. Your tango dancing. Your piano playing. Teacher Mercy this. Auntie Mamie that. Is that all you want? To imitate Anglo ways? To become an Anglo? Do you care nothing for your parents, your tradition?"

"Don't worry," I said, returning to my book. "I won't be playing the piano anymore."

"What's that got to do with anything?" she shouted. "I know you're still playing it in your head." Clutching her stomach as if she'd just been stabbed, she stumbled into the bedroom and slammed the door behind her.

Again I wondered if my mother had been comparing notes about me. Mrs. Baba Sheen had made a similar accusation. It must have been a day when she'd mislaid her ruler: my punishment this time involved kneeling, not offering my open palm for the whack. She kept glowering at me. "Trying to pull the wool over my eyes, what? Kneeling on the outside, but standing on the inside. You can't fool me."

All these women with their penetrating vision of what went on in my head! Auntie Mamie at least did me the favor of inquiring. She sensed I was down that day but misread the cause.

"So what is going on inside that head of yours, Tango, my girl? Lemme guess. Big plans, innit? Planning conquests, if I'm not mistaken. Yes. Conquests—all well and good. Trouble is, who you going to catch in godforsaken town like this? Who worth conquering? Hah? I mean, talented girl like you can afford to put up her price. Anyone try to bring you down, you just tell them, 'I got bigger fish to fry!' Hear?"

At my next piano lesson, I had barely pulled up the stool to the piano when Mercy said, "Okay, Tango. Let's shake out of it. You've been dragging your tail ever since we got back from Anika."

"I'm not getting anywhere," I said.

"What? You want me to sing your praises day in, day out?" she said. "Not enough I spend all my time bringing you along? Why you think I keep you here under my eye, four hours a day, five days a week? Your parents are not thanking me for this; certainly your Baptist schoolmarms are not thanking me. What's in it for me? Only one thing, Tango. Your ability. Your talent. The thing is, you're not serious enough.

You're still a bit of a flit. But I'm hoping you'll grow out of it.

"You're very changeable, see?" she went on. "I won't say fickle, but definitely on the changeable side. All well and good to have several irons in the fire, but mind you don't become jack-of-all-trades. First it was tango. Then it was accordion."

"Bandonion," I couldn't help saying.

"Bandonion, accordion, call it what you want. Point is, you don't stick to one thing. I'm not saying you don't have determination, but I worry you'll lose interest in piano, too. You can't just go through life counting on a good ear, picking up things like a parrot. You want to be cheap accompanist, fine. You want to play at sing-alongs, fine. You want to vamp like some nightclub performer, fine by me. But to be serious you got to know what you're doing.

"Sit up straight, will you?" said Mercy. "And while I'm on the subject, I think it's a bad sign that you keep changing your handwriting. Every time I look, it's different. Small differences, okay. But yours! One time it's straight, another time it slants backward like a lefty's, another time it's all fancy pantsy. You have to stick to your own style."

I remembered Thurani: "Style, my dear, is not so easy as it looks, not something you can learn. You must have potential."

"Are you listening to me?" said Mercy. "I'm only telling you all this because I care for you. Because you have potential. I'm banking so much on you; I don't want you to let us both down.

"Come on!" she pinched my cheek. "No more long face. There's work to do. Let's try the Shopang again."

I looked down at the stool. "I don't want to," I said.

"What?! What blooming cheek! Go on and play or I'll give you a good . . ." She slapped me on the shoulder. "Enough of this nonsense. Come on. One, two, three . . ."

I played. And it was only after she'd stopped me again and again, getting shriller and more impatient by the minute, that she let me continue to the end without interruption. "I see," she said at last. "You're giving up, aren't you?"

I said nothing.

"So you *are* giving up. I was afraid of this."

I went on staring at the sheet music in front of me; it seemed the safest thing to stare at.

"I thought you had more spine than this," Mercy said. "So you can't take it, eh? One little setback, one miserable little insult from some low-class concert pianist—Byzantyne prince, my foot!—and you go to pieces? Shame on you, Tango. I'm disappointed in you.

"Well? What do you have to say for yourself? You going to sit there and give me the silent treatment? All right, two can play the game. You just sit there and sulk and I'll just bite my tongue. Let's see what good that's going to do."

"I'm not sulking," I said, turning to face her. "I just don't think I'm meant to play the piano."

"Meant to?" she barked. "Who is *meant* to play? Moseart was *meant* to play, if that's what you mean. But the rest of us play anyway, don't we? You're a very vain girl, I'm sorry to say. 'Look at me, the great Tango! If I can't be first, I want to be last! If I can't be best, I have to be worst!' No middle ground. Why can't you just say to yourself, 'All right, I'm not the Blessed Virgin, but I'm not Mary Magdalene, either. I'm just . . . Tango, doing . . . doing . . .' "

"Doing the Lambeth walk," I sang and was about to laugh when I saw Mercy's face caught in a sort of spasm.

"It's no use, is it?" Her eyes had filled up. "You've already given up. Oh, Tango, don't do this to me. We've worked so hard. I've had such hopes. Don't throw it all away, I'm begging you."

But I was bored by the piano; by the long hours of repetition and monotony, the impossible standards, the refinement beyond my reach, the ridicule earned instead of praise. I was tired of all that sitting in one place in the pursuit of some lofty feat. I was fed up with sitting still.

I stopped going to Mercy—and went back to Carlos.

"Dance with me, Carlos," I begged. Sadly, as though he'd failed me somehow, he gave in. And once more I was back to dancing. But dancing in a way I hadn't before: defiant, confident, insolent.

Carlos held me now very close, now very far apart, as though torn between wanting and not wanting to look into my eyes.

"Oh, Tango, Tango," he murmured, "you're growing up." It sounded like a halfhearted reprimand. A reprimand for finding me out at something underhanded but secretly to his liking.

Cloddy too was giving me the eye—not saying anything, but ogling on the sly. I caught him right in the middle of a game of rounders one day. I was fooling around with the Hula Hoop as usual, when I noticed he was transfixed. Plastic Hula Hoops were the new thing then. Under Cloddy's gaze, my hips took on a life of their own.

"Hey, Clod!" someone had to yell finally. "You playing or not? What's the matter? Never seen a hoop before?"

Then the players all laughed as one, and I was pleased to see that Cloddy's face reddened on my account. I wondered how his pet was faring.

If Thurani could see me! Those sly little glances of hers seemed so silly now. With my recently acquired skill I could give her a pointer or two. I could tell her that it wasn't necessary to tilt your head and slide your eyeballs to the corners; it wasn't necessary to keep licking your lips or fiddling with your hair. All it took was a bold gaze that met a man head-on; the rest was fluff.

. . .

When news of the talent competition in Anika came along, it was Mamie who prodded me to enter. She saw it as an opportunity that could well lead to one of those bigger fish I was destined to fry.

My mother of course saw it as the unprofitable fishing of a fool. "Dropping a fishhook wherever a bubble appears!" she said. "You mean to tell me you're prepared to go back to Anika and make a fool of yourself again? This time you want to expose your thighs and knees in front of hundreds of people?"

Because it was Mamie's idea, it was my mother's duty to belittle it. It didn't really surprise me. But she did something else far more unexpected.

One day, as the contest drew near, my mother left for her annual retreat at the monastery. This time, instead of returning as usual after her week-long stay, she sent word back to us, in writing, that she had decided to renounce all worldly needs, obligations, and desires—including, sadly, her family—to devote herself to a life of celibacy, meditation, and prayer. She had decided to become a nun for good.

She added a postscript especially for me: be devoted to my father; think of her fondly; remember the Four Noble Laws, in particular the Law of Desire and its dangers of sensual love, which only lead to suffering; and—whatever I did—hold on to a sense of shame. She loved me; she wished to be left in peace.

My father took the news with noble resignation, drawing the sympathy of friends and distant relatives. But a visible effect of my mother's decision was to rob him of what little interest he'd had in me.

The effect on me was that I danced like a dervish—with Carlos, every chance I got, or, in his absence, alone.

"So who's going to pay for this joke?" was all my father had to say about the upcoming competition.

Thanks to Mamie, the Gopal brothers were going to pay.
I'd had my doubts about soliciting them, but Mamie was
confident. "Businessmen always publicity hungry," she reasoned. The Gopals bought in.

"Publicity stunt," explained the fat one to his brother, who
was slower to strike any new bargain.

"Ah, publicity stunt," said the other, seeing the light.

In return for underwriting the costumes and the train fares
for Carlos and me, the Gopals' sponsorship would be announced at the contest, over the loudspeaker, and in the printed
programs:

SPONSORED BY GOPAL BROTHERS

LEADING PURVEYORS OF DRY GOODS

HEADQUARTERED IN IRRAWADDY

Next, Mamie went to Mercy, whom I hadn't seen in close
to two years.

"I thought you weren't speaking," I said.

Mamie shrugged. "Business is business. I said to her,
'Mercy, your former pupil entering talent contest in Anika. She
dancing tango. Got any ideas for costumes?' 'Search me,' she
says. Putting up her price, you know. So I told, 'Look, everyone knows you and I not exactly bosom pals. Amen. But why
not bury the hatchet for sake of talent? You got fashion flair,
I got business sense. Financial backing already arranged, thanks
to me-myself-and-I. How about you make costumes? My son
already working out dance steps, he already composing music
for special tango number; going to be called *Irrawaddy Tango*.
We all put our heads together, maybe she'll be winner, what
say?' "

"And she agreed?"

"Chicken feed." Mamie snapped her fingers. "Tomorrow

we'll choose material from Gopals; next day you go for fitting to Mercy's. And mind she don't chain you to piano again, eh? You got to watch out for dose Goa constrictors."

At last: the big day when it was back to Municipal Hall for me. I waited my turn with Carlos in the very same room backstage where I'd first met Nikiforos Focas. The sofa on which he and Mercy had sat was gone. Only the folding chairs remained; and only three of them were taken up now, by the finalists: Carlos and me, and the magician who called himself the Royal Wizard. (The third finalist had just gone onstage for her last act, the classical court dance.)

All others had been eliminated. The group of elementary-school girls who ran in circles with multicolored crepe streamers was gone. The three-fingered man playing the three-stringed crocodile zither was gone. (The applause was generous, but as Carlos pointed out, his only real distinction was his missing fingers. It didn't quite amount to the handicap he was milking them for: to play the three-stringed zither, after all, you didn't need even three fingers on the strumming hand; one finger would have done just as well.)

And gone was the animal trainer with the somersaulting poodles and the tightrope-walking goat. The poodles had scurried onstage in plaid vests and matching bow ties, yapping and tripping over each other in panic. They dashed repeatedly back into the wings, spilling little puddles on the stage before nerving themselves for the half somersaults and the bunny-hop finale.

As for the goat (a seasoned performer, to judge from the swagger), it surveyed the rope, which was stretched across the stage about three feet off the ground, then turned to the audience with a deadpan look: *Surely you jest.* To reach the level of the rope, it climbed a footstool manned by the trainer (clad, for undisclosed reasons, like a mahout in a turban and loincloth), who produced a drumroll from a tin drum hanging from his neck. The goat took a bold step onto the rope; paused; picked its way a little less surely on the swaying line; then froze, glass-eyed.

"Go!" said the trainer, giving it a whack broadside with one of his drumsticks. "Go, go!"

That set off the wild seesaw leading to the fall. The goat rode the rope on its belly for a moment, legs splayed—and landed with a heavy thud, on its side. With scarcely a moment's hesitation, however, it scrambled to its feet, limping on its way back to the footstool for another valiant try.

Carlos had given a low whistle. "Man, that's what I call showmanship!"

Now the wizard was sitting on the other side of the waiting room. He reached for his bag of tricks—a tattered suitcase bound with twine. He hadn't said a word so far—not even onstage, where he chewed razor blades, scattered grains of rice that turned into silver coins, and blew a duck egg through his nose. He was glaring at us with something like criminal intent. He seemed the kind of magician who would saw a person in half and coolly walk away without putting the two halves back together again. I tried not to meet his gaze: I'd heard he was also a hypnotist.

The wizard brought out of his bag a foot-high stack of mirrors the size of playing cards. He held up the stack horizontally, then startled us by flinging his arms out; and the mirrors, instead of landing on the floor in smithereens, were strung out, clinking, between the full reach of his arms like a swag of miniature glass banners. He turned slightly, and I saw that the pieces were held together by a double band of ribbon glued to the backs. The wizard played this string of mirrors like an accordion, folding and unfolding from side to side, from top to bottom, without breaking or cracking a single piece.

I saw my costume reflected in the mirrors: fragments of the

beaded white halter top with the sparkling stars and suns and moons, and the black satin skirt with the petticoat of multicolored netting underneath.

The mirrors rose and fell, swinging now like an accordion, now like a Jacob's ladder, from the wizard's hands—and catching the glitter of my bodice, my skirt's rainbow flashes of red, blue, lavender, and green.

Suddenly the wizard was holding the mirrors down in my direction in such a way that nothing but my black skirt was visible to me. All I saw now was a row of black frames, a darkened hall of mirrors. He stared spitefully at me as he held up his glass game like a charred banner.

I looked away uneasily and found Carlos staring at me, too.

Carlos had been very downcast of late. His pompadour was flat from unemployment. At this moment he was cross-eyed with sadness as well. It annoyed me to be causing a gloom I didn't intend.

"Two sad faces, four happy legs," he had said about the formula for tango. I just hoped he wasn't going to forget the part about the happy legs out there in front of the audience.

He shook his head morosely and whispered, "Tango, my little Tango, you going to go far."

He further annoyed me by staring at my halter and singing softly, "Don't let the stars get in your eyes, don't let the moon break your heart."

Everything reminded Carlos of a song. He'd stare at a melon his mother was slicing and sing, "Come to me my melon-choly baby . . ."

At last we were summoned to the wings, to stand and wait our turn. The classical dancer, a woman with a child's body and a man's face, was on the last bout of her performance. The white makeup was running down the sides of her cheeks as she kicked away at the long train of her skirt.

She was all fire and whimsy, with a saucy snap to her limbs. But it struck me for the first time that this was the dancing of puppetry. She was jerking, twitching, kicking, and bumping across the floor as if pulled by strings from above.

I felt a rush of affection for the tango, a dance that allowed me to stand up straight and tall. It didn't oblige me to crouch as if in pain, as if my back had just been broken. I wasn't pulled by invisible strings; I was guided and wooed by a partner who strode and leapt as one with me. A partner from whom I could swivel or twist away in seeming pique but could still trust to sweep me off my feet.

"There! See? He can't take his eyes off you." The voice in my ear belonged to one of the stagehands, a thin, spinsterish woman from the Ministry of Culture who had said a few friendly, encouraging words to me.

"Who?"

"The colonel there down in the front row, the four eyes. Big man in the army. Just look at the medals. He's been asking about you. Careful. They say he's looking for a wife."

Among a group of army officers in the front row was an intent-looking man in tinted glasses who wasn't watching the classical dance at all. He was watching me as I stood hidden from most of the audience behind the curtain.

"How come he's not married?" I asked. He looked middle-aged.

"Came close," said the spinster. "Engaged. But she died."

"Of what?"

"Heart."

"Heart?"

"That's what I said. Heart."

It wasn't clear what she meant, but our time had come. A voice called our names—and out we scampered onto the stage, to strike our dramatic pose on which the curtains would open.

How we danced, Carlos and I—missing not a step, not a

beat. Our movements felt both risky and natural, like the stunts performed in dreams: walking on the ceiling, say, or coasting on a wind current from mountain peak to mountain peak. We danced as never before, striding and swaying, prancing and dipping our way across the stage without flaw or seam. We were three-legged, double-jointed Siamese twins—joined now at the hip, now at the elbow, now at the knee—kicking up our heels, holding our heads high, then snapping them smartly for those about-face turns.

"*El jiro,*" Carlos whispered the step in my ear, and I twirled in the spotlight, with the suns, moons, and stars winking from my bodice, and the rainbow whipping around my knees. "*El hoop,*" warned Carlos, and our legs entwined. "*La corrida!*" and we took those tiny playful steps backward and forward, forward and backward, ending in *el sandwich,* with Carlos hooking my foot with his. Then we eased into our two-legged tease, that circling, stirring, probing motion as though testing with our toe tips the waters of a pool.

The shouts and applause rang out, and the flowers rained down on the stage even before we'd taken our bow.

When they announced the winner and it was the classical dancer, not me, I held my hand up to silence whatever it was Carlos was trying to say, to wait for the correction bound to follow the mistake. But there was no correction, and when at last I heard my name, it was as winner of third place.

The spinster squeezed my arm. "You should have won," she said. "But we have to encourage national culture, not foreign dances. Never mind; I'll introduce you to the colonel. He's already crazy about you."

Later, when I'd picked my face up off the floor, what came to mind was that afternoon by the river inlet with Cloddy and his friends. The boys had dared me to grab hold of a stout creeper and try to swing clean over the water to the other bank.

I grasped the creeper and took a running leap. In the

moment my feet left the ground, I knew I wouldn't make it. And I didn't. I fell in.

But I didn't let go of the vine, either; I didn't just fall in and flounder. I held on to the tip of the vine until I reached land—wet but still gripping the creeper. The instinct that drove me then, in the wake of my flop, returned to me now: the sense to hang on to the vine in hand.

To come all this distance from Irrawaddy, only to go back? No, I wasn't going back—not to that compound life and its dearth of potential.

So I kept up the good-sport smile throughout the awards, and even while accepting my prize (a length of coarse, stiff silk the color of sick-baby stool). But when refreshments followed, I lost no time in positioning myself alone with the colonel, to turn directly to the business at hand, the urgent business of getting myself back on my feet. "You have," I said, "so many medals."

4

We were married three months later, in Anika. The private ceremony—prescribed by the astrologer—was a brisk transaction in a dingy room of the Court of Appeals. The judge read from a sheet of mimeographed paper that we then signed.

We shook hands all around and took leave of the serenely smiling judge (who might have been considerably less serene had he known that scarcely a year later, this bridegroom with the nervous blink and the unsteady hand who signed the marriage document would be the new boss of the land, the man who would charge him, the judge, with declaring martial law in the name of his military government).

Afterward came the banquet at the Jade Palace Restaurant downtown, attended mostly by army officers and their wives. The wedding presents took up two long tables; whiskey flowed freely; on the menu were bird's-nest soup, Peking duck, and fresh eel flown in from Hong Kong. The president himself, dressed in the old-fashioned attire for which he was famous—and with his hair in the quaint topknot dating back to his revolutionary student days—put in a brief appearance. He clasped the colonel's hand in both his hands and wished him health, wealth, and serenity. The old politician had a way of fixing a long, expectant gaze on you, as if hoping for the answer to a consuming question on his mind. He subjected me to that hopeful, inquiring scrutiny now as he pressed my hand between his palms. But all he said was "May you live long."

A band played the national anthem. Then the president, flanked by the presidential guard, climbed into his limousine, and through the window waved good-bye—waved with a gesture I'd seen on the newsreels preceding the bioscopes: that semithreatening gesture used by kings, queens, and heads of state when acknowledging crowds.

The captain who drove us to the hotel where the honeymoon suite was reserved also escorted us up to the room. He was careful to keep a straight face as the bridegroom, who had had too many scotch and sodas, kept insisting that he needed to return to the restaurant because he hadn't yet tried the eel.

Alone with me in the fancy hotel room, my husband made for the nearest support, stumbling as he reached an armchair. Braced against its back, he swayed.

"What's the main point?" he demanded. "The main point, in my opinion, is that you are now my wife. Is that agreed? Can we at least agree on that?"

I noticed there were no windows in that room; the only opening in the wall had been plugged up with a humming, throbbing machine that was throwing out a lot of cold air. It was freezing.

"So!" my husband continued. "That being the main point, tell me why I was denied the eel? Just give me one reason why, at my own wedding banquet, I was not given any eel! *Why?*" He seemed to be fighting back tears.

"They're trying to make a monkey out of me, that's why." His voice broke as he landed heavily in the armchair.

"Come to me, my life, my little dancer." He waved me over to him.

He took my hand, leaned his head back, and closed his eyes as if in a swoon of emotion. He'd dropped off. A moment later he was up again, hastily unbuttoning his jacket. "I have something to show you," he said. "A secret. I have . . ." He was rushing to undress now, but his pants were caught on his boots, which he'd neglected to remove. "I have . . . on my person . . . the sacred marks . . . the thirty-two sacred marks of the hero. . . . Now *find them all* . . . !"

He toppled backward and hit the bed snoring, flat on his back but still in uniform: the jacket with the medals and ribbons across his crotch, the fallen trousers girdling his ankles, his tightly laced boots planted pigeon-toed on the floor.

Of course I found them all. Not that night, which I spent shivering under the starched bed sheets in the arctic air of that wedding suite, but later. I unearthed all thirty-two of them; I wasn't stupid: a mole here, a wart there, the stain of a birthmark, the occasional speck, the odd nicks and scars all adding up to the holy number thirty-two, which distinguishes the body of a hero, or a universal monarch. There were other little spots and spoors, naturally, that I could have counted, to say nothing of those I had counted that didn't deserve to be. But something told me this was one equation I had better not flub. Thirty-two marks was the assignment, so thirty-two marks it would be—not one more, not one less.

My hero was awash with gratitude. "You're the only woman," he said, teary-eyed, "who's found them."

Power had just been conferred on me: the same sort of power he would be moved to acknowledge later in the marriage. This was during a wallow of remorse after splitting my lip open in a fit of fury. "Oh, my heart, my life!" he snuffled. "Don't dare leave me! You're the only woman who has ever known exactly where my back itches, exactly where to scratch without even being told!"

I kissed the hand that had just given me a fat lip. It was a small hand—surprisingly small, like a child's fist that packs an unexpected wallop. He had hit me with the back of his hand, I noticed.

The palms of Dayan males are very precious to their owners. The smooth soft hand is not only a measure of the good life, it's a prerequisite for Buddha hopefuls who must think ahead to the day when they'll have to strike that classic pose, palms outstretched in all their noble purity.

This Buddha hopeful's blow left me snuffling; from gratitude as much as anything. He could have knocked out a front tooth or two. But he'd spared me that loss. My hero.

"My general," I blubbered (his promotion had just come through and the new title never failed to please). "My general!" I was dripping blood, tears, and snot onto his hand.

My God, I'd married a maniac!

The next minute he was on his knees, begging forgiveness. "Don't, General, don't!" I said, confused by the turnabout. At once he was back on his feet, managing as he rose to push me down on my knees. Then came the benediction. He stroked the top of my head with one hand, while pushing me away with the other—the one I was groveling over—just far enough to the side so as not to risk soiling his starched uniform with my messy discharges.

But as official back scratcher and mole finder, my position—for the moment, anyway—was secure. (Not sufficiently secure, however, to accept his invitation, at the close of this particular drama, to smash him on the mouth and hurt him as he'd hurt me, in order to grant him some small atonement. "Hit me; hit me so it hurts!" he pleaded. I tapped him lightly on the lip, no fool I.)

Not long afterward there was a picture of my husband, the

newly promoted armed forces chief of staff, on the front page of *The New Times*. He was shaking the hand of a Muslim rebel leader, a member of the Communist Party Alliance, who had just laid down his arms and "entered the light."

My husband, turned three-quarters toward the camera, was baring a lot of teeth; the defector, facing front, was baring mostly the whites of his eyes in their ambushed, sidelong look. I understood that look: it was a response to my husband's smile, the same toothy spasm he'd flashed at me just prior to his backhanded blow.

That was no smile, as I found out. That was a snarl. The two were practically indistinguishable.

Oh, there were compensations. The glitter of city life. The shows and parties and public appearances. The gifts that poured in—the eternal radios and clocks and watches and gold and silver lighters and cigarette cases. And the jewelry, not least.

Long before the Revolution, the jewelers' agents—those plump, perspiring pseudo-aunts—were beating a path to our door. Out of their cloth bags —deliberately ragged, for camouflage—came star-sapphire necklaces as intricate as lace collars; bracelets encrusted with pigeon-blood rubies; gold bangles etched with minute butterflies and bouquets; double and triple strands of blue pearls harvested from the waters of the southern archipelago; brooches and rings of jade from the legendary mines up north; jacket buttons studded with emeralds chiseled out of the rocks of the northwest frontier and transported by mule-back across the border to the markets in Hong Kong. . . .

"Please," they would urge, "just wear them, just try them out!" They'd leave their loot with me for months at a time, to model in public as if the dazzling items were really mine. After I'd exhausted a consignment, I simply turned it in for a new set of bracelets, necklaces, brooches, bangles, buttons, and rings . . . and so on.

Of course these wandering merchants knew, in their immemorial wisdom, that sooner or later we'd buy. And so we did. But when I think of our purchases of those days! The odd bangle and uncut stone, the uneven set of multicolored zircons, the spinels with "sores" in their crude "pagoda" settings. . . . These were child's play compared with the general's full-blown buying-and-hoarding mania of later years, the bushels of diamonds and boulders of jade, if the rumors can be believed.

It didn't require much arm-twisting for me to accept the extravagances that came my way, some from my husband, some from those legions of well-wishers and brownnosers that sprang up around us like jack-in-the-boxes. Not that I was in the same league as an Imelda Marcos or an Elena Ceausescu (for whom I imagine the bribery on our scale would have been small potatoes). But I was on the take long enough to see how power confers almost overnight a sense of natural entitlement, a confidence that one is almost duty-bound to enjoy its bounty.

I delighted in the envy my privileges inspired. (Those stealthy once-overs by women who thought they could disguise their scrutiny! The pedestrians who jumped like crickets to make way for the motorcades bearing me through the streets, as though a palanquin and not merely a Czechoslovak automobile were advancing down the avenues!)

The general himself of course was above greed. Like every other fact of life in the land he governed, it had to be true because he said so. He only desired material rewards for me, his wife. The same selflessness, presumably, that drove him in later years to his religious building frenzy. In time he would put up ever more lavish pagodas, stupa upon gem-studded stupa, in the name of his beloved people—while the wretches watched stupefied from their places in the food lines that inched their way around whole city blocks.

For himself he wanted next to nothing. Power, riches . . .

it was all illusory. The good Buddhist. He used to go on about the paltriness of his own desires: "Just give me rice, salt fish, pickled bamboo, a thatch hut," et cetera, while he fingered his Omega watch, smoked his 555s, and downed his Johnnie Walker Black Label.

"Everything I do," he used to say in his speeches, "every breath I take, is out of love for my people. Yet people will always question and criticize. 'Why have we done this or that?' "

It was always the same speech, the same interview. "The question comes up," he would say, after the sweeping nationalization, "whether a state-controlled economy is really necessary. These doubters must have very short memories. It seems they have forgotten that private enterprise has brought our bountiful nation to the brink of ruin.

"Then the same doubters say, 'Is it really necessary to restrict the foreign presence in our country?' When will they learn?! In order to achieve genuine independence, to stand on our own feet, we must rid ourselves of alien elements, we must expose the profiteers and racketeers who have no deep roots in our soil, no real love for our country, who come to plunder like vultures.

"People, in their simplicity, ask simpleminded questions. For example: Why is martial law necessary? The answer is so obvious! We have martial law for the safety of the people! These are dangerous times, times of unrest. So many groups and factions all out for their petty interests, all making selfish demands with no thought for the greater welfare of the state, the unity of our nation. And yet they wonder why I refuse to enter into negotiations with these traitors and insurgents until they lay down their arms.

"My answer is: there are some things a parent must do for the good of the child, things that may not always be pleasant or even understandable at the time. In the same way, there are steps a leader must take which may be misunderstood, but which are taken for the sake of the nation as a whole, not to satisfy small individual whims. It is what I myself experienced as a child. My father was a strict but wise man. He beat me often and painfully. But he kept me out of trouble. He did this by half killing me with his cane."

The father he was referring to was not his natural father. That man, a worker in the tin mines, had been killed in a mining accident before his son could even walk. The man with the golden cane was the new father—the one who shared his mother's bed soon after the accident. Except that this stepfather and his mother never did marry. Being brother and sister, they couldn't.

The general wouldn't have mentioned the bit about the incest, naturally, but the plug for corporal punishment was earnest. A survivor of beatings, he spoke proudly of its ultimate rewards. *Look at where I am now! Look at what it taught me!* As a boy he'd once talked back to his stepfather who taught him never to make that mistake again by knocking two teeth down his throat.

At age twelve, when his stepfather had sent him to the monastery for his novitiate, he'd chanced upon a wad of money under the abbot's bedroll, which he took and promptly spent. When the theft was discovered, two young monks stripped him of his saffron robe and pummeled him with sandbags until an older monk took over with a jute whip.

Yowling in pain, he made his way, half running, half limping, back home. His stepfather had already received word of the disgrace and was waiting at the top of the hill with a length of rope, silhouetted against the harsh light of noon like the hangman himself. He bound the boy hand and foot and caned him senseless. He spared the face (which was already swollen and throbbing) and the back (which was already bleeding) but went for the fresh areas—the arms and legs and soles of the feet—until the boy passed out. When he came to, there was his mother washing his wounds and welts. And singing. At least that's what her lament sounded like. *What did I do wrong? And I even rinsed his umbilical cord on a gold plate; the Hindu midwife said it would bring greatness, the bitch!*

He'd learned his lesson, all right. He'd learned not to get caught. The best teacher in the world, the cane. And soon enough he had his turn at it.

While apprenticing for an umbrella merchant after he'd finished with school, he caught one of his fellow apprentices, a scabby Indian boy, trying to make off with a bundle of umbrellas. Seizing one of the uncut rods, a species of hardy cane shipped to the factory from up-country, he personally whipped the little thief almost senseless.

Some fifteen years later, while posted to the western provinces, he'd come across the selfsame miserable fellow in a tea shop. The Indian (still scabby and thin, but smartly dressed with gold rings on his fingers) recognized him right away. He fell to the ground and actually kissed his feet. *Sahib, sahib! You taught me a lesson I'll never forget. Thanks and blessings to you, sahib!*

He told the cringer to get up off the ground.

"Show me the scabs on your face, man; not the lice on your head," he said. He thumped him on the back and even bought him a cup of tea. He was a major by then and inclined to benevolence.

"Don't call me sahib," was his parting advice. "The days of the sahib are over."

They weren't quite over, but the independence movement had begun. From foot soldier he rose to freedom fighter in the Free Forces of the Interior. Masterminding the FFI was that legendary underground group popularly known as the Watermelons. ("We may be green on the outside, but we're red, red, red on the inside!" Just how red was proven by their blood pact: into a crock of moonshine the members let fall a few drops of their own blood. They passed it around and drank.)

He became a Watermelon.

After the war, he was appointed commander of the remote Northeast Region Three, not exactly a plum posting, but then he hadn't exactly been a favorite among his Free Forces peers, now the new leaders of the independent republic. (As one of these heroes, a Colonel Sandhurst—so nicknamed because of his Sandhurst Royal Military Academy training—later recalled, "Lord, the fellow had a habit of trimming. A schemer from the word go. But that was the least of it. Rats in the upper story, don't you know.")

But in that free-for-all following independence, Region Three turned out to be an ambitious field commander's dream. All those marauding bandits, paramilitary forces, minority armies, village defense leagues, parties within parties, robber clans, and central government regulars shooting it out across the length and breadth of the region! Chaos brought the commander a chance to make a name for himself.

He had the loyalty of the troops. He got down on the ground with them when they ate; without a grimace he plunged into their jungle fare of weevil-specked rice, boiled roots, fish paste, and roasted cricket, sucking the food off his fingers and rubbing them in the dirt to save water in that drought-ridden region. He bantered with them in the language of the barracks, always stressing his humble past. He brushed his teeth with strips of tree bark. He slept on the bare floor of bamboo slats, his arm for a pillow, leaving his bedroll to mildew in a corner of the officers' quarters where the rain leaked through the rotten thatch.

He sent his men into the paddy fields to plant and sow, heave and ho, with the peasants. Meanwhile, he set in motion a merry-go-round of peekers, eavesdroppers, tipsters, squealers, and snitches who kept him abreast of developments in the rival camps, then slithered back into those camps to stir things up and speed along the process of mutual elimination. Only when the vulture-shredded bodies had piled up in the jungled hills, when the flags drooping in the hot, breezeless air of open fields were down to just one or two different emblems—only then did the commander move in to wipe out the spent, ragtag rebels that remained. Only then did he secure his position as protector and savior of the people, allowing his men, those kindly paddy planters, the run of the towns and villages, allowing them to reap not just the rice harvests but all of the bully's due: stealing, raping, commandeering livestock and food supplies, dragging children into slave labor for the building of new roads and bridges, and whipping, shooting, hanging, or beheading any suspected ingrates at will.

The medals won for this heroism in the service of national unity were stored with the scrapbook of yellowed newspaper clippings in a big velvet-lined box that reposed under his bed. In the early, less eventful days of our marriage, I welcomed the doldrums of those rainy afternoons when he'd get out the box and browse through these mementos to amuse me.

He had a way of using the tip of his delicate forefinger to sort through the paraphernalia that reminded me of the father of the soft-headed Jewel when he was handling his stamp collection. They had the same dry and absorbed air in common, the stamp collector and my husband.

Needless to say, the latter's version of history was somewhat at odds with the ones I came to hear elsewhere over time—just as all the theories about the final inspiration for his coup never did match up with my own conviction that it was really the dog detail that did it.

5

The general loved shad. The beauty of a bony fish with edible bones—and narcotic properties as well (to relieve his chronic insomnia)! The cook had served it the night before: a big dark chunk pressure-cooked to perfection, with slivers of onion, ginger, and garlic clogging the thick, oily sediment of the sauce. But I was the only one who ate any of it that night; none of the others would touch it. I wondered about that—and why my husband fumed about being served one of his favorite dishes.

Afterward I enjoyed the dream-laden sleep induced by the rich meat. In my dream we were back at the table, the general, his deputies, and I, and out of the kitchen came the cook, wheeling a trolley on which was displayed a whole cooked shad. A whale of a shad.

"General, sir," the cook was saying, "please avoid the bones; they are not soft enough to eat."

At which the general picked up the whopper by its tail, leaned back, and opened his mouth wide to receive it headfirst, swallowing it whole.

Then I was listening to his voice as it delivered a lesson

listing points one, two, and three; asking questions not meant to be answered; lecturing on and on, repeating the same words. Security. Unity. National pride. Patriotism. Peace and harmony.

Once or twice I opened my eyes briefly, just long enough to sense the difficulty of shaking off the heavy sleep. The drone woke me finally, and after a while I sat up to the realization that it was my husband's voice issuing from the radio, around which the servants were crowding. He was announcing the success of the Revolution—and the program for the transfer of power.

Power till then had been in the hands of the president of the ruling party—one of the original Watermelons and an old rival. He was a dangerous man, the president—one of those intellectuals who tried to make you feel inferior by quoting Buddha, the Bible, Mahatma Gandhi, and all sorts of Western philosophers. The sort of dabbler who wrote poetry and plays and treatises on Pali texts for recreation. And a shameless name-dropper! *My friend Nehru; my friend Chou En-lai; my dear friends Sihanouk and Rockefeller and Lord Mountbatten and Princess Alexandra and Dag Hammarskjöld!*

But it wasn't these traits my husband found as disturbing as the president's increasingly weak and conciliatory tone with regard to the minorities. Recently, there had even been talk of a peace initiative with the secessionists.

"Look at that topknot!" my husband would shrill, seeing a picture of the president shaking some hand or presenting some award in the pages of *The New Times.* "The old patriot in his topknot and village muslins! What a phony!"

But in the end it was to the president that he owed his successful takeover. It was the president who unwisely put him on the front pages of papers and periodicals, on life-size posters pasted on building walls, on illustrated pamphlets scattered from the air, in wire service stories that appeared in the newspapers of the West. What started out as a campaign to eradicate the rampant stray-dog population turned out to be the best publicity campaign any politician could have hoped for.

Not that the general had seen it quite that way when he first came home with the news that he'd been charged with the dog campaign.

"He's trying to humiliate me!" he screamed. "The fucking hypocrite! The Buddhist sage! He follows the noble Eightfold Path of Compassion, he wouldn't slap a flea, so what does he do when he wants to kill? He gives me the dirty job so I can be blamed if I do and blamed if I don't. If I wipe out the dogs, everyone will damn me and ask what kind of a Buddhist I am. If I don't wipe out the dogs, they'll damn me for incompetence.

"So! You want the blood on *my* hands, not yours, Mr. President? I'll give you blood on my hands, then. Let me get through with those louse-ridden, shit-eating, sore-sucking, motherfucking mongrels and you'll be swimming in it!"

He was beginning to rave in that increasingly familiar way—spit flying and eyes blinking uncontrollably—that presaged a migraine. I ran to get his bottle of pills. What did he do with the bottle, though, but try to stuff it into my mouth?

"Lesson number one," he said with that famous snarl of a smile, one hand engaged in prying my teeth apart, the other in ramming the container of capsules through them. "Lesson number one. Stop treating me like some kind of cripple!"

Yet the next moment he was on his knees just like a cripple, clutching at my waist, praying for forgiveness and tolerance, praising my beauty, my brilliance, my back-scratching talents.

With the bottle out of my mouth, I hastened to distract him. The trick I had learned was to invite him to sit back while I casually dropped my sarong on the floor. It drove him wild to see me pad about the room attending to the most ordinary of chores and urges—rearranging the plastic flowers in the vase, fiddling with the radio, dusting a tabletop, drinking a glass of water, and such—as if oblivious of my nakedness from the waist down.

Eventually I was expected to announce, with a slightly absentminded air, "Hmm . . . I think I need to take a pee. . . ." and squat down right there and then to water the floor. But I tried to avoid this ultimate excitation. Peeing on demand wasn't that simple; besides, it left a stain on the polished floor.

Once I had him in that state, though, I was the one giving the orders. In public I walked several steps behind him; I knew never to speak out of turn. In private too I knew my proper, inferior place. My clothes always remained on the lower shelves of the closet or at the foot of his bed. I'd never dare steal his holy thunder by sitting in a higher chair or touching his sacred head.

But when I had the upper hand after reducing him to that quivering state, I could make him beg ("Don't stop, don't stop, I beg you!"). I could even make fun of him. "Take off your boots," I could say, "you're not riding a horse. You're just the opposite of your crazy granduncle!" (In his dotage, that old vagabond had once shown up at the general's office in the city barefooted and looking like Charlie Chaplin in his baggy nankeens. His shoes—a pair of Bata canvas sneakers—were tucked into his belt. *Wear them?* The old codger is said to have giggled at so preposterous an idea. *And get them all dirty?*)

How the general loved his boots! He sighed whenever he sat down to unlace them. The warrior's reluctance to unbuckle his armor, perhaps. Or maybe he was shy of exposing such small feet (whose tender, infantile toenails it was my weekly privilege to trim). And he sighed—with relief, I thought—as he laced them up in the mornings, stomping each foot twice on the floor, a signal that he was ready for the day's onslaughts. Given the many times he left the big heavily cleated things on in bed, it was fortunate, I guess, that once he actually got down to business, his feet at least remained stable and firmly planted on either side of me. Perhaps he needed the hobnails for traction as he pumped and heaved over me in a state verging on panic.

My spine took the impact of the floorboards. *He'll break a bone*, I thought as he slammed into me, slammed and slammed and slammed in a sweat of overheated frenzy and exertion. I waited for the inevitable anticlimax, for the wilting and shrinking of the thing I'd managed to massage into a stiffness that lasted just long enough for entry. A few thrusts and the stiffness was gone; yet he kept on thrusting and slamming despite the futility of it all. He might have been banging his head against the wall out of sheer frustration.

I tried. I tickled his nipples by blowing on them as earnestly as if the stoking of a fire were at stake. I worked his temperamental organ up and down, up and down. I spread my legs by letting him knee them apart; I squeezed them together when (again with his knees) he slammed them shut. (He did both somewhat testily, as though kicking his way through a tiresome gate.) A bootless exercise if there ever was one (except that he still kept those damned boots on!).

Later, during the dog campaign, those boots, close to immaculate in the mornings, would be thick with muck when he returned home late at night, bright-eyed and ravenous from the day's exertions.

The three-point program of the campaign was uniquely his: (1) poison; (2) shoot; (3) burn. Just the sort of program a person with his obsessions was bound to devise.

Because he carried the destiny of the universal monarch he was vulnerable to the classic attempts on a monarch's life. He particularly feared being poisoned in the manner of the Last Great Unifier and Builder of Ten Thousand Pagodas (whose array of titles, like his reign for life, was self-conferred). At the zenith of his power—and in the feverish grips of a quest to find the secret elixir of immortality—this Great Unifier was poisoned by his queen, slowly going blind before the datura finally did him in.

On the verge of sleep, *my* universal monarch once sat up and turned to me. *Darling!* He said it in English, but pronounced it in the slack-tongued way of the uneducated Dayan, dropping the *r* and the *g: Dahlin!*

Dah-hlin! He said the word again, a different way now, giving it another inflection to mean the Dayan word for "swift knife." *Dah-hlin!* he repeated, struck by a revelation. "All this time I've been afraid of the day when you might poison me. I never thought you might take up a knife. You're not going to knife me one day, are you?"

"No"—I laughed—"I'm not going to knife you," as that inviting image crossed my mind.

Poisoning of one sort or another was ever on *his* mind. He was proud of his expertise in the poisoning of pests: crows, sparrows, squirrels, slugs, ants, but especially rats. Given the choice between setting a rat trap or using poison—a choice he could easily have left to the household staff—he'd always go for the poison. Death on the trap was instantaneous—a snapped neck and that was the end of it—whereas poison allowed him to watch the rodent in its throes before it went belly-up. I remember the pains he took to try to outwit one particularly hardy bandicoot.

One night he came home with a folded piece of newspaper containing some grayish pellets. He had it on good authority, he said, that they would stop a boar in its tracks. He set the bait in the closet where the rat appeared at night, left the light on, shut the closet door, and stayed up to wait.

I fell asleep watching him crouch behind the closed shutters to the closet, one eye pressed to an opening between the slats. When I woke up hours later, he was still peering through the shutters, lying in wait with a patience that made my skin crawl.

I found myself rooting for the rodent, whose days of course were numbered.

By the time the challenge of the dogs came along, my husband was a seasoned exterminator.

The stray dogs had become a plague on the city no longer possible to ignore. With the alarming spread of rabies, the government was forced to take action. Whether it was the same wild boar pellets the general ordered in bulk to spread along the sidewalks, alleys, gutters, cesspools, and rubbish dumps of the dog-infested city and its suburbs, or whether he'd managed to lay his hands on an even more streamlined dogs' bane, the result was that the campaign worked where all others before had failed.

The program involved no half measures, no citizens' committees, no youth volunteers, no street sweepers, latrine cleaners, or grave diggers, no paid labor of any sort. It involved only the Union Forces. Military efficiency. That explained everything.

The soldiers stayed with the task and followed their orders down to the last letter. They scattered the toxins in the cool, discreet hours past midnight, and by noon the next day the dead mongrels would be strewn across town, one on every sidewalk, it seemed; in twos and threes around the trash heaps; in packs of five or six—or more—at points along the railroad tracks. The pedestrians, street vendors, and motorists, only too relieved to abide by the official warning not to touch the carcasses, gave the stiff bodies a wide berth, and by midnight the dogs were gone—to be replaced by the carnage of the following day.

In vans and covered trucks the crew had picked up the dead dogs and headed for the army depot behind the old tire factory. There they hurled the carrion onto the heap of burning rubber that would outstink the burning flesh.

The poison was spread in quantities that would have

eliminated the stray population twice over, but in the event not every stray died from poisoning. In the last days of the campaign, any stragglers still found alive were shot. Teams of military dogcatchers were dispatched to round up these hangers-on and deliver them to the site of the crematorium. There the dogs were released into a narrow corral put up around one side of the whipping orange flames of the pyre. Outside the iron-link fence stood the firing squad, whose members poked the barrels of their rifles through the mesh to shoot down their fear-crazed prey. The orders were to fire and keep firing until every last mongrel had either gone down in a salvo or leapt onto the flames.

Years later I met a lieutenant, a defector who'd been among that firing squad, who described the scene.

The dogs were not what mattered, he said. It was a test of stomach. The general could have picked the Muslims, the Chinese, or the Christians among the troops to do the shooting, but it would have told him nothing. Instead he picked the Buddhists (because that's where the mettle needed testing), to determine which ones among them would balk at the cold-blooded taking of life, which ones would put religion before their soldier's duty.

He wanted to pick out the good Buddhists who shot into those helpless packs . . . and watched as the dogs incinerated themselves . . . and kept shooting—all without a word or shudder of protest. These were the ones he knew would have the stuff. . . .

"That smell!" said the lieutenant. "There's never been anything like it! That smoke from burning rubber and dog meat! I had to burn the uniform I was wearing that night. Still the smell wouldn't go away, it stayed in the skin, in the scalp, no matter how many baths you took! I'll think about that night even now and feel sick because that smell will be in my nose again."

On this point I knew the lieutenant wasn't exaggerating. I could still recall the bitter odor that clung to the general in those campaign days when he came home so wild-eyed at those predawn hours, with all that mud—and worse—on his boots. A putrid smoky odor of unmentionable wastes burning.

But the plague was gone!

Now the man responsible for the deliverance was the man of the moment. The time—and the confidence—had come to clean up the government as he'd cleaned up the city.

Time for the Revolution.

"Right, tell us you didn't know what was afoot, what your own husband was up to," I was used to hearing in later years—from the men at the camps, for example.

But it wasn't my place to know these secrets. I remember only the frequency of his council meetings just before the takeover.

"I'm off to the council," he'd say, using the English word "council." He mispronounced it "councy," suggesting—maybe because it rhymed with "bouncy"—a chummy little get-together. No doubt it was, since the councy in question turned out to be the People's Party Council, the new ruling junta.

He kept it very quiet; I'll give him that. From start to finish it wasn't one of those noisy, messy takeovers with shoot-outs at strategic centers, megaphones blaring through the streets, bodies on the pavements, and choppers in the sky. It never came to that. You can't muffle the rumble of armored cars, of course; you can't put silencers on trucks transporting troops back and forth across the city. You can't avoid the minor blunders, like the one giant explosion caused by accidentally blowing up the oil refinery across the river. It killed fifty-odd people—a tragedy. But the government took full responsibility, offering both an official apology and a promise of reparation for the victims' families.

Otherwise, the streets were quiet, the skies were quiet, the protests—if there were any at all—were quiet; and there was nothing to contradict the reports that even the midnight arrests went quietly. Nobody resisted. Not a single one of the cabinet ministers, party chiefs, factory and mill owners, publishers, journalists, or even student leaders. They weren't being arrested, after all. They were being taken into protective custody.

The voice announcing the coup—the voice of the general himself—came through low, solemn, and commanding over the radio later that morning.

The hush had descended.

6

The takeover put an end to a lot of old ways, including my daily loungings by the swimming pool of the Yacht Club. Here, under an umbrella rotated periodically by attendants in white monkey jackets to provide constant shade, I used to sip iced sweet lime juice all afternoon, stunned by the heat and flattered by the stares from the mostly foreign members of the club—the diplomats, technical advisers, engineers, spies, and minor embassy personnel.

I was consumed with self-fancy, with the satisfaction of seeing heads turn as I rose from my chaise longue, lifted my arms to remove one by one the pins holding my hair so that it fell down my back to its full thickness and length—then ambled up to the diving board where, preening to the last, I'd plunge.

I knew exactly how I looked standing up or sitting down; how I looked with my hair down—or up and pulled back to flaunt my atypical features: a Tartar tilt to the eyes and cheekbones, a high-bridged Western nose, and puffy Latin lips pushed by an overbite into a pout (which I used to try to correct, until Carlos confessed that pouting lips on women *drove men crazy*).

I especially knew how I looked as I emerged from my dive, with my smooth hair shining and my wet skin glistening. I knew because once, in a copy of *National Geographic* that Carlos had brought home to show me, I'd seen a girl from some island in the South Pacific, a girl with a look of both daring and cunning, her hair and her sarong soaked from a swim. That same day when I was climbing out from a swim in the river in my sarong, there was Carlos standing on the rocks above me, his head inclined in that sad resigned way, saying, "You look just like that beauty in *National Geographic*."

"What beauty?"

"Doan gimme that," laughed Carlos. "The girl from Tahiti, the one you were staring at."

"She's not a beauty."

"She got more than beauty, that girl. She got mystery, sex appeal. She got potential. Just like you, Tango, if you don't mind my saying."

I didn't mind. I sensed that beauty in the ordinary sense wasn't in the cards for me. My features were odd —not neat and not always agreeable. They stood out and seemed downright foreign at times. My body too was assuming a foreign shape: not wasp-waisted and low slung like most girls my age, but short waisted and long limbed: long in the legs but long in the arms, too.

It appeared it wasn't Carlos alone who thought I had potential.

"Madame has great potential, General," exclaimed the Frenchwoman who came to tutor me now that I'd become first lady.

She'd been hired soon after the Cambodian visit. Princess Monique's savoir faire had planted the idea in Supremo's head that the grooming of a leader's wife might enhance a leader's image. It was the way she made Prince Sihanouk look better, like less of a boy: a charming boy, granted, but naughty,

naughty. He pulled the most extravagant faces. Seeing him from a distance, beyond earshot, you'd never guess he was speaking of weighty world affairs; you'd think he was deep in some boyish transaction, needling and wheedling. He wagged his head; he made big eyes; he squinted; he frowned; he pouted; he giggled and sputtered till tears rolled down his cheeks.

Monique yawned discreetly. She seemed to me the type to sulk and oversleep: there was that faint puffiness about her face, the slightly dazed, out-of-sorts smile.

"But did you notice the way she called me *mon général?*" My husband gloated.

It impressed him that she had started out an outsider, a commoner, and a mixed breed at that. But for the cut of her clothes and lilt of her French accent she could have been a local Anglo girl. Supremo had pounced on a tidbit of intelligence—a remark made to one of his colonels by a member of the royal delegation—suggesting that private tutoring was what had transformed the princess from rough rock to polished gem.

If Monique could do it, maybe I could do it: heighten his aura in public, now that he was head of state.

He'd never been at ease in society, especially at those diplomatic functions where we were well-known *habitués* when he was armed forces chief of staff. The practice then was for him to repair to one of the back rooms to smoke Havanas and drink Tanqueray and tonics with the military attachés, leaving me to make the rounds on the dance floor.

What disappointing dancers they were, all of them. There was Larry, the American air attaché, a tall, freckle-faced Texan who stamped his foot, shook his fist, and said "Dang!" whenever the music came to an end. There was Günter, the West German trade attaché, for whom the cha-cha-cha seemed just an excuse to click his heels. ("Ah, Dayan women!" I once overheard him say. "So graceful, and such beautiful long hairs!") There was Alain, the French chargé d'affaires, a vain snob who danced with a grimace, as though he smelled something even worse than his own potent BO. There was Vladimir, the burly Russian naval attaché, who whispered sweet vodka fumes into my ear. There was Francisco, the Spanish consul, who sulked whenever I assumed a swaybacked posture to avoid his eager groin. And there was Mordecai, first secretary, embassy of Israel, a tiny man with bat ears, and shoulders raised in a perpetual shrug.

He once rubbed my palm on the dance floor and said something that sounded like *huff!*

"Come with me," he said conspiratorially and slowly danced me away from everyone—and into the bathroom (the house, on that occasion, was his). He shut the door behind him and reached into a cabinet above the sink—for a jar of Nivea cream. Breathing hard—whether from the exertion of the dance or from the excitement of the task at hand I couldn't tell—he unscrewed the top, dipped his fingers into it, and slapped the cream into my palms. "Now they won't be so huff," he beamed.

There was no one to tango with, no one remotely approaching the talent of a Carlos. No one with that little swing of the hip, and turn of the heel, and bend of the knee—with that small movement, so unexpected but so right, which took your breath away. Certainly no one among the few other Dayan guests invited to these affairs—the ones who'd learned the latest numbers and steps abroad or simply from frequenting enough parties of this sort.

I was always on the lookout for another Carlos. But Carlos himself was hors de combat these days, being gainfully employed. On the general's recommendation he'd been inducted into the army.

It was worse after the takeover, when I moved up to dance with the ambassadors—a dreary, lead-footed lot if ever there was one. But this unbridled contact didn't last long.

The general was rethinking his notions of culture.

It began as early as the Ethiopian visit, when at the last minute I had been obliged to change what I was wearing all because he suddenly got it into his head that red was not an appropriate color for first ladies of socialist nations to wear at state banquets for Ethiopian potentates. He'd ordered changes in the welcoming parades and banquets too—no more big drums and dancing girls and elephant parades.

More and more his disapproval was aimed at things foreign. He disapproved of fraternizing with foreigners—even those who'd once been friends. He disapproved of their parties, their food, their liquor, their privileges, their servants, their compound life. He feared any taint of dependence on the Americans or the Russians or the Chinese. One shot of PX Tanqueray and he imagined being labeled a capitalist; one Stolichnaya vodka might put him, as far as his public was concerned, in the pay of the Soviets; one Chinese banquet and it might look like the Chinese—the Reds one minute, the Formosans the next—had him safely tucked into their pockets.

On the other hand, he didn't want to release his hold on the diplomatic grapevine entirely; so he grudgingly left the hobnobbing and glad-handing to me. But he was keen to know if he was missed. "So, was the ambassador upset?" he'd ask, after a function he'd declined to attend. The fewer his public appearances, the greater the aura of the strongman, the mystery man, the remote and independent autocrat.

He was of two minds about the way he perceived my effect on men, too. "*I've* got the most beautiful wife in the world," he'd boast when we were alone, jabbing a thumb at his chest. "She makes men drool and fall at her feet."

Then he'd have my neck in a stranglehold, accusing, demanding, threatening. "I saw the way that American son of a bitch had his big hand on your flesh, there where the back of your waist was bare. Did it feel good? Tell me how it felt and don't lie. Did it make you itch? Did you feel that nerve running down the center of your crotch swelling and twitching? Were you thinking what it would be like to have a huge American prick up you for a change?

"Tell me, tell me!" he'd be panting now, having mounted me for that crippled ride, lashing the waves, crying for the moon. "Tell me what you'd do."

So I'd feed him the stimulant in little doses. I'd give him the lowdown he wanted. I'd describe step by step, from foreplay to climax, the imagined infidelity.

"Oh," he'd whoop, "go on, go on!"

At last the whole fantasy would crumble. "It's useless, I can't do it! I'll kill you, you witch, if you ever try anything like that, do you hear? I'll cut his balls off and feed them to you. I'll make you swallow without chewing, till you choke."

Then he'd wind my hair around his fist and jerk it back (so that to avoid his gaze I would have had to shut my eyes), demanding, "Love me?"

What else to answer but "Always!"?

Madame, the Frenchwoman who remarked on my potential, had said something about love I still remembered. Some years earlier, while employed as a teacher at the International School, Madame had left her English husband, an engineer with Lever Brothers, for the trishaw man who pedaled her children daily to school and back. The Englishman had packed up the children and returned home. Madame had remained with her trishaw man in a one-room flat downtown, near the main trishaw stand at the railway station where he picked up his daily fares. But the scandal had cost her her job, and in the end it was just too hard. Unable to take the strain, the trishaw man fled to his village up-country. Madame, however, stayed. She took in students by day and worked at the Grand Hotel by night.

Once, in the midst of putting me through a drill, Madame fell silent. She rested her cheek on one hand; the other doodled on a page of her exercise book. How disheveled and beaten she looked now, this Frenchwoman with a scandal in her past. Her hair sprung out like copper wires frizzed by the heat. The skin on her face had almost the same texture as her well-worn leather handbag.

"Love," she said—in English now—smiling tenderly in recollection. "It never makes sense until it happens to you. You can't give reasons or explanations; it just happens. Of course you can make things up. I could say I loved him because he loved my children. And he did love them! I saw it in the way he lifted them into their seats every morning and lifted them out every afternoon. But you don't go around falling in love with everyone who's kind to your children. One day, I don't know why, he was taking me somewhere, I was sitting in the seat slightly behind him, when everything changed. How many times I had seen his back, the muscles working, the sweat running down and darkening the waist of his sarong, the knots in his calves from pumping the pedals. But that day we stopped at a light and when he rested one leg on the pedal, it was trembling from the strain. I started trembling too. I couldn't stop shaking; it was like a fever. That was that. When I got home I had to tell him what I felt for him. 'Lady,' he said, looking down at my feet, 'I can't speak; you honor me by returning my love.' He had never spoken of his love; I doubt if he'd felt love for me before then. But that was his way of doing me a courtesy. Imagine."

It wasn't hard to imagine. What was a half-starved trishaw man supposed to do when a redheaded, white-skinned woman declared her love except to relieve her of some of the load? Didn't he rush to spare her the burden of a heavy shopping bag? One acted sometimes out of habit or courtesy or accommodation. True, it occasionally backfired.

I love you! I'd say even now to the general. It was often self-preservation. But courtesy had entered into it too. And habit. And accommodation. And fear. The fact is I kept saying it. And it wasn't as if I gagged on the declaration. I hardly gave it a second thought.

He wasn't always fooled. Sometimes he'd push my face away, spreading all five fingers across it as though wanting to wipe it out entirely.

"Ah, I know what will happen," he'd say with bitter dejection. "You'll be the death of me."

"Why talk nonsense? I love you!"

"You don't love me enough."

"That's true," I replied once, in an excess of daring. "I can't love you enough in this life. But if I killed you, I could worship you. Just think: I could make images of you, thousands and thousands of images like those millions of Buddhas made by the monastery boys outside Irrawaddy. I've seen them do it; I could have them do it. I'd have a beautiful mold of you made. They'd take the best clay and slap it into the two halves of each mold; they'd turn the molds out in the sun and bake the images to the brightest whiteness. There'd be whole populations of you in the purest white. Then I could love you more."

His right eye went into such a spasm that I almost felt sorry.

"God, you are a witch," he whispered.

But he had the last word; he always did.

Witness the *dak* bungalow incident.

He was on an official tour of the northeast, to inspect the newly established LSD, the Local Self-Defense units, charged with policing the rebel-plagued regions—the Punished Provinces, as they were called. I was accompanying him.

We had stopped for lunch at an old *dak* bungalow on the road where the foothills began.

Inside, pains had obviously been taken to air out the place in readiness for our arrival, and the creaky ceiling fan was doing its best to keep the air circulating, but a sour mustiness prevailed, as though trapped there from its better days—the days of British rule—and ripening since.

After lunch—a bland English meal of mutton stew, mashed potatoes, and boiled squash in a gummy sauce, with blancmange for dessert—the general had gone outside and I was looking through the bookcase when the old Muslim cook crept up behind me so quietly that he startled me when he spoke.

"Missy," he said in English, shyly twisting a curry-stained rag that hung over one shoulder, "you want see cockadoodle?" His face was caught in a pained grimace that I realized was a smile.

I nodded. Not that I had any interest in roosters, but it was something to do. I followed him through the kitchen, out the back door, and down the plank stairs. He had a limp so severe that with each step he took I was sure he would lose his footing and plunge his game leg through the space between the treads, but he descended without mishap. He led me through a covered walkway leading beyond the servants' quarters, out to the weedy expanse of what once had been a garden. There in the scrub was a miniature pool, too shallow for swimming, but with tiles and steps at one end, just like a regular swimming pool. Clumps of wild onion grew out of the cracks along the cement apron, and the pool was half-filled with scummy water of putrid purples and greens.

The cook pointed to some lily pads and beckoned me closer. I could see nothing at first, but then the lily pads moved and part of a log surfaced.

"Cockadoodle," he said triumphantly. It was a small crocodile.

"Hassan!" he hollered without warning, next to my ear.

A boy of about thirteen came running out from the servants' quarters, rubbing his eyes. "Papa?"

"Call cockadoodle," the cook commanded in English.

Hassan squatted by the side of the pool, cupped his fingers

around his mouth, and made a sound between a bark and a howl. He waited, repeated it several more times, waited.

The crocodile flicked its tail and nosed its way to the steps, climbing with ungainly sideways movements. Hassan went to meet it, holding his arms out as though encouraging a child just learning to swim. When it had crawled up the side, Hassan put his hands around its snout and wrestled it playfully.

I looked up to see the general standing behind me, flanked by two officers. Behind them, keeping a respectful distance, a group of soldiers from the convoy had gathered to watch.

"What? A nonbiting crocodile?" asked the general.

"My son has tamed it, General, sir," said the cook. "He tamed a mongoose once."

To confirm his father's boast, Hassan swung a leg over the beast and straddled its back. The crocodile was very still. It was only about five feet long, but the grin on its mouth seemed intended to exhibit its formidable teeth.

"Sweet, isn't it?" said the general to me.

Hardly. But I nodded and smiled.

"Then go and stroke it."

I looked up at him. I thought he was joking.

"Go on. Go and stroke it."

I shook my head. A titter from the soldiers in the back.

"Do you hear what I'm saying? I want to see you stroke the crocodile."

"But I don't want to."

"Whether you want to or not, go do it."

He reached down and gripped my elbow, steering me toward the crocodile, where Hassan was posing like a cowboy in his saddle. "It won't bite," said the boy, slapping the snout to convince me. He was radiant from attracting so much attention.

I jerked my elbow out of the general's hand. "I said I don't want to."

He recaptured my arm with a snarl. "Then I'll have to make you."

He was behind me now, one hand on either elbow, marching me forward. The soldiers were laughing. Maybe they thought they were watching a joke, a game. Reaching the crocodile, he shifted his grip to my wrists and pushed me forward under his weight until I fell over, landing with my palms on the ridges of its back. The terror of the contact made me see stars. I fell backward onto the dirt.

By then he was walking away—hitching the strap on his wristwatch, tugging down his jacket, and walking away.

Later, as we were preparing to leave, he called me into the dining room.

"What is it?" I said, avoiding his eyes.

I didn't realize I was standing so close to the wall until I felt my head whip around and bounce off it from the blow he'd just given me. "Don't you ever again disobey me in front of people," he said through gritted teeth. My head hit the wall again—harder this time—just as the cook walked in. It was the old man's presence, I suppose, that kept me from crying out.

The general turned on his heel and went outside, while I stood trembling against the wall for support. I felt the back of my head. A large lump was forming, and it was wet.

The cook had disappeared. He came back now with a moist warm towel, twisted dry. "So sorry, missy," he said as he handed it to me. "All my fault."

I could hear the engines running outside; they were waiting for me.

We drove on in a cloud of dust and heat, under a sun that bleached the horizon. The hills up ahead had paled literally into insignificance, seeming to get farther, not closer, with approach. The road took us past acres of teak and rubber plantations—the sight of which appeared to restore my husband's good humor. "Look at that," he said, pointing out the window at the vast symmetrical stands. "Our bountiful land, our golden country."

"Natural resources," he added in English. "Natural resources." He seemed pleased as he repeated the phrase, as though he'd just recovered a lost bon mot.

He said it again when we reached the bleak expanses of the oil fields. "Natural resources!" He breathed in deeply. "Smell, just smell!" He exulted at the powerful stench from the refineries, as though sniffing perfume. "I swear the oil smells cleaner now, with those fucking capitalists gone." Again he used the English word—"ka-pee-tah-liss"— there being no Dayan word for that plague.

Up above a cluster of smokestacks loomed a large British Petroleum sign that hadn't been taken down. He stuck his hand out the window, pointed an imaginary pistol at it, and pulled the trigger. Then he waved exuberantly. "We can run our own affairs, thank you," he called out the window. "Ta-ta, BP, ta-ta!"

Then he leaned over and gave me a pinch below the ribs. "Lost your tongue like the crocodile?" he teased. "Will the cat find it, heh?"

The crocodile of Dayan myth was a lazy oaf, tricked by the crow who lured him onto land and there left him beached, to die of starvation and thirst. With the help of a stupid bullock-cart driver, the crocodile managed to wangle his way back into the river, but no sooner had he slithered off the cart than the ingrate turned to bite the cart man's bullock on the leg.

At that moment, along came the rabbit to the cart man's aid. "Hit him with your driving stick, hit him with your driving stick," he shouted. The cart man hit, the crocodile let go, and the bullock was free. But the crocodile was after the rabbit now. He caught the little troublemaker in his jaws finally and swam up and down the river with a gleeful "Hee, hee, hee."

Inside the crocodile's jaws, the rabbit rearranged himself to straddle the great tongue, and when he'd got it in a firm grip, he said, "Oh, sure you can laugh hee, hee, hee, my friend. But can you laugh ha, ha, ha?"

The crocodile opened his mouth to meet the challenge, and the rabbit jumped out of his jaws, plucking out the tongue with a mighty yank.

The rabbit, unable to think of a use for the big heavy organ, buried it under a bush. Later, meeting his friend the cat, he decided to reveal the hiding place. But when the cat got there, he could find no trace of the tongue—just a strange-looking squash with a scaly skin, growing out of the ground.

Thus the origin of the vegetable known as the cat-tongue squash.

"Maybe we'll have some *cat-tongue squash* tonight, heh?" my husband was saying. "Heh, heh, heh."

But can you laugh ha, ha, ha? I thought, noticing how very sharp—almost filed to a point—his canines looked when he bared them to laugh.

Sunset was under way as we rounded a bend in the road . . . and playing like a mirage through the illusory waves of heat was a vision: the old Portuguese town of Milonga.

Its buildings were strung out like a necklace of assorted stones—coral, amber, turquoise, jade—threaded through a sparkling little ribbon of a river. Beyond: a tiny bridge, so delicate and ornate it gave the impression of lace. The sun in its descent had expanded into an enormous red plate—and against it, like an etching on that plate, was a trio of spires rising way above the tallest roofs of the town: the spires of a pagoda, a minaret, and a cathedral.

Less than a year later, when the general had decreed Buddhism the state religion—a decree that signaled the first wave of religious persecution, when mosques were wrecked and Chinese temples burned down by mobs chanting nationalist slogans—I remembered his words upon coming across that twilight vision above the dusty plains.

"Tolerance!" he said. "Bah! To think of all the crimes committed in the name of tolerance! Tolerance, the great Buddhist virtue. Bah! I'll tell you something about tolerance. The enemy of progress—that's tolerance."

Pleased with this pronouncement, he gazed out the window drowsily, his mouth hanging open in a way that recalled what Hassan, the crocodile boy, had said earlier in the day. One of the soldiers had asked why the crocodile held its jaws ajar for such long stretches.

"To keep its head from overheating," Hassan had explained.

7

Our next trip up-country had a much more serious purpose. We were going to visit the shrine of the Viriya Bell.

The bell was one of my husband's obsessions. The original had been cast back in the days of Buddha's wanderings and housed in the same niche that once had housed a famous Buddha image. That extraordinary sculpture was supposed to have been created by none other than the Lord of Paradise, to commemorate the Buddha's sojourn through the area. The reason the image had borne such an uncanny likeness to the Buddha was that the Omniscient One had given it life by breathing upon it.

This holiest of holy statues (the cause of bloody wars in centuries to come) had been removed some two hundred years ago to the old walled city of Naungda, the then capital. There it had drawn a steady flow of pilgrims until its destruction by the earthquake of 1922—the year, as it happened, that Supremo was born.

But back at the site of the original shrine remained a copy of the old Viriya Bell, believed to have been cast at the same time as the famous image: a big bronze dome etched with astrological charts determining exactly when and how it should be tolled in the event of imminent attack on the kingdom. If rung according to the precise formulas set out in the inscriptions, the notes sounded by the bell would repel the attackers by upsetting their astrological force fields.

Sometime in the eighteenth century, the bell disappeared. Fortunately, a true copy had been made. Unfortunately, the copy—while true in every detail—had somehow lost its efficacy as an enemy repellent. But the original squares containing the diagrams and charts were extant, etched into the underside of the copy. Supremo's interest was in investigating those squares, to see if something could be salvaged from the old science of state magic.

The Viriya pagoda was an overnight journey—some three hundred miles northeast of the city, up in the hills. We left in a convoy consisting of jeeps, trucks, and the Land Rover reserved for Supremo and me, driving for the first hour or so along the road running parallel to the river and the railway tracks.

As the convoy slowed down near one of the satellite towns, where the road had collapsed into a rash of potholes, I saw the game a group of children were playing. Half of the group would raise their arms in the hands-up position demanded by robbers, while the other half circled them, patting them all around the front and back of their bodies. Then the two halves would switch roles.

They were enacting a scene more and more characteristic of the times. The days had become a series of senseless searches. Anybody at all could challenge the next person on the street, demanding "Hands up!" and almost without fail hands would go up compliantly for the familiar frisk. One had to be cautious; one never knew if the searcher was a fake, or a robber, or an undercover State Security Office agent.

Of course this citizens' search was a weapon with something of a twin-edged blade. The victim himself could turn out to be SSO, could then turn around and search the searcher—or even if he wasn't SSO, what was to stop him from calling a bluff . . . and so on?

It was a slow drive through parched land. Rain was badly needed. The white husks of the bamboo lining the road rattled as we drove by. Cows stood stupefied in the middle of the road, trailing long beards of saliva. Sulfur sand and dust coated every bush, every leaf, every surface along the road. The hills up ahead looked blistered.

I was fighting a powerful drowsiness when the shooting and chaos began.

My first thought—after the screeching stop, the shouting, the panic, the cross fire, the leap out of the Land Rover, and the roll downhill—the first important fact to lodge in my mind was that someone was hit, but it wasn't me.

It was the scrawny soldier in front of me. I saw him go down wordlessly, as in a silent film. I saw him slap his head, like a clown miming forgetfulness, before his knees buckled and he dropped on his side. Just when I thought he'd turned up his toes, up came his hand—the index finger raised to register one last point—before it fell like a rag doll's.

They were around me suddenly, a riffraff crowd, tattered but armed. Their weapons were standard issue Stens, Brens, Thompsons, Enfields—but their uniforms were a disgrace: frayed sarongs and ripped khaki shirts, camouflage pants rolled up to the knee, sleeveless undershirts riddled with holes. On their feet were mostly rubber sandals made from old truck tires, an ignominy for which our men would have been shot.

"Get up!" ordered the one with the barrel closest to me— not in an especially threatening tone, but the tip of his barrel was pointed at the bridge of my nose. He was wearing green galoshes, patched at the toes with tape.

I stood up slowly, noticing the dust and bits of grass that clung to my body. My sarong was white, with widely spaced clusters of pink and green blossoms. What a choice for a day like this! And the sandals were white too. At the moment I had only one on, the one with the broken strap; the other was nowhere to be seen.

Maybe I was moving too slowly. "You're not hit?" asked the same man in a different, almost anxious voice.

I shook my head. "No, I'm not hit," I wanted to answer, but my throat was too clogged to swallow or speak. My elbows were beginning to sting from the scrapes and cuts of the long tumble. The midges were flying thick and fast around my face. It was almost too hot to breathe. I itched to clear my throat, brush my elbows off, shake out my sarong, and swat at the midges, but was chary of making the wrong move. Something wet crept down my cheek and dropped onto my white blouse, just above my breast. I looked down. Blood—and I hadn't felt a thing.

The marksman shifted the barrel site down now to the bloodstain on my chest. I could meet his eye at last. He gave me a wink.

"Your earrings," he said, pointing with the barrel. "I must ask you to remove them." He winked again.

Should I wink back? But as I unscrewed the stopper at the back of my ear, I noticed he was winking furiously.

No, it wasn't a wink; it was a tic. And it wasn't a game; it was real. An ambush.

Where was Supremo? Where were the others? What had I missed?

I handed over my earrings. A heavily tattooed fellow came forward now with a little yellow notebook to which a pencil had been tied with twine. He wrote something, tore out the page, and thrust it at me. It said, in English, "Received, one pair earrings, diamond, white-gold setting," and was signed with a snaky scrawl.

Someone threw me a pair of rubber-tire flip-flops.

"March," said the leader, motioning me to turn around and fall in with the men who had encircled me. We shuffled off from that parched little clearing toward the jungle ahead.

Soon a dark dream had descended: monstrous branches and creepers and vines; unearthly noises of things flapping and rustling and crashing in the bush; a diamondback snake coiled around a tree; thorns at my elbows and thorns at my feet; a gun at my back.

My abductors too were part of the dream: shadow soldiers explaining nothing, speaking a language I couldn't understand, by turns threatening and protective. When we stopped to rest and pluck the leeches off our feet, the man with the patched galoshes unhooked a khaki canteen from the knapsack on his back and offered me a drink. I took a swig and found it was empty—part of the same dream? When would I wake?

At last, after hours—five hours, I found out much later—we emerged from the thickets onto a cleared embankment. The river below looked steely in the twilight—steely and still and deep. The jungle foamed on the banks beyond—the same jungle foaming at our backs.

Two long-tailed boats were docked below, on a shallow sandbank where passengers were already waiting with the boatmen: three teenage boys, machine guns slung over their shoulders, in the same ragtag uniforms my captors were sporting; five peasants—two men, three women—surrounded with baskets of rice and fish.

I climbed into the first skiff with most of our party. The second skiff took the overflow, along with the waiting passengers. One after the other the engines leapt into a roar, and off we shot downriver, our boat in the lead. The hills on either side, chunky silhouettes now, converged in the distance in a sort of trick V, a neat point where the river appeared to narrow down to a clean-cut end. All that remained of sunset was a thin mauve band of light rimming the sky just above the peaks of the hills. That too was smudged out in short order. Night spread in a quick black stain over every visible surface of earth and sky.

One of the men in our boat stood up at the bow, facing forward, very straight, as though to take a salute. He was holding a flashlight pointed directly ahead, throwing off a little patch of brightness in the dark void to guide the boat. I turned around and saw a similar feeble beam cast by the second skiff. Lights were coming on, too, in the solitary huts here and there along the banks—small firefly flickers that seemed destined to die out after a wink or two in that great black fastness of jungle, invisible now but still palpable, that walled us in on both sides.

We'd been on a straight-arrow course. Now the boats slowed to take a sharp ninety-degree turn, and suddenly the river spray misting our faces was no longer tepid but cold enough to sting. I crouched down in my seat, arms crossed, shivering and gritting my teeth.

When a swarm of fireflies appeared up ahead, the boats went into low gear and moved toward the tiny flickers, which turned into a cluster of huts on stilts right above the landing where we pulled in.

I stepped out of the skiff onto soft, wet ground that sucked in the soles of my flip-flops, releasing them with a stubborn *plop*. The steps hewn into the steep path uphill were shallow and irregular; they needed close watching. I was almost at the top before I saw, in the light of kerosene lamps hanging from the thatched eaves, the rows of faces lined up along the open porches of the huts above. More and more silhouettes appeared as I picked my way between the raised huts, led by a man—a different one from the leader with the green galoshes—wielding a small flashlight. Laughter and banter—again in that foreign yet not entirely unfamiliar tongue—between the gallery of men from above and the ones bringing up the rear in my path.

We crossed an empty expanse the size of a soccer field, arriving at a sentry box manned by two guards. One of them shone a bright flashlight into my face, exchanged a joke with my guides, and waved us through. We stopped at the stairs to a hut that appeared to be the largest of the ones we'd passed, shedding our sandals at the foot of the stairs before going up. I heard the crackle of a shortwave radio broadcast and caught "BBC" just before someone turned it off.

Three men were sitting in deck chairs on an open veranda. The one who got up to greet me was a tall, gaunt, white-haired figure clad in black pajamas. He held out his hand. "How d'you do?" he said in English. "I'm Colonel Sandhurst. Trust your journey wasn't too . . . taxing?

"Let me introduce you to our President Boyan . . . ," he said. I had turned to the older of the two men in the deck chairs—a bulldog of a man with swollen lids and lips who was chewing betel nut and leaning forward in his seat—and was about to bow in acknowledgment. But he was looking at the third man, the much younger one—the one lolling back in his chair and fixing me with the blankest of stares. Catching on just in time that *he* was the president, I inclined my head in his direction. He didn't move.

"And this," said Black Pajamas, turning to the bulldog, "is our vice president."

"Sit," said the young president finally—in Dayan—still staring at me.

I lowered myself onto the wooden plank that ran along the sides of the veranda. A boy in an oversized army shirt came up the stairs bearing a tray with four glass tumblers on it. Crouching low, averting his eyes, he set the tray beside me.

"Please," offered the colonel.

I helped myself to one of the glasses—it was half-filled with hot, weak tea.

"You know who we are?" growled the bulldog, masticating. He too spoke Dayan, but with a thick accent.

"No." I shook my head, unable to sort out the jumble of pictures still taking shape in my mind. This was no band of *dacoits*—too much protocol and hierarchy here.

"Who do you *think* we are?" asked the president. His accent was not as strange as the vice president's—but the flatness in his eyes was foreign. In the light of the kerosene lamps, they loomed bright, blank, and disembodied.

"I really don't know."

"I really don't know!" he mocked, turning his face to the side. With a shock I saw it in profile: he had almost no nose. The nostrils were intact, but the bridge looked blown away.

"Why would she know anything about us, just because we're her countrymen?" he said to the bulldog. "She probably thought we had horns and tails and lived in trees besides." The colonel laughed; the bulldog sputtered. The president trained his eyes on me once more—those blank, bare eyes with no mitigating nose. "Am I right?"

"Are you rebels, then?" I asked.

This time all three men burst out laughing—the president in an empty, mirthless way that didn't involve the eyes. "Rebels?" he said. "Of course not. We're a famous song-and-dance troupe, resting in the jungle between engagements. We brought you here because we heard you were a famous dancer."

"My husband will be very angry about this," I said in English, directing this absurd statement to the colonel.

"Alas, you may be right," replied the colonel in his clipped English. Then he turned and conferred with the other two.

"Look here," he said, switching to English again. "We've

nothing against you. But we need to keep you here until—well, until certain of our demands have been met by your—your esteemed husband."

"What sort of demands?" I asked.

"Oh, simple demands, really. The right to live like human beings. You know: to speak our own language and say our own prayers without fear of getting killed—that sort of thing. Not what you'd call outrageous. . . ."

"What *is* your language?" I interrupted. "May I ask? What group are you?"

"Amazing," said the colonel. "You really haven't a clue, have you? The ignorance, the arrogance, of you lowlanders." But he sounded tolerant. "We're the Jesu. You've heard of the Jesu?"

I nodded. "Yes, of course." The Jesu! Weren't they the tribe that sang Negro spirituals every evening, believed in a blue-eyed Messiah, and punished adulterous women by strangling them in a pit? Or maybe I was confusing them with the Mana—another tribe—who were said to force their senior citizens onto high scaffoldings, then shove them to their death with long sticks?

"Anyway," he said. "All *you* have to worry about is making yourself at home while we sort out the nitty-gritty of your release. It won't be very long. The general—your husband— isn't going to let you remain here one minute more than is necessary." He smiled. "Is he?

"It's not asking too much, I hope? To relax here without causing any trouble? While we work for your freedom? Seek ye shelter in the hills, as the Bible says. You'll be well treated, well protected. We've nothing against you. But—bear in mind: our president here is a sincere man. Most sincere. He means what he says, and does what he means to do. He doesn't just threaten executions; he sees they're carried out. And he doesn't just order them to be carried out. He carries them out himself; each and every one of them. A very sincere man."

I couldn't tell whether the president spoke English. He wasn't giving our conversation any attention at the moment. He'd turned his chair around, to face the shortwave radio again, his back to us. He'd tuned in to a Voice of America broadcast in Dayan.

The bulldog's eyelids were drooping. "It's late," he said. "Shouldn't we feed her?"

"Yes, feed her," the president concurred without turning around.

"You must be famished," said the colonel. Famished? My last meal seemed like a lifetime ago. "Come and have a little something to eat." He picked up a light—a small oil lamp sitting on the floor next to him—and led me inside the hut. We passed through the main room—the flame illuminating only the passage and not the details of what lay on either side—and out to another veranda in back.

On the floor, set out on the lid of an aluminum pot and lit by a hurricane lamp, was my meal: a bowl of rice, a dish of greens, and a chipped teacup containing a dollop of something black—fish paste, I guessed. Next to the tray was a tin cup of water.

"Point of etiquette—that's your finger bowl, not your drinking water," said the colonel as I knelt to my primitive fare, laid out on the ground like animal feed.

The squalor was comforting in a way. What a sorry meal, and what a pathetic group—as if they'd ever stand a chance against our Union Forces. And to resort to this crazy, desperate gambit involving me, the Supremo's wife! What a sad miscalculation! The coarse rice, slimy greens, and crude fish paste made me pity them.

Pity rose up in me once more in the small hut out back

where I was to spend the night. As I rigged the mosquito net over the rush mat on the floor, a teenaged girl appeared, bearing a basin of water. She set it down on the split-bamboo floor near my feet and bade me step in. I stood ankle-deep in warm water that acted like balm on the aches and stings left by the jungle hike while she crouched at my feet, bathing and massaging them gently, and afterwards patting them dry with the edge of her soft sarong. The top of her head glistened like the lacquer on a begging bowl; her shoulders seemed so meek and defenseless; and again I thought how regrettable it would be for this silent, servile child to be among those holding me hostage, who surely would have to bear the brunt of Supremo's wrath. But when she picked up her basin and candle and stood to face me, it wasn't a child's eyes I confronted. There was nothing defenseless at all in their hard, assessing look as she backed out the door.

I blew out my candle, crawled in under the well-patched mosquito net and lay on the mat, listening to the sounds from the adjacent huts—the voices of men laughing, talking, singing. When these had subsided, I listened to the clatter of leaves in the wind, the shrilling of crickets, the yawping of frogs— the complicated din known as the stillness of the night. I ached with fatigue and the desire to sleep. Waking from sleep might mean waking from that long dream.

It had been awhile since I'd slept on a bamboo floor. There was a time when I'd slept as easily on bamboo as on foam. But I'd been spoiled in recent years; now it took a lot of shifting and squirming to dodge the slats chafing through the thin rush mat. But exhaustion got the better of me and at last I went under. Yet it was not quite the sleep of the dead. From turn to turn I was aware of the paralyzing fatigue in my limbs, the damp cold in the air, the bamboo strips under me. Nonetheless, I sank eventually into a sleep deep enough to confuse me when I woke to the cock's crow in the half-light of dawn. For an instant I thought I was back home in Irrawaddy.

Then the patches in the mosquito net took shape, and I remembered where I was. It was real, then; it was serious. I had to think seriously. I went over every detail of the escapade, wanting to commit as much of it as possible to memory. Once back home in Anika—in a matter of days, at most—I'd be called upon to recount the misbegotten little episode, the teapot tempest. When would the first news of the ambush hit the stands, I wondered. My picture—more than likely one of those standard glossies supplied by the Ministry of Information—might already at that very moment be on the front page of *The New Times*.

Outside, directly under my window, a clanking and rattling had begun. I got up off the floor and went to look. Three scarecrows appeared through the ghostly mist, sweeping the ground with broomsticks. Chained to one another by the feet, they worked in tandem, each at the point of a triangle, moving as a triangle across the ground. In the gathering light huts appeared on all sides of a cleared quadrangle with a flagpole in the center. A figure at the flagpole held a bugle to his mouth and sounded out a reveille, and out of the huts came the men in their threadbare fatigues to take up formation and salute the flag. It went up the pole in a droop, its emblem obscured.

The leaf sweepers in chains went on with their purposeless sweeping. They swept the leaves into piles only to have the chains undo it all by dragging through the piles and spreading the leaves across the ground again. One of them was a small boy—a child of about ten, I guessed.

He let out a yowl as a soldier kicked him in passing. A chicken appeared at that moment, jerking its way through the leaves. Without warning the boy hit it with his broom, sending it squawking into a bush at a corner of the square where it pecked away with a vengeance at a worm.

"Circles of torment." Now I understood the phrase. The soldiers tormented the prisoners, who tormented the chickens, who tormented the worms, who burrowed their way into the ground where the soldiers would be buried. . . .

"Slept well?" came the unmistakable voice behind me, the voice of Colonel Sandhurst.

"Ah, so you've seen our prisoners, what?" he said, looking out the window over my shoulder.

"Prisoners of war?" I thought that's what he'd said.

"Heavens, no! Not prisoners of *war*! Just prisoners—common criminals: thieves, rapists, murderers, deserters. We don't take prisoners of war. Too troublesome, too costly. Keep them alive here by taking food away from our men to put into their mouths? Hardly worth it, don't you see?

"Except, of course," he said with a smile, "under certain, shall we say *special* circumstances, when the benefits may outweigh the, er, the, er, the, er, nuisance.

"Well, do make yourself at home. Dali, the girl who brought your hot water last night, will be here shortly to show you around—where to bathe, where to walk around for exercise, that sort of thing."

He looked out the window thoughtfully. "Come to think of it, you can walk around anywhere you please, really. You're safe here, at GHQ."

"GHQ?"

"General headquarters; couldn't be safer." General headquarters! This cluster of shacks in the bush!

"We're protected here, you see. Look over there, towards the river. Nobody comes upriver without passing through our patrols. Now look behind you: the mountains in a circle all around us. Not easy for the enemy to come through those hills. And even if they did, they'd have to get through the mine fields. We've been planting them like mad ever since we got here. Trouble is, we can't seem to remember the exact spot of every mine. Makes it a bit risky for us to get through, if we need to. Bit of a double-edged sword, I'm afraid."

Pretentious old fool, I thought. Trying to sound like a Tommy, down to the ridiculous stammer ("the, er, the, er, the, er . . .") out here in the middle of nowhere. Trying so hard to impress. Touching, in a way.

Outside, the mist was clearing; daylight was just around the corner—and with it, the nearness of rescue.

I waited all day; then day after day, all week; then week after week. The atmosphere thickened; I felt its pressure in the dull headache I awoke to each morning, in the sore puffiness around my eyes, in the crushing staleness and stillness in the air. The tension built. By day: electric charges in the air. By night: blazes of lightning. Meanwhile, the odd gusts of wind were like blasts from an open furnace. The sky dropped lower and lower without releasing a single drop of rain.

There was a mood, and I was causing it. At the sight of me, men fingered their weapons, women whispered, children jeered or ran away crying, and even the chickens and pigs turned tail. We were all waiting: I for rescue, they for an end to the long dry season, abnormally long and dry that year.

If the monsoons came first, they would be the winners and I the loser—at least for the length of the long wet malarial season to follow, when the best of plans would be washed away and the world would come to a standstill.

The monsoons exploded before the month was out. Sitting on the floor of my hut, my hands over my ears, I trembled at the thunder, rumbling overhead like divisions of tanks; at the flashes splitting the sky; at the shrieking wind; at the rupture that finally let loose the rain.

I trembled because I knew I was there to stay.

8

My captors' demands weren't nearly as vague as Colonel Sandhurst had made them out to be. Self-rule, religious freedom, human rights—those were the old demands. What they wanted this time, in exchange for me, was something more tangible: the release of three of their leaders still being held in Anika jail.

The response my captors were waiting for, the reply to their proposed hostage exchange, never came—no rejection, no counterproposal, no protest. Just silence.

I waited. Doubted. Waited anyway. *I've been abandoned; of course I haven't; I've been abandoned; of course I haven't. He'll come for me; he's leaving me here to rot; he'll come for me; he's leaving me here. . . .*

I tried assessing my own worth. Was I equal in value to three political prisoners? Or did one of me amount to less than one of them?

The monsoons ended. The slow estivation of jungle life began. The cock crowed at dawn, sounding the wake-up call—and at once the camp roused itself: obedient, on schedule . . . for what?

The prisoners dragged their chains through the dead leaves; the soldiers spat and hawked, gargled and rubbed their teeth with bits of charcoal or the bark of neem trees; the bugle sounded; the flag went up in a droop; the morning calisthenics and training began.

They were boys, mostly—shuffling through laps around the quadrangle, then taking up their make-believe guns, their bamboo poles, to play their war games: the marches and formations, the hand-to-hand tussles, the mock maneuvers and attacks that sent them sprawling and crawling on their bellies through the dirt.

The rest of the day went to housekeeping: cooking quantities of rice over bamboo fires, planting vegetables, washing clothes and pots and pans in the river, mending frayed uniforms and frayed thatch roofs, polishing and cleaning guns, building bunkers, digging trenches, attending meetings and lectures, cooking more rice. . . .

Twice a week, Wednesdays and Sundays, they took me downriver to the village where the families of the officers at GHQ lived. There, the children who once ran from me now sat obediently on their schoolroom floor, rubbing their ringworm and scabby legs as they sang their ABCs after me, scratching the letters onto their slate boards, which they erased with spit. Sometimes I was allowed to lend a hand in the dispensary.

Dispensary! I'd imagined a sort of outpatient clinic where the villagers went for aspirin, quinine, bandages, snake serum, vaccinations—not a dormitory for maimed, amputated, skeletal boys lying on bamboo pallets along both sides of the hut. On one occasion, as I approached the corner occupied by a boy with a patch over one eye, a bandaged chest, and an amputated leg, he sat up with enormous effort—to spit at me.

But generally they tolerated me as I took temperatures, felt pulses, changed blankets and bandages, and adjusted the sandbags used as weights for the pulleys holding their arms and legs in traction.

Sundays there was chapel: under a thatch roof marked by a wooden cross, the officers and their families congregated for service and the singing of hymns. *Onward, Christian soldiers* . . . rang the words across the valley, *marching as to war.* . . .

From the back, where I stood, I watched Boyan and his common-law wife—the girl who had washed my feet the night I arrived, the girl whose clothes I was still wearing. The baby on her hip was a boy, his mocking eyes an imprint of his father's. She was short limbed and thickish around the waist— but what a Chinese calendar beauty! I watched the president's blunt, noseless profile as he turned to look at her.

His gaze followed me back at the camp when I walked past his hut. One night he caught me bathing at the cistern. I had just finished. In my wet sarong, I was stepping over to the tree a few yards away where the lantern and a dry change of clothing were hanging; I was slipping out of the wet cloth into the dry one—when a flicker of light caught my eye from up above, from the veranda of the main office where they'd fed me that first night.

I grabbed the lantern and held it up high. The flicker came from a lit cigarette; smoking it and staring down at me was the president.

"You scared me," I said, unable to set the lantern down at once, unable to tear myself away from that look of raging hunger—those eyes stripped naked by the kerosene light. He continued to stare, smoking his cigarette, saying nothing. I began to shiver and turned to set the lantern down. When I glanced back, I saw the flicker of his cigarette as it arced toward the ground, and the silhouette of his back as he went inside.

In daylight, face-to-face, he was all mockery and sarcasm.

"Not getting bored already?" he asked, seeing me sitting on the steps of my hut and staring vacantly into space. "Not missing the big city?"

The big city! What an illusion—those three improbable years I'd spent among its enticements and dangers! The big city. The memory of it was fast dissolving as I sat on those steps. Anika, I knew it now, was forever lost to me.

Another thing I knew: nothing would ever happen here; no one would ever escape; no goals would be achieved. All these uniforms and rituals and drills—what did it amount to except a spinning of whirligigs in the temperamental breeze?

Sometimes, of an evening, I'd look out my window and there they'd be: the leaders themselves—the president, the vice president, the chief of staff, the camp commander, the brass— some in sarongs, some in pajamas, reclining in their deck chairs, under the snug green dome of a mango tree. Taking the air. Lounging. Smoking. Chewing betel nut. Chatting. Laughing. Scratching themselves. Yawning. Not a care in the world, the layabouts!

The scene would have brought on a seizure in Supremo. I imagined him looking over my shoulder at that jolly little gathering. At the sight of his enemies at ease, could anything keep him from storming out of the hut and running up from behind to kick those recumbent backs, every one of them, through those moldy canvas slings of the deck chairs?

"Get up!" he'd snarl through his teeth. "Do something! Go stir up your stupid rebellion, go lay a few mines, instead of lolling in your easy chairs like invalids!"

The monsoons came round once more. On the night they broke, there I was in the same hut, in the same spot practically, as the time before. *A year has passed,* I thought, *and I haven't moved.* The flares and volleys slugged it out in the skies again; the bottom fell out as before, letting down cataracts of rain.

My face in my hands, I didn't see Boyan come in. I felt only a presence, a steaming weight, settle itself on the floor next to me. He sat, knees up, elbows on his knees, mimicking my position. His clothes were dripping.

"Where's the profit in crying, hmm?" he asked close to my ear. That suggestion of futility got me going again.

His elbow nudged mine. "Come on. I thought you liked it here. A roof over your head, peaceful surroundings, food, drink, light work—what more could a prisoner ask?"

"Why punish me?" I cried. "What did I ever do?"

"What did I ever do?" he mimicked.

"Why keep me here? I'm no use to anyone. Let me go. Please. I'm dying here."

"Dying!" he laughed. "You're tough as an elephant, you can't fool me! You haven't even caught malaria! Now that's what I call tough—or lucky."

"Send me home," I pleaded. "I'd say only the best things about you. I'd say how well you treated me."

"Really? You'd do that?" he mocked. "Why didn't you say so earlier?

"Listen to me, Tango." It was the first time he'd called me by my name. "This home of yours—stop pining for it. Your beloved doesn't want you anymore."

I almost smiled, in spite of myself. That Jesu accent! In Dayan, the word for "want" is distinguishable from the word for "fuck" only by a half tone. "Your beloved doesn't want to fuck you anymore" is the way he'd made it come out. *These hill people*, I thought, *even their tongues are lazy—they'll never get anywhere!*

"And as you know, what your beloved wants, your beloved gets. He's the law of the land, your beloved.

"Your beloved," he went on, almost spitting out the term now, "has graciously given you up—to us. He's divorced you. It's in the papers. We got word today."

"I don't believe you!" But I did.

"But why divorce? Why?" I cried.

"You'll have to ask him that."

"But on what grounds?"

"Desertion, he says."

"Desertion! I was captured! You captured me!"

"Oh, that's what happened, then? I wasn't sure."

"Tell me, please! Why has he really done this?"

"You want a simple answer? Maybe he'd rather keep our leaders. A wife you can pick up easily enough. Rebel leaders— now that's a different matter. Who knows, though? Maybe it's a ruse.

"Will you stop crying?" He sounded more tired than annoyed.

"When I was young," he said after a while, "my mother made me stop crying like this." He reached for the candle and held it up to my face. "She smoked these big cheroots. She brought the smoking tip to my mouth and waited for me to open and bawl."

I lowered my forehead down on my knees—and felt his hand stroke the back of my head. I didn't move; I didn't want him to stop.

The touch shifted from my head to my back. I kept my head down, but my eyes open, and after a while I could see from the candle's erratic flicker how unevenly he was breathing.

"You shouldn't stay in wet clothes," I said.

"You're right." Still, he went on rubbing his hand over my shoulders and back. He blew out the candle. "You're right," he repeated. "They might get you wet."

Then we were under the mosquito net, where it was pitch-black and airless as a mine.

He stayed till the rain let up; then he went, leaving only the smell of brine on my skin. The next night he came back for more—crawling in under the mosquito net long after I'd blown out the candle, crawling out almost immediately after he'd spent himself and caught his breath. Again he was gone—this time for weeks.

It was harder now, by daylight, to meet his gaze. I read in it mockery and cruelty both. The men too were regarding me, I thought, with stifled smirks and leers. Even the vice president, that betel-chewing bulldog, seemed compelled to spit more than the usual amount in my presence.

On my next trip to the village, when I passed by the president's hut, there was Dali squatting over a mortar and pestle, pounding something. She looked up just long enough to meet my eye, then quickly dropped her gaze back to the mortar and pestle, revealing nothing except for a twitch at the corner of her lips as she went on pounding.

What pudgy calves she has, I thought with some satisfaction. *Dali—what a name. The president's woman—his little dolly.*

Sandhurst knew—of that I was certain. He was kinder to me now. He'd sit with me in those useless midafternoon hours, perched on the railing of a hut, puffing on a cheroot and recounting the past—the distant past of his childhood in the south; his Sandhurst days, when the bitter English cold brought on a painful tingle in the depth of his bones, an itch impossible to scratch—and when the very thought of rice, which he craved, was enough to bring tears to his eyes; finally the recent past of jungles, and city jails, and jungles again.

"Colonel," I said, "what makes you go on?"

"The tiger's tail. We caught it and now we can't let it go."

"But what, really?"

"When I was a young man," he recited looking out toward the river, "I defended our state. In my old age I shall not abandon it.

"Cicero," he added, raising his ash tin as though in a toast as he turned to leave.

"I've been learning some things from the colonel," I said one night as I lay with Boyan.

He came always under cover of night; apart from this, there was no pattern to his visits.

He made a noise in his throat: he'd heard what I said, but without the slightest interest.

"Want to know what I've been learning?"

"No." He gave a short laugh.

"I've been learning about guerrilla warfare."

"Guerrilla warfare!" He whistled.

"So what do you know about it?" he asked after a while. "Guerrilla. Warfare."

"I know enough to see it's what you're doing to me. I never know when you're coming; you keep me guessing. Each time it's an ambush. You treat me like the enemy."

"How else should I treat you? You *are* the enemy."

"Is that why you come to me?"

"Is this an interrogation?" he said. "Who's the prisoner here?"

"I am! I'm the prisoner! Why don't you just chain me to those wretches who sweep the leaves? At least they get the nights off."

"I can't do that," he said.

"Why? You can do anything you want. You're the president, aren't you?"

"I can't chain you to them."

"Why?"

"Think about it. How would I do this if you were chained to those men?" he said, stretching out on top of me. Before I could say anything he'd clamped his hand over my mouth.

And there it remained, his hand on my mouth, like a holdup.

Then it was dawn. He was gone, and the net was fluttering at the edge of the mat.

The wind picked up, carrying with it a sound I'd come to expect at that hour. It came from the direction of the river, a noise like an excited panting followed by a long sigh, an *ah-ah-ah-ah-ah-ohhhh!*

What kind of creature would let out so ecstatic a call? Was it bird or beast—or a woman reaching climax in her hut somewhere downriver . . . the president's woman, say?

I fell into a pit of loneliness so deep, so black, so airless I could scarcely breathe. *I must not suffocate. I must breathe. I must get out of this pit—pull myself out by the hair, if necessary.* I turned this droll image over and over in my mind . . . and soon I fell into another pit—the obliterating pit of sleep.

9

 The attack came on a Sunday, in the middle of service.

We were singing "Nearer My God to Thee" when the first crump sent a flutter through the thatch walls of the church. The singing stopped; a child cried; a woman's voice shouted out an order; and suddenly everyone went down between the pews and in the aisles. Crouched near the rear wall close to the entrance, I huddled in a corner with three others. A second concussion went off, but farther away.

Somewhere from the front pews a chorus resumed: *Nearer to thee* . . .

The first to stand up was Boyan, facing the rear, looking more annoyed than alarmed as he gave commands. The rush for the door was orderly—a brisk procession rather than a stampede. Outside, I was herded along with a group bound for the jungle, gripped at the arms by a man on either side of me.

We ran inland, away from the river, into the teak stands bordering the camp. Then, leaving the columns of those thick trunks, we entered a sparser plantation of thin betel trees. Behind us, the volleys of mortar shells were growing weaker and the machine guns stammered faintly as we plunged into dense bush. There were eight of us, I counted when we stopped to catch our breath: seven soldiers and I. The other civilians had apparently gone a different way.

"Where are we going?" I asked the man nearest me.

"To the front."

The front! Why was I being led to the front? To be handed over to the enemy? There was a time when this crisis, an attack by the Dayan military, would have sent my pulse racing with hope. Now I thought of *them* as the enemy and sensed no hope in the prospect of delivery.

No hope here and no hope there. Where did hope lie now?

We pushed on, through bramble and thicket and over rotting jungle floor, stopping only to extricate ourselves from the branches and thorns caught on our clothes. At last we emerged into a clearing where the sun was burning a hole in the bleached sky. As we climbed a slope in dust as thick as fog, I heard voices.

"Ah, Second Brigade!" said one of my captors.

It relieved me to discover that the Second Brigade waiting for us at the foot of the slope was Jesu—a good hundred men who stared at me, bewildered, amused, a little embarrassed, the way a crowd will gawk at a freak. Under a lean-to, a peasant family was cooking huge pots of rice and busy serving dried rusks and tea. Someone handed me a spoonful of rice laced with shreds of dried salt fish and a single green chilli pepper on a banana leaf. While I ate in the shade of a tree, stragglers from a village appeared over the slope in twos and threes: mothers and grandmothers in woven tunics with wicker baskets on their backs and small children at their sides. A bullock cart lumbered by in a cloud of dust, bearing villagers sitting on bags of rice and salt. They seemed at ease with the soldiers, calling out pleasantries before disappearing down the road.

"What's that thing?" one of them—a very old man—shouted, pointing at me.

"It's Irrawaddy Tango!" said a voice from the crowd, producing laughter—though not from the commanding officer. The CO was the one who had been in charge since our flight from church; now he was strapping on a lot of extra gear: a bandolier with bullets the size of small bananas, a canteen, a couple of grenades, a knife in a metal sheath, a gun at his hip in addition to the one slung over his shoulder. He was clanking about in ill humor, shaking his head, spitting on the ground, and muttering under his breath. I could tell he was complaining about the nuisance of having me along.

"Front section!" came the sudden shout. The men were grouping and ready to move out.

"Rear section!"

The CO jerked his thumb at me, indicating I should fall in behind him.

Back we went into the jungle, slogging this time along slippery paths that zigzagged through steep hills. The men were wrestling with their unwieldy arsenal. Apart from the guns—assorted shotguns, M1s, carbines, British Enfields, Thompsons, Brens, and Stens—they had boxes of ammunition, base plates, and bazookas. Humping the big tubes and plates uphill, slipping and sliding and dragging them down the sharp inclines, they struggled on.

A boy ahead of me stumbled under the weight of the rockets he carried. I offered to relieve him of some of his paraphernalia, but he shook his head, hoisted the tube onto his back once more, and hobbled on. I was glad he refused. Winded and sore myself, barely able to keep up, I was in no position to take up additional weight.

The boy stayed beside me now. He had the most refined hands, the hands of a court dancer, and the sensitive face of a Hindu movie star.

"I'm Sherman," he offered, blinking to keep out the sweat trickling into his eyes.

"Sherman?" Named after a missionary, no doubt. "Unusual name."

"Name of a tank," said he. "My father was a tank man during the war."

More trudging along dusty trails, crossing and recrossing parched riverbeds and muddy streams, wading through a spongy mess of jungle floor, slapping away the leeches and fire ants, watching for snakes . . . until, parched and spent, we collapsed for the night. We camped at a village where I was billeted with a family whose teenage daughter acted as my attendant and guard, bringing me a set of men's fatigues to change into, showing me where to wash and bathe and eat and sleep.

The march ended at twilight the following day, at a spot up in the foothills. Across the valley was a mountain ridge. Bald patches pocked the scrub where deep, narrow holes had been dug in the earth. It looked like an unfinished burial ground. Enclosing the area was a barbed-wire fence—rather, the remnants of a fence: the bamboo stakes had collapsed in places and rusty double strands of barbed wire lay twisted on the ground.

The ridge across the valley was the focus of interest now. The officers pointed, paced, passed the binoculars around to scan the view. The sky held an uncertain glow while moonrise and sunset clashed.

It cheered me a little to spot Sherman nearby, leaning against a rock. He was sucking on a reed and massaging his knee.

I walked over to him. "How much longer to the front?"

He frowned, puzzled; then broke into a grin. "This is the front," he said, pointing to the ground.

I looked around: *This* our destination? This desolate, bombed-out hill?

"This *is* the front," Sherman insisted, seeing my disbelief. "And that's the enemy." He pointed to the ridge across the valley.

The men were already at work in the fast-fading light: digging foxholes and Bren-gun emplacements; laying mines; building lean-tos; setting up tripods and base plates and adjusting mortar rounds. As always, more than a few were just sitting around. I felt anxious and awkward, unsure of what to expect— and what was expected of me. The CO was busy talking to another officer. I waited for a break in their conversation before going up to him. "Can I do anything?" I asked.

"Sit quietly. That's the best thing to do," he snapped.

Night fell completely then, soon it was time for the evening meal, and soon after that for bed.

Sandhurst had told me that one of the rules of guerrilla warfare was never to sleep where you cooked. The rule evidently did not apply in this case; cooking trenches were sleeping trenches as well. I had watched them build guerrilla fires by digging narrow tunnels that came up in a hole in the ground some distance away from the trench, to discharge any little amount of smoke that wasn't absorbed by the earth. In these same trenches where the men had cooked rice, watercress, bamboo shoots, and snake meat, they wrapped themselves in plastic sheets for the night. Some others curled up in blankets strung like hammocks between trees.

At a loss as to where or with what I should make my bed, I loitered near the barbed wire, pretending interest in the mountain ridge whose outline was visible in the rising moonlight. Finding a bed would be less awkward, I figured, once the men had settled down. I was wondering how to go about relieving myself, surrounded as I was by man and bush, when Sherman appeared at my side, holding a flashlight. "Come," he said, "I've made a bed for you." I followed, dodging bodies on the ground. At a secluded spot halfway down an incline, he stopped. With his flashlight he scanned the shrub. "All clear. No scorpions, no snakes. Do you want to, uh, do a light one?" was the way he put it. He turned his back on me pointedly. "Take your time; I'll wait up here."

Afterward, he led me to the hammock he'd hitched, holding it steady as I climbed in. Then he handed me his blanket, saying, "Wake me if you want anything—I'll be sleeping over there."

"What about you? It's too cold."

"Be thankful for the cold," he said. "No mosquitoes."

I watched him crawl into a rice bag—the roughest kind of jute sack—that reached no higher than his waist.

Fires were still going in two of the trenches: their faint glow stained the edges of the holes. From a distance, the holes looked like the burning eye slits of some nocturnal monstrosity. The bodies on the ground settled into dark unmoving mounds, the voices into murmurs and whispers, the silence into the alternating hush and racket of the jungle at night. A wind rose and rattled the leaves; a wildcat snarled; an owl whooped and flapped its wings; a tree squirrel shrieked; insects whined and hummed. At intervals, from a swamp across the valley, came the *ong-ing, ong-ing* of frogs—building, building, until their leader's basso profundo shut them up with a great resounding *bong*.

I shivered for a long time before falling asleep.

Sherman woke me in the middle of a dream I was having about being locked up in the bowels of an ice factory. My limbs were stiff from the cold. The stars had disappeared; the sky was lightening into an icy blue. "It's about to break," he whispered, and I knew he wasn't talking about daylight but about the fighting. "The CO wants you in the command bunker."

On our way downhill to the rear-line bunkers, we were just in time to join the group standing around the mortars to watch the first round fired. We stood back as the mortar sizzled and spat; but instead of a blast came a dull thud as the round toppled onto the earth two feet away. The mortar sergeant stared at the heap of metal expectantly, as if hoping it might still take off. Jeers and cheers from the bystanders—one of whom landed a playful kick that knocked the squatting sergeant off his haunches.

"Ten-percenter, ten-percenter!" someone called out.

Ten-percenter? I turned to Sherman.

"They call artillerymen ten-percenters," Sherman explained. "Ten percent of the shells fall short; they never even make it to the enemy side."

The next one did, though. A hiss, a blast, a shattering boom—and then it began: rifle and machine-gun fire, flares, and the pounding of artillery. . . .

Sherman and I reached one of the bunkers, where we crouched with two men trying to fix a radio receiver. The commotion seemed to abate a bit, reduced to the sporadic barrage of automatic weapons, a ten-percenter's minor concussion, pops and bangs like a round of firecrackers . . .

. . . and in one of the lulls, a rooster crowing *aw-ee-ee-ooh!* clear and triumphant, cocking a snook at all the hullaba-loo . . .

. . . which shifted suddenly to the yelling of obscenities back and forth across the valley:

Mother-fucking Jesu!
Corpse-fucking Dayans!
Sons of bitches!
Yes, raise your flags, those dirty menstrual rags!
Come eat shit! We'll feed you cunt shit! . . .

The radio repairmen were chuckling as they worked. Sherman, stooped across from me, was holding his hands in front of him, eyes modestly downcast, as though tuned in to a liturgy. At last he looked up at me with a brave smile. *"Psycho,"* he explained, "they're just doing *psycho*—you know, to scare the enemy." Above us, the scrawny legs of young boys were kicking and bending in what looked from down below like a dance of glee.

Static crackled in the radio receiver. One of the men slapped his thigh. *Success!* And off he went, scrambling out of the trench, the second man close behind—leaving just Sherman and me. "They'll be needing me soon," said Sherman. "I'd better go. You stay. Don't move. I'll be back in a while."

Alone, I cowered under an apocalypse of cross fire, and in a flash it was right over my head—an explosion that left a tremor in the ground above, and a face full of dirt. *I'm trapped in this hole, I'm waiting to die,* I thought. And through the mindless panic came a command heard in my head.

Run—run into the field of fire!

I remembered what Colonel Sandhurst once said: If a machine gun opened fire on you, the thing to do was not to run back to your own lines or hit the ground—neither of which would save you in the end—but to run straight into the field of fire, which might just force the enemy to raise his barrel, might just confuse him long enough for you to get off a grenade that saves your hide in the nick of time. . . .

The throbbing of the mortars set off a throbbing in my head that left space for one thought only—the all-important thought of heading for the field of fire. In a seizure of mad inspiration, I pulled myself out of the trench and started running in a crouch—into the field of fire, wherever that might be.

The explosions all around me became muted now, contained. I felt enclosed as in a heavy-lidded pot, with kernels around me popping one by one; and I, a mere kernel, at popping point too. Steam filled the pressurized pot, almost blinding me. But I could smell. I smelled smoke and cordite. The popping went on while I went on running . . . until the steam lifted . . . and rising from a trench along the barbed-wire line, like a wraith out of a grave, was Sherman, mouth agape, eyes agog, hurtling toward me—but with excruciating slowness. He was taking big, lumbering strides, arms outstretched, shouting something at me I couldn't catch.

What I did hear was a double-barreled yell from a voice along the frontline bunkers. *"Mine! Mine!"*

Sherman turned his head, doing a swift side step that filled me with admiration. *Just in time,* I thought as the explosion went off, and Sherman, though knocked to the ground, made a point of sitting up suddenly, as though to show it had missed him after all. But in an instant he was flat on his back, rubbing himself in the dirt as if scratching an itch, while under him the ground darkened as the blood spread.

A delicate momentary silence was shattered by a fresh clamor—the guns going flat out, the voices in an uproar—as the two men bellying up to him from either side managed to drag him into one of the trenches.

Oh, careful, careful! I thought as I caught a glimpse of the near-severed hand, the ragged, bloody shred attached to one of Sherman's arms by little more than a filament or two of flesh. Someone knocked me down, then I too was dragged along—down into one of the trenches.

The CO had a grip on my neck; he was muddy, sweating, and breathing raggedly while fighting what I knew to be an impulse to strangle me. When he pushed me away, it was so violently that for a while I was unable to swallow.

"Dumb corpse face," he wheezed. "I'll tell you when it's time to die! You leave that to me!"

The CO left; the battle raged; how long I remained there—panicked no longer, only dazed and numb—it was impossible to tell: maybe half an hour, maybe half a day. I reached for the back, then the crotch of my pants: dry. So at least I didn't lose control.

After an immeasurable wait, they came to fetch me from the trench, to move out past the rear lines for the retreat. I followed the column of men bearing Sherman in a cloth-and-bamboo stretcher. I trotted alongside, afraid to take my eyes off the wounded boy whose gaze was fastened on me. Staring—*glaring*—at him, I prayed. *Stay with me, Sherman. We're almost there.*

The boy's lids grew heavy, his mouth began to droop at the corners, and with alarm I realized he was going to cry. *No, Sherman, please! No tears! Anything but tears!* He tried to smile, his face crumpled, his eyes filled up, they blinked, they shut. . . .

By the time we reached the Second Brigade hospital, Sherman was gone, I knew—and I was the only one crying. Running and crying and pulling at the seat of my pants—wonder of wonders, still bone-dry.

Behind the timber and thatch hospital—where I was allowed to catch my breath alone, untended—the scene was normalcy itself. Two young women—one with a stethoscope around her neck, the other with scissors and keys hanging from her waist—were stirring a pot of rice over a wood fire. An old man with sagging breasts and scarlet gums sat cross-legged on the ground nearby, chewing betel nut and threading sections of nipa together. Behind him lay a length of khaki-colored canvas, frayed and heavily patched, which two boys were crawling all over, trying to mend. Chickens staggered around, scratching and pecking in the dirt. A bamboo enclosure, filled with muck and bits of straw, may have been a pigpen; in another smaller enclosure, square and tidy, mustard greens were sprouting. Smoke hung in the air, homey smoke from cook fires, not the smoke of violation and battle. It was too wholesome, too tranquil, to be true.

Some hundred feet beyond, though, the ground dropped off to a wide field, and there I found the officers: some crowded around a wireless, some seated behind a plank table under a lean-to, some conferring over maps. Recent arrivals from the front—dazed, mud spattered, and chalky with dust—were collapsed on the ground, sprawled on their backs, or sitting up for a smoke while recounting the skirmish just survived. One of the boys who had carried Sherman's stretcher sat apart from the rest. He never took his eyes off the ground as he massaged his shoulders with his arms crossed over his chest.

Boyan was with a group on the far side of the field. The sight of his back, with his khaki shirtsleeves rolled up above his elbows, overwhelmed me with a muddle of gratitude and need. He was involved in a debate, with arguments flying back and forth and louder, angrier accusations erupting at intervals, followed by heated denials.

It wasn't until I got beyond the lean-to that I saw the prisoners. Four men sat shackled and cramped, each in a separate bamboo cage. Two others were tied side by side to the thick trunk of a tree, one bleeding across his ribs and half-asleep; the other straining toward a lit cigarette that a soldier was teasing him with, holding it close to the prisoner's lips, then pulling it away. A trench had been dug near the tree, and along the edge of this trench were six men on their knees, all with their hands tied behind their backs. All except the one at the end, whose hands were up and pressed together, begging. The officer listening to this overwrought plea was distracted. Someone had interrupted, a colleague seeking advice. The officer seemed to have forgotten his business with the kneeling men. Instead, something about the new subject under discussion made him smile and shake his head while languidly scratching, scratching away at his crotch.

Shock upon shock upon shock made me queasy and dizzy at once. Boyan was studying some papers. I saw him notice my presence; then turn back to his papers, trying to ignore me; then abruptly give up the effort, pushing the whole sheaf into the hands of the officer at his side. He came after me—reaching my side just as I got sick.

He helped me the way my mother had done: by pressing down hard on my back, to ease the heaves. All the while he looked without flinching. Afterward, he made me sit down. So it didn't agree with me, he said, war? Not a good taste, was it? Especially the first time. He made a face, shuddered, as though tasting something inedible.

"I wish to die," I said, wiping away the tears induced by vomiting.

"Exactly," he said, raising his finger like a doctor who's just had his diagnosis confirmed. "The very feeling you're supposed to have. Wishing to die is part of it. You *must* wish to die. That's how you know you've come through it." There was a laugh in his voice; he was trying to make light of things for my sake.

"I thought you didn't take prisoners of war?" I said.

"What!?" He mimicked surprise. "You must have got it wrong. Who said we don't take prisoners of war? We take them. We just don't keep them."

"What sort of . . ." I hated the fact that I couldn't think of a word. "What sort of *beings* are you?"

He laughed. "I'm going to say something that will startle you. I'm going to say we're human beings."

That night, watched by a pair of guards, I stayed close to the dying embers of a fire, pretending to crave the warmth while I waited, hoping he'd come. I had almost given up waiting when I heard his voice telling the men, "Go now, I'll take over."

He gathered some twigs and got the fire going again before settling down next to me. Without speaking we watched the igniting—slow at first, then erratic, then fierce. The glowing coals burst into flame in one gusting leap, sending out sparks that landed on my knee. I swatted the fatigues I was still wearing.

"Irrawaddy Tango, famous dancer, burned to death at front lines," he joked.

When the flames had abated once more and what remained of the fire had been banked for what remained of the night, he rose without a word, pulled me up by the hand, and led me to the bamboo revetment behind us. He swung himself down first, into the shoulder-high pit, and reached around thinking to help me in, but I had already slid in behind him.

"Let me see where you burned your knees," he said, though I hadn't burned them.

Scarcely were they exposed when he was all over me, touching my face, my neck, my shoulders, with closed fists as though afraid of what the fingertips might feel, or of what the unclenched hand might do; plunging his hands at last into my hair, for something to hold on to. I felt crushed and smothered in the grasp of some beastly force that dragged me down into an airless, fathomless depth. At last he let go, gasping and releasing a sudden odor of brine along with a taste of salt on his skin.

As we lay side by side, pressed close together by the narrowness of the pit, it wasn't confinement I felt, but its opposite: an immense breadth of openness, of detachment. The air in that trench was not close at all; the air was anything but confining and close. Underneath that swath of sky framed by the rectangular pit, I felt weightless, lost and abandoned to the elements. I floated in a vision—a foretaste, not a foreboding— of no longer being myself. I was part of the infinite, of oblivion. It wasn't death; it wasn't scary like death; it was beyond death. It was pure nothingness. Would it be like this when pain and sorrow were gone one day, leaving only this void, of no longer being, or thinking, or feeling—especially feeling?

"Look how bright the stars are!" I said, at once feeling foolish for expressing the obvious.

Then, "Do you love her?" I asked suddenly.

He didn't answer for a long time. "Do you know the Lepcha?" he said. "The Lepcha of Sikkim?"

I shook my head.

He didn't either, he said. He'd never been anywhere up near their part of the world. But he knew a Lepcha once, someone the American missionary in the Jesu area had adopted, a sort of servant-son. The funniest little fellow with fox ears and a pointed chin. The Jesu townspeople thought him a simpleton, and the boys in particular, Boyan among them, used to love goading him into displaying his simplemindedness.

"We'd ask him if he missed his parents," said Boyan, "and he'd look baffled. What did missing mean? Did he care for his parents, we'd ask, and he'd nod. Yes, of course he cared for them, he said; didn't they give him food? What about his wife, we'd ask the Lepcha then. We knew he had a wife he'd left behind. Did he think about his wife? He remembered her, too, he said, because she gave him food also. When he went out to work and came home tired, she had a good meal ready for him, and then he always thought, *This is my wife and I am pleased in my belly.*

"This simple fellow was the laughingstock of our town, but secretly I admired him. He spoke in a way we ourselves were not allowed to speak."

"And all this has something to do with whether you love Dali or not?"

"You want to hear what's pleasant to your ear," he said. "Even if it's not true. I can understand that. But speaking as a Lepcha, the truth, Tango, is that you are the enemy. I don't just mean we are on opposite sides; I mean you are one of those people who cause trouble wherever they go. You provoke desire and envy, and these only lead to trouble and strife."

I hated him suddenly, his disfigured nose. He reminded me of a leper I'd once known, a man whose nose had been eaten away. He used to haunt the old pagoda ruins downriver from Irrawaddy, staking his claim among the rubble, scavenging for food, scaring the locals, becoming a bogeyman rather than return to the leper colony he'd fled. I'd sit on the bank across the inlet from the ruins, spying on him while he pottered about among the bricks and stones.

I found some excuse to bring up the leper, mentioning in particular the nose, but Boyan saw through me immediately. "Well, it's not leprosy that took my nose away," he said cheerfully. "It was a grenade. But I know you're just saying this because you're angry with me that I won't tell you the false flattering things you long to hear."

But in the next minute he surprised and confused me with his gentleness. "Come, let's see those burned knees again," he said. "In another existence, I would blow on them to heal them; I would kiss them; I would lick them."

You'd lick my wounds? I asked silently, on the verge of an oceanic sadness. It brought back the story my mother used to tell me about losing her first child, the one that came before me, to smallpox. Her robust eight-month-old baby, her soul of souls, had broken out in boils she had thought were chicken pox. She wasn't thinking of smallpox because since the dread epidemic, everyone had been innoculated—everyone except the baby. But when the doctor finally came, he could tell right then and there, standing at the door, from that distance he could tell just by the smell that it wasn't chicken pox but the other. Demented. I'll never forget that word she used to describe her state. Demented, she licked her baby boy's sores off and on throughout his remaining days.

Every time I heard that story, I'd think to myself, *Would she lick the same wounds on me? Would she have the same compassion?*

Thinking of my mother, just for an instant I wished her dead—not to anticipate her dying, or experience it, but simply that I might have it behind me, have that one aspect of her dead and buried, the plaguing, haunting aspect I could no more touch than I could shun. Answering a higher call than the call of one's family; vanishing into a monastery; renouncing all ties with the past—these were disappearing acts, not death. Somewhere, improbably, heartlessly, she was still alive; only not alive to me.

It would be easier, I thought pitilessly, *to visit her in a cemetery instead of a monastery*. At least in a cemetery you could go when you wanted, take flowers, and cry.

10

The gods have a way of mocking a prayer by answering some small portion of it. So it was that in a matter of months I was granted the cemetery and the flowers—but the grave was Boyan's.

His death was confusion itself—true to the turmoil of that time. Confusion had marked the preceding months; confusion followed the assassination.

The Jesu were no longer dealing with routine harassments by Dayan forces. The JLA, the Jesu Liberation Army ("every man jack of them," as Sandhurst put it), was engaged in fending off a massive Dayan offensive on all fronts. The attacks were hitting one Jesu outpost after another, all down the border.

Jesu territory was an area of shifting borders, with towns, villages, or bridges on the periphery lost in one skirmish and recaptured in the next. But outside this flux, the land under Jesu control had remained impregnable, shielded by a combination of buffers. The terrain was one; the neutrality of the neighboring Thai was another. The mountain ranges protecting the Jesu strongholds were still reliable, but Dayan forces were attacking now from new positions—from areas *inside* Thailand.

Boyan had gone northeast—not to the front, but to a border town, to confer with Thai officials from the border police and the Supreme Command concerned with Dayan affairs.

He was killed by a bomb in a Chinese restaurant.

News of the explosion changed almost daily. A bomb had gone off, killing senior border police officials. An accidental explosion in a restaurant had left three men, including two military officers, wounded. Two bombs had gone off, killing two border police and wounding three civilians. An explosion in a Chinese coffee shop had left two cows dead. A bomb had gone off and Boyan had been killed. . . .

He was dead. He was alive, but in a Thai hospital. He had disappeared, captured by the Dayans. He was being held in a Thai prison for questioning in connection with the bomb.

I was convinced he was alive. It was altogether too inconvenient, too *unjust* a time for the Jesu to lose him. It was too unjust for me. I couldn't believe that anyone as badly needed as he would allow himself to get killed. He wouldn't be that careless. I wanted to believe it was a ruse, with all the confusion simply part and parcel of it. Some sudden revelation would confirm the fact that he was of course still alive.

Even on the day, that exceedingly clear and cloudless day, on which they brought back his remains, when I watched the procession bearing the box of ashes climb from the riverbank slowly, so slowly, uphill; when I saw the wretched container— the cheap betel box with the design in the dark green lacquer that was actually visible from where I stood, the day was that clear; when Dali appeared with her son crying and clinging to her leg as she tried to meet the procession; when she peeled him off finally and kicked him aside so he fell, sitting, on the ground; when she then flung herself in a dive at the man bearing the betel box and began an absurd tug-of-war over it, screaming and crying, until they had to drag her away . . . even then I held on to the possibility of a trick.

Ashes! What proof were ashes?

I can't say at what precise moment the reality of Boyan's death took hold in me; only that as the doubt lingered, so did a grudge, a rancor against him for leaving so much unanswered and unfinished.

In this welter of anger and bereavement I stepped into the breach to become the Jesu spokesman—a role created by the unusual attention we were getting. The outbreak along the Thai border had raised troubling issues for those worried about the spreading war in Indochina. The Southeast Asia Question now included the Dayan Question, which in turn included the Jesu Question. It was Sandhurst who decided that I had the right stuff—the languages, the color of my past—to become La Liaison, as a French mercenary referred to me. It was Sandhurst who grilled and groomed me for the interviews and public communiqués.

For the first time since my capture, I felt alive. After the long drawn-out uncertainty of my fate, it was a relief to be taking certain action, to know which side I was on at last, having cast my lot with it. I felt alive to new challenges, new dangers. And free. Free because I was no longer captive among the Jesu—and because I began to understand what Boyan had said about the nature of freedom.

"I'll tell you something about freedom," he'd said. "I've known what it is to be 'free.' Free to come and go and make a living without the daily fear of getting killed. I've had that, in times away from the jungle, when I lived in the city. But freedom without purpose is no freedom. One person's liberty—the little choices in the course of a day about what you eat, what you wear, which friend you'll visit, which bioscope you'll see—that kind of freedom counts for very little if there is no purpose, no meaning to the choices. That kind of freedom can even become a burden and leave you empty.

"But when you're part of something bigger than yourself, a purpose bigger than your own single life, you feel free in a different way—even in worse straits, with fewer choices."

"I know what it is not to have a choice," I had said.

"You still don't understand. That's just you. Just one person. One unlucky person. I'm talking about a whole race not having a choice."

The world's interest in the Jesu race was fleeting. By the end of the year of Boyan's death, with losses and damages to both sides—equally minimized by both sides—the Dayans had withdrawn their forces, and the JLA had returned to the daily grind of guerrilla life.

By then I had achieved some status as Irrawaddy Tango, the Rebel Queen. Colorful stories appeared in the press, branding me as a Joan of Arc. Another legend claimed that the government had put a price on my head. In reality, my contribution to the insurgency amounted to drawing a little more attention to the cause than it might have drawn without me.

Sandhurst gave me a new title: head of liaison, in charge of minority relations. The job involved sitting in on meetings—a few of them tricky and heated, most of them excruciatingly dull—with representatives of whichever other ethnic army might come to call. Sometimes it required long treks through the jungle for visits to *their* camps, with endless waits in safe houses in between.

Safe houses were beginning to seem increasingly unsafe to me when I came to the one that seemed unsafest of all.

It was in a town, not a village—and towns, with their many strangers and few escape routes, were full of dangers. This was a large town, moreover—large enough for a post and telegraph office . . . and a regional police headquarters.

"Colonel, is this wise? The police headquarters nearby?" I asked more than once. But Sandhurst seemed unperturbed. Here we were holed up for almost a week, far longer than planned. A bridge along the next stretch of our journey had been blown, causing the delay.

The town was in one of the southernmost provinces, where Muslim insurgents were active. Of late they had been setting fire to the docks, disrupting shipping and causing shortages.

Muslims! Such a strange breed: so easily unhinged—and by religion, of all things! Only the Communists had been capable of doing business with them: they had the do-or-die zeal in common. Recently, the two factions had formed a new alliance and now were seeking a broader coalition. They had come to us with proposals. At their invitation we—Sandhurst, a young JLA major, and I—had taken the long trip south to their region for more talks.

One afternoon, two student representatives of the alliance—a Muslim and a Chinese Communist—came by to report on the latest road conditions. The cabin fever induced by the ceaseless rain that week had taken the form of a stunning lethargy. Sandhurst and the major had passed the days in sporadic animal slumber—while I sat for hours, too listless for activity, too restless for sleep.

I suggested a walk when the students arrived.

"You can't be serious?" said Sandhurst, yawning and rubbing his eyes. "It's still raining."

"All the better. Now's the time to go, when no one's about."

"A very foolish idea, in my opinion," he said in Dayan now—addressing the two students. "Don't you think?"

Why couldn't he ever look me in the eye when he disagreed with me? And why would he never trim those blackened toenails, calcified over the edge of each toe?

"I think I'll go anyway," I said, thinking how much like an old woman Sandhurst looked at that moment, with his pursed lips and dismissive little about-face.

"Suit yourself," he said.

The major was still stretched out on the floor like a convalescent. "Coming?" I asked. If I could just give him one smart kick! He raised himself on an elbow dreamily. "No, don't come," I snapped. "Stay. I'll be gone for just a while."

As I turned at the doorstep to step into my flip-flops, both the colonel and the major seemed cemented to their respective spots: the major on the floor, Sandhurst in an easy chair. They were regarding me in an uncannily similar way, their eyes heavy with a kind of sad, helpless plea. All the irritability of a moment ago was washed away by a wave of something like nostalgia.

The thongs of one of my rubber flip-flops came loose as I stuck my foot in. Bending over to push the grommet back into its hole, I realized I had assumed a position close to kowtowing. Just a little lower and I'd be doing my duty, like any good Buddhist, by paying my respects to these two seniors.

I'd also be sending them into a state of shock to see me, Tango, stooping in obeisance.

The rain had turned into a light mist. I followed the two students—the Muslim with the skinny, hairy arms; the Chinese Communist with the rabbit teeth—out into the street. All that needless worry about being seen! The town was practically deserted. The bungalows, the godowns, the office buildings, were all shuttered against the rain. But the stillness seemed eerie, not safe; and the disquiet, the foreboding, alerted me to the ordinary. By the time we turned toward the river, every object, every scent, every sound worth noting, landed heavily on my senses like a series of blows.

I noticed the muddy runoff flowing like swift rivers in the ditches; I noticed the light—the drab light of dusk following heavy rain. I noticed the shrouds of starlings darkening the air. I noticed the skeletal bitch, ribs poking through her mangy skin, trotting furtively down a side street with a dead pup in her mouth. I noticed the fishy gusts blowing in from the river as we headed toward the wharf. I noticed the pontoon, the teak-and-tin structure of an old godown, the cluster of paddy barges sitting low in the water, the few stick figures tottering about with cane bushels on their heads, the white pagoda rising from the banks beyond. I noticed these unremarkable things because it was as if a giant banner were hung across the horizon, emblazoned with the words: REMEMBER THIS.

We were not, of course, bound for the wharf. That would have been too dangerous. Instead we turned down a side street, a wide one—and treeless, it seemed to me, save for a single old acacia with spreading horizontal branches. Or did the tree stand out as the only tree because of the black sedan parked under its canopy—the only car on the street?

Out of this car emerged three men, one in a sarong, one in a Hawaiian shirt and khaki pants, and the third with a submachine gun.

"Comrades!" said the one in the sarong. The salutation froze me. It was the language of the Dayan forces. "Comrade Lin? Comrade Hussein?"

My God, he was addressing the students by their first names! The blood roared through my head. They hadn't said my name, though. *Keep calm—it's only the students they're after. Now's the time to turn, very slowly—easy, easy—and walk away.*

I had barely taken two steps in the other direction when someone called out, "And you, too, comrade. *Little* comrade."

The man with the submachine gun shepherded us toward the car. "Comrade Hussein, in the front. You, Comrade Lin, in the back." He patted me on the shoulder. "And you. After me."

"What's this?" said Lin. "What's the meaning of this?" He was grinning while demanding an answer. No, not grinning, I realized. In his anxiety he couldn't get his lips to meet over his unruly teeth. "Have a warrant?" he said, chomping.

"Yes," replied the man in the sarong. "Show him the warrant," he said to the one with the Uzi.

"Here's the warrant," said the other, knocking Lin into the back seat with a blow from the butt of his weapon.

The Hawaiian shirt took his place behind the wheel. "You wish to see a warrant, too, Comrade Hussein?" said the man in the sarong, as he got in on the other side, next to Hussein. In the backseat, the man with the Uzi sat between Lin and me, his hand on the trigger, the barrel pointed across my knees. He stared straight ahead; I did the same. Even so, I could see that Lin was bent over in his seat, clutching his ribs.

The streets were dark as we drove back toward town, away from the river. I wondered if we were bound for the safe house. Would Sandhurst and the major still be where I left them, lolling about in their unsuspecting lethargy? And how would we all fit into the car?

But it wasn't the safe house we were headed for; it was the post and telegraph office. The Hawaiian shirt pulled up in front and left the engine idling while he went inside. We waited for an eternity, nobody saying a word. At last he reappeared. Leaning in through the window of the driver's seat, he said to the man in the sarong, "Too many words, Big Brother. We have to cut. They won't take more than twenty-one."

"How's that? Only twenty-one?"

"Post and telegraph rules," said the Hawaiian shirt. "Any cable more than twenty-one words goes regular mail."

"Son-of-a-bitch rules!" said the man in the sarong.

"What to do?" said the other.

"Use your brain, animal! Cut out some words!"

"Which ones?"

"Mother! Do I have to think of everything? Just send three words: WE CAUGHT TANGO. What more do you need?"

So they knew after all. It was me they were after. It was all over, then.

11

The warden was an Anglo-Indian. A civilian, he was eager to impress the military brass committing me to his charge. "Maximum security," he kept repeating as he rattled off the special features of his domain. "Maximum security. *Model* jail, officers. Prisoners are permitted music lessons. Under strict supervision, naturally. Each cell block permitted one zither, one xylophone, one mandolin, one harp, two brass flutes." He ticked off the items on his fingers.

"And we have also instructions in Buddhist scriptures," he boasted. "And facilities"—he looked around joyously—"for weight lifting."

He turned to me and bowed. "Welcome to our model jail."

Now, what is the task here? I asked myself as I signed the admission form acknowledging my name and the day's date. The task, I decided, was to save energy. "Facing grave danger requires energy," Sandhurst used to say. "Save energy and take the path of least resistance if you want to stay alive."

What else had he told me? More of Cicero's wisdom. "Be timid in guarding against dangers, not in facing them."

Too late to guard against dangers; here was the facing part.

With the warden leading the way, and the colonel who had removed my handcuffs and blindfold behind me, we went through massive iron doors that led past a row of crowded cells. The faces pressing up against the bars were green in the bilious light. *How can they stand it?* I thought—not the crowding so much as the reek? The impossible, inhuman reek?

At the end of the row the warden unlocked a half door the size of a hatch and told me to watch my head as I stooped to pass through. Here even the colonel had to clap a handkerchief to his nose as we came out into a tunnel with cesspools at the edges. Fighting the urge to get sick, I looked up toward the only source of light, an open trapdoor above.

It was then that the whole configuration of the place made sense to me: I recognized it from the tour they had given me back in my palace days, right after the lion-presentation ceremony.

I was back in the zoo, the famous zoo project that had begun toward the end of my time in Anika. To make room for the mass arrests, the Department of Prisons had taken over the zoo, cleared the animals out, and put up a warren of cement bunkers over the old cages. Almost nothing of the old grounds were to remain: no gazebos, no fountains, no riotous plantings of hibiscus, dahlia, zinnia, and canna. The moat was widened—the old moat circling the grounds at the foot of the zoo—but the stone bridges were gone.

The switch was made after my capture by the Jesu: the animals to the old annex of the central lockup, the criminals to the renovated zoo.

I understood now the smells, the spirit, the odd layout of the jail. I knew it was a cage they were locking me into.

Living in a cage reveals extraordinary facts. One is that a human being can actually drop off to sleep and even dream while sitting up in the midst of her own wastes, with urine in one corner, vomit and shit in another. Not that the gorge doesn't rise at first—not that the civilized being doesn't protest.

You shout and hammer on the door, your bladder, bowels, and lungs at bursting point, long after it's clear that you can end up in a model jail with access to zithers, xylophones, and weight-lifting facilities, but not to a latrine. Yet even when it becomes unbearable, and—eyes stinging, cramps shooting through the gut—you let go, you still hold on to some little show of neatness.

You urinate in one corner, defecate in another (over the dried-out puke)—hoping that liquids here and solids there will somehow aid evaporation. Neatness has its place in a cement cage too cramped for an adult being to lie down with legs outstretched. You need two good corners, diagonally across from one another: one to lean your back against, the other for leg extensions possible otherwise only when standing.

For a while you even try controlling your intake, hoping thus to limit the messier bodily functions. You take the smallest of sips from the morning tea; you limit yourself to a spoonful or two of the day's gruel. But within a week you find yourself salivating at the sound of the jailer's keys, and by the second week, when he announces "Meat day!" you're mentally clapping your hands in delight. No sooner does the door slam shut as he leaves than you start sucking on the one piece of chicken leg. Not the upper, meatier part, which they wouldn't ever waste on criminals, but the scrawny piece above the claw, the piece with its thin tendon and its pale, scaly skin—hairs included. When every bit of flesh has been picked clean you worry at the little smear of marrow in the bone as if it were the very marrow of life.

All the while, you're less than two feet away from the stinking lava of shit in one corner and the stinking piss pool in the next.

When at last they let you out for your first visit to the public latrine—"Outing!" the jailer shouts to announce this surprise excursion—you reach that hallowed ground only to find it spattered and caked with excrement. Is this, too, part of the punishment? Have they sent an advance goon squad to spray shit all over the place just on your account?

There you squat, straining to no avail, realizing that the privileges you so shrilly insisted upon—latrine privileges, for example—are not all they're cracked up to be. All you long for then is to return to the cell, to the familiarity of your very own refuse and squalor.

Sister, that's nothing! said another prisoner, the Chinese woman they used to let loose into one of the rec rooms with me ("rec" for "recovery," not "recreation"). *They led me to one of those toilets once, six holes in a big open room, four of them occupied—by men! I had to go, I couldn't stand it, so I lifted my sarong, what could I do, and squatted side by side with them. You think that's bad? Wait. The attendant comes in at that moment, an Indian. He's wearing a dhoti and swinging a big bucket. Before we can finish he throws water from one end of the room down the other, dousing our bucksides with Phenyl. A burn like that will make you suck in your breath for a week every time you go— number one or number two.*

She showed me the other burns: the pockmarks on her arms where they'd stubbed out their cigarettes during one of the early intro sessions ("intro" for "interrogation," not "introduction").

My own interrogators weren't so uncouth as to subject me to those intro sessions right away. They followed procedure; I'll give them that.

How sedate it all seemed in the first "interview," conducted in a teak-paneled office with the gallery of framed photos of our national heroes—including of course a photo of *him*, the same old black-and-white portrait that every child, every peasant, every village idiot in the farthest provinces of the nation, can recognize. His picture was no larger but hung slightly higher than the rest and was centered on the horseshoe-shaped table where the members of the military tribunal were seated—two colonels, an air force brigadier general, a major, and a civilian. They offered me an armchair with antimacassars.

"Small cakes," said the major. "Have some small cakes." On the table at my elbow was a covered dish and, under a cozy, a pot of tea.

"A few questions, Comrade Sister," he said after a considerate interval.

Ask away, Brother Comrade, I wanted to say, giddy over the attention I was being given after the weeks of solitude and neglect—and the small cakes. It was difficult not to feel self-important, what with those five judges facing me so expectantly and hanging on to my every word, which a stenographer took down.

"You have a right," said one of the others, "to a court-appointed attorney. Unfortunately, he is on leave."

I stated my name (the one given at birth)—and confirmed that I was also known as Irrawaddy Tango. I stated my parents' names, my date and place of birth, my periods of residency (1) in Irrawaddy Township; (2) in Anika; (3) in the Punished Provinces.

They pressed me to have another cup of tea. The man in plain clothes looked like a schoolteacher. He stared through thick eyeglasses and seemed in the habit of explaining the obvious. "Tea," he proclaimed loudly more than once, "is best drunk hot."

The eyes of the elderly air force brigadier general hopped to the teapot. The four other men continued to stare at me. Above them, *his* hawkish gaze preyed upon the room. The stenographer remained hunched as though in the presence of royalty, scratching away at his machine.

More small talk while I polished off the coconut cakes, a few more unstartling questions, and I was politely dismissed.

One of the colonels—the beady-eyed one with the mangy mustache—suddenly grabbed a fly that had been buzzing over the papers in front of him. He closed his fist over it, pushed back his chair, and went to open a shuttered window a crack, just long enough to release the fly.

A heartening sign, I thought. At least there was one good Buddhist, one man among the judges, who seemed opposed to the taking of life—even a fly's life. And the judges all looked like reasonable men. They believed in protocol; wasn't that a start? I took heart from the fly, the tea and cakes, the harmless questions, the protocol, the stenographer, the attorney I had yet to meet.

Another fact in my favor: no need to subject myself to any ordeal of evasion. What conceivable questions could they ask me that I'd have to refuse to answer? What sort of secrets about the Punished Provinces could I possibly harbor that the State Security Office didn't already know? None that came to mind immediately.

What an odd insurrection they were up against: a war with no military secrets to speak of. The rebel headquarters wasn't secret; the rebels' numbers weren't secret; even their tactics— the ambushes, the bombing of the bridges, roads, and rails— weren't secret. The underground war was really aboveboard, out in the open, with little left to lose or hide.

"Tell us your hopes and fears," I remember one relief worker, an orange-haired American woman, saying to a major at the Jesu camp.

Sandhurst was there to translate. "She's asking about your hopes and fears," he said to the young major.

"We have lots of fears, tell her," said the Jesu, a sardonic type. "And no hopes anymore. Not a single one."

The men had a good laugh, then Sandhurst turned to the

American woman. "He fears the tyranny of the central government and hopes for democracy."

The relief worker took this down in a notebook, wasting
a whole page, I noticed, on a few lines of her long, extravagant,
slanting script.

But I had misunderstood the purpose of the intro room. The
intros—the same questions despite the same answers—were
not the point. It wasn't information they were after; it was
something else. But what? The brain-numbing repetitions made
it hard enough to think straight, much less speculate. But the
effect was benign compared with what the noises could do, the
noises from the other intro rooms.

The noises could make you bleed as you bit your own lip
or tongue when the whimpers turned into groans, the groans
into shouts, the shouts into screams, the screams into yodels
. . . and when at last the absurdity of a rousing polka or march
came blaring through the loudspeakers you felt the charge of
the current full in the temples, an assault that left you quaking.

The noises were the point; they had to be.

After each session, a rest in the rec room. Here you could
relax in a chair and reflect on the good that could come of a
speedy confession. On a table was paper and pencil. The sooner
the confession, the sooner the chances of release.

But confessions were not the true purpose here, either. The
opportunity to confess was just a formality, a step in a ritual. No one showed the slightest interest in seeing whether the
sheet of paper I always left facedown on the table had been
written on.

More often than not they'd bring in the Chinese woman at
that point, a woman whose arrival both excited and frightened
me. She was further along in the intro process than I was: she
had been to see the circus.

She had an unusual way of winding up for her stories about the circus—her fingers got busy telling off invisible worry beads and her eyes fluttered about like moths with no place to alight.

All manner of acts were performed in the circus she described, the room with the stage, the lights, the pulleys, where the real intros took place. She impersonated, *recaptured,* the woman and the girl on the iron bedsteads—their inertia, the way they just lay there on their sides in lazy siesta positions, not turning even once to watch the spectacle on stage.

Meanwhile, stagehands called back and forth, discussing technicalities.

"Combo?"

"No; DYNAMO. Where's DYNAMO?"

DYNAMO appeared: a black box on wheels with a lid that opened up, a lid with meters and knobs and needles, as on a dashboard.

"No, take it away," someone said. "No need for DYNAMO."

"We're doing Combo then?"

"Not Combo. Not DYNAMO. We're doing Houdini."

"Houdini!" The Chinese woman faced me squarely now, her eyelids in a spasm of concentration. "Let me tell you what Houdini means!"

They bring in a man, she said, shackled both at the ankles and the wrists. He lets out a howl at the sight of the women. "Wife! Daughter!" the man is crying. He doesn't say their names, just keeps repeating "Wife! Daughter!"

He tries to shuffle toward them, but is jerked back by the guard who holds him in position, near the door, while something from the ceiling swings down in front of him, a great metal hook attached to a rope that passes through a pulley.

One of the guards knocks him down suddenly with a kick; the hook swings lower; the guards get down on their knees. When they stand up the hook's been passed through the chains on both his hands and feet and he's hoisted like livestock prepped for slaughter.

They work the pulley to swing him over the older woman's bed. The IO, the interrogating officer, stands beside the bed, looking down on the woman he's kicked over now onto her back.

"Poor poor woman!" He clucks. "The trouble a bastard husband can cause! Look, talk to him; tell him not to be so pigheaded next time. Tell him to answer nicely the next time he's questioned. Tell him."

And casually—the Chinese woman shows me just how casually, how almost absentmindedly—he puts his cigarette out on the reclining woman's cheek. The woman flinches and sucks in her breath but doesn't cry out, just goes on crying softly. . . . (And here my informer reproduces a low, bitter hum of misery.)

Now the IO goes over to the other bed, where the girl is lying stone still. "Pardon me, little one," he says. "This will only take a minute. There's something I want your father to see." He shoves her onto her back and pulls down her sarong with one quick tug, exposing her from the waist down. He snaps his fingers at the man working the pulley, motioning him to swing the writhing figure over his daughter's bed.

"Take a good look, Uncle," he says, giving the man a slap on the back before prying the girl's legs apart. "Tell me what you see. Just hold still for a minute, won't you? And tell me what you see? A hole, am I right? A little hole? By tomorrow it might be much bigger; it might be stretched wide from the pumping of a dozen swollen pricks. Now is that what you want? To see your little daughter's hole all red and distended? All because of your stubbornness?

"Think about it," he says, pulling the sarong up to cover the girl again. He snaps his fingers and this time the pulley jerks the man up and back across the room, to swing over the cement tank.

"Houdini?" says one of the attendants.

"Houdini," confirms another.

The hook thrashes about as they lower it into the tank—and there the load remains until the splashing stops.

"So now you know about Houdini," said the Chinese woman a little coyly, as if she had just initiated me into the facts of life.

She was deranged, I could see. An inspired storyteller—and completely off her rocker.

"Do you know the airplane act?" she said, flinging herself across the table till her feet were off the floor. Then she spread her arms and legs wide, holding them stiff. "They make you stay in this airplane position for hours, breaking the first limb that moves."

She got off the table and began pacing. Her fingers were working secret castanets now; she could barely keep her eyes open. "Do you know the motorcycle?"

She squatted down low, on an invisible toy cycle, and worked her wrists. "*Vroom-vroom,*" she said. "They make you sit on this make-believe motorcycle, going *Vroom-vroom!* till your back breaks. Try sitting like this for just one minute; see how long you can take it!"

But she herself continued in that position for an alarmingly long time, shifting gears and singing *Vroom-vroom!* with the spit flying out her mouth—until they came to fetch her.

O God, help me! I cried out in my cell—always feeling not better afterward but worse, much worse. Senseless and spineless! I thought. Senseless because I knew better than to expect God to be within hearing distance; spineless because some bone of resolve broke with that plea, causing me to cry uncle and beg mercy of a power, a resource I had so brazenly denounced. Then I reasoned with myself that to call out to God was just an expression, a reflex. If there were a frog in that cell, another breathing presence, I'd be calling out, wouldn't I: *O frog, help me!?* But there was no one else there, no other being, not a frog in sight, and that was why—the only reason why—I called out to God.

It calmed me a little to think that giving voice to despair wasn't just an involuntary expression of pain, like the grinding of teeth. There was actually a purpose to it, that shouting out. After a while I felt myself heard, really listened to and heard, by someone. That someone, of course, was just me. But in the depths of abandonment I heard myself, I reached myself, and oddly this comforted me.

Between visits to the intro and rec rooms, then, I took to talking to myself—rather, saying things out loud, not making conversation but reciting words that came to mind automatically: words of songs, times tables, nursery rhymes, even prayers, all sorts of prayers. The lauds my mother intoned in her devotions came back to me. The prayer Teacher Mercy used to recite every day over the keyboard, before our piano lesson:

> *Remember, O most gracious Virgin Mary,*
> *That never was it known*
> *That anyone who fled to thy protection,*
> *Implored thy help, and sought thy intercession,*
> *Was left unaided.*
> *Inspired with this confidence, I fly unto thee*
> *O Virgin of virgins, my Mother.*
> *To thee I come, before thee I stand*
> *Sinful and sorrowful.*
> *O Mother of the Word Incarnate!*

Despise not my petitions,
But, in thy mercy, hear and answer me.

I remembered songs I never thought I knew completely, sayings I wasn't aware I had memorized. I remembered Madame the tutor's favorite poem:

Quelle est cette île triste et noire?—C'est Cythère,
Nous dit-on, un pays fameux dans les chansons,
Eldorado banal de tous les vieux garçons.
Regardez, après tout, c'est une pauvre terre.

One morning a jailer with cancerous feet came in, and I knew by the way he stood over me that he was trying to prepare me for something.

"Sister, I don't hate you," he said, while I stared at the tops of his blistered feet. "That's why I'll tell you something now. It might help. I'm not saying it will spare you. But it could shed a little drop of comfort. They're coming for you; it's your turn today. Be brave, try to—how can I say this? When you can't bear it any longer, when you've sunk so low that you think you're eye level with hell, remember what you are—not a beast, not a bug, but a human being."

I'm a human being, I thought, after I'd been led to the room where I watched them take off my hair. They insisted that I watch. Not enough to take their rusty shears to me; they made me watch as well. They had a mirror holder: someone just to hold up a mirror for me to see how they hacked and chopped away as though clearing a path through bush. *A woman would never cut another woman's hair that way,* I thought. *So brutally, so mercilessly.* But I was the only woman present.

"For your own good, Little Sister," one of the barbers whispered. "We're shaving you so you won't worry about getting hurt. We don't hurt nuns; good Buddhists never hurt nuns, see?"

"It's only hair," I said to the mirror as they took the razor to my head. With my hair gone, I felt surprisingly weightless. And worthless . . .

So that when I was stripped, it wasn't as bad somehow; a naked body was not much more shameful than a shaved head. But shorn and stripped and weightless, I felt unbalanced, without a keel, and found myself swaying as I got up, as ordered, to enter the next room.

A billiard table stood in the center. In one corner of the room was a sink; in another, a globe on a stool. No windows— just solid walls of perforated board. A black electric fan swiveled slowly up high on a corner shelf.

"On the table!" said the IO in charge, waving his gun at me. I pulled myself up over one side, feeling not the slightest desire to resist—only the instinct to protect myself from the fan's stiff breeze that swept back and forth across the table and especially chilled my head.

I sat on the billiard table, my arms folded across my chest, trying to remember the question that wanted asking. Remember the question: *What's the task before me?* Answer: *Save energy, above all save energy.*

And so I did. I lay on my back, spread-eagle, while someone bound me at the ankles and wrists to each of the four corners of the table.

Save energy. Breathe deeply. Concentrate on breathing. What's happening isn't important. No one's in a hurry; no one seems nervous; not the guards—they're standing at ease now, their guns are lowered; not the lieutenant who keeps coming in and out to consult the IO; not the IO himself who keeps flipping through a folder for a piece of paper he can't seem to find.

Concentrate on objects. On the globe. Look: the world. There's Africa; there's the Indian Ocean. . . .

The globe was spinning suddenly, and all the world was a

blur. The lieutenant, on his way out the door, had just given it an idle twirl.

The world's gone out of control right here in this room. It's in their hands entirely. It starts and stops at their touch.

I'd lost my rhythm—the rhythm necessary to keep breathing evenly; I'd lost my footing suddenly. I was stumbling, struggling for breath, gasping, suffocating. . . .

No, not suffocating; just sobbing.

It's just sobbing; let it happen. It won't kill you. What's the worst that can happen now? Pain? But pain has an end too. It ends—in death if necessary. Doesn't the body just shut down when it can endure no more? Why the great terror of death then, when death offers an end to what's beyond enduring? God save me from enduring all that it's possible to endure!

But there's something else besides death and pain. What is it again?

Something revealed by that woman in the rec room, the nonstop talker. The veteran. Wanting to recount every horror in detail, for why should you be spared when she hadn't? Let-me-tell-you-what-it-was-like-and-if-you-think-that's-bad-listen-to-this. She paused now and then but not to catch her breath; more to show she had some modesty. She paused to say, "I don't mean to brag . . . ," before describing the next atrocity. A torture bore.

"Dynamo!" she chatted. "Sure, sooner or later everyone gets Dynamo. How many times I had it myself. But I'm talking about something different now. I'm not trying to make myself important, Little Sister, but they gave me special treatment. They gave me an injection one day—of course I've had all kinds of injections, it's not even worth mentioning—and when I woke from this one I was in some rich person's kitchen. Believe me, you haven't seen a kitchen like that. Clean as a hospital room, Formica everywhere, and nice white linoleum on the floor. But it was a kitchen, no question about it. Electric stove, shining pots and pans, and all the latest gadgets. Mix-master, toaster, automatic can opener, I'm not exaggerating.

"I thought I was dreaming. 'Why am I here?' I kept asking. And someone explained, 'The outlets are better here in the colonel's new kitchen. Two hundred and twenty volts and no transformer needed.'

"The wires came straight out of the sockets. Someone got a spoon from a drawer—not a porcelain Chinese spoon, an ordinary tin spoon. I felt them press it to my big toe and wrap a wire around it.

"It wasn't the worst thing when they turned on the current. God knows they could have taped the spoon anywhere they wanted. It was only my toe. But I'll tell you what happens afterward. In the middle of the night, every time you feel a nightmare coming on, you get a warning from the toe that conducted the shock. It starts trembling and twitching, having a convulsion all on its own. Oh, my God, here comes the nightmare, you'll say to yourself—and before you can reach down to squeeze it and stop the tremor, you've dreamed the terrible dream.

"Wires, wires! How they love playing with wires! And telephones—have you noticed? How they love their gadgets! One of them had me hold his thing while they had me plugged in and turned on the charge. Some of them almost fell on the floor, laughing. 'Try it,' he said to one of the others. 'It's nice—just a little buzz.'

"You get used to it, Sister. You get used to anything that doesn't kill you. But here's something I hope you'll never have to endure. Please don't think I'm making it up. I'm speaking as one who's had it all. Have I said what it's like when they apply their wires to your gums, your nipples, your birth hole? The jolt? They first have to put a piece of rubber in your mouth to keep you from biting off your tongue. I've had them douse me with water before the shock, to heighten the charge. The noises that come out of you, then! Animal noises you can't control. The things they can do just short of killing you.

"But what I'm trying to say is that none of this compares with what happens when they've got you bound hand and foot with your legs spread apart and they touch you down there with a wire that's giving off a current they've managed to turn down very low, so low that you feel little more than a tickle, a hum. They hold it there right on that nerve. . . .

"Say anything you like, think any thought, pray any prayer, but you can't avoid what happens, Little Sister. You have—how to say it? A climax. A low moment for a woman. But what can a woman do? Nothing."

Shh, shh, said a voice in my ear. The IO was bending over me, rubbing his hand gently over my naked head, which felt as peculiar as an open wound he could touch without hurting. He was telling me to stop crying.

"You're worried," he said softly. "You think we're going to hurt you. You're thinking rape." He tapped my cheek lightly. "Aren't you?

"You mustn't *worry!*" He gave me several slaps now, as though trying to get through to an inattentive child. "Didn't we tell you we don't fuck nuns?"

Then he turned his back on me crisply, like a magician preparing a disguise, and when he swirled around to face me again it was the face of a cross-eyed lunatic, slobbering and screaming with rage. "Especially we don't fuck whores!" he shrieked. "Whores who betray their countrymen just to have their itchy cunts scratched!

"Not enough you betrayed us," he said more calmly now, but close to tears as he squeezed my cheeks in one hand. "You took up arms. Like this!" He thrust a gun up to my face. "See? Revolver. Webley. Thirty-eight caliber. Nice half-moon site, no jagged point at the tip. Don't tell me you've never seen one before? You had better ones in the jungle, I suppose? Newer models, I suppose? Three-fifty-seven magnums, I suppose? What? *What!?* Never mind. This one will have to do.

"Comrade, comrade! Where is your courage?" he said almost tenderly, turning the gun in front of my face like a bauble, a bribe. "Can't you pay attention? Now, don't shut your eyes. I don't like that. Here I'm taking the trouble to explain things, and you're daydreaming. I'm troubling to talk to you because you're not just some helpless, ignorant little thing, you're one of us. Come now, you know what's what, don't tell me otherwise. I'm extending a courtesy. Professional courtesy, let's call it, because you're one of us.

"I'm reminding you how this gun works. Six chambers, remember? But what I'm going to do is put in one bullet, just one, do you follow? Remember how the cylinder moves? Clockwise, Little Sister, clockwise, see? Look, I'm spinning the thing now just to show you how.

"So you're catching on at last, Sister Tango? You can guess the game we're about to play? Think of it as a raffle, a lottery. What do they call it in English? *Lucky dip?* That's good, because luck is on your side already. See? I'm going to fire five times only, not six, five; just five—to increase your odds. Just so your chances will be better than six to one. And you think we have no mercy!"

"Major!" said a voice high with anguish from somewhere near my feet. It was the lieutenant, the globe spinner. "Don't do it, Major. Please! What good will this do?"

"Get him out of here! Now!" said the IO to the guards, without turning around. A scuffle, then the lieutenant's voice again: "Don't do that to me. There's no need." The door banged, opened, banged again. At last: no more voices, no more noises other than the rattle of the electric fan turning above me this way and that, shuddering in midcircuit.

A terrific crunch, like the breaking of a bone, occurred deep in the interior of my being, in an area at the back of my nose. Yet the gun was nowhere near my nose, it was between my legs. *One!* I counted, thinking he had fired the first shot; but it was only the impact of the barrel pressed against me, down below where it should not have felt like the point between my eyes.

I intended to keep on counting, but counting was out of the question now because of all that desperate screaming. Somewhere a woman was screaming her head off. Screaming and screaming, damn her to hell! Somebody shoot her, finish her off, for God's sake!

Somebody does. The screaming stops, praise God's mercy. They've silenced her! I'm ready to sing.

"Click," I hear the major say playfully. "What a big mouth you have, comrade! What a set of lungs! My poor eardrums! And what a karma! Five clicks from a thirty-eight and you're still here!" He's laughing into my face; I can see deep into his mouth, into the bits of shrapnel lodged in his teeth.

"Now get up," he says, frowning as he inspects his gun, "and take your slimy little mess with you. Your fright-shit."

12

Lawrence was my liberator. Lawrence of Daya, I'd call him, after we'd seen *Lawrence of Arabia* together. (But this was some years later, after he'd gotten me out of jail, and we'd returned to America to stay.) I could imagine him donning a burnoose, like the other Lawrence, if burnooses were worn in our part of the world. But sarongs being the Dayan equivalent, it was in a sarong of course that he had appeared when I first met him at the Jesu camp some three years before my imprisonment in Anika.

He was so proud of having mastered the knot, tying and retying it with a careless flourish. (I didn't know then that part of the elaborate homework he'd done in anticipation of his travels, even before leaving home in Washington, was to acquire a sarong, for practicing the knot.) Good intentions aside, however, there are those little subtleties separating the native from the newcomer. How was Lawrence to know that it wasn't simply a matter of getting the knot right? It was the frequency with which the native wrapped and rewrapped a sarong around his waist—not because the thing kept coming loose, but to air himself, letting out the fabric like a cormorant its wings.

Lawrence missed the point about spitting too. He was so eager to squat on the ground with the soldiers and spit nonchalantly. But he was an inexperienced spitter; the thin, unconcentrated spray gave it away. Still, he did try, and we liked him for that.

Sandhurst had warned me about his arrival. "There's a chap coming from an outfit called INRI. A Yank."

"INRI?" Those were the initials printed under the crucifix that hung in the camp chapel. "Jesus of Nazareth, King of the Jews?" I said.

"Don't blaspheme, girl," said Sandhurst mildly. "You never forget a thing, do you?" It was he who had told me, during service, what the letters stood for.

"No, this INRI is some kind of do-good group," he said. "They roam around the world preaching nonviolent protest to scoundrels like us. *'Lay down your arms. Lie down on the streets like nice people, and when they drag you off to jail, don't kick up a fuss.'* Get ready for a lot of preaching about the evils of armed struggle."

Lawrence was one of the first visitors during my early days with the Jesu. And the most serious. The others that later wandered through were oddball drifters: Kees, the dour Dutch globe-trotter; Pierre and Boudouin, the smelly Belgians who hinted at dark escapades in the Congo, when their true occupation there—we later discovered—was owning a coffee shop in Léopoldville; David and Inge, the husband-and-wife team from *Life* magazine; Bruno the Swiss photographer with the big Hasselblad and the jaunty harelip. . . .

None stayed as long, though, as the couple from Stoke on Trent. He'd come to relive wartime memories. He'd been with the British Fourteenth Army in its successful attack on Japanese transport and communication lines to the delta, during which he had fought shoulder to shoulder with a Jesu who had passed away in his arms. Nostalgia and a sense of duty had brought

the old boy now to see what he might do for the Jesu as a
people.

He stayed and stayed, contributing nothing except the joke
of removing his glass eye and passing it around like a magician
his gimmick. As a last resort he'd hitch up his khakis and bare
a porky thigh to flout old shrapnel wounds. He'd brought his
sister along: a watchful little spinster with feather-fine hair and
nervous fingers that pecked. He called her Mums. Every time
she was faced with a dish of stewed lizard or boiled snake or
roasted beetles or fried sparrows, the movement in her lips and
throat suggested that she was fighting bile.

"She's not much of a meat eater. Are you, Mums?" said the
brother, shoving his elbow into her ribs with broad winks.

"These are my blood brothers!" he said about the men,
confiding in her with one hand cupped blatantly over his
mouth. He seemed to be trying to pull a leg. Whose leg that
might be—ours or hers—wasn't clear. Personally, I had no
reason to complain. I drew from him only howls of admiration:
"Ow, ooh, aren't you a clever girl?"

Sandhurst was feeling the strain of the visit. His jaw became
stiffer and his accent thicker in the man's presence.

"Ever 'ear the one about the vice admiral's vice?" inquired
old Glass Eye one afternoon in desperation, faced with one of
those cheerless silences he couldn't abide.

"Don't believe I have," said Sandhurst glumly.

"The rear admiral's rear!" yapped the man from Stoke on
Trent, jousting with his elbows to the left and right.

"Too funny, old boy," Sandhurst said, gazing into the
middle distance with that absent look characteristic of dogs
engaged in humping.

After them came Amos the Nigerian, who was circling the
globe on a motorcycle and had dragged the hefty machine like
a mule through the jungle. He collected autographs of "lady
crusaders" and desired to add mine to his scrapbook. He was

making his way south toward the Malay archipelago, where he hoped to acquire the signature of Dewi Sukarno.

Was Dewi Sukarno a crusader?

"Technically?" said Amos, thoughtfully picking through a massive beard that might house any number of curiosities. "No. But she's one beautiful lady."

I remember one of our men asking me in his presence, through politely clenched teeth, if Amos came from the part of Africa where people ate people. From the way the dust made Amos sneeze, I somehow doubted it. He sneezed primly, into a surprisingly white hankie, which came neatly folded from under his belt.

His Triumph was covered with decals and labels from all the countries he'd conquered. "Look here, I'm a happy man," he said. His exuberance was frightening. "Turning dreams into reality—that's the whole idea, the secret to happiness. I dreamed about this for years and years. My father gave me hell for being lazy. I wasn't lazy, my dear; I was plotting and planning for this big trip. One day I got so sick of his nagging, I just shouted at him, 'Keep quiet! I am tired of your co-mahnds! You are not ruling my destiny!'

" 'Go!' my father said. 'Allow me not to watch your downfall!'

" 'Don't worry!' I told him. 'The downfall of a man is not the end of his life!' "

We couldn't afford to turn away visitors. The diversion aside, some publicity might come of it; if not publicity, at least some little traffic with the world beyond. Some preview, if nothing else, of the latest gadgetry in the arsenal they brought with them: Swiss army knives; Leica and Canon cameras; Akai tape recorders; Samsonite cases; Ronson lighters. To say nothing of the odd handgun and explosive device so lovingly demonstrated by the mercenaries.

Still, not many found it worthwhile to come slogging

through the bush to seek us out. We had nothing then like the tourist trade thriving in the region nowadays.

Anyone can get to the camps in this day and age. It simply requires flying to Bangkok. There, the Minorities Alliance has a liaison man who meets you in the lobby of one of those heartless hotels on Sukhumvit Road once frequented by GIs on R and R from Vietnam. He asks you the routine questions, takes down your passport number, negotiates the fee depending on whether you pay in baht or dollars, and sets the time and place where a jitney will pick you up for the six-hour ride to the rebel GHQ. Follow the liaison man to his car in the parking lot outside, and you'll see a Volvo station wagon, equipped with bulletproof windows and a cellular phone on which he can direct dial Kunming, if the tour requires arrangements for more northerly border crossings.

Back in my time, visitors were seasonal. They came only in the dry season, when malaria was less of a risk, when the stagnancy of the monsoons had passed. But Lawrence was serious. He braved the rains.

He stayed for two weeks, and—since this was in the early days of my capture by the Jesu—it was with the men he conferred mostly, not with me. But two memories stand out from that time.

One: the three of them—Lawrence, Boyan, and Sand-hurst—are in the Meeting House, seated at the table and looking through some papers. I'm on the floor toward the open veranda, helping one of the old drill sergeants patch a sheet of tarpaulin. A rustle and flutter in the ceiling suddenly—and out of the thatch drops a gray snake that lands smack on the floor, between the table and the tarpaulin, where it lies stiff and unmoving. The drill sergeant and I spring to our feet; everyone's eyes are on the snake. But when I look up, Lawrence is staring at me, not at the snake—and Boyan is watching Lawrence and me. His cool gaze sweeps back and forth between us like a silent oscillating fan. (Was Boyan seeing the future then? A future involving Lawrence and me, without him?)

The other memory: Lawrence out on the parade ground, playing wicker-ball with the men. They're standing in a circle, passing the ball around, keeping it aloft by bouncing it off their heads, shoulders, elbows, knees, and feet. Lawrence, a full head taller than the tallest of the men, is in the game, but seems caught up in a private activity as he leaps sideways, forming acute triangles with his elongated limbs. He couldn't look more like a praying mantis if he tried. Watching him brings on a twinge of pity in me—the kind of tenderness one feels for an albino, say. He is after all so pale, his eyebrows and lashes so bleached and defenseless.

Yet five years later this was the man who got me out of jail. Not single-handedly, of course. The team negotiating my release also included Amnesty, the Red Cross, the American embassy, the UN, the Buddhist Peace Council, the Swedish Institute for International Peace, and Prisoners of Conscience International. But Lawrence was the driving force: it was his one-man effort for nearly a year on my case that brought things to a head.

It was the late sixties—a most inopportune moment for stirring up public sympathy toward a case like mine. What call, in those Vietnam War–crazed days, for any serious interest in the affairs of yet another paddy-farm nation?

Daya? Where was Daya exactly? Ah yes, the Haiti of the East, with its grinding poverty, its Tontons Macoutes-like secret police, and its very own crackpot strongman for a Papa Doc. And wasn't there trouble with the hill tribes—some scattered ethnic rebellion led by the Supremo's ex-wife? A family feud, undoubtedly.

This was the climate in which Lawrence negotiated the terms of my release and deportation, leaving room for Supremo to save face by declaring me stateless and forcing me to leave.

But when they officially delivered me into Lawrence's custody, my gratitude toward him was for another, more immediate kindness. I came through the door to the room in which he'd been waiting, and he rose to greet me with a courtesy I'll never forget—the courtesy of keeping in check the shock he must have felt at seeing what had become of me.

Earlier that day, I'd been allowed the first look at myself in close to a year. In the hand mirror—provided along with an innocent-looking white blouse and navy-blue sarong I was to wear—was the face of some nocturnal creature with dark-ringed eyes, the kind I remembered from books on Australia. My hair had grown out of the stubble but offered no protection, no disguise to mask the severity of the bony head and neck, the hollow eyes and cheeks. I bared my teeth. Just as I suspected from the taste in my mouth: the gums were swollen and bled along the tooth line when poked with the tongue.

Yet all he said to me, his blue eyes sparkling as he gave my hand a long, double-handed shake, was, "Great seeing you again. Really great."

For that alone I thought I could never thank him enough.

What I didn't know then was that he *preferred* me in that state. A year or so later, noting my weight gain—avoirdupois, as he put it—he would recall almost wistfully, "You were such a gamine then, Tango, with your tomboy haircut. Such an alluring little wisp of a thing."

In less than an hour after boarding our plane, we were in Bangkok, in a wholly unfamiliar zone: the zone of air-conditioning. The expensive atmosphere pervaded every interior space—in hotels, offices, shops, restaurants, and in the Japanese taxicabs that got us there. In the bracing chill that lofted me through the city's heat and noise and fumes, I felt rid of petty concerns.

We gave endless interviews, going from breakfast at one hotel to lunch at another; from drinks in lobbies to dinners at private clubs. While I stood deliberating over the cornucopia of meats and seafoods, breads and vegetables, fruits and cheeses, pastries and desserts, Lawrence held forth for the journalist or official at hand. He was most at home when holding forth: explaining, expounding, enlarging. The air-conditioned haze meanwhile preserved me in a chill of well-being, indifferent to the content of those interviews—even when the resulting stories were untrue.

I had pointed out to Lawrence an error in one of the early AP articles, which had me saying "I was scared as the dickens" while in jail.

"What's not true?" said Lawrence.

" 'Scared as the dickens.' I never said that."

"But it's true you were scared, isn't it?"

"Yes, I was scared. But I didn't say it that way. I've never used those words: 'scared as the dickens.' "

"Splitting hairs, Tango; splitting hairs. It's true, isn't it? In essence? You don't know much about journalists, I guess. Journalism, by definition . . ." and off he went on the complexities of the trade.

I went back to enjoying my banana split.

We were seated at a window of an ice-cream parlor, looking out onto the street. Across the way were the boutiques. The Thai cottons and silks were patterned with the brilliance of hallucinations. The jewelry was so ornate, so abundant, it all looked fake. But the tiger- and leopard-skin rugs, snakeskin belts, and crocodile handbags and shoes looked only too real.

In and out of the shops swarmed the tourists, balancing cameras and shopping bags while trying to sidestep the puddles on the street—and the snarl of taxis, jitneys, mopeds, and three-wheelers all spewing black smoke.

I didn't dare openly admire the Western chic of the Thai women—the stylish miniskirts and hip-huggers, the subtle makeup, the coiffed hair. I knew what would follow: a lecture.

How could I admire a culture that aspired only to imitate? I heard about fakery. I heard about venality.

Still, I longed to shed my sarong—the long, dignified, tiresome thing—for a miniskirt with the waist below the navel and the hem above the knee. I longed for stiletto heels, false eyelashes, and painted nails. I especially longed for a wig. The night markets were full of them—page boys, bouffants, braids, ringlets, tight curls, loose waves, chignons, French rolls, and luxuriant, blunt-cut tresses—all made of real hair. I couldn't understand Lawrence's objection. What was so fake about real hair?

"A wig?" Lawrence recoiled. "Why would you want a wig?" He had a point; I had my own head of hair; I wasn't exactly bald. Lawrence always had a point.

"Oh, look: sweet mango rice, Lawrence!" I said, passing a food stall.

"I'm not hungry."

"But mango . . . just a taste?"

"I never eat when I'm not hungry."

To eat only out of necessity and not out of whim—here was a virtue, a discipline I had associated only with monks. Like a monk, he sat serenely on a mountain of wisdom and facts and from there enjoyed a truer view of things—the patterns and connections of life.

It showed in the grand pattern, he said, that we were meant to come together in marriage. Didn't I see the thread: our meeting at the camp three years ago; his coming to my rescue; our togetherness now that I was finally free?

"I wanted to save you the moment I set eyes on you," he said.

"Not back at the camp?"

"Back then."

"But I wasn't looking to be saved."

Not by him, anyway. I dreamed of a savior, but he was

nothing like Lawrence. I dreamed of an impresario. A man prepared to risk more than escorting me safely through the outposts and mine fields and jungles of the home camps, on past the jungles and mine fields and outposts of the enemy camps, and beyond the borders to freedom. I envisioned escape on the arm of an Argentine. A mercenary from Buenos Aires with a passion for the tango would have been the ideal. Someone who would take me down the grand avenues of B.A. and into the best of the tango cafés.

Not Carlos, though. I couldn't picture poor Carlos hacking through the bush to rescue me, especially now that he was a member of the Dayan armed forces. But not someone like Lawrence either. Certainly not someone like Lawrence.

Yet here I was, free against all odds—and indebted to him for my freedom. And he was saying, "I have one mission; that mission is you."

Men with a mission made me very nervous. But in Lawrence's eyes was such a fascinating play of light. I'd never been so close to anyone with blue eyes before. Looking into them had the novelty of a kaleidoscope.

So I said yes, I'd marry him.

He went out of his way to plan a ceremony outside the city and its taints. "It's a surprise" was all he would say as we sat in our blue Datsun taxicab that lurched and idled through the brawling traffic with its machine-gun exhausts, backfiring engines, bells ringing like fire alarms, horns blaring like war clarions, people screaming death threats and laughing with the uproariousness of the damned.

Once out of the city we stayed on the two-lane Southern Highway and followed an arrow-straight course along miles of tin-roofed, cement-fronted stores on one side and canals glowing with neon wastes on the other. Here and there, overloaded trucks and vans had slid off the soft side of the road, wheels mired at a tilt in the clay.

It was near noon, but the windows of the cab might have been tinted, so smoky was the glare of smog. An eerie twilight had fallen along stretches of the road—a pinkish phosphorescence lighting up some of the buildings. Lawrence pointed to its source: giant fluorescent bulbs with long metal covers over their tops, jutting out over the façades.

Noticing our interest, the cabdriver adjusted his rearview mirror to bring us into view. "You like?" he said. His previously bellicose mood caused by the city traffic seemed to have passed.

"Like what?"

He took a hand off the wheel to point out the twilight buildings. "Shalimp?"

Lawrence and I looked at each other. "Shalimp," he repeated. "*Kung,* we call in Thai."

"Ah, shrimp," said Lawrence.

"Yet," he affirmed. "Shalimp. Make many, many shalimp here for sell to market." It was only then I noticed the holding tanks for the shrimp hatcheries under the fluorescent lights.

"How do you do?" said the driver in a bright new tone, having broken the ice. "My name Jumsai. But better call me Joe."

He turned his mirror again to look at me this time and posed a long question in Thai.

I shook my head and shrugged. *Sorry, don't understand.*

He turned around to face the mystery—a deaf-mute, maybe?

"You no speak Thai?" He was seeing me for the first time.

"No, no speak."

"How come you no speak Thai?" he said into the mirror. "You Pilipino?"

"No."

"Indonesia?"

"No."

"Japanese lady!"

"No."

"Chinese?" he said doubtfully.

"No."

Shifting gears, he pressed on: "Spanish?"

"No."

"Yugoslob!"

I shook my head. He looked relieved. "Yugoslob people no good," he explained, his lips curling in disgust.

"So . . . you not Yugoslob." He scratched his head, then pleaded: "Where you *from*?"

"Daya," I said.

"Daya!" Once again he turned around, incredulous. "But Daya so poor!" he protested. "So bad gowerment, am I light? One time you have too much lice, too much oil, so many wude for furnitures. Now you no have—nothing."

He kept shaking his head. "So poor!"

He turned his mirror to see Lawrence. "You mally?"

"We are on our way," said Lawrence, "to marry."

"Aw, I understand!" Joe nodded. "You go now to famous wat for mally!"

I turned to Lawrence. "We're getting married in a temple?"

"A *Buddhist* temple," Lawrence stressed proudly.

I smiled; I should have known.

"What's funny, Tango?"

"I didn't know you were a Buddhist."

"Well, I'm not. But it's for you."

"Who said I'm Buddhist?"

"You're not a Buddhist?" Lawrence looked as if he might cry with disappointment.

"No."

"Then what are you?"

"A free tinker," I said.

"Freetinker? What do you mean?"

"Someone who's free to tink what she wants," I said.

But Lawrence wasn't smiling. "Well," he said, standing his ground. "I still think it's the way to go."

Joe wanted to get across his approval of the wat in question. "You hava nice wetting in wat," he promised. "Maybe you see famous monk. Wery wery holy man. He fart all day.

"Yet, yet, he fart," Joe insisted. "You no believe? All day he eat no food so he wery thin. Lart time I go to wat, I see: he fart all day!"

Joe stopped at the foot of a hill on which stood the *wat*—a bright orange temple with a curved gilt roof, brassy and theatrical in the afternoon sun. "Good lahk," he called, as we got out—to be surrounded immediately by a half-dozen young men, all pulling at Lawrence's elbows and plucking at his belt. And talking at once.

"You like Thai culture?"

"Holy monk?"

"You want Coke? Fanta?"

"Taxi? I have taxi, I wait here for you, okay?"

"Hey, big man, where you from? You like Thai girl?"

"I show you wood carving from up-country, you want?"

They followed us all the way up the winding path that led from the wrought-iron gates through exquisitely tended grounds where giant sprinklers sprayed every square inch of cultivated soil: flowering bushes and ornamental plants, lily ponds and rock gardens, thick lawns and thin palm trees. The boys followed and badgered us with the same tenacity shown by the young men soliciting people along Patpong Road.

Lawrence and I were walking through that celebrated strip one night, when the door to one of the neon-lit bars swung and stayed open long enough for me to see four naked girls in high heels gyrating on the glass surface of a raised platform. Under the brute pulse of the music and the strobe lights, they seemed both thunder- and lightning-struck, their bodies caught in the throes of electrocution, their eyes blank and lifeless from shock.

But we weren't on Patpong Road; we were on the grounds of a temple famous not only for its fasting monk but—as Lawrence was explaining now—for the spiritual retreats, special lectures, and films offered anyone wanting to escape the materialism of city life for an afternoon of reflection and meditation. With advance notice, one could even arrange a private wedding—a simple ceremony costing only a modest donation.

Joe's fasting monk never appeared, and our marriage ceremony took place not in the glittering chambers of the temple proper, but in the annex halfway down the hill, a building with the look of a renovated pillbox. The young monk who did the honors had a name that sounded like "Somesuch."

Afterward, he ushered us back to the temple, where we sat cross-legged on a cool marble floor, under a giant screen on which the feature film was projected. The subject, evidently, concerned the corruptions of city life. Scene upon grainy scene of massage parlors and nightclubs flashed by. Then came the final message, a moral I couldn't quite piece together, which involved vistas of chanting Buddhist nuns—row after row of them, filling the wide screen.

A knowledge of Thai was not necessary to benefit from the program, we had been told. True or not, the music was inspirational enough. It was the theme from *Exodus*, the movie.

"Happy?" said Lawrence.

I smiled and nodded. I felt a little disturbance in the throat—a kind of heartburn. But maybe it was happiness; what did I know?

Outside it was pouring rain. There was no way to get downhill to the nearest taxi without a thorough drenching. "This is what Joe meant, I guess," said Lawrence. "A nice wetting in the wat."

The next day I felt uneasy about what else was in store when all he would say about the honeymoon was "It's a surprise!"

This time he had rented a chauffeured Land Rover. Once more we inched our way through the gridlocks and deadlocks of city traffic, once more we made it to the Southern Highway, but now we kept going—past the road leading to the wat, past the ragged edges of the suburbs with their smoking factories and tin-and-thatch shanties, past rice fields and one-buffalo villages . . . till the paved road came to an end. Then we were in jungle, bouncing and grinding our way through rock and mud, crawling over streams and riverbeds, bridge by bridge. We crossed stone bridges, brick bridges, bamboo bridges, cannibalized steel bridges, and the flotsam and jetsam of old bridges—a rotting plank here, a sagging railroad tie there.

Air-conditioning had spoiled me. I felt sickened by the heat and dust that whipped through the open Land Rover with a smothering force, a force that required straining against just to withstand, like gravity itself. Then the road began to climb, and the Land Rover seemed to be straining against all three: heat, dust, and gravity. At times the road was so narrow that leaves and branches poked through the open sides of the jeep; other times we came into an open space or to the edge of a drop where we could actually see into the distance—to familiar puffs of smoke. The perennial jungle fire! Someone or other was always burning something or other in some war or other.

I used to be able to tell when the burnings involved human settlements. The smoke was different: dark brown over smoldering villages, gray over mere foliage. But brown or gray, that sight of smoke over jungle brought home once more a sense of inescapable strife. Impossible to imagine jungle without war. What an idea! As absurd as a jungle without ambush. The terrain was meant for ambush, earmarked for it—as I well knew.

It was exactly on a stretch like this that I was taken: an ideal spot for an attack. There on the right, the dead space they've got covered by mines, booby traps, machine guns, maybe mortars; to the left, up on that hill, the command post; below, the assault units, already in position. There to the left of the road they hide, waiting to fan out for the hit: cut off reinforcements up ahead and to the rear, halt the advance guard, block the withdrawal route, cut off retreat, and stop the target in its tracks—an easy target in our case, an open Land Rover plodding along our condemned course.

So they'd got me after all, lured me while my defenses were down, across the borders and back into the trap I thought I'd escaped for good.

I stared at the two men sitting in the front seat—the driver on the left, Lawrence on the right—and all at once their alert postures, the rigid backs of their heads, told me they were in on the treachery, the bastards! The old symptoms of panic were upon me—the kicking heart, the burning eyes, the roar in my ears, the rising gorge. *Easy; it's just panic, that's all.* But it was no use. I had to lean forward and grip Lawrence's shoulder.

"Lawrence!" I had to plead. "Stop! Stop here! I have to get sick!"

I felt better almost immediately, thanks to the warm bottle of Fanta produced by the driver. On we drove, Lawrence by my side in the backseat now, holding my hand and craning his neck to see through the windshield.

"We should be seeing a Brophie shortly," he said.

"What's a brophie?" I asked.

Lawrence laughed. "One of our hosts. The three Brophie brothers. Never heard of them? I'm surprised. They're legends by now—they grew up in this part of the world, been here practically all their lives. Missionary kids. Of course they went to the States part of the time for schooling and such, but they all came back to settle. They know the area like the backs of their hands. Great guys—white-hunter types. Speak half a dozen languages and hill dialects. I think one of them even speaks Dayan. The youngest one, Jack, is the one that went to school with me. He's an adviser to the border police on ethnic relations. He's the real daredevil; I could tell you some stories. . . ."

"The one that jumps out of planes with a snake wrapped around his neck?"

"God, you remember everything."

"Not everything. Just men who like to fall out of the sky with snakes around their necks."

"Anyway, they've got this plantation out here; I thought it'd be a treat for you."

The driver was pointing up ahead. Through the thinning stands of trees I could see running water . . . and on a rise beyond, a single thatch hut—a large hut; but a hut, nothing more.

"The plantation!" said Lawrence. His eyes were alight. "Bob!" he shouted. "Hey, Bob, old buddy!"

For a shocking moment I saw the tall, tanned man with narrow-set eyes and wavy yellow hair and thought it was Sanders, the missionary back in Irrawaddy who had tried to fondle me. But it was only the oldest of the Brophie boys, waving and smiling in welcome. The other two were out back behind the hut, sitting—no, lounging—in deck chairs under the awning of a mango tree. They were wearing sarongs.

My God, I thought. *It's the camps all over again. Here I am back in the bush; there they are, the rebels, the warriors in repose. Taking the air. Scratching their crotches. Sucking on beer bottles. I'll never get out alive.*

Lawrence could scarcely wait to slip into a sarong too and join the Brophies in their cocktail hour. We went inside—he to change, I to unpack. I remained in our room longer than necessary, sitting on the bed and staring once more at the dreary, all-too-familiar details of a thatch hut: the layered leaves of the roof where scorpions and snakes and other vermin nested; the woven walls that buckled in a high wind; the windows that failed to keep out the heavy rains. . . . In a terrible, disheartening way, I felt I'd come home. This matchbox abode, this sham dwelling, was a birthright I could never escape.

A vile little cat with yellow eyes crept out from under the bed and scratched at my bare heel. I gave it a kick and went outside.

The men were in their element—and in their cups. The sun was setting across the stream; a breeze was blowing; the ice was clinking in their whiskey glasses. They were into their first round of jokes and tall tales.

Over the next days I heard them again and again—jokes about outsize genitalia of one sort and another, tales of the Brophie brothers' great barbaric feats—the drinking of fresh buffalo blood, the eating of fresh brains scooped out of the heads of live monkeys, et cetera. I heard about weird local customs they'd witnessed—men offering their wives to visiting guests out of hospitality; mountain villages arrived at through avenues lined with human skulls impaled on stakes; animal sacrifices that required first the starving, then the beating, and only then the eating of chickens, dogs, and pigs . . . and so on. I thought I heard something about riding on the back of a tiger—but maybe by then I was confusing the jokes with the yarns.

They did rouse themselves from time to time to walk around the edges of the clearing—the "plantation grounds"— or bathe in the stream or get in a little target practice by firing at beer bottles. They did take time out for an afternoon nap. But it was always to return to the deck chairs, where they reclined late into the night, burning mosquito coils, shooting the breeze.

I'd turn in early and be half-asleep by the time Lawrence crawled in underneath the mosquito net, smelling of caramel and yeast—the smell of Mekong whiskey. But I was still awake when he came in on our last night there.

"Let me get something off my chest, Tango," he said. "You've made me feel like this honeymoon was a real bust."

"I thought you were having a good time."

"One of us had to be cheerful. I mean, what is this thing you're dragging around? You've been uptight from day one, Tango. You snubbed Bob when he came out to greet us and gave you a *wai*. You ignored it completely. That's pretty rude, if you ask me."

"But what was he doing, giving me a *wai*? It's not something we do in Daya. Or doesn't he know that? It's like expecting me to salaam."

The truth is I hated returning a *wai*, that praying gesture—*I greet the God in you*. Each person's god was his own business, I figured.

"Oh, what's the big deal?" said Lawrence. "Why be such a snob?

"And it's snobbery," he went on. "What else but snobbery when you smile and say nothing, nothing at all, to Boon."

Boon was the second Brophie's wife, a hill-tribe matron about my age. The thought of resorting to sign language, of trying to strike up an interest, tired me. I knew the girl already; I knew her whole story. She reminded me of Dali—Boyan's Jesu wife. She could have been Dali's double.

I still dreamed of Dali and her baby sometimes. That defiant-looking baby with his father's mocking eyes and a nose flat enough to resemble his father's lack of one.

13

Lawrence and I left at last for Los Angeles, he clutching the large brown envelope containing my chest X ray—a U.S. immigration requirement. He'd had it in hand at Anika airport; he'd held on to it on the plane to Bangkok and in the cab from Bangkok airport to the hotel. In our hotel room he'd hidden it in a drawer, under the spare blanket and pillows.

Now, on the plane to San Francisco, the brown envelope was ever at his side again. He did hand it to me once at Tokyo International Airport. (Or I should say, in deference to Lawrence, Haneda International, as the airport was called then. He liked to establish his familiarity with airports around the world by using their specific names. *I was flying out of Don Muang . . . ; when I was passing through Kai Tak, on my way to Fiumicino . . .*)

He had asked me to hang on to it while he went to the men's room, but lost in the wonderland of transistor radios and tape recorders, I set the envelope down on one of the sales counters and forgot about it.

Lawrence's face was drained of what little color it had—

and remained bleached even after I'd retraced my steps and recovered the X ray.

Then he became angry—with the cameras and radios and tape recorders.

"What, Lawrence?"

"The temptation, the corruption. All these gadgets, these toys, that make you lose your head. The materialism . . ."

"I didn't lose my head. I just forgot my X ray."

"Without this X ray, Tango, we are lost."

I wondered about one thing. "Have you looked at it?" I said.

"What, the X ray? No, of course not."

"Don't look like that. I'm not accusing you."

"But why would I look at it?"

"Why wouldn't you? Don't you want to see?"

"See what?" He was gearing up for the effort of appearing at ease—I could tell from the jogging of one knee.

"Whatever there is to see. Maybe you'll see a spot on the lungs. Maybe you'll see a broken rib or two."

Not a flicker of expression in those cut-glass eyes. But he was nodding now: thinking, preparing himself. "Did they?"

"What?"

"Break any bones?"

I laughed; I don't know why. "Not bones, no."

"I didn't think so," said Lawrence, allowing himself to exhale. He twisted around in his seat, looking for a stewardess. "Do you want anything to drink?"

"You didn't think so," I said, ignoring the drink offer, "but you didn't want to ask."

Lawrence looked out his window. From where I sat, there was nothing to be seen but a wasteland of cloud. "Look, Tango—we can let what you've been through poison our lives, or we can put it behind us and get on with all the things that need doing. I'm for putting the whole nightmare behind us. It's over now; we're together; you're free."

I studied his fingers as they rubbed my hand—such long, officious fingers they were, the tools of a busybody twitching with the urge to fix.

"Change seats with me, Lawrence," I said, catching a glimpse of lightening sky over his shoulder. "I want to look out the window."

We changed, and I looked down to a blanket of sunstruck, blue-white fleece—transformed, before my very eyes, into acres of rain forest covered with snow. Here and there were rifts in the cloud, canyons as sheer as jungle ravines. I shut my eyes, wanting to leave that landscape behind me, and pulled the shade down to sleep.

I woke to a beam of daylight that someone had let in by raising a window shade across the aisle. The sun hadn't quite risen but was visible only through a glow, an intimation of light behind a thick wall of cloud that stretched like a fortress wall. Some distance behind was the horizon, fragile and reflective as a sheet of glass. In between wall and glass lay the enchantment—in between was an ethereal city of light, its skyline the backdrop of a distant magic lantern show.

And what a skyline! Mile after mile of rooftops recalling all the cities from all the ages of the world: towers and castle turrets; pagodas and minarets and Chinese temples and church steeples; the fanciest gables and the simplest domes.

"Lawrence, come look," I beckoned. But by the time he came, a big brutish sun had leapt clear out from behind the long fortress wall of cloud, and the city of rooftops and hushed lights was gone.

14

To put my papers in order and secure my citizenship was not the chief reason for our trip to the States. The chief reason was Hollywood. We were about to "negotiate with a studio."

Lawrence's Hollywood contact was a high-school friend, an adman who was taking a year off to study film at UCLA. This phase of the negotiations consisted of long afternoons spent by the side of the UCLA swimming pool, while Dick expounded on film history and technique and ogled the bikini-clad coeds.

"Jesus, look at the SAM factor on that one," he'd mutter.

"What's the SAM factor?" I asked.

"SAM. A boob measurement. Standard American Mouthful. Christ, and look at that mons veneris. The succulence."

"Somewhat hirsute, wouldn't you say?" added Lawrence pompously. He wasn't entirely comfortable with his friend's running commentary, but laughed along obligingly and from time to time tried to contribute.

In private, he allowed that Dick was crude, but not a lout.

"Rabelaisian," he said. "Dick's a Rabelaisian character." It explained a lot and excused everything, apparently—including the way Dick would grill me every time I emerged from the women's dressing room. "So what's the story, Tango? Miss Kuwait have a bush on her? Bet she could use a lawn mower, huh? Well, hell, didn't you even manage to find out where she was from? She hangs out with those greasy mustachioed Middle Eastern oil-sheikh types, so I'm guessing she's Miss Kuwait, but who knows? Maybe she's Mary Lou Jones from Muncie, Indiana. But nah! The schnoz on her. I mean, it's a good thing she's built. That face definitely won't launch a thousand ships. Christ, it could pass for the rear end of a camel."

"Dionysian," said Lawrence of his friend, fondly. "A classic Dionysian character."

"What's Dionysian, Lawrence?"

"The opposite of Apollonian. Which of course is what I am."

"Oh."

I had no complaints. The weather was perfect, sunny, cool, and dry, and the afternoons were languid; they reminded me of those indolent days by the pool of the Anika Yacht Club. When it was dark, we'd walk the half mile home to our apartment in our flip-flops—a great comfort to me, since one of the things I had feared about life in the West was the necessity of wearing closed shoes, which I abhorred. On the way home, we'd stop for groceries: a head of lettuce, a bottle of Kraft's Green Goddess salad dressing, a package of ground beef, and a box of Lipton's onion soup mix to doctor the beef into a dish Lawrence called instant Stroganoff.

Lawrence seemed disgruntled at the table. He was immensely disappointed that I couldn't cook. "How can you not know how to cook?" he'd ask me, again and again.

"I never needed to cook, I told you. I was never allowed

to. My mother never let me cook, we had a cook at Government House, and they had cooks at the Jesu camps. In jail I offered to cook, but guess what? They refused my offer."

"All those spicy dishes?" he'd persist, longingly. Then he'd shake his head as if he'd been deliberately misled, while reaching for a piece of lettuce with his chopsticks. Eating with chopsticks put him in touch with the cuisine he admired and was so cruelly deprived of.

"Why set out silverware, Tango?" he'd say. "Who needs it when we have chopsticks?"

"I prefer not to eat salad with chopsticks."

"But why? Chopsticks are so efficient."

"Wrong, Lawrence. Not for everything."

"Oh, come on. You grew up picking up grains of rice with chopsticks from the time you were this high."

"I hate to tell you this," I said, pushing away the salad, for which I'd lost my appetite. "But we don't use chopsticks the way you think. You're confusing us with the Chinese, maybe? We only used chopsticks in Chinese tea shops and restaurants. The rest of the time we tried to do without utensils. We ate with our hands."

"I wish you wouldn't make those sweeping statements, sweetie." He sighed, implying that I didn't know what I was talking about, even when it concerned my own past. Lawrence was confident of his insider's knowledge of matters Asian. He was full of theories and nuggets of lore about the smallest points of etiquette—many of them wrong. But it didn't matter: nothing could prove him wrong, once he had espoused a belief.

The movie Lawrence envisioned changed from day to day. His original idea of a sweeping epic about an American hero who leads an Asian war of liberation had already undergone major alterations by the time we reached Los Angeles. Extensive poolside discussions with Dick had steered him in yet another direction. "Listen, Larr," said Dick, "people are too bitter and twisted about Vietnam to want to know anything more about Asia than they have to these days. The climate's lousy for any kind of Asian *Doctor Zhivago*. The only thing that'll sell is a story playing the ChiCom connection or the KMT opium connection."

The ideal solution, therefore, was for Lawrence and Dick to collaborate on a screenplay that incorporated both the espionage *and* the opium angle—a sweeping Cain-and-Abel saga, say, about two brothers who end up fighting on opposite sides of the Chinese civil war, one rising to power as the secret police chief in the Peking politburo, the other to a different kind of notoriety as a KMT general who becomes an opium warlord.

Dick found a potential producer, a high-strung man named Wesley Block.

Wesley seemed eager, but he was burdened with a hiatal hernia, several phobias, and a tendency to hives. Lawrence mistrusted him ("I have questions about his bona fides," as he put it), but chiefly because the man mispronounced key foreign words, in particular some Chinese proper nouns. Every time the subject of Teng Hsiao-P'ing came up, for example, Lawrence would interrupt him. " 'Dung,' Wesley, 'Dung.' Not 'Teng.' "

"Sorry. Dung. Well, as I was saying, I thought Dung and Mousey Tung were buddies on the Long March."

"Maotza Dung, you mean?"

"That's what I said. Mousey Tung."

One of Wesley's phobias concerned the ChiComs. He believed their agents operated as far afield as West Los Angeles, where our apartment was located, necessitating unusual security measures every time he and Lawrence met to discuss the screenplay. He was worried that the ChiComs might construe the screenplay to be a cover, a bogus project fronting for an infinitely more complex propaganda campaign masterminded by the running-dog capitalist warmongers of Hollywood. That's how they thought, those crazed fanatics.

Wesley arrived one day with two potential coproducers. Wesley was a teetotaler (a tooteetler, he kept saying, referring to a joke that apparently only I hadn't heard), but his friends had been drinking. The one with the thin chest and the thin hair was wearing an Indian shirt that looked and smelled like cheesecloth. His name was Milan. The other had curly gray hair and wore a perpetual grimace, like Victor Mature. His name was Herbie.

Milan and Herbie hiccuped and snorted with laughter, repeating the punch lines to private jokes, in particular one involving the words "focus" and "bofus." By the time the conversation turned to the screenplay, they could barely contain their hilarity.

"Now wait a minute," said Herbie. "Let me get this straight. Are we talking about a movie about warlocks or warlords? I thought this was going to be about a Chinese warlock."

"You mean . . . ," Milan sputtered, "you mean like Fu Manchu meets *Bell, Buke and Kendle?* Come on, Herpie. Gimme break."

"Ahoy, ahoy," chortled Herbie. He seemed to be smoking from the nostrils, ears, and neck, where little puffs of gray hair showed.

They were joined presently by Herbie's girlfriend, a florist called Barb. Barb smoked and coughed a lot.

"Enough of show biz," she said finally, reaching for a big bag from which she brought out an object wrapped in green tissue paper. Considering my origins, she thought I might be able to identify something from her collection of Oriental antiques. The object in question was a Buddha of some sort, remarkable to me only for its chipped nose and missing ear.

"Do you suppose," she said, searching my eyes, "that it's Indian? Or Thai?"

I shook my head and shrugged helplessly, unable to shed any light whatsoever on the mystery. But Lawrence's long arm had reached out to rescue the artifact from my ignorant grasp. Turning it around in his finicky hands, he began following one of his laborious lines of inquiry. *You have to ask yourself . . . is this a feature you're likely to find . . . then you say to yourself . . . but you have to remember . . . then you figure . . .*

He dropped names of periods and dynasties—Sukhothai, Mon-Khmer; he speculated; he hazarded; he opined. But the upshot was he didn't know.

Warming to his subject, he expanded on Buddhist scriptures and Pali texts. After several mentions of the word "Pali," Milan suddenly found an escape. "Speaking of Polly," he said, reaching for the saltines, "anyone want a cracker?"

Barb laughed so hard that the wet cough turned into spasms, and her face went scarlet. "Meelin!" she gasped. "Meelin!" I thought she was choking.

Lawrence's movie did get made in the end. It wasn't the saga he'd envisioned, but it *was* set in Southeast Asia—right across the border, in fact, from the northern tip of Jesu territory, in the far more accessible and convenient jungles of Thailand. It took us back to Asia within the year, where the filming was done by an Australian crew. It was a joint Thai-Scandinavian production, a documentary designed to promote both tourism and the teak industry in Thailand.

The movie was a half-hour feature on the Asian elephant. I had a walk-on part as a village girl in a bath sarong, dreamily crossing a bamboo bridge at sunset while an invisible elephant trumpeted in the background.

We had planned to stay on in Thailand for a few months. Instead we ended up staying four years.

"Why are you so desperately unhappy, Tango?" Lawrence said on the day I let the gibbon go.

He had been upset about the gibbon for a while, but it was my state of mind that continued to needle him. The gibbon was only the latest in a long series of provocations—most of them caused by my resolute lack of interest in things that Lawrence felt should have mattered to me. Like the tae kwon do.

He had taken pains to find the right instructor for me and was scathing in his disappointment when he discovered that Mr. Kim had devoted several classes to teaching me how to make kimchee instead of improving my form. How could I be so . . . "cavalier" was the word he used, when he wanted to say "shallow."

But the gibbon was the last straw. It was a gift for me— brought back from his most recent visit with the Brophie brothers. Together they had journeyed through a Wa village, where the headman had untied his pet gibbon from its tether to a tree and presented it to Lawrence. The string was still tied around its pelvis when Lawrence brought it out of its cardboard box and attempted to hand it to me.

"I hate monkeys, Lawrence," I said, recoiling, which sent the gibbon shrieking back into Lawrence's arms and clinging to his neck.

"Gibbons aren't monkeys, they're apes," said Lawrence, wounded, stroking the creature's back. "I thought you said you grew up with gibbons."

"I said there was a gibbon in Irrawaddy when I was growing up, and I didn't like it one bit."

The house we were living in at the time was a Thai-style bungalow in one of the older, more rural sections of Bangkok, where mosquitoes were fierce and rents were low. Lawrence kept the gibbon outside, tied to an acacia tree that made for ideal climbing and swinging. "Brachiation" was the word I tried not to forget.

One afternoon I was watching it from the kitchen, remembering the Gopal gibbon, when I noticed something odd about this one's movements. It was a female, and the other had been a male, but that didn't explain everything. Lawrence had said she was only a year; yet there was a stiffness to her movements, an economy. Suddenly I guessed why and went outside for a closer look.

She was perched on one of the lower branches, shelling an acacia pod, and at my approach sourly pelted me with a seed. As I drew close she stood up—anticipating tit for tat, possibly—and reached for the limb above. That revealed what I had suspected. The length of twine around her pelvis was tied so tight that the abrasion was deep and raw.

I went inside, for scissors, and when I returned it was as though she intuited some purpose. She began screeching. Dropping the scissors on the ground, I tried to beckon her down with coaxing words, but it was pointless. Grabbing the string as close to her waist as I could, I yanked her down, frantic and screaming, from the tree. I clutched the string with one hand and with the other picked up the scissors. Then, while she scratched and struggled, I thrust the scissors into a space between her waist and the string—and cut.

"Why did you do it, Tango, why?" Lawrence said, hard-pressed to believe that the gibbon was really gone. The sight of the bites and scratches on my arms seemed to make him angrier. "You could have waited till I came home. I would have untied her, adjusted the string. It was a gift to me from the Wa chief. It was my gift to you. Don't you value anything?"

"Oh, Lawrence!" I said. "I can't describe the way it looked at me when it realized what I'd done. It fought tooth and claw and suddenly realized I had taken away the pain. We stared at each other, you should have seen us, panting. For a while it couldn't grasp that it was free—*and* free from pain. Then it just—I don't know how to describe it—unleashed this noise at me, as if it wanted to express something truly . . . big, something so full of feeling. It faced me and went on and on, pouring its heart out. And then it swung away."

"I'm glad, Tango, sincerely I am," he said sarcastically, "that you can be moved to a selfless act like that. But you never liked the gibbon, and I can't help thinking it's hostility directed at me."

I cried then—and shrugged off his arm when he tried to comfort me.

That's when he said, "Why are you so desperately unhappy? What is so miserable about your life that you shut yourself off from everything that should matter, from doing things, getting involved, making a contribution, being *useful* for God's sake?"

"What is so miserable about my life, Lawrence," I cried, "is that I hate being here in this country. It's too close to home, too much like home, but it isn't home. I don't feel safe; I don't feel free. I'm like that gibbon. You could have loosened her string, given her more rope, let her roam. But if I hadn't cut her loose, she still wouldn't have been free. I'm not free, Lawrence, can't you understand that? I'm too close to that terrible place to be free."

"That terrible place happens to be home," he said. "You can't run away forever."

"Easy for you to say. You have a home you don't *have* to run away from. Can't you try to imagine that there are some places in the world where you might never wish to return to, even if it's home?"

"Okay, Tango," he said, looking defeated. "I can't take this much longer. We'll go back to the States."

. . .

Distance did not make our hearts grow fonder. On the contrary, with distance—in effect, the distance from home I had so harped on and craved—another distance fell between us, and lengthened. I could see Lawrence struggling to overcome the sense of defeat that returning to the States spelled for him, while I struggled to prove that I was a different person now, a happier person, more energetic, more purposeful, willing to take useful action and rise above the past.

The fundamental difference between Socrates and Sartre, someone once said, was that Socrates woke up in the mornings and saw a worthwhile world. I resolved to wake up like Socrates. In Washington, D.C., where we settled, I took extension courses at first; later enrolled as a full-time college student; then quit in my sophomore year.

Lawrence had been offered a position to head up a refugee relief organization back in northern Thailand. Using my unfinished studies as justification, I remained in Washington while Lawrence returned to that part of the world where he felt most useful, most at home. By then we both knew what the mistake had been: Lawrence had seen in me a link, a ligature, to the East, where he thought he belonged, and I had looked to him as my bridge to the West, where I thought I'd be free. With his departure, we were relieved at last of the daily reminder of our mutual disappointment.

15

For a while I thought I was rid of the yoke of Lawrence's zeal that kept me fettered to a world I wanted only to forget. Yet before long I was back in the loop again, keeping house for a group of Dayans recently arrived in America.

Lawrence himself had just left to return to Asia, following his most recent rescue mission: the emigration of these six Dayan refugees. The official sponsors of the effort, for whom he had worked behind the scenes, were a chapter of New England Buddhists. It was the house they provided in Washington, D.C., that I got roped into running—because Lawrence felt it was the least I could do for my fellow citizens, and I felt it was the least I could do for Lawrence. I was grateful to him—for not dragging me back to Asia, for his decency in our separation, for leaving me a stipend to live on.

The house was a leaky, drafty old bungalow on Sixteenth Street. Once a school for juvenile delinquents, it had been through the wars. Names, expletives, and symbols were gouged into walls and woodwork; the windows were a patchwork of mismatched panes; the floors a mess of paint and water stains. The building seemed doomed to frequent states of emergency caused by roofing, plumbing, heating, and assorted other problems—to say nothing of the periodic break-ins. I called it the Safe House because, like all safe houses, it was anything but safe.

My charges too were proving to be an accident-prone lot. They went to the Greyhound bus station to pick up a suitcase one day—and returned some six hours later. While waiting for the bus, they had gone to the Burger King across the street. Just as the metal gate came clanking down precisely at closing time, Bartholomew had managed to get his forehead in the way of the descending bars. Bleeding profusely, he had been taken by the Burger King manager to the emergency room for stitches.

They brought him home with an impressively bandaged head. He eased himself into a chair like a man just home from the wars.

"A dangerous, dangerous country" was his pronouncement after taking a sip from a glass someone had brought him. "My God, the things that can happen when you're just trying to get a hamburger. A hamburger!"

"Jackass!" said Mon, whose hands were still shaking from the ordeal. "Don't blame the Burger King. You put your head under a steel grate anywhere and it'll split just the same."

"No!" said the wounded one, struggling out of his chair and almost tipping it over in his excitement. "No! I'm telling you. Remember the guy in the papers who went to get a hamburger and ordered a milk shake? Chocolate, the flavor was, I think; yes, chocolate; that's why he couldn't see. Remember how he swallowed six fishhooks?"

"Swallowed!?"

"Swallowed."

"Oh, go on. Six fishhooks I believe. Caught on his tongue I believe. But swallowed?"

"Don't listen to him," someone else said. "He's delirious from the head wound."

Before long, though, they began to look at me as though I were the one with the head injury. Increasingly I found myself going off the deep end, yelling at them for some stupidity or cowardice or ineptitude; slamming doors intemperately; banging things down on the table hard enough to leave dents in the wood; throwing books and papers and banana skins across the room to make more of a mess than the mess I was protesting.

They were driving me berserk, all of them. Boys, they called themselves, but they were grown men (all except Soe Soe, who was seventeen). Bartholomew had an advanced degree in geology. Lwin had even been abroad once before, in his youth, as a Boy Scout representative to Copenhagen. Wu Jing Jang, the Chinaman, may have been the oldest—or just prematurely gray; we couldn't tell, because he was secretive about everything, including his age. Sonny and Mon had left behind wives and children, and as mature married men, they felt especially qualified to blow hot air.

Sonny was the intellectual. He had the hair with the middle part, the horn-rimmed glasses, and the scruffy mustache to prove it. His favorite thinkers, whom he often quoted, were Neatsy and Sartray, as he called them. But it was to Pascal he turned whenever obliged to defend inaction. Pascal knew that most of life's evils arose from man's inability to sit still in a room. Sonny was firmly committed to sitting still in a room. Mon and he were natural allies: both family men, both devoted to bodily functions. In clerical detail they compared notes about the pattern and yield of their visits to the toilet, followed by theories on indigestion and flatulence.

I was maddened by the boys' bizarre obsessions, by their littlest blunders and flaws: their unprofitable efforts to grow a banana tree; their bungling of any new task from driving a car to working a gas stove; their fear of the elements, snow, rain, sleet, or fog; their ignorance and delusions; their petty squabbles.

At night, I almost always regretted my ill temper and resolved to be more tolerant and compassionate in the future—a resolve that unfailingly failed. At night, I could be moved to feel protective and even fond of them—*The poor things, doing their best to survive a transplanting not even their banana tree can survive,* et cetera. Often there arose moments of irresistible humor and fun. Over meals, the day's mishaps were recalled and turned into comedies. On winter evenings, we looked forward to reruns of "Hawaii Five-O" on television, the tropical setting soothing us with images and reminders of warmth. Occasionally we looked to Lwin for entertainment. Beginning always with a tribute to Copenhagen (where his musical talent had been awakened when he won a guitar at a raffle), Lwin threw himself wholeheartedly into his Elvis Presley numbers. He was faithful to the Elvis style, no matter what he sang.

"Oh-oh-oh yes, I'm the great pretender," he sang, knees knocking, pompadour bouncing,

> *Pretending that I'm doing well;*
> *My need is such, I pretend too much*
> *I'm lonely but no one can tell*

Sometimes, with a fire going and Sonny and Mon hunched over the chessboard, a comfortable familiarity reigned, and we were simply a family in the security and warmth of home. But in the midst of serenity a minor incident, a mindless remark, would set me off. Once, during one of their interminable chess games, Bartholomew, the geologist, called across the room, "Hey, Sonny, did you ever hear the saying that life is too short for chess? What do you say to that?"

"The time of life is short," said Sonny, twirling the scant hairs on his upper lip, "only for the idle. Life is long if it is full."

"Who said that, professor?" said Mon. "Neatsy or Sartray?"

"Seneca," Sonny replied. I could hardly believe it. Sandhurst too had quoted Seneca, but that was not nearly as absurd, or outrageous, as the idea of Sonny—soft, foolish Sonny—arrogating to himself the wisdom of a flinty Roman statesman-scholar.

"Did anyone see the diving today?" someone asked. An international diving competition was being televised at the time. The winner, a Greek, had enjoyed an astounding victory a mere half hour after splitting his head open on the diving board.

"I did!" said Bartholomew. "Did you see the guy choke up when he took the prize? I couldn't help it; the stupid fellow made me cry."

"He's not stupid," I shouted, startling everyone. "He's very *intelligent*. What's more he's a *competitor*. He *pushes* himself so that *losing* is *not* a choice."

How dare this self-pitying, moist-eyed, so-called geologist talk about himself and the athlete in the same breath? Didn't he see the immeasurable difference separating them? When he had been hit on the head by the Burger King grate, he had lain abed for weeks. The Greek diver hit *his* head on the diving board, immediately got four stitches, and within half an hour was diving again to win the championship.

Increasingly, I felt trapped. How was it possible to end up once again as figurehead and mascot to a group of well meaning but utterly powerless, defenseless men?

I railed in the house mostly, but, when crossed, I wasn't above railing in the streets—or behind the wheel, a good place from which to hurl insults and throw obscene hand gestures at antagonists, while gunning the motor with murderous defiance. When a rude, officious woman began yapping at us from her car for some infringement as she saw it, I told her to go take a flying fuck. Sputtering, she expressed the hope that I would get hit by a truck, to which I yelled back that I would never say a thing like that to her because if *she* were hit by a truck, it would only disappear up her giant asshole.

At the first signs of trouble, the boys would rush to placate or divert me, only making things worse. The blood would pound louder and harder in my head when I felt them pluck at my sleeve with entreaties to calm down, too stupid apparently to know that nothing is so enraging as thwarted rage.

Why else would I have let fly the way I did at the big angry black woman outside the Safeway? She thought we were stealing her groceries when one of the boys mistakenly lifted a bag out of her cart. Useless to apologize, useless to explain. Still, I might just have walked away, if Lwin—the nervous biddy, the peacemaker—hadn't begun pushing me away from the danger at hand, whispering, "Leave, it, Sister, leave it. Let's go."

I shook him off and turned on the woman. I remember the enlarged whites of her eyes, the O of her mouth, as I stood shouting into her face. *Why would we want to steal your stupid fucking groceries, you stupid fucking woman?* Then, to prolong the grisly satisfaction of anger, I lashed out at Lwin for having incited me with his pacifism.

Seeing how group outings tended to shorten my fuse, I should have avoided Disney World. But the New England Buddhists had arranged the trip, and I was the only one lacking enthusiasm.

All throughout that first day I tried not to notice the manifold ways in which a person could be driven crazy in that supposedly benign playground. I tried to stay calm in the face of the deafening brass bands, the marauding Mickeys and Plutos brandishing monstrous hands and feet, the raucous teenage performers in western outfits of red, white, and blue, singing and dancing for the most extraordinary collection of grotesque human beings I had ever seen—a world convention of the lame, the halt, and the unspeakably obese.

I was already experiencing sweaty palms and shortness of breath when the boys stumbled on an unexpected treat: a ride we couldn't possibly pass up. This was a boat ride on a steamer named *Irrawaddy Irma*.

They nudged each other with private delight as we piled in for the journey into the wilds of a spooky tropical interior. Our "river" cut through jungle walls overgrown with apple-green creepers and vines, with ruins, part Mayan, part Cambodian, poking through, and, around each bend, some mechanical jungle beast poised to scare. There was a tiger with glowing eyes, elephants at play in a kangaroo stance (with their two front feet up in the air), monkeys that grinned and waved, and snakes with affable faces. At the end of the ride, around the last bend, up popped a fat, agreeable American Indian in Hawaiian shorts and shirt, his belly exposed, swinging a bunch of shrunken heads in his hand, those faces, too, smiling broadly.

I was the first to step off the boat onto the landing, and as I looked back at the rest of my countrymen—some of them still twisting in their seats for a last glimpse at the wonders just passed—an irrational fury and shame overtook me at the sight of their uncritical expressions, their tolerance of so inane and debasing an image of our origins.

Back in the car, on our way to the motel we were staying in that night, I managed to get stuck in traffic, going in the wrong direction. The boys in the backseat had begun one of their senseless little squabbles, while the car—a decrepit Lincoln—kept stalling. *Please!* I kept muttering. *I'm having problems. Stop it, please!* But my protest wasn't loud enough, apparently. I continued muttering; they continued arguing.

The familiar tightening across my forehead and eyes had begun. It was the same old argument, about Daya's future. The same little squeaks and hisses leaking out of the same windbags. I kept hearing the idiot phrase "nonviolent protest."

I slammed on the brakes, shook the steering wheel as if rattling a cage, and yelled at the top of my lungs, "Get out! Get out! All of you! Out!"

I leaned over and opened the front door on the passenger's side. "Out!" Then I reached across the backseat and opened that door. "Out!"

"Okay, okay, Tango; calm down, please. . . ." I heard someone say. Someone else began to laugh.

"Out!" I continued to scream. "I'm sick of you—all of you. Out! Now!"

"Please, Tango, please!" But they were getting out. Doors slammed shut.

"You'll harm yourself."

"She's a lunatic. Let her be." That was Mon, the BM king. *Noted!* I thought, knowing even in my witless state that I would forever hold that remark against him.

"Stop, Tango! You can't leave us here. How will we get back?!"

Mindlessly, I drove for hours, along highways and over bridges, past commercial centers and through silent neighborhoods—until, exhausted, I came to my senses and realized it was St. Patrick's Day.

Blind with rage was what I had been. Seeing red—I'd done that too. Those expressions described the state exactly. Fury had an aura all its own, as dazzling as a vision that blotted out the surrounds. And when it was gone, the colors were gone; the blinding lights were gone; the roar in the ears was gone; the heart stopped its chopping.

What remained was an emptiness, a feeling of being left behind, a sense that worlds had turned in that lapse when the aura reigned. The celebrations and parades passed on our way to Disney World seemed like events of long ago. The floats, the bands, the hundreds of thousands of good-natured spectators, all wearing a touch of green, were ancient images. And

Disney World was merely a mirage. Hunger came over me suddenly; I felt weak.

I drove back to our motel, worried now about whether the boys would ever be able to find their way home. In one of the two rooms we were occupying, I found Sonny alone, seated at the small table with the lamp on it, his back to the door.

In as neutral a voice as I could manage, I asked, "So, what shall we have for dinner?"

He was eating something. At least I thought he was eating, because he was wiping his mouth. No, he was wiping his nose and mouth. He was weeping. Tears hung on his mustache.

I pulled up a chair wearily and sat in front of him.

"You're so, so hard, Big Sister," he cried, his voice breaking. "Sometimes I think you hate us all, and I don't know why. You expect so much, you treat us like nothing, like worms. But do we have a choice except to stick together? Do you think it's easy—depending on you?"

His arm on the table, his head on his arm now, he broke down, sobbing. "Almighty God, we are such wretches! What's the use, Tango, what's the use? Our families back home so far away. No one to help us, no one to care!"

So now it's self-pity, I thought, reaching for the facecloth that someone had used to wipe up a spill. It had a yellow stain, I noticed, and I thought with annoyance how every dishcloth in the Safe House had yellow turmeric stains on it—and now, even away from home, they managed to stain and discolor clean white towels, the slobs. I handed him the facecloth. He waved it away.

"Where's hope for our poor country, comrade?" he cried, falling into the old salutation in his misery.

Comrade?! I thought of a scene from *Doctor Zhivago*, which I had seen with Lawrence. "Oh, Sasha darling," says Lara tenderly when Strelnikov, bitter and correct, addresses her as "comrade," "I am not your comrade."

Oh, Sonny darling, I am not your comrade. Have you ever danced the tango? Do you dare to eat a peach? Don't laugh! I said to myself, quivering with the urge. *Whatever you do, don't laugh!* I was worried about the wrong urge, as it happened. The next thing I knew I was crying into the facecloth Sonny had rejected, taking us both by surprise. In the end it was he who did the comforting. He placed his stubby little hand, still sticky with tears, over mine.

"No, no, Tango, Big Sister; it's not for you to despair. What will become of us if you give up? We look to you, our leader. Our Irrawaddy Tango."

The Jesu believe that man is made up of two parts: physical body and butterfly spirit. While the body plods through the lumpish tasks of living, the butterfly soul ranges unfettered through the open spaces of dreams, trances, wishes, reveries, unconscious desires.

In my days among the Jesu, seeing how butterflies were drawn to moisture, to dung or urine of any sort, how they decorated dung heaps and floated like showers of petals around the outhouses, I used to tease Sandhurst at the sight of any butterfly on manure: "There's your butterfly spirit."

Once, on a jungle trek, we came upon a corpse, the still intact body of a woman dead, most likely, of natural causes. While the men talked over what to do, I thought for one long mesmerizing moment that they were mistaken, that she was still alive. It wasn't just the graceful positioning of her limbs—the legs together and slightly bent at the kness, one arm across her middle, the other hand by her cheek—it was the drowsy fluttering of her eyelashes. But on cautious approach, for a closer look, I saw that slowly opening and shutting, opening and shutting over each eyeball were the wings of two dark butterflies.

Now it was Sandhurst, catching me startled, who teased. "Took you off guard, did it? The butterfly spirit?"

The butterfly spirit that hovered about me in America, that kept alighting and vanishing and realighting always somewhere nearby, came in the guise of a man called Rex.

I had first spotted him one summer afternoon during the Safe House days, on the roof of the house next door. We had been sitting out on our own roof patio, a sagging affair of warped planks and rotting planters where the boys carried out their experiments with tropical plants.

"What is that?" someone asked. The "that" in question was perched astride the ridge of the roof near the chimney, so still as to look like a scarecrow. Then it moved.

"Maybe it will slip and fall," said one of the boys hopefully—betraying the Dayan appetite for witnessing disaster.

"Oh, look, look—it's sliding. . . ."

Seeing us, the creature waved a twiggy arm—and slid down the chimney.

That was our first sighting of Rex. He turned out to be the fixer for our stretch of Sixteenth Street, a series of group houses shared by college students, Carmelites, Maryknolls, Sri Lankan Buddhists, Vietnamese Buddhists, American Sikhs, Orthodox Greeks, White Russians, Ukrainians, and Moonies. But we at the Safe House came to enjoy special status. Little by little he sought to educate us, helping us decipher maps and directions and bus schedules as we found our way around the city, leading us on walks through the parks, pointing out statues and landmarks and buildings, bringing used books and magazines and news clippings that might be of interest. In return we stuffed him with the usual gingery, garlicky Dayan dishes, whose potent fumes reached every corner of the house and out into the street before drifting back homeward to penetrate all bedding and clothing, where they permanently settled.

The boys dispersed in time to sponsors and jobs in far-flung parts of the country, and I was free to move to a place of my own, an apartment on Canal Road. Rex had disappeared some time ago, but one afternoon, I saw him near the Reservoir, crossing the street. I knew him at once, that spindly scarecrow with the ancient Gladstone and the oversize raincoat flapping and luffing like a sail. He still walked as though heading into strong winds, leaning forward with his head turned a little to one side.

But Rex, once an ageless sort, was ageless no longer. He had come from a job that left him covered with plaster dust, and the white hair and chalk skin gave him an air of having turned abruptly, abstractly old. His eyes were bloodshot and he smelled of stale alcohol and neglect.

"What have you been doing with yourself, Tango?" he asked, in a way that suggested I was showing my own signs of decline. What I had been doing since I'd seen him last was drifting: from job to job, home to home, man to man—unable always, in the end, to sustain the necessary interest or attention or compassion. I had learned to go through the motions with the minimum of soul-searching; I had mastered the sham of interviewing and putting the right foot forward—the foot required to meet the needs of the hour, for employment or companionship. *You want someone to clean? I can clean! You need a companion? I'm a good companion! A typist? I can type! And shorthand? That too! Am I capable of a warm, nourishing, intimate relationship? Of course I am!*

At the back of my mind was the excuse that all I was missing was a knack, a trick that would turn things around and shunt me onto the right path. At low points—at the desks of countless office cubicles, booths, and tellers, struggling to focus on the files and papers in front of me; by the beds and wheel-chairs of the old invalids I served as companion and read to; in my own bed at night, listening to the police sirens and hearing in those wails the hooting of gibbons; waking to rains that caused a dull ache of association, each and every time, with monsoons past—at such times I comforted myself with the prospect of that knack, that lucky break, which would lift me out of the circle of defeat.

The miracle that finally occurred—soon after my reunion with Rex, as it happened—was pregnancy. The accident beggared belief. After all those years of infertility—thanks first to Supremo's impotence, then later, with Boyan, to what I thought was the efficacy of papaya seed contraceptives!

After jail in Anika, of course, after the shooting, what need for any more worries about contraception?

What else to call it but The Shooting, even though not a bullet was fired, not a scar left as evidence—not a scratch, not a nick?

Did that stop me from wishing that someone, just once, would care enough to want to look? If only Lawrence had said, "Where did they hurt you, Tango? Open your legs, let me look, let me see." But how could poor Lawrence, even afraid of what my X ray might show, bring himself to peer into that dread cavity, to find what might be a sucking war wound?

He preferred to lie there on his back, with me squeezing his left hand helpfully while he masturbated with his right. "Shouldn't we be making love, Lawrence?" I used to ask, admittedly with less than raging desire. "This *is* making love, sweet," he'd say, eyes shut tight to conjure up who knows what fantasy—and his hand pumping away until the split second before he was ready to mount me. And then he wasn't one for lingering.

No, I wasn't worried any longer about conceiving. It

wasn't imaginable: the idea that something could take root and grow in a womb that's been shot at point-blank, even if the shots were empties.

But I was wrong. Miracle of miracles, I was wrong! Pregnant—and at age forty! The surprise of it, the sheer wonder of it, brought sensations I had never known. In sleep I dreamed literally heavenly dreams, wherein it seemed natural to find myself mooching about in the unfamiliar territory of clouds, aimless but not confused. Waking, I felt a prickle on my skin, a light in my eyes even before the lids were open, a tingle of well-being —those long-forgotten symptoms of hope. Throughout the day, now and then, without warning, I felt a sudden draft blow through my rib cage, followed by the flitter of many tiny wings.

That such a blessing could flow from so uninspiring a night.

The man responsible for this state was not someone important; I scarcely knew him. In the early hours of dawn, he had gotten up to prowl through the kitchen in search of food. After a while he came to stand over the bed.

"I'm hungry," he said. "Don't you have anything like crackers?"

"Not crackers, but other things," I offered.

"No crackers? What kind of place has no crackers?"

"A place like this."

He sank into a chair and brooded. "I don't know. I could never live like this." His eyes paced the room, making the small space seem even smaller. To conceal the long cement wall that ran the length of the apartment I had hung some printed bed sheets from a rod. The flaws in the design that marked them as seconds were suddenly glaring.

"You really want crackers, don't you?" I said. "Nothing else will do, will it?"

He shrugged.

"I'll tell you what I'll do," I said. "I'll get you some. I'll go to the Seven-Eleven right now."

"Well . . ." He hesitated, annoyed that so simple a craving had to involve complications.

"I'll go," I said, putting on my clothes and ignoring his halfhearted protests. It was dawn, the lights in the lampposts were still on, and nobody else was about. Alert to the dangers of that hour, I walked briskly toward the 7-Eleven, where the incurious Korean teenager behind the cash register rang up the four different boxes of crackers I had swept off the shelf.

Back at my place, I set the boxes on the table and sat across from him to watch him eat.

"Four boxes!" He whistled. "You didn't have to get four boxes! I just wanted a few crackers."

Nonetheless he sampled them all while I watched, saying nothing. Slowly it dawned on him that maybe something was wrong, that maybe my interest was not altogether benign.

"Well," he sighed at last, "I guess I just got really hungry."

"But you're satisfied now?"

"Yes."

"Then go."

"What do you mean?"

"I mean leave. Now. Just go."

"Am I missing something? I thought we had a great night. What's come over you?"

"I'll say it another way, then. I want you to leave."

"You're nuts," he said. "Nuts." But he gathered up his things and left.

He left me bent over with a cramp, a burning that no crackers would ease. It kept me from rushing out the door and calling down the street, "Wait! Don't go! Come back and tell me what to do about *my* hunger!"

I didn't of course do that simple thing. I didn't call out for help.

Not then. But some months later, when another kind of cramping started, then the bleeding that wouldn't let up, it was Rex I looked to for help.

Rex was the sort of friend who asked no questions—the only kind possible for me in those days. He made no demands for intimacy, no clamors for an exchange of confidences. He was kind, considerate, and secretive. Like a butterfly spirit he was gone one minute—always moving without a forwarding address, always referring to himself as his own zip code—and back again, with uncanny timing, when he was most needed.

Making one of his timely appearances that night, he leapt to drive me to the hospital in a borrowed car. In the dark it escaped me that he had been drinking. The doctor I was seeing was a former neighbor now practicing in Baltimore. The drive would take, at that hour, no more than forty minutes by the Beltway.

The pain was already coming in stabs as I climbed into the backseat of the ancient car, where I could stretch out if necessary. But less than halfway to the hospital, the cramping was so bad that I went from writhing to clawing the air just to breathe.

He began taking one wrong exit after another, swerving and doing U-turns to the outrage of blasting horns, muttering to himself a string of curses that might have made me laugh at another time. "Jesus! Black-hearted Christ!"

Disoriented by drink and badly rattled by my moans and cries, he was completely lost. How long we continued circling the Beltway I'll never know, but in the end he gave in to my pleadings to just go home.

The minute he turned into the driveway that led to my apartment building, the minute I saw the lamplights with their fake-candle bulbs, the pain subsided. It washed over and out of me in one rolling, receding wave. The cessation was so exquisite it left me trembling. I waited for the return of that dread tide but felt only little ripples of relief lapping through me.

Rex opened the back door to help me out. A few feet from the door to my apartment, I had to stand still and just let it occur. I felt it bearing down on me—a pressure, painless but irreversible. I felt it take shape between my legs with a kind of important deliberation. I felt the final gush, in a form that turned warm and solid and snug, to be cradled by the pad I was wearing.

Very slowly, very carefully, I moved inside, into the bathroom. In a shivering sweat, I removed the pad without looking and set it on the floor, under the sink. I was sweating at the thought, the suspicion, that the thing I had given birth to was not human. In my mind was an image of a stillborn cat.

I opened the door and went to my bedroom where I drew back the cover on the bed and got in.

Rex appeared after a while. "It's in there," I said. "I can't touch it, I can't look."

I heard him opening and shutting drawers and doors in the bathroom. Once more he appeared at the door, a lanky, courtly figure, half knight, half jester, twisting his cap in his hands.

"Rest, m'dear. I've taken care of—things."

I turned and faced the other way.

" 'Twill get better," I heard him say. "What wound did ever heal but by degrees?"

We kept in touch less frequently after that; then he disappeared altogether for another long stretch, for another episode in his ongoing butterfly act.

16

It wasn't till eight years later, when Rex realighted, that I began to see him regularly. We ended up working as a team—he as the subcontractor and handyman, I as the cleaning person—for rental properties in the Glover Park area. We got our hire as we went: I with my cleaning tools and solutions —the collapsible mop, wire brush, steel wool, putty knife, sponges, Spic and Span, Ajax, Pinesol, and WD-40; he with his array of tools and widgets and ratchets—some in the Gladstone, some in the red toolbox.

It was the longest stretch of steady employment I'd known in years. The partnership with Rex meant no job security, no benefits, no dependable routines; it also meant no more bosses and coworkers breathing down my neck day after day, no more contracts to sign and break over and over again, no more reminders of failure and enslavement. Day labor was only as bad as that day, in a matter of hours I could count on an end.

We'd meet in the mornings at the job site—a renovation or rental property, usually. I'd bring the sandwiches and the thermos of coffee; he'd bring his old KLH radio with the torn speaker grille and plug it in, for music and call-ins to work by.

Then we'd get down to work: Rex sawing, hammering, drilling, sanding, or painting—me scraping paint off windows and doors, taking a knife and scouring pad to grime and rust and grease, wiping down dusty surfaces, washing and waxing floors on hands and knees.

It took its toll, yes; it took the skin off my hands and clogged my throat with dust and was agony on the shoulders and back. But it was rewarding in its way, the thoughtless oblivion of the toil—the chipping away at a blob of dried paint or the rubbing at a stubborn stain so that all thoughts of past and future fell away and only the present—the paint blob, the stain—consumed the moment.

At the end of each day, in the space we had tackled, were the tangible, visible results of our labors: a freshly painted wall; the wood on windows or floors sanded down and stripped of old layers of varnish, paint, and stain; fridges, ovens, and stove tops scrubbed clean of crud and congealed grease; bookshelves now level after years of sagging; and trash bags all overflowing with the day's detritus—newspaper and wallpaper, old rags and stiff sponges, empty cans of paint and thinning solutions, lumps of plaster and piles of wood scraps and shavings and dust—all evidence, real evidence, that something had been done to make a difference to an empty space.

The day's work done, we'd go our separate ways—I to my musty basement apartment in one of those Canal Road row houses; he to wherever it was he spent the nights.

From empty houses we graduated to furnished spaces— servicing the interiors of Victorian and colonial mansions and luxury town houses. I continued to clean; Rex continued as handyman, but with a difference.

He now had keys. He had become not only fixer and subcontractor but occasional house sitter, too, with his own set of keys to every household. He could let himself in and out at any time—to attend to routine jobs or sudden crises, to relieve the owners from the nuisance of waiting for delivery or repair men to arrive, to water their plants and feed their pets while they were away. He also had the run of their liquor cabinets, the chief consequence for me being that I no longer had to wait for him to produce from his pocket the bottle wrapped in a brown paper bag before seeing him change from scarecrow to knight, with a looser, grander, more expansive air. He had a sly leprechaun smile to match that mood: "Catch me if you can and I'll lead you to a crock of gold."

The gold hinted at—or so I imagined—was a secret, a way of *not* belonging to the world as I found it, of renouncing its plenty. It was one thing to renounce, like a good Buddhist, the "plenty" of what life in Daya held—quite another to know how to renounce the material world of America, with its temptations and seductions that could never be resisted and never be fulfilled. Rex knew how to do it: to live with nothing, aim for nothing. He knew how not to belong—and, more and more, it seemed that not belonging was the right place for me to be. He led the life of a guerrilla—owning little, expecting little, always on the run. I understood that life. It spoke to my condition.

Anyway, he had style. He may have been homeless, but he wasn't one of those rag-and-bone figures camped out on the steps or thresholds of churches, surrounded by tattered bedrolls and scavenged belongings—or one of those bearded mountain men who huddle over the hot vapors of open grates and shake tin cups at passersby. He wasn't a park-bench regular who rummaged through the trash bins for meals or settled for a cardboard crate to sleep in.

I watched, I followed—from a distance at first—as he took his chances and spent his nights at houses to which he had keys. He stayed at times when he knew the owners to be away, when he was supposed to be feeding their pets, picking up their newspapers, setting their sprinkler systems in motion. . . .

Strange, how easy it was for me to make the leap from observer to accomplice, how one day I could say to myself in surprise, "So that's where he sleeps! That's how he stays off the streets!"—and, not long afterward, find myself accepting his invitation to "stay over."

So from time to time I stayed—Rex showing me to the best room or bed in the house, then graciously repairing to the second-best. He was the host and I his guest always: I left it to him to work out the safest times for arrival and departure— also whatever alibis might come into play. It was he who took pains to cover our tracks, who checked the wastebaskets for any foreign trash, the bathrooms for incriminating hairs, and the ashtrays for stray cigarette butts, who remembered the exact state of each bed—how it was made up or left unmade—before each use.

There was a difference, of course, in our actual circumstances. I was not technically homeless—just playing at it, becoming ever more willing, meanwhile, to stay away whenever I could from the increasingly unhomey place I called home.

The particulars of this reckless, hopeless stint in my life are not worth recalling. But I did make an extraordinary discovery. I discovered solace in the stolen contact with those invisible owners whose beds we slept in, and whose pots and pans we cooked with, and whose tables we sat at, and chairs we lounged on, and sinks we washed at.

Burying my face in those borrowed pillows, I found a most forbidden, most gentle intimacy. The human presence—so soothing in its absence! Despite the risks, despite the whole crazy business, I slept—and soundly too.

If Rex had remained the same, how much longer we might have gone on playing house in our sordid little way is anybody's guess. But he wasn't the same. Week by week I watched the downward spiral as he drank himself stupid. Week by week he was less reliable, less careful—and not just in matters of concealment and subterfuge (diluting liquor bottles, duplicating keys, faking repairs, fudging bills, concocting alibis, and so forth). He couldn't be trusted now on another point: he couldn't be counted on to leave the past—his and mine—alone.

This rankled more than the bright, bloodshot eyes, the bitter laugh, the memory lapses, the disconnected thoughts, the digressions, the stupors. Now came his maudlin return, again and again, to the distant days when he was a boy in Maine. Each time I had to hear it through from the beginning—all the charms of that idyll called Fiddlehead Island, where his family spent the summers: the early morning fog lifting over the dark-green banks of the other islands; the cry of sea gulls; the fishing boats and multicolored buoys; the mustard seaweed on the rocks along the shore; the glassy waters with shag carpets of mussels below; the pools in the pits of the quarry; the hikes through the woods along pine-needle footpaths; the wild berries and mushrooms; the seals and foxes and deer. . . .

Then the happy family: a father who taught school and read the Bible out loud for an evening's entertainment; a mother who sang at church, knew the names of every plant and flower and tree, and baked wonderful breads; their adored only child, the curly-haired Rex, who was given to wandering off for hours to collect stones and shells and butterflies—a trait the father warned him about, saying it might make him like the monk who went for a walk in the woods and was so distracted by the trill of a bird song that when he got back to the gates of the monastery he found that fifty years had gone by. . . .

It was usually about here that Rex choked up, seized by a memory—of the turning point, perhaps, when things went awry.

In the Mark Twain story about the old ram—a story Rex

had introduced me to in the Safe House days—the boys always wait for the man to get drunk before asking him to tell about his grandfather's old ram. The man starts out to tell the story, goes off on endless tangents, and of course never does finish the story.

Rex couldn't ever get to his old ram either. When he'd calmed himself after reaching the choke point, he'd turn to me expectantly as if to say, *Show me your past now that I've shown you mine.*

I can still see him, sitting across from me on the marble steps of some downtown edifice—one of those elaborate Pennsylvania Avenue buildings in whose landings and stairs and complex spaces we often took refuge at night.

"In the secret places of the stairs . . . ," I can hear him say, "let me see thy countenance, let me hear thy voice." (Why was it my luck, I wondered, to get mixed up with Bible-quoting men: first Sandhurst, then Rex?)

I see the flicker of his cigarette in the dark as he waits for some sign of weakening on my part. Then he invites again, more bluntly this time, "Well, m'dear? You have a story to tell?"

I was damned if I was going to tell it.

Our *Wanderjahr* came to an end on the night of the tango concert.

Rex had seen ads of the coming performance by the celebrated French-Argentine troupe Tango Heroico and, without telling me, had bought tickets.

I dreaded the event. I had become used to anonymity, to transparency, to passing people on the street who looked *through* me or *past* me, rarely *at* me—a strange myopia, I always thought, given that I felt so alien.

Once, taking a shortcut through Rock Creek Park, I came upon an apparition. Heavy rains had fallen most of that week, and as I crossed the Japanese bridge, I stopped to look down at the thick cocoa-colored current that had risen high enough to flood a stretch of road.

It was late afternoon in summer, the air heavy and humid and sour with the smell of fermenting leaves, the sun slanting down on the bamboo brake that ran along the footpath below. I was thinking of the village paths in Daya, bordered by tall bamboo brakes, thinking of the way the afternoon sun flecked their uppermost leaves, thinking of the same fermenting smells that rose after a monsoon rain . . . when it took shape in the distance. Walking up the footpath was a monk. A Buddhist monk, no less—saffron robe, begging bowl, and all.

A Buddhist monk near an old mill in Washington—how could that be? The closer he came, the more I was convinced that it wasn't just a Buddhist monk but a *Dayan* Buddhist monk. Yes! That dark lowland face with the flattened back of the head and the swollen lips.

I fidgeted in anticipation. But how slowly he was walk-ing—fairly dragging his feet, for some undiscernible reason. Why wouldn't he hurry? Surely he had seen me and was eager to meet.

At last he was at the foot of the bridge, looking up at me —not curiously at all, looking *through* me, rather—looking past a person on a bridge, an obstacle in his path. I stood aside to let him pass, struck dumb with sudden shame—shame first of all at having forgotten the formal language in which the laity must address the clergy. (What was the proper term for "walk" when directed to a monk, for example? Was it "progress"? "stride"? "amble"? Is Your Holiness enjoying his *progress/ stride/amble* today?) Shame also from crossing paths with a fellow vagabond from a land of common disgrace. Shame at having lost face in the worst sense: I was faceless now. Shame finally at owning up to who I had been and what I had since become. Irrawaddy Tango—what a laugh!

The monk went by, and I went hot with humiliation. I remained for a long time where I was, in the middle of the Japanese bridge, clutching the rail, bypassed by my own kind, my exile complete.

How to make the leap now from faceless nonentity to respectability—for an evening at the National Theater in Washington, D.C.? What to wear, how to act in public? And what to expect of Rex? Could he lay his hands on suitable clothes; could he remain sober; could he sit still in such closed, stiff quarters for that length of time?

We met at the theater, an odd couple if ever there was one: Rex in a suit—a most appalling suit (wide lapels, green and purple stripes, deep creases) with a most appalling smell (of which camphor and mildew were the milder components)— and I in one of my relics from Bangkok days, a long bottle-green number, cut like a caftan but stiff as a tent, on account of the inferior Thai silk. Edging the neckline was gold braid the seamstress had sewn on as an afterthought, to conceal a ragged join. I had bought, for this extraordinary occasion, twenty Indian brass bangles from a street vendor in Georgetown, at a dollar a pair. The man had thrown in the earrings free: brass hoops supporting a row of miniature sovereigns that jingled.

I knew it was all wrong the moment we walked into the theater and I saw what others were wearing. Too late it struck me that I must have missed some essential directive—fine print on the tickets, maybe—that everyone else had seen. They were dressed, all of them, in staid, muted colors—and even the fabrics had a harmony, a homogeneity to them. Clearly there had been prior discussion and agreement about the dress code.

The turning of heads as we walked down the aisle to our

seats was further confirmation that I not only looked but *sounded* wrong—thanks to the jangling earrings and the silk that chafed like crickets with every step I took.

Then the lights dimmed; the curtains parted. . . .

And I was someone else, somewhere else altogether. In a flare of lucidity, like a jolt out of a dream, I remembered who I really was and where I really belonged.

The orchestra floated center stage on a terraced platform: the piano on the highest tier, the strings on the tier below, and, down at stage level, the bandonions. The bandonions wailed; the violins swooped in; the musicians, all dressed in black and white, played against the backdrop of a red sky. . . .

There was a red sky on the night I'd last danced the tango, at the Monsoon Madness Ball back in Daya. The ball was an annual charity event; its theme that year was linked in some way with the moon.

It was a night of moons. The ballroom walls were festooned with huge iridescent cloth paintings of a red sky aswirl with star clusters, planets, comets, nebulae, the signs of the zodiac—and moons of every stage and size: full moons, crescent moons, gibbous moons, horned moons, satellite moons, and moons enclosing the outlines of rabbits and the profiles of hook-nosed men.

I sat at the head table facing the stage with my entourage for the evening: a trio of movie stars and their consorts; some senior SSO types. My husband the general had not seen fit to attend, but wasn't averse to my going. I was enjoying myself. After dinner came the variety show: no acrobatic animals or impaired zitherists here but spiffy American banjo players in straw hats and blackface, and European girls with bobbed hair, short tasseled dresses, and feather boas who sprang into a knock-kneed Charleston, singing "Five Foot Two, Eyes of Blue."

Then the stage was cleared and the guests were free to dance. As the band struck up, the committee chair, an Englishwoman,

*appeared at my side with a swarthy, silver-haired man in tow. I
thought at first he might be an Anglo, but then he kissed my hand
with authority—something no Anglo would have dared.*

*"Madame," said the Englishwoman. "May I introduce you?
Mr. Pereira—from Brazil. A marvelous dancer."*

Pereira bowed. "May I request the honor?"

*A signal must have gone out in the time it took to leave my
seat. The room went dark except for the colored lights sweeping
the bare dance floor; and the band was playing a tango. . . .*

"Softly as in a morning sunrise . . ."

And here was Pereira now, up on this stage—Pereira's
double, anyway, in the same tuxedo; a somewhat older and
stouter Pereira, but a better, much better dancer than before—
moving with an economy of means, with improbable grace. . . .

*Pereira at the Monsoon Madness Ball of the distant past took
my hand. Wait—did I even remember how it went? But I did.
Some things can never be unlearned; the tango was one. How it
all came surging back as Pereira and I cut a swath across the
dance floor—tentative at first, but only at first. How it all came
together: the reckless passion; the sweet collusion of the embrace;
the languor and the swagger; the backward plunges and forward
dips; the pauses in the tempo like the catch of a breath . . . and
through it all the flight—that giddy flight of the small white bird
swooping around—slow-QUICK-slow-slow—inside the cage of
one's breast, swooping to the tango's syncopation.*

*Pereira was no Carlos. He lacked that swing of the hip. And
turn of the heel. And bend of the knee. That small movement, so
unexpected but so right, which took your breath away. And I? I
too left much to be desired. The proper dress, for a start.*

*Ah, for the chintzy costume I had worn that fateful night—the
night of the talent competition—the sparkling bodice and the
riotous petticoat whipping about my knees! Oh, for the freedom
of stepping wide and kicking high! Instead—this sarong, this rich*

brocade affair: alluring, yes, expensive, yes, but unfit for the tango. . . .

Whereas up on this stage now, in Pereira Senior's arms, was the woman I might have been, in the dress I might have worn, a vision of sequins and silk and chiffon—silk for the backless top, chiffon panels for a skirt that fell open to reveal the shimmering stockings. Yes, that's the woman I would have been—the insolent seductress, temperamentally swooning and stamping her feet, kicking her leg head high one moment, hooking it around his waist the next; that languorous, smoldering beauty—*emitting* music and light.

. . . Round and round I sailed back at the ball in a pool of lovely tawdry light that changed from blue to green to red as the cellophane beams followed our course and the assorted moons spun through their painted orbits. . . .

I remembered the day Carlos taught me the tango—remembered waking that night, as I often did, to the remotest of music. Until then, hard as I tried, I never could crack the mystery of its origin. The sounds were so subtle as to die on the ear. That night I stepped out onto the veranda and stared in the direction of the river—the source, I thought, of those scarcely audible strains. All I could see puncturing the great blanket of darkness were the pinpricks of hurricane lamps flickering from the fishing boats. At last it dawned on me: it wasn't from the river or the banks beyond that the music was coming; it was from the sky itself, from the crackle and hum of all those stars warming the emptiness above.

"Go back to bed. You know what happens to stargazers," said a voice behind me—Thurani's voice. I knew all right. Mrs. Baba Sheen had read us the parable of Aesop's astronomer in class: the one so intent on stargazing that he fell into a well . . .

. . . Someone was tapping me on the back. Turning, I looked into the face of the man in the seat behind me—a coarse, simian face, with one long continuous eyebrow instead of two, and a big bully's mouth deliberately forming the words: *Would you quit moving your head!*

"Sorry!" I said, without thinking and faced forward again. Had I been moving my head? I must have been, I realized as I took in the fact that the woman in front of me had been obscuring my view of the stage by rubbernecking from time to time. The fault wasn't mine, then; she was the one to blame.

I shouldn't have apologized. Had I lost all my old spirit and edge? How eager I was to accept blame; how quick to be civil—an abject Dayan trait. I remembered a recent dispute with a bitter cabdriver who, as I got out, had said under his breath, "Cunt!"

"Yes?" I replied. I thought he'd called me "Aunt"—and so ready was I to accept appeasement that like a fool I turned and said, "Yes?"

Here I was once again, too quick to appease; too slow to take offense. What gave that ape behind me the right to object to the way I sat in my own seat—the seat I'd paid for? My skin began to crawl with the rash of an anger I hadn't known since the Safe House days.

I turned to look at Rex, who merely shook his head and raised his eyebrows to show he had witnessed the exchange. In the semidarkness the expression on his face came across as passive, tolerant, and weak. How I despised that look—the same hunted look I remembered from the night of the miscarriage when he'd blundered round the Beltway without getting me to the hospital. What sort of friend, what sort of companion, was he to let an insult like that go, without coming to my defense? Not even a glare in the offender's direction—not even a look.

I was keenly aware of a smell, suddenly—the smell of nervous sweat; *fear-sweat,* as it's called in Dayan. Rex was putting out a powerful odor of fear and cowardice—a hateful, intolerable odor. I thought I might get sick and got up to leave. Startled, he followed.

Outside the theater, in the fresh air, the nausea passed. It was an early fall night, with a crispness and definition to everything from the clear cobalt of the sky, to the decorative white lights blooming in the bare trees, down to the shed leaves crackling underfoot. The snap in the air suggested a mood of hope and expectation I recognized but did not share.

"Nothing," I said in answer to Rex's question about what was the matter. "I didn't feel well."

He had the sense to leave it at that and, sparing me further questions, followed alongside as I walked briskly, silently, down Pennsylvania Avenue. I had no destination in mind—only the impulse to keep walking. We came to the National Archives Building, and here, under the ponderous statues of the two Roman figures representing Past and Future, Rex made his first mistake.

"Study the past if you would divine the future," he read out loud; then, passing the second plaque, he intoned: "What is past is prologue."

Rex's habit of reading signs and notices out loud was not new to me, but in this instance it was a glaring affront. I decided to ignore it.

At Ninth Street, we turned up Constitution Avenue—and at the main entrance to the Department of Justice, looking up at the inscription above the door, he resumed the aggravation. "*Lege atque ordine omnia fiunt,*" he read, then, to make matters worse, translated. "By law and order all is accomplished."

I looked at him to see if he was teasing; he wasn't. He had recited the saying with sincerity and pride, without a trace of mockery. Did the man really believe such idiocy?

But why wouldn't he believe those empty inscriptions, carved into the façades of those lofty institutions we passed one after the other? They were meant for him, bequeathed to him, after all.

I had thought we were alike because we were both dispossessed, both drifters. But he wasn't really dispossessed—just pretending to be. Home was everywhere around him. The Archives, the Departments of Agriculture and Commerce and Justice, the streets we walked, the buildings we took shelter in, the statues and fountains in the parks where we sat—the Canova lions, the Proctor Tigers, the Cathedral gargoyles, the Anderson Sphinxes, the Henry Adams bronze, the Bernard Baruch Bench of Inspiration facing the White House on Lafayette Square—the White House itself . . . all of it belonged to him. All of it was part of his legacy. And all the time he was posing as a vagabond, an unsuccessful alien, like me.

"Take a break?" Rex said and stopped to sit on the stoop of the Gatehouse. We had come farther than I had realized—as far as the Ellipse. The park was deserted at that hour, and the traffic on the avenue had thinned.

He reached into the inside pocket of his jacket and brought out a pint-size bottle of bourbon. "Cheers," he said and knocked back a sip. I could see his eyes moisten as he dared to look at me now, from the distance the liquor had put between us.

Rex was still smiling when I lunged at him and wrested the bottle away. I flung it against the sandstone gate with such force that he ducked, then brushed bits of glass from his hair.

After he straightened out, he stood staring at the shards, shaking his head. His lower lip was quivering, but he affected a smile and a breezy tone, saying, "All that energy, m'dear. So unproductive, don't you think?"

Back in the Safe House days, referring to my tantrums, he used to tease, "Who is she that looketh forth as the morning, fair as the moon, clear as the sun, and terrible as an army with banners?" But he was the enemy now, and I was going to make sure he knew it.

"You sniveling drunk!" I screamed, baring my teeth in an uncontrollable grin. "You're a fraud! A fake! A liar!"

Standing and shrieking at him was not enough. I had to damage and destroy. I pulled the brass bangles off one arm and flung them at him, then wrenched them off the other arm and flung those too. I reached for my earrings, but they were gone. Crazed, I began plucking at the gold braid on my dress, shredding and ripping at the same time.

I was not screaming anymore, but stammering incoherently, as if between bouts of laughter. Laughing noises were coming from my throat now. "Run, run!" I chortled, as Rex turned and bolted. "Coward!"

The last I heard from him was the note he sent me: "I have done as you have done; that's what I can—*Coriolanus*."

17

Isolation breeds meanness, not generosity, and the more isolated I became, the more I sought to keep everything in, everything to myself. My experiences were exclusively mine.

But Americans were such vicarious experience seekers. Endlessly they appeared on television: men, women, and children in some significantly altered state, recalling some former trauma, predicting some catastrophe, stoutheartedly plunging back into the snake pits of memory in hopes of *experiencing* old cruelties and grievances and abuses—and *surviving* to tell the tale. To share, share, share. *Confessions* of experience; *strivings* for experience; *faith* in the power of experience to defang what frightens and heal what sickens.

A retired assistant secretary of labor told how under hypnosis he had returned to past incarnations of his life, the most vivid one being his career as a Roman centurion in A.D. 75, where he was present for the laying of the first lawn in Western civilization.

Another bureaucrat, the father of six, took two weeks off from his job as a lawyer with a government agency for an experiment in blindness. For fourteen days he wore special eye patches while he muddled and stumbled through as many daily rituals and activities as he could in his handicapped state —all for the *experience* of blindness. Animal welfare activists described the wretched *experience* of birds and beasts in farms, slaughterhouses, poultry-processing plants, research laboratories, zoos, carnivals, and pigeon shoots. Former skeptics *experienced* faith and spirituality as a result of a single seminar, and computer sophisticates applauded virtual reality, in which seeing was truly believing, truly *experiencing*.

I read about a woman, a devotee of the home-birthing movement, who planned things so that when her baby was born—at home, naturally—and the midwife had left, she could sauté and eat the placenta. Not such an outlandish practice, she insisted, when you considered that it was a powerful form of bonding, a fitting conclusion to the natural childbirth process, and a wonderful way to share the ritual of a family meal at birth—by consuming part of the birth. She was only too happy to share the recipe ("just a quick sauté in a little butter; I try to stay away from animal fats, so mostly I used PAM"); the accompaniments ("lima beans, for protein, a small green salad, and a Chianti"); and the taste ("really very mild, milder than liver or kidneys").

Call it a spiritual experience, she said of cannibalism. Yes, cannibalism. Not hostile cannibalism, of course, not the kind where you kill and eat slain enemies, but the loving, unthreatening kind. And even to call it cannibalism was not right. True, the placenta was human flesh, but it wasn't *part* of anyone, didn't *belong* to anyone—to the mother or the child—anymore.

To what end, this mania for experience? To explain it all away, it seemed. Not a single practice, a single facet of human behavior, was beyond explanation. There was nothing that couldn't be analyzed, rationalized, neutralized, and finally trivialized.

Every experience was given equal time, equal weight:
Holocaust survivors, torture victims, relatives of involuntarily
tattooed youngsters, mothers volunteering to act as surrogate
mothers for their own infertile daughters, single fathers suing
for paternity leave, grandparents accused of sodomizing their
grandchildren, single women angered by the fact that only
bimbos get dates.

Accompanying it all, the exhortation to feel, feel, feel.
What did it feel like then? How does it feel now? Allow
yourself to feel. All feelings are valid. Acknowledge the feelings. Above all, share every feeling, every little suspicion or
hint of a feeling. Leave no feeling unearthed, unfelt. Trust the
feeling. Feeling is all. All feelings—I once heard—are "on
schedule."

Since everyone, sooner or later, must divulge his feelings
in public, it was inevitable that even my fellow Dayans, that
most minor of minority groups in America, would have their
day on TV. What catapulted them into sudden fame was not
the most recent turbulence in Daya. That event, as luck would
have it, that spectacle of protest and massacre, was overtaken
by the more relevant, more absorbing spectacle of protest and
massacre in China.

What brought my compatriots into public view finally was
another disaster, far more newsworthy than anything the internal affairs of our country could have generated: the disappear-
ance of an American rock star in the wilderness of our northern
jungles. It became necessary to inquire into the nature of this
mysterious country that had swallowed without a trace the
famous rock musician whose concerts had done so much for
world peace. Where was Daya, and who were the Dayans
exactly?

Coming up next: a look at this forgotten land, through the
eyes of some exiles, living here in the United States.

The panel consisted of an American anthropologist from a

small college in Washington State, whose lifework had been among several of Daya's ethnic minorities, and three Dayans: an assistant professor of political science at a New England college; a Dayan-born Pakistani doctor, now resident in California and a pioneer in heart research (studying the benign effect of alliaceous foods on blood circulation); and Sonny. Yes, my own Sonny, the intellectual—now apparently a spokesman for something called FAD, or the Foundation for Asian Democracies.

It was the American anthropologist who dominated. He distilled; he inquired; he examined; he suggested. He had the grace to defer to his Dayan friends, allowing that they were of course better informed than he. The Dayans shook their heads *no, no!*—sincerely doubting that to be the case. They seemed mortified by his superior knowledge of their country and countrymen. Mortified and tongue-tied.

Then came the inevitable question—a question specifically for the Dayan guests. How did it *feel*, asked the interviewer, to have escaped from a country known for having one of the worst human rights records in the world?

The Dayans looked at one another and giggled anxiously. How did it feel? *Good!* said the doctor, at last. *Yes, good, good!* chimed in the other two eagerly, gratefully—until all three were nodding in agreement that it felt good indeed. "But!" said Sonny, injecting a somber note. "We have many problems, very difficult for people in Western world to understand, many problems in the Turd World."

"Although," said the political scientist, eager not to appear ungracious on network television, "we are of course very fortunate, very very fortunate to be neutralized, I mean naturalized, Americans."

There it was: the unintended truth—the testimony of a neutralized American.

Sonny's sister had been raped, then shot, during the upris-

ing; both his brother and his best friend had disappeared. Yet
here was Sonny, unable to get across the merest hint of his
experiences, able only to express solidarity with the Turd
World, his entire history neutralized, trivialized in one sound
bite.

It was this that scared me increasingly: the fear that one day
my turn would come; I would be called on to reveal my own
experience, to explore my feelings about it, then by naming and
sharing the feelings to defang and ultimately to degrade them.
The more I saw of growing trends—not just trends but whole
movements, whole belief systems—toward the confessing and
exorcising of experience, the more stubborn I grew in my own
belief that it was essential in some way I couldn't fully defend
to remain steadfast to my experience in all its shameful in-
humanity.

I didn't want to be rehabilitated; I didn't want to be healed.
I wasn't drawn to therapy to find out why I was wounded and
angry. I knew why I was wounded and angry; and it was my
right, in some way my salvation, to hold on to that wound, that
anger. I didn't want to be an activist or a born-again crusader
for human rights and other civil liberties or to go on the torture
circuit. I shuddered, turned sour in the stomach, at the thought
of taking part in the kinds of panels and roundtables and talk
shows on which survivors of the most exotic tortures from the
most repressive nations came forward to recount their or-
deals—all for a good cause, naturally. Even for a good cause,
I wanted no part of it. Even if the point was to educate the
humanitarian American public on inhuman practices in other
parts of the world. Even if the public could then get involved
by writing to their congressman or calling an 800 number to
pledge support.

A perfect example of one of those gabfests I so dreaded
appeared on a popular television talk show. The guests were a

group of women whose common bond was having survived various forms of state-sanctioned torture.

Faced with the open-ended question "What does torture mean to you?" the panelists begin to ramble. "It means," says one, "the loss of freedom and dignity and will, the loss of hope, the disappearances of innocent people." It means, says another, "the psychological torment of women separated from their children. . . ."

Here the host interrupts to steer them in the right direction. "What I'm asking is," she says, turning to the first of her guests, "exactly what was done to you?"

Stoically, the woman recounts the horrors: electrodes, beatings, and—this she mentions almost in passing—being raped by rats.

"Raped by rats? Excuse me, did I just hear you say raped by rats?" says the host a little dully, trying to find the right expression, the right intonation, to express such a horror.

But there are no right words, no right facial expressions, for the violations that follow, one upon another. In the end another guest is brought in, a specialist on torture, a medical doctor who has treated victims all over the world. The expert speaks in a peculiar monotone, as though he himself has had the screws put to him in some godforsaken Third World lockup.

"Doctor," says the interviewer, straightaway getting to the point, "you have seen—what?"

The doctor tells of the four-and-a-half-inch nail driven into the forehead of a victim in Southeast Asia, a nail that hit the back of his brain, robbed him of his speech, and paralyzed half his body.

But time, unfortunately, is running out, so the interviewer prompts the doctor about an atrocity too important to be missed.

"Uh, burned babies?" she reminds him.

"Burned babies? Oh, burned babies." What he meant by burned babies was not so much torture per se but the fact of babies being burned during the Gulf War. As a result of the embargo on propane gas, the use of kerosene had increased, resulting in the burnings. Perhaps it might be called *accidental* torture.

I was beginning to learn the nuances, the shades, the varieties of torture—not simply the garden variety kind practiced on political prisoners, but accidental torture, psychological torture, the tortures of sexual abuse.

Once, in a bookstore, I overheard the following conversation.

CUSTOMER: Do you have a book called *A Miracle, A Universe?*

PROPRIETOR: Don't think so; haven't heard of it. What's it about?

CUSTOMER (*lowering her voice*): About torture in Paraguay. Or maybe it's Uruguay. And Brazil, I think.

PROPRIETOR (*exultant*): Torture! Are you interested in the subject?

CUSTOMER (*still trying to keep her voice down*): Well, no, not really. Only for a project I'm working on.

PROPRIETOR: Oh? What project is that? See, I'm working on a torture project too. A personal project. I'll be honest with you. I was tortured as a child, by my father and uncle. They were part of a Masonic cult that sacrificed children in rituals? The rituals involved forcing the children to have sex with animals? I was one of those sacrifices. I'd blocked everything out until a few years ago. It all came back to me in therapy. Hypnosis. I confronted my father; he denied everything, but disowned me. I ask you why. I could tell you his name. A pillar of the community. You wouldn't think it possible. You can't tell, can you? Looking at me? That's the thing—you can't easily see someone else's pain.

I certainly couldn't see it. The young man stood up from behind the counter where he'd been sitting. I saw a softish, roundish, bespectacled face expressing nothing of the dark night of the soul, only the bland musings of a bookstore clerk. No, the pain of others was not easy to see, but hearing about it had become as unavoidable as the drone of mosquitoes in a swamp.

You couldn't turn on the radio or television without hearing about pain of one sort or another: chronic pain; psychic pain; self-inflicted pain; cosmic pain; thresholds of pain; past, present, and projected pain; pain doctors; pain clinics; veterans of pain. You couldn't ride a bus or train without the person in the next seat instantly regaling you with the most intimate causes of pain—operations survived, procedures endured, this organ lost, that organ revived—a veritable organ recital.

Standing in line once at a train station, I heard the man behind me let out a conversational sigh. No sooner had I turned around than he confided that this was his first vacation in ages ("donkeys' years" was the phrase he used) on account of his lover's long illness.

"He was in a lot of pain," he said, waiting for me to ask about the pain, about the nature of the illness. Cussedly, I refrained from asking.

"He died," he said finally, still hoping maybe for some kind of response, if not over the death at least over the gender.

"I'm sorry," I said, trying not to stare at his toupee, which was slightly askew.

"Yep, I'm still in a lot of pain," he said brightly, "but I've met someone special. A wonderful person. We're very happy. He's really a secure sort—not threatened at all by my past. Just really good about allowing me to grieve. Doesn't make a big deal out of it, but I know he feels my pain."

"That's very fortunate."

"Hey, I know how lucky I am. Of course there are tensions. Nothing serious, though, just the usual rough spots that people go through when they start living together."

From the speed with which the chiming lights over the available ticketing agents were coming on, I calculated at most a minute left to spare.

"Well, you know the thing about beds?" he said. "How one likes a hard mattress, the other likes a soft bed? I've always had to have a really firm mattress, and it has to be queen-size. *He* prefers coziness, a double. Well, we worked it out. I keep the firm queen. But I've had to bend too. Any love relationship is a two-way street, right? I have to put up with his dogs. Dogs! I mean, they're horses. But I love them because they're part of him.

"Although," he added, just as the light indicating my turn came on, "one of them is sick right now. Poor baby, she's in a lot of pain. And she's so big, so the pain is so—like—large."

"Four kinds of pain," I said over my shoulder.

"What's that?"

"You just described four kinds of pain," I found myself muttering at the ticket counter, when he was out of earshot.

Something was happening to me in that once-tender region of the heart. The crust of the old days, the occasional crust, the hardening and cooling that would build up but then peel off before forming again, was now an insulation, a shield of calluses. Compassion was a state I had to talk myself into feeling—especially compassion for the wounded. I had lost the instinct for pity.

I once sat among total strangers, in a drafty room above a church in Georgetown, listening to the serial confessions of men and women trying to overcome addictions and demons of various kinds. One by one they took their turn at the podium to recount their failures and triumphs, the difficulties met, the progress made, since the last meeting. Out came the life histories, the grueling intimacies, all compressed into orderly five-minute segments—all claiming equal time, given equal weight.

Midway in this parade came a middle-aged woman who told of how good she was feeling, having swum earlier that morning in the Chesapeake Bay and written a long epic poem besides. She did exude contentment, with her wide smile, her flushed, freckled cheeks, her buoyant red hair.

What was so good about feeling so good, she said, was realizing that it was a year to the day on which she'd killed her father, the father who had sodomized her when she was two. *Only a year!* she had said to herself that morning in the bay. How far she had come in that year. How much healing had taken place. She still had bad days of course, but that was okay, she knew that too: she could allow herself now to have bad days. But the swim, the poem—how good it all felt. That morning she was at one with the universe.

At one with the universe! What universe was that? The universe of soul barers? But I was envious. Envious of her story in which the crime was so clear, the revenge so complete, the healing so swift—Daddy was a dirty bugger, so Daddy deserved to die, and look at me a year later, writing poetry!

How would I tell my own story? What words to supplement that limited vocabulary of feeling? Which wounds to reveal? Exposed, flaunted, aired out like the rest, would they too become as banal as the rest? What would I be then but just another recovering victim? The wounds I had were not closed, not bound up, not mollified by ointment, as the Bible would have it. They were important to me, unique to me, and I was afraid of what I might become on being healed.

I didn't want to become what Thurani had become. It was Thurani who had taken me to the meeting, on one of her visits to Washington. In New York, where she'd been living for the past twelve years, she attended such meetings several times a week. They'd helped her come to terms with a lot of anger. She'd had so much anger.

Thurani had been twice divorced, but the anger she was referring to was unrelated to bad marriages. "I was denied my roots," she said. "First because Daddy dragged me all over the world. Then"—she put her hand over mine to soften the blow—"then we couldn't go home because of you, Tango, because we were related to you. This made me persona non grata. I'm not trying to make you feel guilty. But the fact is I'm an outcast. My heritage . . ."

"But Thurani! I thought you hated living in Daya. Small-town mentality!"

"You don't forget anything, do you? What did I know then? I was a princess; the world was my oyster. Things looked different. Don't you feel sentimental about home? I mean, as terrible as things are, it's still our birthplace. This uprooted life has been so hard."

I wondered which life she meant. Her first husband, the Dayan diplomat with the scarred lip, had turned out, she said, to be a weak philanderer. During their very first posting to the embassy in Bonn, he had rekindled an old affair with a Dutch woman, a secretary at the Netherlands legation. A coarse woman with hairy legs and unshaven armpits, trying to look young in flouncy floral dresses. Mutton dressed as lamb.

Scarcely a year after the divorce, Thurani had married Gavin, on the rebound. Gavin was a young Canadian mining engineer from Vancouver. The mistake was instantly magnified upon returning to live in Canada. Apart from some good Chinese restaurants, the region had so little to recommend it. She felt trapped in an unbelievably dull life; Gavin himself turned out to be such an unbelievably dull fellow. Decent, yes. He did the laundry, the dishes, even the weekend shopping. But his idea of fun was fishing. That, and taking pointlessly long walks in foul weather. She didn't mean to bad-mouth him, because he really was a considerate sort, Gavin, always ready to give the other person the benefit of the doubt. Like the time she accused him of stinking up the bedroom.

"We'd been away on a trip somewhere. We came home late at night and went straight to bed, but I couldn't go to sleep; I kept tossing and turning. After a while I couldn't stand it. I just had to tell him. 'Gavin,' I said, 'I hate to tell you this, but your butt smells.' Of course I did, Tango. I had to tell him. It was bothering me so much I couldn't go to sleep. But I don't think he thought I was serious. He just laughed and blushed and said, 'Oh, Thurani!' He blushed so easily."

"I don't know, Thurani," I said. "I don't blush that easily, but I think I might if someone told me my butt smelled."

"But it was true. I had to let him know. When he finally realized I wasn't kidding, he was quite nice about it. He just reached down and pulled the sheets up, to cover himself. 'Thanks, baby,' I said, and turned around to go to sleep. But you know what? It was still there—the smell. So I had to tell him again. He was half-asleep by then, and sort of grumbled, but he did reach for his undershorts and pulled them on quickly. Then he got back under the sheet again. I guess he thought that would be the end of things. But I tell you, it got worse. I didn't know what to do. A bad smell is not something you can block out, like the light. You can put a pillow over your eyes, but you can't clamp your nose shut when you're trying to sleep. I woke him finally. 'Gavin,' I said. 'I'm really sorry, but your butt really smells. I'm getting a terrible headache from it; I can't sleep.'

'Oh for God's sake, Rani' was all he said, shaking his head as if he couldn't believe it. He got up, went to the bathroom, and washed. Then he came back into the room, put on a pair of fresh undershorts, got back into bed, and went to sleep.

"So now he's done everything he can do; he's sleeping like a baby; and guess what? The smell's still there. And I'm beginning to feel sick. So I turn on the bedside light and get up . . . and there on the table next to me is a glass of awful, rancid, curdled orange juice. It must have been there all that time we were away. It was foul. That was where the smell came from.

"The thing is, though—and here's my point about Gavin—he was willing to give me the benefit of the doubt. He never insisted he was in the right. Quite a rare thing in a man."

I thought about Lawrence and how unlikely it would have been for him to entertain in the first place the idea that anyone might find his smell offensive. Lawrence was very tolerant of his natural attributes, good or bad. He used to sniff his armpits approvingly and say, "I seem to be putting out a musk," when someone else would have said, "I stink." He was unapologetic even in the most compromising situations.

I remembered the day in Bangkok when Nit, our cleaning girl, quit in a huff. Nit was a hard worker. She had a crew cut, a blunt, canny face, and wore black Bermuda shorts that set off her lumpy knees.

"I look like girl," she said to me the first time we met, making a quick sign of the cross over her breasts, "but inside"—she patted her heart—"I feel like boy."

"What an earth mover!" said Lawrence admiringly as he watched her scrub the floor on her hands and knees with a ferocity that I myself thought was uncalled for. The admiration was not mutual. I noticed that Nit's eyes would narrow whenever she inquired if Mither Lawrence—Mither, as she called him for short—was going to be home for dinner.

She waited for Lawrence to leave before bursting into my

room one morning. "Too much work!" she shouted. "Too much cook, too much clean!"

Looking around for evidence, she swooped up one of Lawrence's shoes and shook it at me. "So many chews for chining!" Suddenly, her mood turned. Buoyed by her imminent freedom, perhaps, she burst into good-natured laughter as she disclosed the final straw. "Mither!" She chuckled, pointing to the laundry basket. "All a time Mither leave chit in chorts!"

"Nit's gone," I told Lawrence that evening.

"Gone?! Why?"

"She said she was fed up with finding chit in your chorts."

"What?!"

"Dirty underwear."

"Oh, skid marks!" he said, smiling sweetly, recalling a talent, not a failing.

"What are you smiling about, Tango?" Thurani was saying.

"About the past."

Thurani's look softened. "I'm glad there are still things to smile about in our past. Aren't you? God, you especially—the tough times you've been through."

We were at Union Station, waiting for Thurani to board her train back to New York. Thurani looked at her watch, then up at the schedule board, and back at her watch again, making some kind of calculation. Then she turned around in her chair to face me squarely.

"I don't know anything about your time in jail," she said. "I haven't asked, not because I don't want to know. It's just that . . . I hope you don't take this in the wrong way, Tango, but . . . you're not the easiest person in the world to reach. You listen, but you give back nothing. You were so hard to figure out, even when you were little."

When I was little, it was Thurani who had seemed so full of mysteries to me. She suggested mysteries of adulthood, secrets of other worlds beyond Daya. It was Thurani who had opened the first door for me, the door that let Potential in. I hung on to her every word, observed her every mannerism. It was hard to connect that consuming influence with the middle-aged woman sitting across from me now, a gaunt, graying woman in an unnecessarily severe suit with exaggerated shoulder pads.

"You were so tough. Remember we called you Mew? You acted like a cat. Attached to no one. Attached to nothing. You didn't seem to care if you lost things. You'll forgive me, but you didn't seem to care one little bit about your mother leaving, for instance. It had to be so sad for you, Tango. We felt for you. Remember I came back to visit during that time? All you could think about was going to Anika for that tango competition. There was your father, confused and heartbroken. He didn't know how he'd failed your mother, what he'd done wrong. It was so sudden, her decision to go and cut herself off from the world. So extreme. I think your father was very hurt that you didn't let everything drop, that you just went ahead with your plans, as if you didn't care. He cried, you know, when you were off dancing in Municipal Hall, or wherever the show was."

"My father was a very stupid man," I said, and felt a curious satisfaction at giving voice at last to a frightening suspicion that had been with me all throughout my childhood—a suspicion I always knew was not in my best interests to have confirmed, just as I sensed it wasn't a good idea to try to prove that God did not exist.

Thurani looked shocked. "Don't say things like that about my uncle," she said, as if the relationship to her made him immune to stupidity. *"Mon Dieu,* Tango! You are hard as nails."

. . .

Thurani had urged me to attend the demonstration. I didn't attend, but I went to watch. It was just another political demonstration—one more disaffected group of Third World exiles venting its obscure frustrations. A common occurrence in Washington, where activists milled about the entrances of their respective embassies, waving their homemade placards.

Here was another one of those embassy rallies. DEMOCRACY FOR DAYA. DOWN WITH THE MILITARY. STOP HUMAN RIGHTS ABUSES. DOWN WITH THE REIGN OF TERROR.

From my strategic post—a bus stand with tinted Plexiglas panels for walls—I could watch, unobserved, the goings-on across the street and listen to the silly catechism blaring through the megaphones (*Who wants democracy? We want democracy! Who wants it now? We want it now! Who condemns brutality? We condemn* . . . et cetera).

The farce of crisis diplomacy, Dayan style: One of the demonstrators jog-trots up the front steps of the embassy and rings the doorbell. In a darkened window on the second floor, the vertical blinds part for a quick peek. The doorbell ringer turns to his colleagues below, shrugs self-consciously, sticks a sheaf of papers—some ultimatum or manifesto—through the mail slot in the front door . . . then trips back down the steps to rejoin the protest.

The papers disappear through the slot, onto the other side of the door—and reappear in the same slot some thirty minutes later. A polite return of unsolicited mail—after faxing to the home office in Anika, presumably.

I want no part of it. What part could I possibly come forward to play in my sorry state? What ties might bind me to the misfortunes of that wretched country at this late date? I'm hiding because I feel degraded, and not just by my own condition. I'm downright ashamed to claim any kinship with my fellow exiles. To follow their plight is a matter of personal disgrace to me.

The infrequent headlines describing the crackdown in Daya; the sporadic pictures and film footage of the shootings and beatings; the statistics and acronyms describing the bleak state of the economy—Daya, that once bountiful nation, now a less developed country, an LDC, with an abysmal GNP and so forth—these aren't the causes of shame particularly. And why should I be humiliated by how useless Daya has become, how irrelevant to the rest of the world? Why should it reflect on me that every other revolution, every other bid for freedom—Tiananmen Square, Wenceslas Square—seem to draw sympathy, but not the one tearing up that stagnant little backwater, the *Eldorado banal,* known as the Republic of Daya?

What shames me is a sickness, an infirmity that cripples us—all of us Dayans—as a race. What others find unbearable we go on bearing; what prods others to action puts us to sleep. All because of a fatal flaw, a blend of grandiosity and lethargy. *We're superior, we Dayans: better than others; what can the others teach us? So, yes, we're on hard times, dreadful times, but why bestir ourselves? Why not just sit back and wait till the tide turns and brings us the recognition, the respect, the good fortune, that are part of our birthright? Let's just dream a little meanwhile and go on hatching our grand plans for those better times to come.*

Buddhism! say the Western experts, trying to account for the long-suffering inaction of Buddhists—and forgetting, no doubt, the levels of violence achieved by disappointed Buddhists throughout Asian history.

But all I could see from afar as the country went under was a kind of insect behavior, the mindless instinct of an entire population to follow one another in a never-ending circle, plodding on without letup, accursed though the path might be.

In one of the safe houses I occupied in my jungle days, I spent a week with nothing better to do than observe a large potted plant for hours at a time. I watched a column of black caterpillars climb into the pot. Following their leader, the insects had reached the rim and were making an endless circuit round and round the lip. Not for minutes, not for hours, but for days they circled that pot, unable to break out of their roundabout, even after collapsing periodically; even after—at long last—one member would actually strike out on its own.

In the end every adventurer returned to fall back in step with the column. And on went the march—an endless looping of the loop by witless troops who'd lost their leader but were simply unable to abandon their path.

No, there was no one—not a leader, not a martyr, not a crackpot—not one miserable soul, to stop him. Him, the Supremo, the architect of misery. Help was not forthcoming from any quarter as far as this eye could see—not from outside, not from inside the borders. Not from the only other men with the guns—those eternally bickering separatist groups (yes, my Jesu included), who couldn't set aside their petty quarrels long enough to gang up on him for the ultimate kick in the head.

Then suddenly, out of the past, out of the blue, came the visitation. He sent his men to find me—and they actually did. Amazing. They weren't exactly swift in the field, my compatriots, at least not when operating on foreign soil.

To see them in action—those State Security Office types working out of the Dayan embassy in Washington, D.C.— you'd think it was their first time abroad.

I overheard a story about Dayan diplomats once. Quite by accident, in a Foggy Bottom park where World Bank and IMF types took their lunch breaks on summer days. Someone on the bench next to mine—a dapper Latino—was describing to his friends a dinner party at the Dayan embassy he'd had the misfortune to attend. What a farce of an evening! The mismatched guests, waiting for a full hour and a half—waiting and nursing their whiskeys and trying to ignore the peeling paint and ragged furniture of the salon—before the host appeared. Then the food! Served in plastic bowls! And labeled—yes, labeled! With little flags stuck into the middle of each dish— like houseplants sold at the florist's. CHICKEN CURRY, MILDLY HOT, et cetera.

It was from this selfsame embassy that the emissaries came, bearing their implausible request, a proposition only a Dayan would entertain.

They began by invoking the all-knowing Board of Astrology. The Board of Astrology had made a momentous forecast. It had cast the prediction that the reign of the Lion was ending.

But the gods were on the side of the Lion. The astrologers themselves had revealed the antidote. The first and best remedy, naturally, would be that sacred elixir of immortality. The age-old brew so sought after by our grand monarchs since immemorial times. Not an easy commodity to secure, however. Who could forget the great kings that had tried?

The alternative cure was where I came in. The cure would be a reunion. A reconciliation between the Lion and the first woman sanctioned to receive his sacred life milk. Put plainly, the first woman on whom he had legitimately spilt his seed.

That woman of course was me.

Would I return to Daya, then? Would I accept the Supremo's most humble and heartfelt request to return—and bestow upon him my compassion, thus freeing him from the fate forecast by the Board of Astrology?

In return: anything my heart desired. Money, serious sums of money; jewelry, any amount of it; a house of my own, an independent life, if I wished; properties and holdings and bank accounts abroad; public announcements reinstating me as first lady of the land and clearing my tarnished name; legal contracts; safeguards for the future; a Rolex . . . anything I wanted within the realm of the possible would be mine for the asking. All he required was my return.

How to refuse such an offer—how to resist him, the man whom no one, nothing, had been able to stop? The man who, on a whim, could turn a nickname (Supremo) into a self-conferred title. The man who went on doing his will and having his way with an entire nation, on and on, day after day, decade after decade. With utter impunity. The Supremo. The People's Patriarch. The Universal Monarch.

How could I ignore this siren song—the chance to see the beast close up, to step through the barbed wire and into the Lion's den once more, to come face-to-face with one of the last great deluded tyrants?

The walls of our famous Imperial Palace, now of course in ruins, had gone up under the aegis of a king who had hand-picked human sacrifices for burial in auspicious spots along the foundation—one at each corner of the fortress, three buried alive under each gate house, four more under the Lion Throne. Calculations all endorsed, naturally, by the Board of Astrology.

Our rulers have always been prone to the madness of numbers, obsessed by numerology. The superstitions go back to that fear-crazed king in the Third Dynasty who, frantic to find the immortal elixir, tried to follow the imperial quack's recipe.

The ingredients called for included two thousand hearts of white doves, four thousand hearts of white cows, and six thousand human hearts. The doves and cows could be procured without too much difficulty. The human hearts, however—in those numbers, especially—required drastic measures, claiming what may have been the first wave of "disappeareds" in history.

That old numbers game was still going on. Supremo, it was said, had ordered the latest demonetization, the one that had caused such chaos, not as monetary strategy but simply in order to create bank notes in "luckier" denominations.

Numerology was only a part of the dementia. There had been reports of weird sightings. He had been seen dressed in the costume of King Maha Bala. He had ordered elaborate custom-made coffins built in shapes representing his special interests: one in the shape of a lion, one in the shape of a Mercedes-Benz, one in the shape of a golf cart. He had engaged an elite corps of "hearers" to infiltrate the streets. These hearers were not common spies but trained eavesdroppers who specialized in picking up chance remarks about the state of the nation, genuinely inadvertent comments, made by persons in the street. Such remarks about the state of the nation usually came from those least ruled by rational thought—women, children, and artists, generally—so it was to these types that the hearers paid particular attention.

He was sending out hearers. He was drugging his soldiers. He was planning his immortality. Those were only some of the legends surrounding my old flame, my universal hero.

Even if none of it were true, even if the whole byzantine story of the forecast and the remedy was nothing but a ruse, a last gasp of lingering revenge, what difference did it make?

Suppose all *he* wanted was to lure me back into his clutches for other reasons and subject me to some unspeakable end? The end I was coming to in my sorry existence in America was not much more speakable anyway.

18

At last, the dates have been set. I'm near enough the end now that I welcome this news. No need for further delay.

The dates have been set: first the elections, then the trial—the trial later, so as not to skew the elections. And what of the chance of things happening in reverse? Suppose the election results affect the outcome of my trial; what then? Either way, I fear my fate's as good as sealed. Whatever happens, whoever wins. If the army stays, the firing squad may be among the more merciful ends in sight for me.

You'd think the firing squad wouldn't be the worst way to go—less awful somehow than being snuffed out in the bowels of the state security system. In the intro room, for instance, where the line between accident and intent is all too thin. The IOs get a little carried away, say. Just one outburst of temper or zeal—one extra blow across the back of the neck, one incremental surge from the black box they call Dynamo—and snap goes the thread. The thin thread connecting the victim with the living.

I've been there. Watching it happen right in front of me. Forced to watch, if that excuses me. A few feet from where you sit, trussed to your chair, a body writhes, then goes limp under the beatings. (They'll use anything close at hand to do the job—sticks, canes, truncheons, rifle butts, ropes, pipes . . . I saw them use a shiny metal pipe once, a thing with buttons and stops, some sort of wind instrument.) You watch until someone says, "He's had it!" Only then—when they've taken the pulse and called in the body disposers, do you grasp what's happened. But the sense gets keener in time. You know it's over before they say "He's had it!" A twinge, that's all you feel—a slight tug on the invisible thread connecting you with the victim, before it snaps at his end.

And now you're coarsened enough to notice the looks on their faces—the almost sheepish look of the man who's been wielding the lethal wind instrument; the sympathetic head shaking from his colleague who gives him a slap on the back. One team member consoling another over a flub on a game field. You're able to look on as they try to diffuse the tension by lighting up and wisecracking.

"Man, what a temper! Did you have to be so rough?"

"The animal was a corpse before I started."

"No, you're good at this. Really. Your peasant training, what? Beating buffalo on the back day after day?"

Give me the firing squad any day. If it's real, that is. If it's both final and swift. If it isn't just a mock execution. Those dress rehearsals do take a toll. Who can forget the first time in the yard? Me, I dropped to my knees. Voluntarily.

I heard someone requesting an adjustment. "Six feet," I heard him say to the presence behind me (the man whose job, I think, was to keep me from falling over), "give me six feet." A baby began to scream. A burst of machine-gun fire put out the noise entirely, and I thought, Good God, they've shot the baby!

It wasn't a baby they'd shot; it was the man who'd been kneeling ahead of me. Imagine: until that moment I'd failed to take him in. Talk about blinding fear! He was down now, on his side, a blossom of blood on his temple; his face was turned toward me. Such a weak, stupid face! It made me want to laugh; I felt a sort of laugh come on, a sudden loosening of the gut, the gush of something warm and wet through the seat of my pants.

"Just doing you a favor, comrade," said the voice that had asked for six feet. "A little practice to toughen you up."

Shaking with gratitude, with immense gratitude, I thanked him. Because now I knew what it was like. One more lesson learned; one more bridge crossed. The next time, I thought, the fear won't—can't—be as bad.

But I was speaking of the elections. Suppose for once the battle is not to the strong; suppose the army loses out and the opposition wins?

Then they'll still have to prosecute me. A show of reform from the new order will require a show of new respect for the law. They'll have no choice but to nail me. Never mind my service to the state. Even though, in the words of Othello, "I have done the state some service, and they know't."

I could be acquitted, of course. There's always that speck of a chance. But why fool myself? They'll find me guilty, turn me into the burnt offering needed at a time like this. It's all in the books, from the beginning of time.

Time is running out, thank God. I'm tired. And grateful for the excuse not to dwell on what it was like in that room near the lion house, the crushing tedium of waiting for news, for a message or signal that the Grand Reunion was imminent; of waiting with perfect uncertainty about what might happen and where.

I'll go back then to the day itself. To the event itself. Not the event of our first meeting following my homecoming—which was formal and stilted and brief, an appearance put in for a minor state guest—but our last, our real union. I'll finish my story.

He came to my room—the one they'd transferred me to just the night before, a room in a bunker (what could be safer?), a room thoroughly scoured and stripped of all but a few pieces of furniture; he came to *this* room.

There was a gross logic to the furnishings. Every item was to serve a purpose, and the purpose was only too clear. The room had the heartless look of a stage boudoir. A king-size Scandinavian-style bed dominated. On it was a paisley spread, machine quilted, which gave off that smothering dried-flower odor of new nylon. The black swivel chair with the ottoman was also new, to tell by the smell and feel of the vinyl. Likewise the almirah with the crude gilt carvings and the matching dressing table with its conspicuously missing mirror. Even the Chinese clock, though handless, I suspected was new.

In a corner of the room was the water supply—not in an earthenware jug, as in the old room, but in a metal thermos now. This one too sat on a stool, under which was the usual chamber pot cum spittoon, stenciled in the Chinese fashion, with ultramarine flowers. In another corner, on the floor, was a rotating black fan.

He got rid of every last one of them in the end, officials and bodyguards, and gave the final "Do not disturb" order that would leave us alone for the night.

He sat on the swivel chair; I sat on the bed. I felt something of the anticipation I remembered from those outdoor theater events of my childhood, when I'd found my little spot of ground among the crowds to set my mat on and could settle down cross-legged for the excitement in store.

I waited now for entertainment of another sort, exactly what sort, I couldn't have said. I knew only that I was obscurely pleased. I could barely stifle a smirk as I watched him edge forward in the swivel chair, leaning over to hook a finger or squeeze a fist in front of him from time to time like some old bedridden butterfly catcher as he reminisced.

He stood up suddenly—as suddenly as a man his age can, pressing down hard on his knees with the heels of his palms and rocking forward and backward once, twice, thrice, for propulsion. Maybe he meant to pace, but the room didn't invite pacing, what with the big king-size bed taking up so much space.

He lowered himself back into the chair. I had the craziest urge to lean over and spin the chair with all my might, just for the fun of seeing him whirl like a dervish out of control for a minute, of seeing his hair—what was left of it—stand on end.

"What's the main point?" he asked. Where had I heard that before? On our wedding night, for a start. (The main point then, as I recalled, was that I was his wife.) "The main point," he answered himself, "is that I spent my whole life cleaning up this country."

So he was still worrying at the main points and totting up the merits in his favor, after all this time. Now I heard it once again, that singsong of boast and harangue so beloved of tyrants still craving approval. The selfless career thwarted by the selfish and small-minded! The good intentions aborted by the filthy legacy of colonialism and capitalism! The economic miracle he could have wrought! The public works he set out to build! The roads, the bridges, the dams, the irrigation canals, the miracle rice projects, the great hydroelectric plant . . . all delayed because of the cleaning up, the endless, thankless flushing out and cleaning up of the muck and rot that had eaten through the flesh and fiber of the nation like maggots spoiling meat. But now at last he'd brought an end to corruption and decay; he'd made the country whole and clean once more. He was ready to build now. Look, he'd already started building: take the pagodas. What other ruler of a Buddhist nation had built so many in this century? And industry! Industry was on the upswing now. The foreign companies were coming in droves, prepared to pay any price for Daya's great wealth, for oil rights, mineral rights, fishing rights, logging rights. The Americans, the Canadians, the Germans, the Japanese, the Thai, the Koreans, all salivating . . .

I let him go on unreeling his long, tangled revisions of the past while my mind wandered. I was only half listening as he shot out his questions. *Who do you think saved the nation from anarchy? Who do you think gave our people some self-respect? Who do you think taught them how to stand on their own feet? Who?*

Misreading my blank stare, he decided suddenly to enlighten me. "Me!" he shouted, stabbing his chest with his thumb. "Me-me-me-me-me!"

Yet when the tumult outside began, he was the first to hear it. "What's that?" he said, suddenly alert to the present.

It was no more disturbing at first than the roar of surf on a distant shore. But wave by wave the roar encroached. A tide was coming in, a swelling, seething tide of voices rising and falling: a *chant-chant-chant* and *SHOUT* repeated over and over, louder and louder, joined in its crescendo at last by a different sound altogether, a sound like the drumming—could it be that famous drumming?—of pots and pans.

They'd banged on pots and pans during the last upheaval—the one ending in the so-called Massacre of a Thousand. What began as a gesture of solidarity, by the housewives of a single city ward all banging their aluminum pots and pans, had spread into a spontaneous citywide jamboree.

What dissonant music we make, I thought. Even in moments of high national purpose, we seemed to achieve only those tinniest noises. When the walls came down in Eastern Europe, the masses in Czechoslovakia's Wenceslas Square held up bunches of keys and jingled them in unison. It must have sounded like the tintinnabulation of a million triangles and celestas.

Ours was the clamor of kitchen implements. But it was growing; the strain was mounting; something had to give.

It came in a tearing blast, a ripping of a mammoth membrane.

The shooting began: cracks, whistles, and pops, a familiar chatter of gunfire, of long and short bursts, a conversation in code.

Supremo had a white-knuckled grip on the arm of his chair. But his knuckles weren't white; they were a livid mess of age blotches. Those little hands in their clutch of fear—so frail, so stained, so smashable now. But he was smiling.

"Listen to those firecrackers!" he said with a snort of feigned humor, even as he jumped as though zapped from an explosion or two. "What, is it Chinese New Year?"

How long the firecrackers went on, I couldn't say exactly. We sat very still—he in his swivel chair that wasn't at the moment swiveling a hair, I at the edge of my outsize, outlandish bed—listening but not looking at each other.

The cross fire ceased. Another silence; then the caterwauling and the banging again. On and on it went, more strident now. More monotonous too. Supremo hadn't moved in his seat. To my surprise, his cheeks were wet with tears. "They're singing my song," he said, his face in a helpless contortion. " 'The Victory Song.' "

He was right. The pots and pans hadn't let up, but the chants had indeed yielded to that rousing wartime ballad of the independence heroes—"The Victory Song." No mistaking the familiar "Mack the Knife" harmonies. "We sang that song when independence was still a dream," Supremo was saying. "We sang it to fight seasickness on the boat coming back from Japan. It was my song."

Except for the tears, he seemed oddly composed as he leaned back a little in his seat, in line with its tilt, his head on the bulge of the headrest, his grip on the arms of the chair.

I watched him dispassionately. The old patriot in a wallow of sentiment. He might have been a fish in a glass bowl or a toad on a log. At last he heaved a deep, ragged breath and turned to look at me. "They'll feed me to the dogs, Tango," he said with an almost wistful smile. So it wasn't the past he was weeping over. It was the future. I wondered if he had a handkerchief. His snuffling was grating on me. I had half a mind to reach over and clamp a cloth to his nose, saying, "Blow."

I did reach over. I reached for that stained, aging hand. Hard to believe: the power it once wielded, the blows it once landed. It gripped mine eagerly in a child's hold. I pulled him up and out of his seat—how ready he seemed to latch on to me—and led him to the bed.

"Rest here," I said. He looked at me, wary. "Rest," I repeated and crouched to unlace his boots, but stopped myself. Of course he would want them on. "Leave them on?" I asked, just to be sure. He nodded.

He was sitting at the edge of the bed. I picked up his legs—boots and all—and set them on the bed until he was prone. Docile but still suspicious, he kept an eye on my movements.

"What are you doing?" he said when I stretched out beside him.

I turned on my side, raised my head on an elbow, and reached out to stroke his forehead. I'd been away for so long that I'd forgotten all about those sumptuary laws and the affront of touching one's superior on the head.

He wasn't past overlooking the breach, though. "My sanctity!" he murmured. "You're bringing down my sanctity; you always did."

Ah, the sanctity of Dayan males! Even at that Damoclean moment, under the sword, under the gun, how they swear by their precious sanctity.

This time it wasn't a serious complaint. I could feel his brow unclenching under my touch. He closed his eyes, freeing me to study the top of his head, that great repository of sanctity—and of a steel plate too (if the rumors were true). The liver blotches had invaded his temples and brow as well, right up to the receded hairline. I felt at liberty to run my hand over the thinning pate, over the bumps and faults that may or may not have appeared since the last official count, when I was tallying up the thirty-two sacred marks. I couldn't have taken such liberties in those days.

I looked down at a slight old man, stretched out on his back at my behest, lying at attention in full uniform, defenselessly at my mercy. And as I took in the details of his clothing—the half boots, the starched uniform that held nothing of the bitter smoke I remembered so well, but smelled of mothballs now— as I saw him thus, dressed so formally yet waiting so humbly, I couldn't for the life of me stir up the old revulsion and fear. It wasn't that I'd willed those sentiments away. There was simply no fear to overcome anymore after all.

My head went down on his chest. I lay there for a long

moment, very still—as was he. I heard his heart, a shuffling beat like the dragging of feet. Then his arms went round me, but lightly, cautiously.

With one hand I felt for the lowest button on his jacket, undid it, and moved up to the next. He stopped me as I approached the collar. "There's no need," he said. "I'm too old."

I loosened the collar anyway. Despite his protests he turned helpfully from side to side as I worked his arms out of the jacket sleeves. How small and sunken he looked in his sleeveless undershirt ("singlet" was the word; it came back to me suddenly)—all hollowed out around the shoulders and collarbone, and puny-chested like a boy.

I started to fiddle with his belt but thought better of the order of things. "I'm going to have to take your boots off," I said.

He replied with a groan. Was it pleasure or protest? I went ahead anyway, feeling—while I gingerly untied the tight laces—as if I were unbandaging and snipping at the stitches of a wound that may not yet have healed. Once I had the boots off, I could hardly bear to look at that equivalent of a wound: those vulnerable feet and little clawed toes. I hastened to pull down his trousers; it was almost kinder to gaze on the loose jockey briefs hanging above the slack thighs and calves.

I carried his clothes to the chair, set the boots under the ottoman, spread the folded trousers over the seat, and hung the jacket across the back of the chair. When I turned around I saw he was shivering a little, his arms crossed over his chest. I made him get under the sheets, turning him like an invalid as I pulled them down and back over him until they reached below his chin. I sat at the edge of the bed for a while, patting the bedspread around his shoulders and wondering how best to get undressed.

I thought of the days when all it took to jump-start his

batteries was to hoist my sarong, squat on the floor, and release a trickle. It would take a lot more to charge them up now—and I wasn't sure that undressing in front of him would help things any. My nakedness would probably frighten before it would arouse him. I didn't want to frighten him now.

I got into bed beside him, and only then, under cover of the sheets, did I shed my clothes. It went much quicker than the shedding of his uniform. With my clothes in their rightful place—on the ground toward the foot of the bed—I turned and pressed myself along the length of his body, feeling the cold in his hands and feet. I stuck the top of my feet under his soles, remembering for some strange reason the peasant woman in a Russian story who was obliged to mount her husband every night. The object was not only to pleasure him but to provide at the same time the surface of her rump for him to warm his frigid, horny feet.

Supremo's teeth were chattering a little, and as I reached for the switch overhead to turn off the light, I saw that his lips had turned a swimmer's blue. In the dark, I placed a hand over his mouth, which he moved in a whisper of a kiss at the center of my palm. I was lying on one of his hands—the one still folded across his chest; I searched out his other hand and held it to my breast. It stung like ice, as though he'd just come in from the snow like that Russian dolt, and like the dolt's wife I left it there against my flesh, which must have felt feverish by contrast.

When his chill had subsided, I reached down with both hands to pull off his jockeys, tossing them in the direction of the chair, and began warming the last of his extremities. They too were cold. Cold, familiar to the touch—and softer than ever. Soon I would begin the massage I remembered so well: the gentle stroking and cupping of the scrotum; the light gripping of his monsoon fungus (as he himself once called it: a variety of mushroom with a stem so soft it toppled over at the slightest touch); the dexterous rubbing and squeezing that would coax it to swell by the smallest of fractions; the driving of my hand like a piston so he could get it up and into me for the few rapid thrusts before the inevitable wilt.

"Ah, that's good," he was saying, although nothing was astir yet in the palm of my hand. I wondered if he was still listening to the noises from afar that came through by fits and starts. The songsters and pot bangers had presumably retired for the night, but new revelers were about—jeeploads, truck-loads, tankloads of them from the sound of things. They were rumbling through the streets, jumping off at points, then rum-bling off again.

Now that I'd taken the edge off his chill, I decided to turn on the fan, keeping it pointed away from the bed. It wasn't the draft I wanted but the brassy hum, to drown out the distant clamor. Before crossing the room, I took care, lest I startle him with a view of my bare back, to pick my sarong up off the floor and wrap myself in it from the chest down. The overhead light was off, but the illuminated clock cast its tawdry nightclub glow.

Bending down to position the fan, I felt a pain go through me—a quick diffuse pain—and jerked my hand away, thinking I'd been shocked. I went back to the bed, leaving my sarong on while I continued my ministrations.

I ran my hand up under his singlet, across the tines of his rib cage, over the nipples on which I'd once wasted so much breath, and down toward the soft waist, where I encountered the long, puckered welt of a scar that hadn't been there in my time.

"What's this?" I asked.

"A scar."

"Go on! I thought it was a beauty mark."

His belly shook a little from the first laugh I'd elicited.

"What's it from?" I said.

He sighed. "I've been cut up a lot since you left, Tango."

I couldn't let the opportunity pass. "In the head, too?"

In the dim light I saw him raise his head in puzzlement. "What are you talking about?"

So maybe the rumors about the steel plate in his head weren't true, after all.

I knelt over him. "Want me to count your sacred marks?"

"Can you still find them?" His voice was tender.

"Not only that. I bet I can find the spot on your back exactly where it itches. Turn around and I'll show you."

He turned away from me, onto his side, offering me his neck and back with the submissiveness of the condemned before the executioner. I picked a spot under his left shoulder blade, in line with his heart, and scratched. "Right there. Am I right?"

His back began to shake. A sob broke out finally. "Why did you betray me, Tango? I never loved anyone else but you."

How alike are the old and the young, I thought, as I continued to scratch that childish old back and answer his childish old accusations with silence. "I heard what they did to you," he was wailing now. "They did it without my knowledge, I swear upon God and everything sacred to me. I'd never have let them harm a hair on your head. The only woman I've ever loved!"

The area I was gently raking my nails across was exactly the area, it occurred to me, into which I might plunge a knife: right between the ribs and straight into the heart.

"Turn around," I said at last. "No use crying now. Here, let me see if I can find the sacred marks."

As he turned, I helped him off with his singlet and pulled down the sheets so that he was stripped bare, fully exposed in the mauve glow of the Chinese clock. Remembering the protocol of starting from the feet up, I turned my back to him and bent toward his ankles to begin the scrutiny, resting one forearm against his crotch while doing so. As I lingered over his shins, gently stroking his thighs while I continued the ostensible search, I felt something stir at my elbow, the one pressed to his crotch. I shifted my arm a little, almost imperceptibly— and found that the mushroom had actually expanded a bit.

It was like tracking a small skittish animal that could be scared off with any sudden movement. I continued bending over his shins and stroking his thighs as if I hadn't noticed a thing, but all the while I kept pressing closer and closer into his genitals, feeling the increasing hardness against my arm. When I thought the danger of a scare had passed, I lay down with my head across his middle and, with my face right up against the blooming bud, slowly began the massage.

Even in tumescence, he was smaller than I'd remembered— or maybe it was just the reduction of age. It struck me that the reverse was true in my case: I'd become larger, not smaller. My breasts, my hips, my arms, my thighs, my face itself—all aspects of my flesh were fuller and thicker than ever. But then I was younger than he; I still had a distance to go.

"Oh," he was saying, "O almighty God."

He was hard now, hard enough for penetration, anyway— but still I worked his shaft, wanting to be sure the moment had come.

"Take that off," he pleaded, tugging at my sarong. I complied, managing to slip the thing off me with one hand, while keeping the crucial momentum going with the other.

The moment I'd stripped, he got on top of me, kneeing my legs open in the old unceremonious way. As small as he'd appeared in my hand, his entry was abrasive—probably because I was bone-dry. It didn't stop him from the frantic rocking (pounding would be too strong a word)—frantic and brief and weaker by the moment, until there wasn't the shadow of a doubt that he'd shrunk without climaxing and was no longer inside me.

He fell on his side, panting from that small exertion. I gave him a minute or two to recover, then went to work again. This time it took considerably longer to obtain an erection, but it lasted longer as I allowed him to remain on his back, while I straddled him for a change, keeping a slow but steady canter. He stared at my breasts, which hung above him, keeping his hands to himself. He kept them palms up and next to his shoulders in the posture of a newborn babe. How large and deliberate I must have seemed to him, looming above with my spreading hips and swinging tits like some Tartar horsewoman swooping down from the steppes astride her steed. No wonder he ended up cowering (his head turned to one side to avert the Amazonian vision, perhaps) when once again limpness prevailed. But it had been a longish ride, leaving both of us sweating.

I got off and went to turn the fan around, to get some air in our direction. I remembered the shock and touched the fan cautiously, but this time felt no pain. When I got back into bed, he'd pulled the bed sheet up to his chin and turned on his side, his back to me. "I want to sleep a little," he said.

I lay on my back, suddenly aware of fatigue. But I was wide-awake.

After a few minutes he was jolted out of sleep. He turned to me, confused. "The locusts are coming! I saw the swarms. I heard them in my sleep."

I stroked his forehead and found sweat at the temples. I didn't have the heart to tell him that what he'd heard in his sleep was not the chirring of locusts but the rasping of his own labored breath. When I moved my hand down to his chest I could feel the aftereffects of his dream in the quick march of his heartbeat. Taking a deep breath he turned to look at me, and though I couldn't see his expression, I knew he was studying me. He reached out as though to stroke the back of my head but instead wrapped my hair around his hand and pulled. It used to hurt; it didn't now.

"Why did you come back?" he said. "Why did you really come back?"

I'd expected the question, and I'd expected to answer by quoting an old proverb. He always liked proverbs; they offered the convenience of ready-made thought. "Seek not to escape the mate that fate has ordained" was the answer I'd planned to give. Instead I moved down once more toward his groin. Time was running out: I sensed we'd used up the night and began to imagine subtle changes in the artificial mauve light itself. I thought I detected hints of dawn.

With Supremo's grip still firmly on my hair, I closed my own grip firmly on his dormant cock and held it up to begin a different kind of treatment from the practiced routine. I started at the top. I touched the head with a flick of my tongue, then ran my tongue all over the surface of the crest, up to and including the fault bisecting it. There lay a spot of secretion. So there was still sap in the old blighted stump after all.

Supremo was sucking in his breath. If he weren't also babbling—in French, no less! *(oh la-la, la-la!)*—I might have thought he was in pain. He'd relaxed his hold on my hair but left his hand on my head as it began the slow nodding that accompanied the slow licking. I licked his shaft, up and down, bottom to top, and all around the circumference.

"Oh ho-ho-ho!" he said, sounding jolly like Santa Claus now. I had moved farther down; I had lifted his balls; I had elbowed his legs apart—I, the invader for a change—and now I was tracking, with the edge of my tongue, the line that ran all the way from his anus, under and over and across his sac, and up along the underside of his organ (fully extended by now), right to the top of its head—a swelled and cracked head, not unlike his other one. They even smelled the same, his two heads—they had the vulnerable, almost touching odor of a scalp that needed washing.

I went on—wanting to leave no stone unturned—to stuff his balls, one at a time, into my mouth . . . thinking how apt was the Dayan name for that hairy and loose-skinned fruit that grew only in the marshlands of the south (the scrotum fruit) and how even a rabid old xenophobe can be so trusting as to lie there with his life in my hands and his balls between my teeth.

He was stone still. For a moment I couldn't tell if he was even breathing. I thought maybe he'd passed out. But then he stirred and groaned, spurring me on to what I could sense would be the final stages of my mission. If he *had* expired, I wondered if the sucking I now gave myself to would have revived him. Did blowing—such a misnomer, it seemed to me—suggest the possibility of blowing life back into a dying man through this open flue?

I sucked; I licked; I blew.

"Oh!" he croaked. "Ah!" he crooned.

Then he pumped his bony pelvis and broke into a sort of song. The time had come. Keeping one hand in a tight grip on the fruit of my labors, I started to mount it, but out of some sense of deference, I decided it would be better, more fitting, for him to end up on top. So I lay on my back and led him to me by the nose, or rather by the hose, which I held on to right up to the moment of insertion.

Despite the shallow thrusts, I knew he was going to make it this time. He pumped away: once, twice, thrice—and more, and more. He pumped longer than he'd ever pumped, and all the time I could feel from the charge of the engine that it was well primed and not destined to stall.

"I'm finished . . . !" he shouted at last. "O my God, I'm finished . . . !"

Then came the seizure, the almost epileptic spasms. Eeriest of all, though, were the cries accompanying the convulsions: they were like echoes of the bellows and the shouts, the groans and protests, of the poisoned lion as it bit the dust that night of my homecoming. I'd never been a believer in reincarnation, but for the duration of that loud and long climax I had brought to a head, I could imagine that the soul of the lion from Ethiopia at its moment of death had actually entered the soul of the Lion of Daya.

This one wasn't dead yet, though. He was either laughing or crying—or both. "Oh, my heart, my life! My precious Tango!" he said at last. "Here I thought you'd come to kill me one day. Instead you came to save me. You've forgiven me, then?"

I sat up and looked at him. We couldn't see clearly into each other's eyes, but I forced myself to look at him.

"No," I said at last, shaking in a sudden fever. "No, I haven't forgiven you."

"My hardheaded little witch!" he said, and opened his mouth in a loud yawn that ended in a whinny. "Now I must really sleep." He turned on his side, his back to me, and in less than a minute had rejoined the chorus of locusts.

As he turned, he took part of the bedclothes with him, wrapping himself in the quilt.

The gods are my witness: that was the moment I knew how I'd do it; until that second, the inspiration hadn't come. I reached under a corner of the bed on my side and ran my hand along the ledge there, to find the thing I'd discovered by accident only the night before. I'd left it where it was, a meaningless object at the time.

Someone—a carpenter, a repair or maintenance man, a divine accomplice, perhaps—must have been using it, must have forgotten and left it there. Now there it was still: a big thick roll of gray insulating tape, the kind that worked on cloth.

I got up to turn off and unplug the noisy fan and noticed the silence. The revelry outside had ceased. I moved the fan to my side of the bed, surprised at how much the heavy cast-iron thing weighed. Immediately I set to work on the bed linen, pulling out the sheets on my side where they were still tucked into the mattress, then pulling up both sheet and comforter so that he would be lying over and not under them.

He muttered a few protests and turned toward me as I struggled to get them into the proper place: all the way up under him, under his head and past the pillows. I walked around to his side of the bed and untucked the sheets there, too. Now he was sound asleep and snoring louder than ever at the center of the bed linen, which hung down unfettered on both sides of the bed. I gathered up one end of the double layer and folded it snugly over his body. Then I did the same from the other side, wrapping him like a papoose. Lastly, I turned on the overhead light which caused him to frown a little but otherwise seemed not to disturb him.

He stirred only once, after he was bundled, to inquire groggily what I was doing.

"Keeping you warm and cozy," I said, as I reached under the bed for the roll of duct tape. I peeled off a length about a foot long and stuck it to the wood on my side of the bed, leaving it hanging by the roll and at the ready. I paused for a moment to take stock of things and when I was sure I had everything I needed—the tape, the fan, the right amount of bed linen above his head—I drew, as gently as possible, the top of the comforter and sheet over his head. I waited a while to see if this would wake him. It didn't. I leaned over then and pulled the hanging roll of tape off the side of the bed. As deftly and quickly as I could, I pressed the tape to the sheets around his neck, bunching the fabrics close into the bottleneck as I unwound and tore off and stuck more and more tape around it.

By the time he began the weak struggle, I'd managed to run strips of tape bandaging the cocoon of sheets from his neck almost down to his waist. Even then his wriggling was surprisingly feeble, his muffled cries even feebler. In a marvel of speed and efficiency, I forged ahead almost unhindered in my frenzy of taping and rolling, rocking the cocoon from side to side, until I was reasonably certain I had him pinned. I stepped back from the bed and watched for a few seconds to see if he would try to roll around on the bed, but the only activity that came from within was a kind of slow kicking.

Now! I bent over to pick up the fan—Lord, it was heavy!

Now! I lifted it overhead with both hands, my arms quivering under its weight.

Now! I hurled it onto the padded and sealed shape twitching on the bed. I aimed for the upper one-third, figuring I would probably miss the true target: the head. The fan landed on its back, astride the area around the bottleneck, with a dull and not entirely satisfying thud. I got up on the bed, picked up the heavy black thing, and flung it back down again, with much more force, onto roughly the same spot as before. This time I heard a crunch, a muted *oompf!* from under the sheets, and felt the bed shake under my feet. I bent down and lifted the fan again, and threw it down again, aiming lower now in pursuit of a louder crunch, a harder impact.

The shape under me was hardly a moving target. But I stayed there on the bed, stark naked, straddling him, picking up and flinging down that big black fan to crush every part of his body with a flaming zeal, an ecstasy. Eventually, my legs grew weak and my arms too tired to lift the fan one more time. I got off the bed sweating and panting with a wild thirst.

They say the chills brought on by malaria reduce the body to a trembling more severe than any other outbreak of shivers. I'd managed to escape malaria all those years in the jungle. Once, before I'd learned about the blood disorder that gave me the immunity, I was boasting to one of the captains—himself a survivor of many bouts—about how invincible I was.

"No one who comes here escapes malaria." He smiled. "Everyone must pay this jungle tax."

Maybe, I thought—as a violent chill came over me now, causing my teeth to rattle and my knees to buckle from the shakes—*maybe I've been carrying the malaria vector all those years.* What a nuisance to come upon it now! I reached for the sarong I'd dropped on the floor, stepped into the circle of cloth, and pulled it up around me, holding it closed around my neck. I felt too weak to cross the room for a drink of water. Huddling under the thin cotton, I sat on the floor at the foot of the bed for a long time —until the chill had passed.

No sooner had it passed, though, than I began to sweat again. I got up, wrapped the sarong around my chest, and set to unwrapping the motionless bundle on the bed.

It wasn't what I'd expected. No gaping lacerations or bruises leapt out at me. Still, to see him in that light— the ordinarily milky but now strangely harsh light—was shocking beyond belief. He couldn't have been more obscenely exposed. Belly-up, with his head twisted to one side, he looked like some desiccated old frog with a snapped neck. I thought I'd never be able to touch him; yet somehow—and with an effort that left me panting and perspiring—I did manage to get him dressed, wondering whether the awkwardness of his limbs was due to broken bones or the heavy absence of life. When I'd fastened the belt on his trousers and buttoned up his jacket, I turned at last to the task of putting his boots back on.

It was only after I'd tied the last lace and placed the feet side by side (it was the least I could do to set his feet in order), after I'd straightened the bed sheets out of some twisted sense of decorum, that it took me by storm—that onset of something so powerful, so sickening, that it knocks you to the floor where you're racked with sobs as wrenching as the dry heaves, and all you can do for quick relief is clutch at your heart and tear at your hair.

Pain severe enough to pass out from—for a while it seemed

the attack had brought on that order of pain. Like a spell of empty retching, it turned me inside out.

What was it I had expected to feel? Not this; anything but this. Panic knocked the wind out of me, hard as a kick in the back. Suddenly I was like one who remembers, just at the moment of plunging headlong to save a drowning person, that he himself can't swim. There I was, having plunged: sinking past help, past hope, saving no one—not those flailing, drowning bodies of the oppressed masses who would always be out there, beyond reach and too numerous for rescue; not my own flailing, drowning self, a cork in a tidal wave.

The Lion of Daya, good and dead now, at long last: the tenacious old martinet who for so long had refused to step down and refused to die. And I was the one finally who'd done the deed. *Sic semper tyrannis*. If ever a death seemed meet and just, it was his. Killing him was as necessary as putting a wounded man-eater out of its misery once and for all: a service to the terrorized and a service to the beast.

But I'd killed the beast out of revenge—nothing but revenge. Had I really done the state some service? Had I even succored the beast? Revenge—what a taste it left! The harshness on my tongue was the harshness of a substance to be tasted once and only once—the harshness of poison itself.

Had I really imagined an end to the sorrows and rages that had dogged me all the years? Look where I was still: sorrowful, enraged, undelivered after all. And filled with a wholly new dread. I had crossed yet another border into yet another place of banishment. On one side were all the people of the world who had never killed another human being; on the other were those who had. I was entering yet another state from which there was no salvation.

I couldn't shake the sorrow; I couldn't erase the stain. It seemed natural finally that this stain I'd carried around for most of my life would seep from the inside out to merge with the real stain upon me now, of blood and semen both. Whatever my fate after the dust storms settled, the stains were there to stay—thick as a sealant, indelible as fate.

The stain between my legs had dried on the trickle down the insides of my thighs and was cruddy to the touch. Just the feel of it made me burst into another round of sobbing and howling—even as I told myself that I should get ahold of myself fairly soon. Before long, they'd be there to discover my deed, and I had to think of what I'd say.

Suddenly, I was in the wild throes of laughter. Through the residual sobs came the raucous, maniacal hooting and gasping—as I repeated the phrase out loud, the phrase I'd offer in explanation. *The fan hit the shit,* I'd say. *The fan hit the shit. The fan hit the shit.*

Nothing being permanent, not even hysteria, not even grief, I was able eventually to gather up my clothes and get dressed. Clothed and composed once more, I sat on the ottoman, knowing I wouldn't have long to wait.

Where I would end up while they sorted things out at the centers of power was anybody's guess—or where I would end up after that. But as I sat there, purposely turned away from the bed, staring out of habit at that imbecile clock, I allowed myself the luxury of a daydream.

The yearning was not for a glimpse of the streets of Anika, which I had yet to see. The yearning was to be back in America when all this was over, when by miracle I might somehow be set free . . . free once more to return to the streets of Washington, where I'd roam in search of Rex.

I will rise now, and go about the city in the streets, and in the broad ways I will seek him. . . .

Maybe I wouldn't have far to look as I headed up along the Tidal Basin, where the Japanese cherries would be foaming with pink and white clouds of rice-paper blossoms in the early spring; along Pennsylvania Avenue with its plethora of buildings that housed our hiding places—*in the secret places of the stairs*; to our old stomping grounds at Lafayette Park. Maybe he'd be there already, among the lunch crowd of men and women in their business suits, with their brown paper bags, all eager to catch a bit of the sun.

I'd spot him as I came through the entrance directly in front of the White House—the entrance with the statue of Andrew Jackson on his horse with that feathery, filigreed tail. I'd look just past the statue, at a corner of the hedge enclosing the square. . . .

"Rex!" I'd call out and wave, for there he'd be, settled on our bench—the Bernard Baruch Bench of Inspiration—smoking a cigarette, legs crossed, tattered Gladstone at his feet. Startled, he'd turn in my direction. He'd nod his head formally as he stood up, but he'd be beaming away, his hands in the pockets of his soiled tan windbreaker—a scarecrow come to life.

"The winter is past, Rex," I'd say, approaching him. "The rain is over and gone. The flowers appear on the earth; the time of the singing of birds is come."

Striking his dandified pose, arms folded, one leg crossed in front of the other, he'd answer, "Who is she that looketh forth as the morning, fair as the moon, clear as the sun, and terrible as an army with banners?"

With his filthy handkerchief he'd dust the seat off for me.

"So, Rex," I'd say as we sat down, "any new inspirations?"

"Possibly," he'd reply with the coy leprechaun smile, after the usual hesitation. He'd light up another cigarette. "Well, m'dear, you have a story to tell?"

For a moment I'd feel chill and low in the shadow of a passing cloud. In that mood, I might say something melancholy. *Once I had a lovely land*, I might say, quoting a poem he'd shown me. *It was a dream.*

Maybe not, though. Maybe this time, as we sat in the speckled light of spring, under elms and oaks just now crisping into multitudinous shades of green . . .

But why am I thinking of spring, when in truth spring has long since come and gone? It's autumn now: the elms and oaks crisping into browns, not greens, the leaves gusting in swirls, the days brisk and short, the dusks fading fast, the night air bittersweet with smoke from fires unseen, the windows of houses lighting up one by one. . . .

The windows of other people's houses! Just to stand outside, looking in, would be enough for me now. Walk me past those windows once more, Rex, the way we did in the fall nights of that year—the year we were alone together. I'm thinking of our route up along the canal—the water on our left, the covered walkway of an office building on our right, the narrow lock spanning the canal, which you once danced across, agile as only a drunk can be. We'd take our time along that stretch, on the lookout for a night's shelter, stopping here and there on the way. We'd pause at a bench while you smoked, or at the water fountain, or on the hidden stairs under the covered walkway to study the bits of broken glass and neon graffiti glittering in the dark.

Blowing on our hands for warmth, we'd come up to the street on which the newest of the town houses fronted, the windows bare and open to public view. A narrow bedroom revealing an open suitcase on a single bed piled high with wrinkled clothes; a living room with immense ceilings and curved walls the color of cinnabar; a small kitchen with a bowl of tangerines on the table. The infinite riches of home.

How did it go again, Rilke's "Autumn Day"?

Whoever has no house now, will never have one.
Whoever is alone will stay alone,

will sit, read, write long letters through the evening,
and wander on the boulevards, up and down,
restlessly, while the dry leaves are blowing.

I'd do without a house now; I'd be content just to look, Rex; to gaze through the glass at the comforts of others—books on a shelf, flowers on a windowsill, a fire in a fireplace, framed pictures on a wall, a table set for dinner—of a life so beyond our reach. To stop under windows is all I'd ask—even the windows of empty rooms. Those empty rooms would be enough. I'd settle for watching the light again—the light transforming the emptiness, setting it here on fire, freezing it there in blue-white ice.

A warm, sheltered spot to pass the night somewhere under a window like that—it wouldn't be the worst thing in the world.

You'd light up, of course. "Well, m'dear, you have a story to tell?" Even in the shadows, I'd catch that look: bloodshot, a little unstable, a little too bright. The look would have turned me off in the past. Not now.

Yes, I might feel chill and low for a moment. In that mood, I might say something gloomy. *Once I had a lovely land,* I might say. *It was a dream.*

Maybe not, though. Maybe this time I'd feel like talking. Maybe this time I'd—feel.

I have done as you have done, I might say, with feeling; *that's what I can.* . . .

A NOTE ON THE TYPE

This book was set in Fournier, a typeface named for Pierre Simon
Fournier, a celebrated type designer in eighteenth-century France.
Fournier's type is considered transitional in that it drew its inspiration from the old style yet was ingeniously innovational, pro-
viding for an elegant yet legible appearance. For some time after
his death in 1768, Fournier was remembered primarily as the
author of a famous manual of typography and as a pioneer of the
point system. However, in 1925, his reputation was enhanced
when The Monotype Corporation of London revived Fournier's
roman and italic.

Composed by ComCom, a division of Haddon Craftsmen,
Allentown, Pennsylvania
Printed and bound by The Haddon Craftsmen,
Scranton, Pennsylvania

Typography and binding design by
Dorothy S. Baker